ANDREW GROSS

Before turning to full-time writing, Andrew Gross was an executive in the sportswear business. Andrew has co-authored 5 novels with James Patterson, all of them reaching Number One in the *NY Times* Bestseller list. He currently lives in New York with his wife, Lynne, and has three children.

Visit www.AuthorTracker.co.uk for exclusive updates on Andrew Gross.

THE DARK TIDE

Andrew Gross

HARPER

Harper
An imprint of HarperCollins*Publishers*
77–85 Fulham Palace Road,
Hammersmith, London W6 8JB

www.harpercollins.co.uk

This production 2012

First published in Great Britain by
HarperCollins*Publishers*

Copyright © Andrew Gross 2008

Andrew Gross asserts the moral right to
be identified as the author of this work

A catalogue record for this book is
available from the British Library

ISBN-13 978 0 00 793014 2

Set in Palatino by Palimpsest Book Production Ltd,
Grangemouth, Stirlingshire

Printed and bound in Great Britain by
Clays Ltd, St Ives plc

MIX
Paper from
responsible sources
FSC® C007454

FSC
www.fsc.org

PART ONE

CHAPTER ONE

6:10 A.M.

As the morning sun canted sharply through the bedroom window, Charles Friedman dropped the baton.

He hadn't had the dream in years, yet there he was, gangly, twelve years old, running the third leg of the relay in the track meet at summer camp, the battle between the Blue and the Gray squarely on the line. The sky was a brilliant blue, the crowd jumping up and down—crew-cut, red-cheeked faces he would never see again, except here. His teammate, Kyle Bregman, running the preceding leg, was bearing down on him, holding on to a slim lead, cheeks puffing with everything he had.

Reach. . . .

Charles readied himself, set to take off at the

3

touch of the baton. He felt his fingers twitch, awaiting the slap of the stick in his palm.

There it was! Now! He took off.

Suddenly there was a crushing groan.

Charles stopped, looked down in horror. The baton lay on the ground. The Gray Team completed the exchange, sprinting past him to an improbable victory, their supporters jumping in glee. Cheers of jubilation mixed with jeers of disappointment echoed in Charles's ears.

That's when he woke up. As he always did. Breathing heavily, sheets damp with sweat. Charles glanced at his hands—empty. He patted the covers as if the baton were somehow still there, after thirty years.

But it was only Tobey, their white West Highland terrier, staring wide-eyed and expectantly, straddled turkey-legged on his chest.

Charles let his head fall back with a sigh.

He glanced at the clock: 6:10 A.M. Ten minutes before the alarm. His wife, Karen, lay curled up next to him. He hadn't slept much at all. He'd been wide awake from 3:00 to 4:00 A.M., staring at the World's Strongest Female Championship on ESPN2 without the sound, not wanting to disturb her. Something was weighing heavily on Charles's mind.

Maybe it was the large position he had taken

in Canadian oil sands last Thursday and had kept through the weekend—highly risky with the price of oil leaking the other way. Or how he had bet up the six-month natural-gas contracts, at the same time going short against the one-years. Friday the energy index had continued to decline. He was scared to get out of bed, scared to look at the screen this morning and see what he'd find.

Or was it Sasha?

For the past ten years, Charles had run his own energy hedge fund in Manhattan, leveraged up eight to one. On the outside—his sandy brown hair, the horn-rim glasses, his bookish calm—he seemed more the estate-planner type or a tax consultant than someone whose bowels (and now his dreams as well!) attested to the fact that he was living in high-beta hell.

Charles pushed himself up in his boxers and paused, elbows on knees. Tobey leaped off the bed ahead of him, scratching feverishly at the door.

"Let him out." Karen stirred, rolling over, yanking the covers over her head.

"You're sure?" Charles checked out the dog, ears pinned back, tail quivering, jumping on his hind legs in anticipation, as if he could turn the knob with his teeth. "You know what's going to happen."

"C'mon, Charlie, it's your turn this morning. Just let the little bastard out."

"Famous last words . . ."

Charles got up and opened the door leading to their fenced-in half-acre yard, a block from the sound in Old Greenwich. In a flash Tobey bolted out onto the patio, his nose fixed to the scent of some unsuspecting rabbit or squirrel.

Immediately the dog began his high-pitched yelp.

Karen scrunched the pillow over her head and growled. *"Rrrrggg . . ."*

That's how every day began, Charles trudging into the kitchen, turning on CNN and a pot of coffee, the dog barking outside. Then going into his study and checking the European spots online before hopping into the shower.

That morning the spots didn't offer much cheer—$72.10. They had continued to decline. Charles did a quick calculation in his head. Three more contracts he'd be forced to sell out. Another couple of million—gone. It was a little after 6:00 A.M., and he was already underwater.

Outside, Tobey was in the middle of a nonstop three-minute barrage.

In the shower, Charles went over his day. He had to reverse his positions. He had these oil-sand contracts to clear up, then a meeting with

6

one of his lenders. *Was it time for him to come clean?* He had a transfer to make into his daughter Sam's college account; she'd be a senior at the high school in the fall.

That's when it hit him. *Shit!*

He had to take in the goddamn car this morning.

The fifteen-thousand-mile service on the Merc. Karen had finally badgered him into making the appointment last week. That meant he'd have to take the train in. It would set him back a bit. He'd hoped to be at his desk by seven-thirty to deal with those positions. Now Karen would have to pick him up at the station later that afternoon.

Dressed, Charles was usually in rush mode by now. The six-thirty wake-up shout to Karen, a knock on Alex's and Samantha's doors to get them rolling for school. Looking over the *Wall Street Journal*'s headlines at the front door.

This morning, thanks to the car, he had a moment to sip his coffee.

They lived in a warm, refurbished Colonial on an affluent tree-lined street in the town of Old Greenwich, a block off the sound. Fully paid for, the damned thing was probably worth more than Charles's father, a tie salesman from Scranton, had earned in his entire life. Maybe he couldn't show it like some of their big-time friends in their megahomes out on North Street, but he'd done well. He'd fought to get himself into Penn from a high-school class of seven hundred, distinguished himself at the energy desk at Morgan Stanley, steered a few private clients away when he'd opened his own firm, Harbor Capital. They had the ski house in Vermont, the kids' college paid for, took fancy vacations.

So what the hell had he done wrong?

Outside, Tobey was scratching at the kitchen's French doors, trying to get back in. *All right, all right.* Charles sighed.

Last week their other Westie, Sasha, had been run over. Right on their quiet street, directly in front of their house. It had been Charles who'd found her, bloodied, inert. Everyone was still upset. And then the note. The note that came to his office in a basket of flowers the very next day. That had left him in such a sweat. And brought on these dreams.

Sorry about the pooch, Charles. Could your kids be next?

How the hell had it gotten this far?

He stood up and checked the clock on the

stove: 6:45. With any luck, he figured, he could be out of the dealership by 7:30, catch a ride to the 7:51, be at his desk at Forty-ninth Street and Third Avenue fifty minutes after that. Figure out what to do. He let in the dog, who immediately darted past him into the living room with a yelp and out the front door, which Charles had absentmindedly failed to shut. Now he was waking up the entire neighborhood.

The little bastard was more work than the kids!

"Karen, I'm leaving!" he yelled, grabbing his briefcase and tucking the *Journal* under his arm.

"*Kiss, kiss,*" she called back, wrapped in her robe, dashing out of the shower.

She still looked sexy to him, her caramel-colored hair wet and a little tangled from the shower. Karen was nothing if not beautiful. She had kept her figure toned and inviting from years of yoga, her skin was still smooth, and she had those dreamy, grab-you-and-never-let-go hazel eyes. For a moment Charles regretted not rolling over to her back in bed once Tobey had flown the coop and given them the unexpected opportunity.

But instead he just yelled up something about the car—that he'd be taking in the Metro-North. That maybe he'd call her later and have her meet him on the way home to pick it up.

9

"Love you!" Karen called over the hum of the hair dryer.

"You, too!"

"After Alex's game we'll go out. . . ."

Damn, that was right, Alex's lacrosse game, his first of the season. Charles went back and scratched out a note to him that he left on the kitchen counter.

To our #1 attacker! Knock 'em dead, champ! BEST OF LUCK!!!

He signed his initials, then crossed it out and wrote *Dad.* He stared at the note for a second. He had to stop this. Whatever was going on, he'd never let anything happen to them.

Then he headed for the garage, and over the sound of the automatic door opening and the dog's barking in the yard, he heard his wife yell above the hair dryer, *"Charlie, would you please let in the goddamn dog!"*

CHAPTER TWO

By eight-thirty Karen was at yoga.

By that time she had already roused Alex and Samantha from their beds, put out boxes of cereal and toast for their breakfasts, found the top that Sam claimed was "*absolutely* missing, Mom" (in her daughter's dresser drawer), and refereed two fights over who was driving whom that morning and whose cooties were in the bathroom sink the kids shared.

She'd also fed the dog, made sure Alex's lacrosse uniform was pressed, and when the shoulder-slapping, finger-flicking spat over who touched whom last began to simmer into a name-calling brawl, pushed them out the door and into Sam's Acura with a kiss and a wave, got a quote from Sav-a-Tree about one of their elms that needed to come down and dashed off two e-mails to board members on the school's upcoming capital campaign.

A start . . . Karen sighed, nodding *"Hey, all,"* to a few familiar faces as she hurriedly joined in with their sun salutations at the Sportsplex studio in Stamford.

The afternoon was going to be a bitch.

Karen was forty-two, pretty; she knew she looked at least five years younger. With her sharp brown eyes, the trace of a few freckles still dotting her cheekbones, people often compared her to a fairer Sela Ward. Her thick, light brown hair was clipped up in back, and as she caught herself in the mirror, she wasn't at all ashamed of how she still looked in her yoga tights for a mom who in a former life had been the leading fund-raiser for the City Ballet.

That's where she and Charlie had first met. At a large-donors dinner. Of course, he was only there to fill out a table for the firm and couldn't tell a plié from the twist. *Still couldn't,* she always ribbed him. But he was shy and a bit self-deprecating—and with his horn-rim glasses and suspenders, his mop of sandy hair, he seemed more like some poli-sci professor than the new hotshot on the Morgan Stanley energy desk. Charlie seemed to like that she wasn't from around here—the hint of a drawl she still carried in her voice. The velvet glove wrapped around her iron fist, he always called it admiringly, because he'd never met anyone, *anyone*, who could get things done like she could.

Well, the drawl was long gone, and so was the perfect slimness of her hips. Not to mention the feeling that she had any control over her life.

She'd lost that one a couple of kids ago.

Karen concentrated on her breathing as she leaned forward into stick pose, which was a difficult one for her, focusing on the extension of her arms, the straightness of her spine.

"Straight back," Cheryl, the instructor, intoned. "Donna, arms by the ears. Karen, *posture.* Engage that thighbone."

"It's my *thighbone* that's about to fall off." Karen groaned, wobbling. A couple of people around her laughed. Then she righted herself and regained her form.

"Beautiful." Cheryl clapped. "Well done."

Karen had been raised in Atlanta. Her father owned a small chain of paint and remodeling stores there. She'd gone to Emory and studied art. At twenty-three she and a girlfriend went up to New York, she got her first job in the publicity department at Sotheby's, and things just seemed to click from there. It wasn't easy at first, after she and Charlie married. Giving up her career, moving up here to the country, starting a family. Charlie was always working back then—or away—and even when he was home, it seemed he had a phone perpetually stapled to his ear.

Things were a little dicey at the beginning. Charlie had made a few wrong plays when he opened his firm and almost "bought the farm." But one of his mentors from Morgan Stanley had stepped in and bailed him out, and since then things had worked out pretty well. It wasn't a big life—like some of the people they knew who lived in those giant Normandy castles in backcountry, with places in Palm Beach and whose kids had never flown commercial. But who even wanted that? They had the place in Vermont, a skiff at a yacht club in Greenwich. Karen still shopped for the groceries and picked up the poop out of the driveway. She solicited auction gifts for the Teen Center, did the household bills. The bloom on her cheeks said she was happy. She loved her family more than anything in the world.

Still, she sighed, shifting into chair pose; it was like heaven that at least for an hour the kids, the dog, the bills piling up on her desk were a million miles away.

Karen's attention was caught by something

14

through the glass partition. People were gathering around the front desk, staring up at the overhead TV.

"Think of a beautiful place. . . ." Cheryl directed them. "Inhale. Use your breath to take you there. . . ."

Karen drifted to the place she always fixed on. A remote cove just outside Tortola, in the Caribbean. She and Charlie and the kids had come upon it when they were sailing nearby. They had waded in and spent the day by themselves in the beautiful turquoise bay. A world without cell phones and Comedy Central. She had never seen her husband so relaxed. When the kids were gone, he always said, when he was able to get it all together, they could go there. *Right*. Karen always smiled inside. Charlie was a lifer. He loved the arbitrage, the risk. The cove could stay away, a lifetime if it had to. She was happy. She caught her face in the mirror. It made her smile.

Suddenly Karen became aware that the crowd at the front desk had grown. A few runners had stepped off their treadmills, focused on the overhead screen. Even the trainers had come over and were watching.

Something had happened!

Cheryl tried clapping them back to attention. "People, focus!" But to no avail.

One by one, they all broke their poses and stared.

A woman from the club ran over, throwing open their door. *"Something's happened!"* she said, her face white with alarm. "There's a fire in Grand Central Station! *There's been some kind of bombing there."*

CHAPTER THREE

Karen hurried through the glass door and squeezed in front of the screen to watch.

They all did.

There was a reporter broadcasting from the street in Manhattan across from the train station, confirming in a halting tone that some sort of explosion had gone off inside. *"Possibly multiple explosions . . ."*

The screen then cut to an aerial view from a helicopter. A billowing plume of black smoke rose into the sky from inside.

"Oh, Jesus, God," Karen muttered, staring at the scene in horror. "What's happened . . . ?"

"It's down on the tracks," a woman in a leotard standing next to her said. "They think some kind of bomb went off, maybe on one of the trains."

"My son went in by train this morning," a woman gasped, pressing a hand to her lips.

Another, a towel draped around her neck, holding back tears: "My husband, too."

Before Karen could even think, fresh reports came in. An explosion, *several explosions*, on the tracks, just as a Metro-North train was pulling into the station. There was a fire raging down there, the news reporter said. Smoke coming up on the street. Dozens of people still trapped. Maybe hundreds. *This was bad!*

"Who?" people were murmuring all around.

"Terrorists, they're saying." One of the trainers shook his head. "They don't know. . . ."

They'd all been part of this kind of terrible moment before. Karen and Charlie had both known people who'd never made it out on 9/11. At first Karen watched with the empathetic worry of someone whose life was outside the tragedy that was taking place. Nameless, faceless people she might have seen a hundred times—across from her on the train, reading the sports page, hurrying on the street for a cab. Eyes fixed to the screen, now many of them locked fingers with one another's hands.

Then, all of a sudden, it hit Karen.

Not with a flash—a numbing sensation at first, in her chest. Then intensifying, accompanied by a feeling of impending dread.

Charlie had yelled something up to her—about going in by train this morning. Above the drone of the hair dryer.

About having to take in the car and needing her to pick him up later on that afternoon.

Oh, my God . . .

She felt a constriction in her chest. Her eyes darted toward the clock. Frantically, she tried to reconstruct some sort of timeline. Charlie, what time he left, what time it was now . . . It started to scare her. Her heart began to speed up like a metronome set on high.

An updated report came in. Karen tensed. "It appears we are talking about a bomb," the reporter announced. "Aboard a Metro-North train just as it pulled into Grand Central. This has just been confirmed," he said. "It was on the *Stamford branch.*"

A collective gasp rose up from the studio.

Most of them were from around there. Everyone knew people—relatives, friends—who regularly took the train. Faces drained of blood— in shock. People turning to each other without even knowing whom they were next to, seeking the comfort of each other's eyes.

"It's horrible, isn't it?" A woman next to Karen shook her head.

Karen could barely answer. A chill had

suddenly taken control of her, knifing through her bones.

The Stamford train went through Greenwich.

All she could do was look up at the clock in terror—8:54. Her chest was coiled so tightly she could barely breathe.

The woman stared at her. "Honey, are you okay?"

"I don't know. . . ." Karen's eyes had filled with terror. "I think my husband might be on that train."

CHAPTER FOUR

8:45 A.M.

Ty Hauck was on his way to work.

He cut the engines to five miles per hour as he maneuvered his twenty-four-foot fishing skiff, the *Merrily*, into the mouth of Greenwich Harbor.

Hauck took the boat in from time to time when the weather turned nice. *This* morning, with its clear, crisp April breeze, he looked off his deck and sort of mentally declared it: *Summer hours officially begin!* The twenty-five minutes on the Long Island Sound from where he lived near Cove Island in Stamford were hardly longer than the slow slog this time of the morning down I-95. And the brisk wind whipping through his hair woke him a whole lot faster than any grande at Starbucks. He clicked the portable CD player on. Fleetwood Mac. An old favorite:

Rhiannon rings like a bell through the night / And wouldn't you love to love her.

It was why he'd moved back up here, four years ago. After the accident, after his marriage had broken up. Some said that it was running away. Hiding out. And maybe it was, just a little. *So the hell what?*

He was head of the Violent Crimes Unit on the Greenwich police force. People relied on him. *Was that running away?* Sometimes he took the boat out for an hour or so before work in the rosy predawn calm and fished for blues and striped bass. *Was that?*

He had grown up here. In middle-class Byram, near Port Chester by the New York border, only a few miles but a lifetime away from the massive estates that now lined the way out to back-country, gates he now drove through to follow up on some rich kid who had tipped over his sixty-thousand-dollar Hummer.

It was all different now. The countrified families who had grown up there in his youth had given way to thirty-something hedge-fund zillionaires who tore the old homes down and built enormous castles behind iron gates, with lake-size pools and movie theaters. Everyone with money was coming in. Now Russian moguls—who even knew where *their* wealth was from?—were buying up horse-country estates in Conyers Farm, putting in helicopter pads.

Billionaires ruining things for millionaires. Hauck shook his head.

Twenty years ago he'd been a running back at Greenwich High. Then he went on and played at Colby, Division III. Not exactly Big Ten, but the fancy degree got him fast-tracked into the NYPD detectives' training program, which made his dad, who worked his whole life for the Town of Greenwich Water Authority, proud. He'd cracked a couple of high-profile cases and moved up. Later on he worked for the department's Information Office when the Trade Towers were hit.

So now he was back.

As he chugged into the harbor, the manicured lawns of Belle Haven to his left, a couple of small boats cruised past him on their way out—doing the same thing he was doing, heading to work on Long Island across the sound, a half hour's ride away.

Hauck waved.

And he liked it here now, though a lot of pain had left its mark in between.

It was lonely since he and Beth had split up. He dated a bit: a pretty secretary to the CEO at General Reinsurance, a marketing gal who worked at Altria for a while. Even one or two gals on the force. But he'd found no one new to share his life with. Though Beth had.

Occasionally he hung out with a few of his old buddies from town, a couple who had made bundles building homes, some who just became plumbers or mortgage brokers or owned a landscaping company. "The Leg," that's what everyone still called him—with a soft *g*, as in "Legend." Old-timers, who still recalled him busting two tackles into the end zone to beat Stamford West for the Lower Fairfield County crown, still toasted that as the best game they'd ever seen anyone play here since Steve Young and bought him beers.

But mostly he simply felt free. That the past hadn't followed him up here. He just tried to do a little good during the day, cut people a break. Be fair. And he had Jessica, who was ten now, up on weekends, and they fished and kicked soccer balls around on Tod's Point and had cookouts there. Sunday afternoons, in his eight-year-old Bronco, he'd drive her back to where she lived now, in Brooklyn. Friday nights in the winter, he played hockey in the local over-forty league.

Basically he tried to push it back a little each day—time, that is—trying to find himself back to that point before everything caved in on him. That moment before the accident. Before his marriage collapsed. Before he gave up.

Why go back there, Ty?

Hard as you tried, you could never quite push it back all the way. Life didn't afford you that.

Hauck caught sight of the marina at the Indian Harbor Yacht Club, where the dock manager, Hank Gordon, an old buddy, always let him put in for the day. He picked up the radio. "Heading in, Gordo . . ."

But the marina manager was waiting for him out on the pier.

"What the hell are you doing here, Ty?"

Hauck yelled to him, "Summer hours, guy!" He reversed and backed the *Merrily* in. Gordo tossed a bowline to him and reeled him in. Hauck cut the engine. He went out to the stern as the boat hit the buoy and hopped onto the pier. "Like a dream out there today."

"A *bad* dream," Hank said. "Lemme take it from here, Ty. You better get your ass up that hill."

There was something on the dock manager's face that Hauck couldn't quite read. He glanced at his watch—8:52. Usually he and Gordo shot the shit a few minutes, about the Rangers or what had made it onto the police blotter the night before.

25

That's when Hauck's cell phone started to beep. The office. *Two-three-seven.*

Two-thirty-seven was the department's emergency code.

"You didn't have the radio on, did you?" Gordo asked, securing the line.

Hauck shook his head blankly.

"Then you haven't heard what the hell happened out there, have you, Lieutenant?"

CHAPTER FIVE

Karen didn't flip out at first. That wasn't her way. She told herself over and over to stay calm. Charlie could be anywhere. *Anywhere.*

You don't know for sure if he was even on that train.

Like a few years back, when Samantha was four or five, and they thought they'd lost her at Bloomie's. And after a frantic, heart-constricting search, retracing their steps, calling for the manager, and starting to accept the reality that something horrible had happened—*that this wasn't a false alarm!*—there she was, their little Sammy, waving hi to Mommy and Daddy, paging through one of her favorite books atop a pile of Oriental rugs, as innocent as if she were on a stage at school.

This could be just like that, Karen reassured

herself now. *Stay calm, Karen. Goddamn it, just stay calm!*

She ran back into the yoga studio, found her purse, and fumbled around for her phone. Heart pumping, she punched in Charlie's number on the speed dial. *C'mon, c'mon. . . .* Her fingers barely complied.

As she waited for the call to connect, she tried her best to flash through her husband's schedule that morning. He'd left the house around seven. She'd been finishing her hair. Ten minutes into town, ten minutes at the dealership dropping off the car, going over what had to be done. So that was, what—7:20? Another ten or so to the station. The news said the explosion had occurred at 8:41. He could have made an earlier train. Or even ended up getting a loaner and driving in. For a second, Karen allowed herself to feel uplifted. Anything was possible. . . . Charlie was the most resourceful man she knew.

His phone began to ring. Karen saw that her hands were shaking. *C'mon, Charlie, answer. . . .*

To her dismay, his voice recording came on. "This is Charlie Friedman. . . ."

"Charlie, it's me," Karen blurted. "I'm really worried about you. I know you took the train in. You've got to call me as soon as you get this.

28

I don't care what you're doing, Charlie. Just call, hon. . . ."

She pressed the end button feeling totally helpless.

Then she realized—there was a voice-mail message on her phone! Blood racing, she scrolled immediately to Recently Received Calls.

It was Charlie's number! Thank God! Her heart almost climbed up her throat in joy.

Anxiously, Karen punched in her code and pressed the receiver to her ear. His familiar voice came on and it was calm. "Listen, hon, I thought as long as I'm gonna be in Grand Central, I'd pick up some of those marinated steaks you like at Ottomanelli's on the way home and we'd grill instead of going out. . . . Sound good? Lemme know. I'll be in the office by nine. I got hung up. Madhouse at the dealership. *Bye.*"

Karen stared at the message screen—*8:34. He was heading into Grand Central when he made the call. Still on the train.* The sweats began to come over her again. She looked back outside at the monitor, at the pall of smoke building over Grand Central, the chaos and confusion on the screen.

Suddenly she knew in her heart. She couldn't deny it anymore.

Her husband was on that train.

29

Unable to control herself any longer, Karen punched in the speed code to her husband's office. *C'mon, c'mon,* she said over and over during the agonizing seconds it took for the call to connect. Finally Heather, Charlie's assistant, picked up.

"Charles Friedman's office."

"Heather, it's Karen." She tried to control herself. "By any chance has my husband come in?"

"Not yet, Mrs. Friedman. He left me an e-mail earlier from his BlackBerry saying that he had to take his car in or something. I'm sure I'll be hearing from him soon."

"I know he had to take his car in, Heather! That's what I'm worried about. Have you seen the news? He said he was taking the train."

"Oh, my God!" His assistant gasped, reality setting in. Of course she'd seen it. They *all* had. The whole office was watching it now.

"Mrs. Friedman, let me try and get him on the phone. I'm sure it's got to be crazy around Grand Central. Maybe he's on his way over and the phones just aren't functioning. Maybe he took a later train—"

"I got a call from him, Heather! At eight thirty-four. He said they were pulling into Grand Central in a while. . . ." Her voice was shaking.

"That was eight thirty-four, Heather! He was on it. Otherwise he would have called. *I think he was on that train. . . ."*

Heather begged her to stay calm and said she would e-mail him, that she was sure she'd hear from him soon. Karen nodded okay, but when she put down the phone, her heart was racing and her blood was pumping out of control and she had no idea what to do next. She pressed the phone to her heart and dialed his number one more time.

C'mon, Charlie. . . . Charlie, please . . .

Outside Grand Central, the news reporter was confirming that it had been at least one bomb. A few survivors had staggered out of the station. They were gathered on the street, dazed, faces smeared with blood and black with soot. Some were muttering something about Track 109, that there'd been at least two powerful explosions and a fire raging down there, with lots of people still trapped. That something had gone off in the first two cars.

Karen froze. That's when tears finally started to roll down her cheeks.

That's where Charlie always sat. It was like a ritual with him. He always camped out in the first car!

C'mon, Charlie. . . . Karen pleaded silently,

watching the screen outside. *People are making it out. Look, they're interviewing them.*

She punched his number in again, her body giving over to full-out panic.

"Answer the fucking phone, Charlie!"

CHAPTER SIX

Her thoughts flashed to Samantha and Alex. Karen realized she had to get home.

What could she possibly tell them? Charlie always drove in. He had a spot in his building's garage. He'd been doing it for years.

That this was the one goddamn morning he picked to take the train!

Karen crumpled her sweat top into her bag and ran out, past the front counter, through the outer glass doors. She hurried over to where her Lexus was parked, the hybrid Charlie had bought her barely a month ago. The console still smelled new. She flicked the automatic lock on her key chain and jumped in.

Her house was about ten minutes away. Pulling out of the lot, Karen kept the Blue Tooth phone on automatic dial to Charlie's cell. *Please, Charlie, please, answer the goddamn phone!*

Her heart kept sinking. "This is Charlie Friedman. . . ."

Tears rolled down her cheeks as she pushed back her worst fears. *This can't be happening!*

Karen made a sharp right out of the Sportsplex's lot onto Prospect, cut the light at the corner, accelerating onto I-95. Traffic was backed up, slowing everything headed into downtown Greenwich.

All sorts of new, conflicting reports were coming in. The radio said that multiple explosions had taken place. That there was a fire on the tracks, burning out of control. That the intense heat and the possibility of noxious fumes made it impossible for firefighters even to get close. That there were significant casualties.

It was starting to scare Karen to death.

He could be trapped down there. *Anywhere.* He could be burned or injured, unable to get out. On his way to a hospital. There were a hundred fucking scenarios that could possibly be playing out. Karen pressed the speed dial again.

"Where are you, goddamn it, Charlie? *Come on, please. . . .*"

Her mind flashed again to Alex and Samantha. They wouldn't have any idea. Even if word had spread to them, it wouldn't occur to them. Charlie always drove.

Karen pulled off the highway at Exit 5, Old Greenwich, and onto the Post Road. Suddenly her car phone beeped. *Thank God!* Her heart almost leaped out of her chest.

But it was only Paula, her best friend, who lived nearby in Riverside, only a few minutes away.

"You hear what's going on?" The sound of the TV was blaring in the background.

"Of course I've heard, Paula. I—"

"They're saying it was from Greenwich. There might even be people we—"

"Paula." Karen interrupted her. She could barely force the words out of her mouth. "I think Charlie was on that train."

"What?"

Karen told her about the car and not being able to reach him. She said she was heading home and wanted to keep the lines free, in case he or his office might call.

"Of course, honey. I understand. Kar, he's going to be okay. Charlie always comes out okay. You know that, Kar, don't you?"

"I know," Karen said, though she knew she was lying to herself. *"I know."*

Karen drove through town, her heart beating madly, then turned onto Shore Road near the sound. Then Sea Wall. Half a block down, she jerked the Lexus into her driveway. Charlie's old Mustang was pulled into the third bay of the garage, just as she'd left it an hour earlier. She ran through the garage and into the kitchen. Her hope was momentarily raised by a message light flashing on the machine. *Please . . .* she prayed to herself, and pushed the play button, her blood pulsing with alarm.

"Hey, Mrs. Friedman . . ." a dull voice came over the speaker. It was Mal, their plumber, droning on and on about the water heater she'd wanted to have fixed, about some goddamn valve he was having a bitch of a time finding. Tears ran down Karen's cheeks as her legs started to give out, and she pressed herself to the wall and sank helplessly onto the floor. Tobey wagged his way up, nuzzling into her. She mashed her tears with the palms of her hands. "Not now, baby. Please, not now. . . ."

Up on the counter, Karen fumbled for the remote. She flicked on the TV. The situation had gotten worse. Matt Lauer was on the screen—with Brian Williams now—and the reports were that there were dozens of casualties down on the tracks, that the fire was spreading and uncontained. That some of the lower part of the building had collapsed, and while they were flashing to some expert about Al Qaeda and terrorism, they split-screened to the dark cloud seeping into the Manhattan sky.

He would've called them, Karen knew, at least Heather at the office—if he was okay. Maybe even before he would've called her. That's what scared her most. She closed her eyes.

Just be okay, Charlie, wherever you are. Just be okay.

A car door slammed outside. Karen heard the doorbell ring. Someone called out her name and came running into the house.

It was Paula. She fixed on Karen huddled on the floor, in a way she had never seen her before. Paula sank down next to her, and they just hugged each other, tears glistening on each other's cheeks.

"It's gonna be okay, honey." Paula stroked Karen's hair. "I know it will. There could be hundreds of people down there. Maybe the phones aren't working. Maybe he needed some medical attention. Charlie's a survivor. If anyone's gonna get out, it's him. You'll see, baby. It's gonna be okay."

And Karen kept nodding back and repeating, "I know, I know," wiping the tears with her sleeve.

They called over and over. What else was there to do? Charlie's cell phone. His office. Maybe thirty, forty times.

At some point Karen even sniffled back a smile. "You know how mad Charlie gets when I bug him at the office?"

By nine forty-five they had settled onto the couch in the family room. That's when they heard the car pull up and more doors slamming. Alex and Samantha burst in through the kitchen with a shout. *School's closed!*

They stuck their heads into the TV room. "You heard what happened?" Alex said.

Karen could barely answer. The sight of them struck terror in her heart. She told them to sit down. They could see that her face was raw and worried. That something was terribly wrong was written all over it.

Samantha sat down across from her. "Mom, what's wrong?"

"Daddy took the car in this morning," Karen said, "for service."

"So?"

Karen swallowed back a lump, or she was sure she would start to cry. "Afterward," she paused, "I think he went into the city by train."

Both kids' eyes went wide and followed hers, as if drawn, to the wide screen.

"He's there?" her son asked. *"At Grand Central?"*

"I don't know, baby. We haven't heard from

38

him. That's what's so worrisome. He called and said he was on the train. That was eight thirty-four. This happened at eight forty-one. I don't know. . . ."

Karen was trying so hard to appear positive and strong, trying with all her heart not to alarm them, because she knew with that same unflinching certainty that any moment Charlie would call, tell them he had made it out, that he was okay. So she didn't even feel the trail of tears carving its way down her cheeks and onto her lap, and Samantha staring at her, jaw parted, about to cry herself. And Alex—her poor, macho Alex, white as parchment—eyes glued to the horrifying plume of smoke elevating into the Manhattan sky.

For a while no one said a word. They just stared, all in their own world between denial and hope. Sam, arms hung loosely around her brother's neck, her chin resting nervously on his shoulder. Alex, grasping Karen's hand for the first time in years, watching, waiting for their father's face to emerge. Paula, elbows on knees, poised to shout and point, *Look, there he is!* Jump up in glee. Waiting with all the certainty in the world to hear the phone she was sure was about to ring.

Alex turned to Karen. "Dad's gonna make it out of there? Isn't he, Mom?"

"Of course he is, baby." Karen squeezed his hand. "You know your father. If anyone will, it's him. He'll make it out."

That was when they heard a rumble. On the screen the camera shook from another muffled explosion. Onlookers gasped and screamed as a fresh cloud of dense black smoke emerged from the station.

Samantha wailed, *"Oh, God . . ."*

Karen felt her stomach fall. She cupped Alex's fist tightly and squeezed. "Oh, Charlie, Charlie, Charlie . . ."

"Secondary explosions . . ." muttered a fire chief coming out of the station, his head shaking with a kind of finality. "There are many, many bodies down there. We can't even get our people close."

CHAPTER SEVEN

Around noon

When the call came in, Hauck was on the phone with the NYPD's Emergency Management Office in the city.

Possible 634. Leaving the scene of an accident. *West Street and the Post Road.*

All morning long he'd kept a close tab on the mess going on in the city. Panicked people had been calling in all day, unable to reach their loved ones, not knowing what else to do. When the Trade Towers were hit, he'd been working for the department's Office of Information, and it had been his job for weeks afterward to track down the fates of people unaccounted for—through the hospitals, the wreckage, the network of first responders. Hauck still had friends down there. He stared at the list of Greenwich names he'd taken down: Pomeroy. Bashtar. Grace. O'Connor.

The first time around, out of the hundreds unaccounted for, they had found only two.

"Possible 634, Ty!" the day sergeant buzzed in a second time. Hit and Run. Down on the Post Road, by West Street, near the fast-food outlets and car dealerships.

"Can't," Hauck said back to her. "Get Muñoz on it. I'm on something."

"Muñoz is already on the scene, Lieutenant. It's a homicide. It seems you got a body down there."

It took only minutes for Hauck to grab his Grand Corona out of the lot outside, shoot straight up Mason, his top hat flashing, to the top of the avenue by the Greenwich Office Park, then down the Post Road to West Street, across from the Acura dealership.

As he was the head of Violent Crimes in town, this was his call. Mostly his department broke up spats at the high school, the occasional report of a break-in, marital rows. Dead bodies were rare up here in Greenwich.

Stock fraud was a lot more common.

At the bottom of the avenue, four local blue-and-whites had blocked off the busy commercial thoroughfare, their lights ablaze. Traffic was being routed into one lane. Hauck slowed, nodding to a couple of patrolmen he recognized. Freddy Muñoz, one of the detectives on his staff, came over as Hauck got out.

"You gotta be kidding, Freddy." Hauck shook his head in disbelief. "Today of all days . . ."

The detective made a grim motion toward a covered mound in the middle of West Street, which intersected the Post Road and cut up to Railroad Avenue and I-95.

"It look like we're kidding, LT?"

The patrol cars had parked in a way that formed sort of a protective circle around the body. An EMS truck had arrived, but the tech was standing around waiting for the regional medical team out of Farmington. Hauck knelt and peeled back the plastic tarp.

Christ! His cheeks puffed out a blast of air.

The guy was just a kid—twenty-two, twenty-three at most—white, wearing a brown work uniform, long red locks braided in cornrows in the manner of a Jamaican *rasta*. His body was twisted so that his hips were swung over slightly and raised off the pavement, while his back was flat, face upward. The eyes were open, wide, the moment of impact still frozen in their pupils. A trickle of blood ran onto the pavement from the corner of the victim's mouth.

"You got a name?"

"Raymond. First name Abel. Middle name John. Went by AJ, his boss at the auto-customizing shop over there said. That's where he worked."

A young uniformed officer was standing nearby with a notepad. His nameplate read STASIO. Hauck assumed he'd been first on the scene.

"He was just off-shift," Muñoz said. "Said he was going out to buy some smokes and make a call." He pointed across the street. "Seems like he was headed into the diner over there."

Hauck glanced over to a place he knew called the Fairfield Diner, an occasional police hangout. He'd grabbed a meal there a couple of times himself.

"What do we know about the car?"

Muñoz called over Officer Stasio, who looked about a month removed from training, and who read, a little nervously, from his spiral pad. "It appears like the hit-car was a white SUV, Lieutenant. It was traveling north up the Post Road and turned sharply onto West Street here. . . . Ran into the vic just as he was crossing the street. We got two eyewitnesses who saw the whole thing."

Stasio pointed to two men, one stocky, sport

coat, mustached, sitting in the front seat of an open patrol car rubbing his hair. The other in a blue fleece top talking to another officer, somberly shaking his head. "We located one in the parking lot of the Arby's over there. An ex-cop, it turns out. The other came from the bank across the street."

The kid had put it together pretty good. "Good work, Stasio."

"Thank you, sir."

Hauck slowly raised himself up, his knees cracking. A parting gift from his football days.

He looked back at the rutted gray asphalt on West Street—the two extended streaks of rubber about twenty feet farther along than the victim's cell phone and glasses. Skid marks. Well past the point of impact. Hauck sucked in an unpleasant breath, and his stomach shifted.

Son of a bitch hadn't even tried to stop.

He looked over at Stasio. "You doin' okay, son?" That this was the young officer's first fatality was plainly written all over his face.

Stasio nodded back. "Yessir."

"Never easy." Hauck patted the young patrolman on the shoulder. "That's true for any of us."

"Thank you, Lieutenant."

Hauck pulled Muñoz aside. He guided his

detective's eye along the Post Road south, the route that the hit-car traveled, then in the direction of the tire marks on the pavement.

"Seeing what I'm seeing, Freddy?"

The detective nodded grimly. "Bastard never made a move to stop."

"Yeah." Hauck pulled out a latex glove from his jacket pocket and threaded it over his fingers.

"Okay." He knelt back down to the inert body. "Let's see what she says. . . ."

Hauck lifted Abel Raymond's torso just enough to remove a black wallet from the victim's trouser pocket. A Florida driver's license: Abel John Raymond. There was also a laminated photo ID from Seminole Junior College, dating back two years. Same bright-eyed grin as on the license, hair a little shorter. Maybe the kid had dropped out.

There was a MasterCard in his name, a card from Sears, others from Costco, ExxonMobil, Social Security. Forty-two dollars in cash. A ticket stub from the 1996 Orange Bowl. Florida State–Notre Dame. Hauck recalled the game. From out of the wallet's divider he unfolded a snapshot of an attractive dark-haired woman who appeared to be in her twenties holding a young boy. Hauck handed it up to Muñoz.

"Doesn't look like a sister." The detective

shrugged. The victim wasn't wearing a wedding ring. "Girlfriend, maybe."

They'd have to track down who it was.

"*Someone's* not going to be very happy tonight." Freddy Muñoz sighed.

Hauck tucked the photo back into the wallet and exhaled. "Long list, I'm afraid, Freddy."

"It's crazy, isn't it, Lieutenant?" Muñoz shook his head. He was no longer talking about the accident. "You know my wife's brother took in the 7:57 this morning. Got out just before it happened. My sister-in-law was going crazy. She couldn't reach him till he got into the office. You roll over in bed for a few more minutes, get stuck at a light, miss your train. . . . You know how lucky he is?"

Hauck thought of the list of names back on his desk, the nervous, hopeful voices of those who had called in about them. He glanced over to Stasio's witnesses.

"C'mon, Freddy, let's get an ID on that car."

47

CHAPTER EIGHT

Hauck took the guy in the sport jacket, Freddy the North Face fleece.

Hauck's turned out to be a retired cop from South Jersey, name of Phil Dietz. He claimed he was up here cold-canvassing for state-of-the-art security systems—"You know, 'smart' homes, thumbprint, ID sensors, that sort of thing"— which he'd been handling since turning in the badge three years before. He had just pulled into the Arby's up the street to grab a sandwich when he saw the whole thing.

"He came down the street moving pretty good," Dietz said. He was short, stocky, graying hair a little thin on top, with a thick mustache, and he moved his stubby hands excitedly. "I heard the engine pick up. He accelerated down the street and made this turn *there*." He pointed toward the intersection of West Street and the Post Road.

"SOB hit that kid without even touching the brakes. I didn't see it until it was too late."

"Can you give me a make on the car?" Hauck asked.

Dietz nodded. "It was a white late-model SUV. A Honda or an Acura, I think, something like that. I could look at some pictures. Plates were white, too—I think blue lettering, or maybe green." He shook his head. "Too far away. My eyes aren't what they were when I was on the job." He jiggled a set of reading glasses in his breast pocket. "Now all I have to do is to be able to read POs."

Hauck smiled, then made a notation on his pad. "Not local?"

Dietz shook his head. "No. Maybe New Hampshire or Massachusetts. Sorry, I couldn't get a solid read. The bastard stopped for a second—*after*. I yelled, 'Hey, you!' and started to run down the hill. But he just took off up the road. I tried to grab a picture with my cell phone, but it happened too fast. He was gone."

Dietz pointed up the hill, toward the heights of Railroad Avenue. West Street went into a curve as it bent past an open lot, an office building. Once you were up there, I-95 was only a minute or two away. Hauck knew they'd have to be lucky if anyone up there saw him.

49

He turned back to the witness. "You said you heard the engine accelerate?"

"That's right. I was stepping out of my car. Thought I'd kill some time before my next appointment." Dietz pressed his interlocked hands around the back of his head. "Cold calls . . . Don't ever quit."

"I'll try not to." Hauck grinned, then re-directed him, motioning south. "It was coming from down there? You were able to follow it before it turned?"

"Yup. It caught my eyes as it sped up." Dietz nodded.

"The driver was male?"

"Definitely."

"Any chance you caught a description?"

He shook his head. "After the vehicle stopped, the guy looked back for an instant through the glass. Maybe had a second thought at what he'd done. I couldn't get a read on his face. Tinted windows. Believe me, I wish I had."

Hauck looked back up the hill and followed what he imagined was the victim's path. If he worked at J&D Tint and Rims, he'd have to walk across West Street, then cross the Post Road at the light to get to the diner.

"You say you used to be on the force?"

"Township of Freehold." The witness's eyes

50

lit up. "South Jersey. Near Atlantic City. Twenty-three years."

"Good for you. So what I'm going to ask you, Mr. Dietz, you may understand. Did you happen to notice if the vehicle was traveling at a consistently high rate of speed prior to making the turn? Or did it speed up as the victim stepped into the street?"

"You're trying to decide if this was an accident or intentional?" The ex-cop cocked his head.

"I'm just trying to get a picture of what took place," Hauck replied.

"I heard him from up there." Dietz pointed up the block toward the Arby's. "He shot down the hill, then spun into the turn—outta control. To me it was like he must've been drunk. I don't know, I just looked up when I heard the impact. He dragged the poor kid's body like a sack of wheat. You can still see the marks. Then he stopped. I think the kid was underneath him at that point, before he sped away."

Dietz said he'd be happy to look at some photos of white SUVs, to try to narrow down the make and model. "You find this SOB, Lieutenant. Anything I can do, you let me know. I wanna be the hammer that drives the nail into his coffin."

Hauck thanked him. Not as much to go on as

he would have liked. Muñoz stepped over. The guy he'd been talking to saw the incident from across the street. A track coach from up in Wilton, twenty miles away. Hodges. He identified the same white vehicle and same out-of-state plates. "AD or something. Maybe eight . . ." He was just stepping out of the bank after using the ATM. It had happened so quickly that he, too, couldn't get much of a read. He gave roughly the same sketchy picture Dietz had of what had taken place.

Muñoz shrugged, disappointed. "Not a whole lot to go on, is it, Lieutenant?"

Hauck pressed his lips in frustration. "No."

He went back to his car and called in an APB. A white late-model SUV driven by a white male, "possibly Honda or Acura, possibly Massachusetts or New Hampshire plates, possibly beginning AD8. Likely front-end body damage." They'd put it out to the state police and the auto-repair shops all over the Northeast. They'd canvass people farther up along West Street to see if anyone spotted him racing by. There might be some speed-control cameras along the highway. That was their best hope.

Unless, of course, it turned out someone had it in for Abel Raymond.

There was a guy in a Yankees cap standing

nearby, huddled against the chill. Stasio brought him over. Dave Corso, the owner of the auto custom shop where AJ Raymond worked.

"He was a good kid." Corso shook his head, visibly distressed. "He'd been working with me for about a year. He was talented. He remodeled old cars himself. He was up from Florida."

Hauck recalled his license. "You know where?"

The body-shop owner shrugged. "I don't know. Tallahassee, Pensacola . . . He always wore these T-shirts, the Florida State Seminoles. I think he took everyone out for a beer when they won that college bowl last year. I think his father was a sailor or something down there."

"You mean like in the navy?"

"No. Tugboat or something. He had his picture tacked up on the board. It's still inside."

Hauck nodded. "Where did Mr. Raymond live?"

"Up in Bridgeport, I'm pretty sure. I know we have it on file inside, but you know how it is—things change. But I know he banked over at First City. . . ." He told them that AJ got this call, maybe twenty minutes before he left. He was in the middle of doing this tinting. Then he came and said he was going on early break. "Marty something, I think the guy said. AJ said he was going across the street to grab some smokes. The diner, I think. It has a machine." Corso glanced over at the covered mound in the street. "Then *this* . . . How the hell do you figure?"

Hauck removed the victim's wallet from out of a bag and showed Corso the photo of the girl and her son. "Any idea who this is?"

The auto-body manager shrugged. "I think he had some gal up there. . . . Or maybe Stamford. She picked him up here once or twice. Lemme look. . . . Yeah, I think that's her. AJ was into working on classic cars. You know, restoring them. Corvettes, LeSabres, Mustangs. I think he'd just been up at a show this past weekend. *Man* . . ."

"Mr. Corso." Hauck took the man aside. "Is there anyone you can think of who'd possibly want to do Mr. Raymond harm? Did he have debts? Did he gamble? Do drugs? Anything you can think of would help."

"You're thinking this wasn't an accident?" The victim's employer's eyes widened in surprise.

"Just doing our job," Muñoz said.

"Jeez, I don't know. To me he was just a solid kid. He showed up. Did his job. People liked him here. But now that you mention it, this gal . . . I think she was married or recently split up from her husband. I know somewhere back I heard AJ mention he was having trouble with

54

her ex. Maybe Jackie would know. Inside. He was closer to him."

Hauck nodded. He signaled to Muñoz to follow that up.

"While we're in there, Mr. Corso, you mind if we check where the phone call he received came from, too?"

There was something in Hauck's gut that wasn't sitting well about this.

He went out to the side of the road, looking back down the knoll to the accident site. It was visible—clearly. The West Street turnoff. Nothing obstructing the view. The assailant's car hadn't slowed. It hadn't made a move to stop or avoid him. A DUI would have had to have been drop-dead out of his gourd on a Monday at noon to have hit this kid head-on.

The medical team from upstate had finally arrived. Hauck went back down the hill. He picked up the victim's cell phone. He'd check the recently dialed numbers. It wouldn't surprise him if the number that had called in would be traced to the same guy.

Things like this often worked that way.

Hauck knelt over Abel Raymond's body a last time, taking a good look at the kid's face. *I'm gonna find out for you, son,* he vowed. His thoughts flashed back to the bombing. There were a lot of people in town who weren't going to be coming home tonight. This would only be one. But this one he could do something about.

This one—Hauck stared at the locks of long red hair, the ache of a long-untended wound rising up inside him—this one had a face.

As he was about to get up, Hauck checked the victim's pockets a final time. In the guy's trousers, he found some change, a gas receipt. Then he reached into the chest pocket under the embroidered patch that bore his initials. AJ.

He poked his finger around and brought out a yellow scrap of paper, a standard Post-it note. It had a name written on it with a number, a local phone exchange.

It could've been the person AJ Raymond was on his way to meet. Or it could've been in there for weeks. Hauck dropped it in the evidence bag with the other things he had pulled, one more link to check out.

Charles Friedman.

CHAPTER NINE

I never heard from my husband again. I never knew what happened.

The fires raged underground in Grand Central for most of the day. There'd been a powerful accelerant used in the blast. Four blasts. One in each of the first two cars of the 7:51 out of Greenwich, exploding just as it came to a stop. The others in trash baskets along the platform packed with a hundred pounds of hexagen, enough to bring a good-sized building down. A splinter cell, they said. Over Iraq. Can you imagine? Charlie hated the war in Iraq. They found names, pictures of the station, traces of chemicals where the bombs were made. The fire that burned there for most of two days had reached close to twenty-three hundred degrees.

We waited. We waited all day that first day to hear something. Anything. Charlie's voice. A message from one of the hospitals that he was there. It seemed like we called the whole world: the NYPD, the hotline that had been set up. Our local congressman, whom Charlie knew.

We never did.

One hundred and eleven people died. That included three of the bombers, who, they suspected, were in the first two cars. Where Charlie always sat. Many of them couldn't even be identified. No distinguishable remains. They just went to work one morning and disappeared from the earth. That was Charlie. My husband of eighteen years. He just yelled goodbye over the hum of the hair dryer and went to take in the car.

And disappeared.

What they did find was the handle of the leather briefcase the kids had given him last year—the charred top piece still attached, blown clear from the blast site, the gold-embossed monogram, CMF, which made it final for the first time and brought our tears.

Charles Michael Friedman.

Those first days I was sure he was going to crawl out of that mess. Charlie could pull himself out of anything. He could fall off the damn roof trying to fix the satellite and he'd land on his feet. You could just count on him so much.

But he didn't. There was never a call, or a piece of his clothing, even a handful of ashes.

And I'll never know.

I'll never know if he died from the initial explosion or in the flames. If he was conscious or if he felt pain. If he had a final thought of us. If he called out our names.

Part of me wanted one last chance to take him by the shoulders and scream, "How could you let yourself die in there, Charlie?" How?

Now I guess I have to accept that he's gone. That he won't be coming back. Though it's so effing hard. . . .

That he'll never get to drive Samantha to college that first time. Or watch Alex score a goal. Or see the people they become. Things that would have made him so proud.

We were going to grow old together. Sail off to that Caribbean cove. Now he's gone, in a flash.

Eighteen years of our lives.

Eighteen years . . .

And I don't even get to kiss him good-bye.

CHAPTER TEN

A few days later—Friday, Saturday, Karen had lost track—a police detective came by the house.

Not from the city. People from the police in New York and the FBI had been by a few times trying to trace Charlie's movements that day. This one was local. He called ahead and asked if he could talk with Karen for just a few moments on a matter unrelated to the bombing. She said sure. Anything that helped take her mind off things for a few moments was a godsend to her now.

She was in the kitchen arranging flowers that had come in from one of the outfits that Charlie cleared through when he stopped by.

Karen knew she looked a mess. She wasn't exactly keeping up appearances right now. Her dad, Sid, who was up from Atlanta and who was being very protective of her, brought him in.

"I'm Lieutenant Hauck," he said. He was nicely dressed, for a cop, in a tweed sport jacket and slacks and a tasteful tie. "I saw you at the meeting in town Monday night. I'll only take a few moments of your time. I'm very sorry for your loss."

"Thank you." Karen nodded and pushed her hair back as they sat down in the sunroom, trying to shift the mood with an appreciative smile.

"My daughter's not feeling so well," her father cut in, "so maybe, whatever it is you have to go over . . ."

"Dad, I'm fine." She smiled. She rolled her eyes affectionately, then caught the lieutenant's gaze. "It's okay. Let me talk to the policeman."

"Okay, okay," he said. "I'm out here. If you need me . . ." He went back into the TV room and shut the door.

"He doesn't know what to do," Karen said with a deep sigh. "No one does. It's tough for everyone right now."

"Thank you for seeing me," the detective said. "I won't take long." He sat across from her and took something out of his pocket. "I don't know if you heard, but there was another incident in town on Monday. A hit-and-run accident, down on the Post Road. A young man was killed."

"No, I didn't," Karen said, surprised.

"His name was Raymond. Abel John Raymond." The lieutenant handed her a photo of a smiling, well-built young man with red dreadlocks, standing next to a surfboard on the beach. "AJ, he was called. He worked in a custom-car shop here in town. He was crossing West Street when he was run over at a high speed by an SUV making a right turn. Whoever it was didn't even bother to stop. The guy dragged him about fifty feet, then took off."

"That's horrible," Karen said, staring at the face again, feeling a stab of sorrow. Whatever had happened to her, it was still a small town. It could have been anybody. Anybody's son. The same day she'd lost Charlie.

She looked back at him. "What does this have to do with me?"

"Any chance you've seen this person before?"

Karen looked again. A handsome face, full of life. The long red locks would've made it hard to forget. "I don't think so. No."

"You never heard the name Abel Raymond or maybe AJ Raymond?"

Karen stared at the photo once again and shook her head. "I don't think so, Lieutenant. Why?"

The detective seemed disappointed. He reached back into his jacket again, this time removing a yellow slip of paper, a wrinkled Post-it note contained in a plastic bag. "We found this in the victim's work uniform, at the crime scene."

As Karen looked, she felt her insides tighten and her eyes grow wide.

"That is your husband's name, isn't it? Charles Friedman. And his cell number?"

Karen looked up, completely mystified, and nodded. "Yes. It is."

"And you're sure you never heard your husband mention his name? Raymond? He did tinting and custom painting at a car shop in town."

"Tinting?" Karen shook her head and smiled with her eyes. "Unless he was gearing up for some kind of midlife crisis he didn't tell me about."

Hauck smiled back at her. But Karen could see he was disappointed.

"I wish I could help you, Lieutenant. Are you thinking this was intentional, this hit-and-run?"

"Just being thorough." He took back the photo and the slip of paper with Charlie's name. He was handsome, Karen thought. In a rugged sort of way. Serious blue eyes. But something caring in them. It must have been hard for him to come here today. It was clear he wanted to do right by this boy.

She shrugged. "It's a bit of a coincidence, isn't it? Charlie's name on that paper. In that boy's pocket. The same day . . . you having to come here like this."

"A bad one"—he nodded, forcing a tight smile—"yes. I'll be out of your way." They both stood up. "If you think of anything, you'll let me know. I'll leave a card."

"Of course." Karen took it and stared at it: CHIEF OF DETECTIVES. VIOLENT CRIMES. GREENWICH POLICE DEPARTMENT.

"I'm very sorry about your husband," the lieutenant repeated.

His eyes seemed to drift to a photo she kept on the shelf. She and Charlie, dressed up formal. At her cousin Meredith's wedding. Karen always loved the way the two of them looked in that picture.

She smiled wistfully. "Eighteen years together, I don't even get to kiss him good-bye."

For a second they just stood there, she wishing she hadn't said that, he shifting on the balls of his feet, seemingly contemplating something and a little strained. Then he said, "On 9/11, I was working in the city at the NYPD's Office of Information. It was my job to try and track down people who were missing. You know, presumed to be inside the buildings, lost. It was tough. I saw

64

a lot of families"—he wet his lips—"in this same situation. I guess all I'm trying to say is, I have a rough idea of what you're going through. . . ."

Karen felt a sting at the back of her eyes. She looked up and tried to smile, not knowing what else to say.

"You'll let me know if there's anything I can do." He took a step to the door. "I still keep a few friends down there."

"I appreciate that, Lieutenant." She walked him through the kitchen to the back door in order to avoid the crowd in front. "It's awful. I wish you luck with finding this guy. I wish I could be more help."

"You have your own things to be thinking about," he said, opening the door.

Karen looked at him. A tone of hopefulness rose in her voice. "So did anyone ever turn up? When you were looking?"

"Two." He shrugged. "One at St. Vincent's Hospital. She had been struck by debris. The other, he never even made it in to work that morning. He witnessed what happened and just couldn't go home for a few days."

"Not the best odds." Karen smiled, looking at him as if she knew what he must be thinking. "It would just be good, you know, to have something. . . ."

"My best to you and your family, Mrs. Friedman." The lieutenant opened the door. "I'm very sorry for your loss."

Outside, Hauck stood a moment on the walkway.

He had hoped the name and number in AJ Raymond's pocket would prove more promising. It was pretty much all he had left.

A check of the phone records where the victim worked hadn't panned out at all. The call that he'd received—*Marty something,* the manager had said—was designated a private caller. From a cell phone. Totally untraceable now.

Nor had the girlfriend's ex. The guy turned out to be a lowlife, maybe a wife beater, but his alibi checked. He'd been at a conference at his kid's school at the time of the accident, and anyway he drove a navy Toyota Corolla, not an SUV. Hauck had double-checked.

Now all he was left with were the conflicting reports from the two eyewitnesses and his APB on the white SUVs.

Next to nothing.

It burned in him. Like AJ Raymond's red hair.

Someone out there was getting away with murder. He just couldn't prove it.

Karen Friedman was attractive, nice. He wished he could help in some way. It hurt a little, seeing the strain and uncertainty in her eyes. Knowing exactly what she would be going through. What she was going to face.

The heaviness in his heart, he knew it wasn't tied quite as closely to 9/11 victims as he'd said. But to something deeper, something never very far away.

Norah. *She'd be eight now, right?*

The thought of her came back to him with a stab, as it always did. A child in a powder blue sweatshirt and braces, playing with her sister on the pavement. A Tugboat Annie toy.

He could still hear the trill of her sweet voice. *Merrily, merrily, merrily, merrily . . .*

He could still see her red, braided hair.

A car door slammed at the curb, rocketing him back. Hauck looked up and saw a nicely dressed couple holding flowers walking up to Karen Friedman's front door.

Something caught his eye.

One of the garage doors had been opened in the time since he'd arrived. A housekeeper was lugging out a bag of trash.

There was a copper-colored Mustang parked in one of the bays—'65 or '66, he guessed. A convertible. A red heart decal on the rear fender and a white racing stripe running down the side.

The license plate read CHRLYS BABY.

Hauck went over and knelt, running his hand along the smooth chrome trim.

Son of a bitch . . .

That's what AJ Raymond did! He restored old cars. For a second it almost made Hauck laugh out loud. He wasn't sure how it made him feel, disappointed or relieved, the last of his leads slipping away.

Still, he decided, heading back across the driveway to his car, at least he now knew what the guy was doing with Charles Friedman's number.

CHAPTER ELEVEN

Pensacola, Florida

The huge gray tanker emerged from the mist and cut its engines at the mouth of the harbor.

The shadows of heavy industry: steel gray trestles, the refinery tanks, the gigantic hydraulic pumps awaiting gas and oil, all lay quiet in the vessel's approach.

A single launch motored out to meet it.

At the helm the pilot, who was called Pappy, fixed on the waiting ship. As assistant harbormaster, Pensacola Port Authority, his job was to guide the football-field-size craft through the sandy limestone shoals around Singleton Point and then through the busy lanes of the inner harbor, which bustled with commercial traffic as the day wore on. He'd been bringing home large ships like this since he was twenty-two, a job—more like a rite—

handed down from his own father, who had done it himself since *he* was twenty-two. For close to thirty years, Pappy had done this so many times he could pretty much guide home a ship in his sleep, which in the darkened calm before the dawn this morning—if it were a normal morning and this just another tanker—would be exactly what he was about to do.

She's tall there, Pappy noted, focused on the ship's hull.

Too tall. The draft line was plainly visible. He stared at the logo on the tanker's bow.

He'd seen these ships before.

Normally the real skill lay in gauging what the large tanker was drawing and navigating it through the sandbars at the outer rim of the harbor. Then simply follow the lanes, which by 10:00 A.M. could be livelier than the loop into downtown, and make the wide, sweeping arc into Pier 12, which was where the *Persephone*, according to its papers carrying a full load of Venezuelan crude, was slotted to put in.

But not this morning.

Pappy's launch approached the large tanker from the port side. As he neared, he focused on the logo of a leaping dolphin on the *Persephone*'s hull.

Dolphin Oil.

He scratched a weathered hand across his beard and scanned over his entry papers from Maritime Control: 2.3 million barrels of crude aboard. The ship had made the trip up from Trinidad in barely fourteen hours. *Fast,* Pappy noted, especially for an outdated 1970 ULCC-class piece of junk like this, weighed down with a full load.

They always made it up here fast.

Dolphin Oil.

The first time he'd just been curious. It had come in from Jakarta. He had wondered, how could a ship loaded with slime be riding quite that high? The second time, just a few weeks back, he'd actually snuck below after it docked— inside the belly of the ship, making his way past the distracted crew, and checked out the forward tanks.

Empty. Came as no surprise. At least not to him.

Clean as a newborn's ass.

He'd brought this up to the harbormaster, not once but twice. But he just patted Pappy on the back like he was some old fool and asked him what his plans were when he retired. This time, though, no glorified paper pusher was going to slip this under a stack of forms. Pappy knew people. People who worked in the right places.

People who'd be interested in this kind of thing. This time, when he brought the ship in, he'd prove it.

2.3 million barrels . . .

2.3 million barrels, my ass.

Pappy sounded the horn and pulled the launch along the ship's bow. His mate, Al, took over the wheel. A retractable gangway was lowered from the main deck. He prepared to board.

That's when his cell phone vibrated. He grabbed it off his belt. It was 5:10 in the morning. Anyone not insane was still asleep. The screen read PRIVATE. Text message.

Some kind of picture coming through.

Pappy yelled forward to Al to hold it and jumped back from the *Persephone*'s gangway. In the predawn light, he squinted at the image on the screen.

He froze.

It was a body. Twisted and contorted on the street. A dark pool beneath the head that Pappy realized was blood.

He brought the screen closer and tried to find the light.

"Oh, Lord God, no . . ."

His eyes were seized by the image of the victim's long red dreadlocks. His chest filled up

72

with pain as if he'd been stabbed. He fell back, an inner vise cracking his ribs.

"Pappy!" Al called back from the bridge. "You all right there?"

No. He wasn't all right.

"That's Abel," he gasped, his airways closing. *"That's my son!"*

Suddenly, he felt the vibration of another message coming through.

Same: PRIVATE NUMBER.

This time it was just three words that flashed on the screen.

Pappy ripped open his collar and tried to breathe. But it was sorrow knifing at him there, not a heart attack. And anger—at his own pride.

He sank to the deck, the three words flashing in his brain.

SEEN ENOUGH NOW?

CHAPTER TWELVE

A month later—a few days after they'd finally held a memorial for Charlie, Karen trying to be upbeat, but it was so, so hard—the UPS man dropped off a package at her door.

It was during the day. The kids were at school. Karen was getting ready to leave. She had a steering-committee meeting at the kids' school. She was trying as best she could to get back to some kind of normal routine.

Rita, their housekeeper, brought it in, knocking on the bedroom door.

It was a large padded envelope. Karen checked out the sender. The label said it was from a Shipping Plus outlet in Brooklyn. No return name or address. Karen couldn't think of anyone she knew in Brooklyn.

She went into the kitchen and took a package blade and opened the envelope. Whatever was inside was protected in bubble wrap, which Karen carefully slit open. Curious, she lifted out the contents.

It was a frame. Maybe ten by twelve inches. Chrome. Someone had gone to a lot of trouble.

Inside the frame was what appeared to be a page from some kind of notepad, charred, dirt marks on it, torn on the upper right edge. There were a bunch of random numbers scratched all over it, and a name.

Karen felt her breath stolen away.

The page read *From the desk of Charles Friedman*. The writing on it was Charlie's.

"Ees a gift?" asked Rita, picking up the wrappings.

Karen nodded, barely able to even speak. "*Yes.*"

She took it into the sunroom and sat with it on the window seat, rain coming down outside.

It was her husband's notepad. The stationery Karen had given him herself a few years back. The sheet was torn. The numbers didn't make sense to her and the name scrawled there was one Karen didn't recognize. Megan Walsh. A corner of it was charred. It looked as if it had been on the ground for a long time.

But it was Charlie—his writing. Karen felt a tingling sensation all over.

There was a note taped to the frame. Karen pulled it off. It read: *I found this, three days after what happened, in the main terminal of Grand Central. It must have floated there. I held on to it, because I didn't know if it would hurt or help. I pray it helps.*

It was unsigned.

Karen couldn't believe it. On the news she'd heard there were thousands of papers blown all over the station after the explosion. They had settled everywhere. Like confetti after a parade.

Karen fixed intently on Charlie's writing. It was just a bunch of meaningless numbers and a name she didn't recognize, scribbled at odd angles. Dated 3/22, weeks before his death. A bunch of random messages, no doubt.

But it was from Charlie. His writing. It was a part of him the day he died.

They had never given her back the piece of his briefcase they'd recovered. This was all she had. Holding it to her, for a moment it was almost as if she felt him there.

Her eyes filled up with tears. "Oh, Charlie . . ."

In a way it was like he was saying good-bye.

I didn't know if it would hurt or help, the sender had written.

Oh, yes, it helps. It more than helps. . . . Karen held it close. *A thousand times more.*

It was just a jumble of stupid numbers and a name scratched out in his hand. But it was all she had.

She hadn't been able to cry at his memorial. Too many people. Charlie's blown-up photo looming above them. And they all wanted it to be upbeat, not sad. She'd tried to be so strong.

But there, sitting by the window, her husband's writing pressed against her heart, she felt it was okay. *I'm here with you, Charlie,* Karen thought. She finally let herself really cry.

CHAPTER THIRTEEN

Down the street a man hunched in a darkened car, rain streaming on the windshield. He smoked as he watched the house and cracked the window a shade to flick the ashes onto the street.

The UPS truck had just left. He knew that what it brought would send things spinning. A short while later, Karen Friedman rushed out, a rain jacket over her head, and climbed into her Lexus.

Things promised to get interesting.

She backed out of the driveway and onto the street, reversed, and headed back toward him. The man hunched lower in the car, the Lexus's headlights hitting his windshield, glistening sharply in the rain as it went by.

Hybrid, he noted, impressed, watching in the rearview mirror as it went down the block.

He picked up his phone, which was sitting on the passenger seat across from him, next to his Walther P38, punching in a private number. His gaze fell to his hands. They were thick, coarse, workman's hands.

Time to get them dirty again, he sighed.

"Plan A doesn't seem to be moving," he said into the phone when the voice he was expecting finally answered.

"We don't have forever," the person on the other end replied.

"*Exactamente.*" He exhaled. He started his ignition, flicked an ash out the window, and took off at a slow pace, following the Lexus. "I'm already on Plan B."

CHAPTER FOURTEEN

One of the things Karen had to deal with in the weeks that followed was the liquidation of Charlie's firm.

She'd never gotten deeply involved in her husband's business. Harbor was what was termed "a general limited partnership." The share agreement maintained that in case the principal partner ever became deceased or unable to perform, the assets of the firm were to be redistributed back to the other partners. Charlie managed a modest-size fund, with assets of around $250 million. The lead investors were Goldman Sachs, where he had started out years before, and a few wealthy families he'd attracted over the years.

Saul Lennick, Charlie's first boss at Goldman, who had helped put him in business, acted as the firm's trustee.

It was hard for Karen to go through. Bittersweet. Charlie had only seven people working for him: a junior trader and a book-keeper, Sally, who ran the back office and had been with him since he'd first opened shop. His assistant, Heather, handled a lot of their personal stuff. Karen pretty much knew them all.

It would take a few months, Lennick advised her, for everything to be finalized. And that was fine with her. Charlie would've wanted them all to be well taken care of. "Hell, you know better than anyone that he practically spent more time with them over the years than he did with me," she said, smiling knowingly at Saul. Anyway, money wasn't exactly the issue right now.

She and the kids were okay financially. She had the house, which they owned clear, the ski place in Vermont. Plus, Charlie had been able to pull out some money over the years.

But it was tough, seeing his baby dismantled. The positions were sold. The office on Park Avenue was put up for lease. One by one, people found new jobs and began to leave.

That was like the final straw. The final imprint of him gone.

About that time the junior trader Charlie had brought into the firm just a few months before, Jonathan Lauer, called her at home. Karen wasn't around. He left a message on her machine: "I'd like to speak with you, Mrs. Friedman. At your convenience. There are some things you ought to know."

Some things ... Whatever they were, she wasn't up to it right then. Jonathan was new; he had started working for Charles only this past year. Charlie had lured him from Morgan. She passed the message on to Saul.

"Don't worry, I'll handle it," he told her. "All kinds of sticky issues, closing down a firm. People are looking out for their own arrangements. There may have been some bonus agreements discussed. Charlie wasn't the best at recording those things. You shouldn't have to deal with any of that right now."

He was right. She *couldn't* deal with that right now. In July she went away for a well-needed week at Paula and Rick's house in Sag Harbor. She rejoined her book group, started doing yoga again. God, how she needed that. Her body began to resemble itself once again and feel alive. Gradually her spirits did, too.

August came, and Samantha had a job at a local beach club. Alex was away at lacrosse camp. Karen was thinking maybe she'd look into getting a real-estate license.

Jonathan Lauer contacted her again.

This time Karen was at home. Still, she didn't pick up. She heard the same cryptic message on the machine: "Mrs. Friedman, I think it's important that we talk. . . ."

But Karen just let the message tape go on. She didn't like avoiding him. Charlie had always spoken highly of the young man. *People are looking out for their own arrangements. . . .*

She just couldn't answer. Hearing his voice trail off, she felt bad.

CHAPTER FIFTEEN

It was September, the kids were back in school when Karen ran into Lieutenant Hauck, the Greenwich detective, again.

It was halftime of a high-school football game at Greenwich Field. They were playing Stamford West. Karen had volunteered to sell raffle tickets for the Teen Center drive for the athletic department. The stands were packed. It was a crisp, early-autumn Saturday morning. The Huskies band was on the field. She went over to the refreshment stand to grab herself a cup of coffee against the chill.

She almost didn't recognize him at first. He was dressed in a navy polar-fleece pullover and jeans, a young, pretty girl who looked no more than nine or ten to Karen hoisted on his shoulders. They sort of bumped into each other in the crowd.

"Lieutenant . . . ?"

"Hauck." He turned and stopped, a pleased glimmer in his eye.

"Karen Friedman." She nodded, shielding the sun out of her eyes.

"Of course I remember." He let the girl down. "Jess, say hi to Mrs. Friedman."

"Hi." The pretty girl waved, a little shy. "Nice to meet you."

"It's nice to meet you too, sweetie." Karen smiled. "Your daughter?"

The lieutenant nodded. "Just as well," he groaned, clutching his back, "she's getting way too big for me to do this for very long. Right, honey? Why don't you go ahead and find your friends. I'll be over in a while."

"Okay." The girl ran off and melded into the crowd, heading in the direction of the far sidelines.

"Nine?" Karen guessed, an inquisitive arch of her eyebrows.

Ten. Somehow she still pushes for the Big Ride. I figure I've got another year or two at best before she'll start to cringe if I ever offer to do it again."

"Not girls and their daddies." Karen shook her head and grinned. "Anyway, it's sort of like a bell curve. At some point they come all the way back. At least that's what I'm told. *I'm* still waiting."

They stood around for a minute, bucking the flow of the crowd. A heavyset guy in a Greenwich sweatshirt slapped Hauck on the shoulder as he went by. "Hey, *Leg* . . ."

"Rollie." The lieutenant waved back.

"I was just headed to get some coffee," Karen said.

"Let me," Hauck offered. "Trust me, you won't be able to beat the price."

They stepped over to the refreshment line. A woman who was running the coffee station seemed to recognize him. "Hey, Ty! How's it going, Lieutenant? Looks like we could use you out there today."

"Yeah, just gimme about twenty of these straight up plus a shot of cortisone in both knees and you can put me in." He pulled out a couple of bills.

"On the house, Lieutenant." She waved him away. "Booster program."

"Thanks, Mary." Hauck winked back. He handed a cup to Karen. There was a table free, and Hauck motioned her toward it and they each grabbed a metal chair.

"See what I mean?" He took a sip. "One of the few legal perks I have left."

"Rank has its privilege." Karen winked, pretending to be impressed.

"Nah." Hauck shrugged. "Tailback. Greenwich High, 1975. Went all the way to the state finals that year. They never forget."

Karen grinned. She brushed her hair back from under her hooded Greenwich High sweatshirt and cupped her hands on the steaming cup.

"So how are you doing?" the detective asked. "I actually meant to call a couple of times. When I last saw you, things were pretty raw."

"I know." Karen shrugged again. "They were then. I'm doing better. Time . . ." She sighed, tilting her cup.

"As they say . . ." The lieutenant did the same and smiled. "So you have kids in the high school?"

"Two. Samantha's graduating this year. Alex is a sophomore. He plays lacrosse. He's still taking things pretty hard."

"'Course he is," the lieutenant said. Someone brushed him in the back, rushing by. He nodded, pressing his lips together. What could you say?

"You were looking into a hit-and-run then," Karen said, shifting gears. "Some kid out of Florida. You ever find that guy?"

"No. But I did find out why your husband's name was in his pocket."

87

He told Karen about the Mustang.

"'*Charlie's Baby*.'" She nodded and smiled. "Figures. Still have it. Charlie asked in his will not to sell it. How about it, Lieutenant? You want your own American icon, only year they made the color Emberglow. Only costs about eight grand a year to take it out of the garage a couple of times?"

"Sorry. I have my own American icon. College account." He grinned.

The PA announced that the teams were heading back on the field. The Huskies band marched off to a brassy version of Bon Jovi's "Who Says You Can't Go Home?" The lieutenant's daughter ran out of the crowd and yelled, "*Daddy*, come on! I want to sit with Elyse!"

"Second half's starting up," the lieutenant said.

"She's pretty," Karen said. "Oldest?"

"*My only*," the detective replied after a short pause. "Thanks."

Their eyes met for a second. There was something Karen felt hiding behind his deep-set eyes.

"So how about a raffle ticket?" she asked. "It's for a good cause. Booster program." She chuckled. "C'mon, I'm running behind."

"I'm afraid I already paid my dues." Hauck sighed resignedly, patting his knees.

She tore one off the pad and penciled his name in the blank. "It's on the house. You know, it was nice what you said to me that day. About how you knew how I felt. I guess I needed something then. I appreciated that."

"Man . . ." Hauck shook his head, taking the raffle slip out of her hand, their fingers momentarily touching. "The gifts just don't stop coming today."

"Price you have to pay for doing a good deed, Lieutenant."

They stood up. The lieutenant's daughter called out impatiently, "Daddy, c'mon!"

"Good luck with the raffles," he said. "You know, it might be good if you actually ended up *selling* a few of them today."

Karen laughed. "Nice to see you, Lieutenant." She shook her fists like imaginary pom-poms. *"Go Huskies!"*

Hauck waved, backing into the crowd. "See you around."

CHAPTER SIXTEEN

It took him by surprise that night, Hauck decided as he dabbed at the canvas in the small two-bedroom home he rented on Euclid Avenue in Stamford, overlooking Holly Cove.

Another marina scene. A sloop in a harbor, sails down. Pretty much the same scene from his deck. It was all he ever painted. Boats . . .

Jessie was in her room, watching TV, sending text messages. They'd had a pizza at Mona Lisa in town and went to the new animated release. Jess pretended to be bored. He'd enjoyed it.

"It's for, like, three-year-olds, Daddy." She rolled her eyes.

"Oh." He stopped pushing it. "The penguins were cool."

Hauck liked it here. A block from the small cove. His little two-story sixties Cape. The owner had fixed it up. From the deck off the second floor, where the living room was, you could see Long Island Sound. A French couple lived next door, Richard and Jacqueline, custom furniture restorers—their workshop was out in their garage—and they always invited him to their parties, full of lots of people with crazy accents and not-half-bad wine.

Yes, it took him by surprise. What he was feeling. How he had noticed her eyes—brown and fetchingly wide. How laughter seemed a natural fit in them. The little lilt in her voice, as if she weren't from around here. Her auburn hair tied back in a youthful ponytail.

How she stuffed that raffle ticket into his pocket and tried to make him smile.

Unlike Beth. When *her* world fell apart.

Hauck traced a narrow line from the sailboat's mast and blended it into the blue of the sea. He stared. It sucked.

No one would exactly confuse him with Picasso.

She had asked him if Jess was his youngest, and he had replied, pausing for what seemed an eternity—*my only*. He could have told her. She would have understood. She was going through it, too.

C'mon, Ty, why does it always have to come back to this?

They'd had everything then. He and Beth. It was hard to remember how they were once so in love. How she once thought he was the sexiest man alive. And he, her.

My only . . .

What had he forgotten at the store that made him rush back in? Pudding Snacks. . . .

Jamming the van hastily into park. How many times had he done that—and it stayed? A thousand? *A hundred thousand?*

"Watch out, guys. Daddy's got to back out of the garage. . . ."

As he headed back to the garage, receipt in hand, wallet in hand, they heard the shriek. Jessie's.

Beth's frozen eyes—*"Oh, my God, Ty, no!"*—as through the kitchen window they watched the van roll back.

Norah never even uttered a sound.

Hauck laid down his brush. He rested his forehead on the heel of his hand. It had cost him his marriage. It had cost him ever being able to look in the mirror without starting to cry. For the longest time, being able to put his arms around Jess and hug her.

Everything.

His mind came back to that morning. The freckles dancing on her cheek. It made him smile.

Get real, Ty. . . . She probably drives a car worth more than your 401(k). She's just lost her husband. A different life, maybe.

A different time.

But it surprised him as he picked up the brush again. What he was thinking . . . what it made him feel.

Awakened.

And that was strange, he decided. Because nothing surprised him anymore.

CHAPTER SEVENTEEN

December

Their lives had just begun to get back on some kind of even keel. Sam was applying to colleges, Tufts and Bucknell, her top choices. Karen had made the obligatory visits with her.

That was when the two men from Archer knocked on her door.

"Mrs. Friedman?" the shorter one stood at the door and inquired. He had a chiseled face and close-cropped light hair, was wearing a gray business suit under a raincoat. The other was gaunt and taller with horn-rim glasses, carrying a leather lawyer's briefcase.

"We're from a private auditing firm, Mrs. Friedman. Do you mind if we come in?"

At first it flashed through Karen's mind that they might be from the government fund that was being set up for victims' families. She'd heard through her support group that these people could be pretty officious and cold. She opened the door.

"Thank you." The light-haired one had a slight European accent and handed her a card. Archer and Bey Associates. Johannesburg, South Africa. "My name is Paul Roos, Mrs. Friedman. My partner is Alan Gillespie. We won't take too much of your time. Do you mind if we sit down?"

"Of course . . ." Karen said, a little hesitant. There *was* something cool and impersonal about them. She glanced closer at their cards. "If this is about my husband, you know Saul Lennick of the Whiteacre Capital Group is overseeing the disposition of the funds."

"We've been in touch with Mr. Lennick," answered Roos, a little matter-of-factly. He took a step toward the living room. "If you wouldn't mind . . ."

She took them over to the couch.

"You have a lovely home, Mrs. Friedman," Roos told her, looking around intently.

"Thank you. You said you were auditors," Karen replied. "I think my husband was handled by someone out of the city. Ross and Weiner— I don't recall your firm's name."

"We're actually not here on behalf of your

husband, Mrs. Friedman"—the South African crossed his legs—"but on the part of some of his investors."

"Investors?"

Karen knew that Morgan Stanley was Charlie's largest by far. Then came the O'Flynns and the Hazens, who had been with him since he began.

"Which ones?" Karen stared at him, puzzled.

Roos looked at her with a hesitant smile. "Just . . . *investors.*" That smile began to make Karen feel ill at ease.

His partner, Gillespie, opened his briefcase. "You received proceeds from the liquidation of your husband's firm assets, did you not, Mrs. Friedman?"

"This sounds more like an audit." Karen tightened. "Yes. Is there something wrong?" The funds had just been finalized. Charlie's share, after some final expenses to close down the firm, came to a little less than $4 million. "Maybe if you just told me what this is about."

"We're looking back through certain transactions," Gillespie said, dropping a large bound report in front of him on the coffee table.

"Look, I never got very involved at all in my husband's business," Karen answered. This was starting to make her worried. "I'm sure if you spoke to Mr. Lennick—"

"*Shortfalls*, actually," the accountant corrected himself, clear-eyed.

Karen didn't like these people. She didn't know why they were here. She peered at the business cards again. "You said you were auditors?"

"Auditors, and forensic investigators, Mrs. Friedman," Paul Roos told her.

"Investigators . . . ?"

"We're trying to piece through certain aspects of your husband's firm," Gillespie explained. "The records are proving to be a little . . . shall we call it *hazy*. We realize that as an independent hedge fund, he was not bound by certain formalities."

"Listen, I think you'd better go. I think you'd be better off if you took this to—"

"But what is clearly inescapable," the accountant continued, "is that there seems to be a considerable amount of money *missing*."

"*Missing* . . ." Karen met his eyes, holding back anger. Saul had never mentioned anything about any missing money. "That's why you're here? Well, isn't that just too bad, Mr. Gillespie? My husband's dead, as you seem to know. He went in to work one morning eight months ago and never came home again. So please, tell me"— her eyes burned through him like X-rays, and she stood up—"just how much money are we talking about, Mr. Gillespie? I'll go get my purse."

"We're speaking of two hundred and fifty million dollars, Mrs. Friedman," the accountant said. "Do you happen to keep that much in cash?"

Karen's heart almost stopped. She sat back down, the words striking her like bullets. The accountant's expression never changed.

"What the hell are you saying?"

Roos took over again, edging slightly forward. "What we're saying is that there's a hell of a lot of money unaccounted for in your husband's firm, Mrs. Friedman. And our clients want us to find out where it is."

Two hundred and fifty million. Karen was too stunned to even laugh. The proceeds had been finalized without a hitch. Charlie's entire business was barely larger than that.

She looked back into their dull, unchanging eyes. She knew they were implying something about her husband. Charlie was dead. He couldn't defend himself.

"I'm not sure we have anything further to discuss, Mr. Gillespie, Mr. Roos." Karen stood again. She wanted these men to leave. She wanted them out of her house. Now. "I told you, I never got involved in my husband's business.

You'll have to address your concerns to Mr. Lennick. I'd like you to go."

The accountants looked at each other. Gillespie folded his file back into his briefcase and clasped it shut. They rose.

"We don't mean any insult, Mrs. Friedman," Roos said in a more conciliatory tone. "What I would tell you, though, is that there may well be some sort of investigation launched. I wouldn't be spending any of those proceeds you received just yet." He smiled transparently and glanced around.

"Like I said, you have a lovely home. . . . But it's only fair to warn you." He turned at the door. "Your personal accounts may have to be looked at, too."

The hairs on Karen's arms stood on edge.

CHAPTER EIGHTEEN

It took just minutes, frantic ones, for Karen to get Saul Lennick on the phone.

It was hard for his office to find him. He was out of the country, on business. But his secretary heard the agitation in Karen's voice. Finally they tracked him down.

"Karen . . . ?"

"Saul, I'm sorry to bother you." She was almost on the verge of tears. She told him about the upsetting visit she'd had with two men from Archer.

"*Who?*"

"They're from something called Archer and Bey Associates. They're auditors, forensic investigators. It says they're out of South Africa. They said they spoke with you."

He made her go through every detail again, injecting a few sharp questions about their names and specifically what they said.

"Karen, listen. First, I want to assure you this is nothing you have to be concerned about. Harbor's partnership dissolution is moving along smoothly, and I promise you it's one hundred percent by the book. For the record, yes, Charlie may have taken a few losses at the end. He bet pretty heavily on some Canadian oil leases that took a hit."

"Who *are* these people, Saul?"

"I don't know. Some overseas accounting group, I suspect, but I'll find out. They could have been hired by some of Charles's investors over there, hoping to hold up the process."

"They're talking about hundreds of millions of dollars, Saul! You know Charlie didn't handle money like that. They were making these insinuations, warning me not to spend any of the proceeds. That's Charlie's money, Saul! It was creepy. They told me our personal accounts might be examined, too."

"That's not going to happen, Karen. Look, there are some details pending that someone could make some issues on if they wanted—"

"What kind of details, Saul?" She hadn't heard any of that before.

"Maybe some plays one could question. A glitch or two in one of Charles's lending agreements. But I don't want to get ahead of ourselves. This isn't the time."

"Charlie's dead, Saul! He can't defend himself. I mean, how many times did I hear him fretting over goddamn nickels and dimes for his clients? Fractions of a fucking point. And *these* people, making innuendos like that . . . They had no right to come here, Saul."

"Karen, I want to assure you there's no basis at all to what they're talking about. Whoever they are, they're just trying to stir up trouble. And they just went about it the wrong way."

"Yeah, Saul, they did." The fury in her blood began to recede. "They damn well did go about it the wrong way. I don't want them back in my house again. Thank God Samantha and Alex weren't here."

"Listen, I want you to fax me that card, Karen. I'll look into it from here. I promise, I'll make sure it doesn't happen again."

"Charlie was a reputable guy, Saul. You know that better than anyone."

"I know that, Karen. Charlie was like a second son to me. You realize I always have your interests at heart."

She pushed the hair off her face to cool herself down. "I do. . . ."

"Send me the card, Karen. And I want to be the first to know if they contact you again."

"Thank you, Saul."

Suddenly something strange came over Karen, an unexplainable rush of tears. Sometimes it just happened like that. Out of nowhere. The thought of having to defend her husband. She let a few seconds elapse on the line while she regained control.

"I mean it, Saul. . . . Really, thank you."

Her husband's mentor told her softly, "You don't even have to say it, Karen."

He didn't have the heart to tell her now. Or the will.

Lennick replaced the house phone in its cradle in the Old World lobby of the Vier Jahreszeiten Hotel in Munich.

A week ago his contact from the Royal Bank of Scotland had called, one of the lenders he had arranged for Charlie, who advanced his firm funds. It sounded perfunctory. The banker had a tone of slight concern.

A random check of an oil tanker by a customs official in Jakarta had reached their attention.

Lennick's heart had come to a stop. He wheeled around back to his desk. "Why?"

"Some kind of discrepancy," the banker explained, "in the stated contents of the cargo." Which was declared to have been 1.4 million barrels of oil.

The tanker was found to be empty, the bank official declared.

Lennick had turned ashen.

"I'm sure there's simply been some kind of mistake," the Scottish banker said to him. It seemed that 1.4 million barrels at sixty-six dollars per had been previously pledged by Charles Friedman as collateral against their loan.

The banker cleared his throat. "Is there any cause for alarm?"

Lennick felt a shiver of concern race down his spine. He'd look into it, he told the man, and that was enough to make the banker feel appeased. But as soon as he put down the phone, Lennick closed his eyes.

He thought of Charlie's recent losses, the pressure he'd been under. The pressure they'd all been under. How heavily he'd leveraged up on his funds.

You stupid son of a bitch, Charlie. Lennick sighed. He reached for the phone and started to dial a number. *How could you be so desperate, you fool, so careless? Don't you have any idea who these people are?*

People who didn't like to be looked into. Or have their affairs examined. Now everything had to be reconstructed. *Everything, Charlie.*

Even now, weeks later, in the Vier Jahreszeiten's lobby, the banker's all-too-delicate question made Lennick's mouth go dry.

Is there any cause for alarm?

CHAPTER NINETEEN

It was the second day of field-hockey practice, near the end of February. Sam Friedman tossed her stick into the bottom of her locker.

She played right forward for the girls' team. They'd lost a couple of their best attackers from last year, so this season it was going to be tough. Sam grabbed her parka off the hook and scanned over a few books. She had an English quiz tomorrow on a story by Tobias Wolfe, a chapter to skim on Vietnam. Since she'd gotten into Tufts, Early Decision 2 in January, she'd pretty much been coasting. Tonight a bunch of them were meeting in town at Thataways for wings and maybe sneak a beer.

Senior slump was in full throttle.

Outside, Sam ran over to her blue Acura SUV, which she'd parked in the west lot after lunch. She jumped in and tossed her bag onto the seat, and started up the engine. Then she plugged her iPod into the port and scrolled to her favorite tune.

"And I am telling you I'm not going . . . ," she sang, belting it out as closely as she could to Jennifer Hudson in *Dreamgirls.* She went to slip the Acura into drive.

That's when the hand wrapped around her mouth and jerked her head back to the headrest.

Samantha's eyes peeled back and she tried to let out a muffled scream.

"Don't make a sound, Samantha," a voice from behind her said.

Oh my God! That scared her even more, that the person knew her name. She felt a bolt of fear race down her spine, her eyes darting around, straining to glance at him in the rearview mirror.

"Uh-uh, Samantha." The assailant redirected her face forward. "Don't try to look at me. It'll be better for you that way."

How did he know her name?

This was bad. She ratcheted through a million things she had always heard in case something like this occurred. *Don't fight back. Let him do what he wants. Give him your money, jewelry, even if it's something important. Let him have his way.*

Anything.

107

"You're scared, Samantha, aren't you?" the man asked in a subdued voice. He had his hand wrapped tightly over her mouth, her eyes stretched wide.

She nodded.

"I don't blame you. I'd be scared, too."

She glanced outside, praying someone might come by. But it was late, and dark. The lot was empty. She felt his breath, hot on the back of her neck. She closed her eyes. *Oh, God, he's going to rape me. Or worse . . .*

"But it's your lucky day. I'm not going to hurt you, Samantha. I just want you to deliver a message to someone. Will you do that for me?"

Yes, Samantha nodded, yes. *Stay together, stay together,* she begged herself. *He's going to let you go.*

"To your mom."

My mom . . . What did her mom have to do with this?

"I want you to tell her, Sam, that the investigation is going to start very soon. And that it's going to get very personal. She'll understand. And that we're not the types to wait around patiently—forever. I think you can see that, can't you? Do you understand that, Sam?"

She shut her eyes. Shaking. Nodded.

"Good. Be sure and tell her that the clock's

108

ticking. And she doesn't want it to run out, I can promise that. Do you hear me, Sam?" He loosened his hand just slightly from her mouth.

"*Yes*," Sam whispered, her voice quaking.

"Now, don't look around," he said. "I'm going to slip out the back." The man had a hooded sweatshirt pulled over his face. "Trust me, the less you see, the better for you."

Samantha sat rigid. Her head moved up and down. "I understand."

"Good." The door opened. The man slipped out. She didn't look. Or turn to follow. She just sat there staring. Exactly as she was told.

"You are your father's little girl, aren't you, Sam?"

Her eyes shot wide.

"Remember about the sum. Two hundred and fifty million dollars. You tell your mom we won't wait long."

CHAPTER TWENTY

Karen clung to her daughter on the living-room couch. Samantha was sobbing, her head buried against her mother's shoulder, barely able to speak. She'd called Karen after the man had left, then driven home in a panic. Karen immediately called the police. Outside, the quiet street was ablaze in flashing lights.

Karen went through it with the first officers who'd arrived. "How could there be no protection at the school? How could they just let anyone in there?" Then to Sam, in total frustration, "Baby, how could you not have locked the car?"

"I don't know, Mom."

But inside she knew—her daughter's fingers tight and trembling, her face smeared with tears—that this wasn't about Samantha. Or more protection at school. Or locking the car door.

It was about Charlie.

This was about something he had done. Something she was growing more and more afraid that he had withheld from her.

They would have found Samantha at the mall, or at someone's house, or at the club where she worked. But they weren't trying to get to Samantha, she knew.

They were trying to get to her.

And the scariest part was, Karen had no idea what these people wanted from her.

When she spotted Lieutenant Hauck come through the front door, her body almost gave out all at once. She leaped up and ran over to him. She had to hold herself back from hugging him.

He placed a hand on her shoulder. "Is she all right?"

"Yes." Karen nodded in relief. "I think so."

"I know she's already been through it a couple of times, but I need to talk with her, too."

Karen took him over to her daughter. "Okay."

Hauck sat down on the coffee table directly across from Samantha. "Sam, my name's Lieutenant Hauck. I'm the head of detectives with the Greenwich police here in town. I know your mom a little from when your dad died. I want you to tell me exactly what took place."

111

Karen nodded to her, sitting next to her on the couch and taking her hand.

Sniffling back tears, Sam went through it all again. Coming out of the gym after practice, stepping into her car, putting on her iPod. The man in the backseat, completely surprising her from behind. Cupping her mouth so she couldn't scream, his voice so chilling and close to her ear that his words seemed to tingle down her spine.

"It was so scary, Mom."

Karen squeezed. "I know, baby, I know. . . ."

She told Hauck that she'd never gotten a good look at him. "He told me not to." She was certain she was about to be raped or killed.

"You did right, honey," Hauck said.

"He said that the investigation was going to start soon. And that it was going to get very personal. He said something about two hundred and fifty million dollars." Samantha looked up at Karen. *"What the hell did he mean by that, Mom?"*

Karen fitfully shook her head. "I don't know."

When they'd finished, Karen eased herself away from her daughter. She asked Hauck if he would come outside with her. The awning on the patio wasn't up yet. Still too cold. In the darkness there were lights flashing out on the sound.

"Do you have any idea what she's talking about?" he asked.

Karen drew a sharp breath and nodded. "Yes."

And no . . .

She took him through the visit she'd received. The two men from Archer and Bey, who had pressured her about all that missing money. "Two hundred and fifty million dollars," she admitted.

Now this.

"I don't know what the hell is going on." She shook her head, eyes glistening. "Charlie's trustee—he's a friend—he promises that everything in the partnership was one hundred percent by the book. And I'm sure it was. These people . . ." Karen looked at Hauck, flustered. "Charlie was a good man. He didn't handle that kind of money. It's like they've targeted the wrong person, Lieutenant. My husband had a handful of clients. Morgan Stanley, a few well-to-do families he'd known a long time."

"You understand I have to look into this," Hauck said.

Karen nodded.

"But I need to tell you that without a physical description from your daughter, it's going to be very tough. There are cameras at the school entrances. Maybe someone around spotted a car.

113

But it was dark and pretty much deserted at that time. And whoever these people are, they're clearly professional."

Karen nodded again. "I know."

She leaned toward him, suddenly so full of questions she felt light-headed, her knees on the verge of buckling.

The lieutenant placed his hand on her shoulder. She didn't pull away.

She'd handled Charlie's death, the long months of uncertainty and loneliness, the breakup of his business. But this was too much. Tears rushed in her eyes—burning. Tears of mounting fear and confusion. The fear that her children had suddenly become involved. The fear of what she did not know. More tears started to flow. She hated this feeling. This doubt that had so abruptly sprung up about her husband. She hated these people who had invaded their lives.

"I'll make sure you have some protection," the lieutenant said, squeezing Karen's shoulder. "I'll station someone outside the house. We'll see that someone follows the kids to school for a while."

She looked at him, sucking in a tense breath. "I have this feeling that my husband might have done something, Lieutenant. In his business.

Charlie always took risks, and now one of them has come back to haunt us. But he's dead. He can't untangle this for us." She wiped her eyes with the heel of her hand. "He's gone, and we're still here."

"I'll need a list of his clients," Hauck said, his hand still perched upon her shoulder.

"Okay."

"And I'll need to talk to Lennick, your husband's trustee."

"I understand." Karen pulled back, taking in a breath, trying to compose herself. Her mascara had run. She dabbed her eyes.

"I'll find something. I promise you. I'll do my best to make sure you're safe."

"Thank you, Lieutenant." She leaned against him. "For everything."

Static from her sweater rippled against his hand as he took it away.

"Listen." He smiled. "I'm not exactly a Wall Street guy. But somehow I don't think this is how Morgan Stanley goes about collecting its debts."

CHAPTER TWENTY-ONE

The call came in at eleven-thirty that night. The limo had just dropped Saul Lennick at his Park Avenue apartment, home from the opera. His wife, Mimi, was in the bathroom removing her makeup.

"Can you get that, Saul?"

Lennick had just pulled off his shoes and removed his tie. Calls this late, he knew what they were usually about. He picked up the phone in frustration. *Couldn't it wait for the morning?* "Hello."

"Saul?"

It was Karen Friedman. Her voice was cracking and upset. He knew that something was wrong. "What's happened, Karen?"

Exasperated, she told him what had happened to Samantha leaving school.

Lennick stood up. Sam was like a grandniece

to him. He had been at her bat mitzvah. He had set up accounts for her, and for Alex, at his firm. Every bone in his tired body became rigid.

"Jesus, Karen, is she all right?"

"She's okay. . . ." Karen sniffed back a sob in frustration. "But . . ." She told him what the man who had accosted her had said, about wanting their money. The same two hundred and fifty million dollars as before. The part about how she was her father's little girl.

"What the hell did they mean by that, Saul? Was that some kind of threat?"

In his underwear and socks, Lennick sank down on the bed. His mind ran back to Charles. The avalanche he had unleashed.

You stupid son of a bitch. He shook his head and sighed.

"Something's going on, Saul. You were about to tell me something a couple of weeks back. You said it wasn't the right time. . . . Well I just put my daughter in my own bed," Karen said, her voice stiffening. "She was scared within an inch of her life. What do you think, Saul—*is it the right time now?"*

CHAPTER TWENTY-TWO

Archer and Bey turned out to be phony.

Just a name on a business card. A call to an old contact at Interpol and a quick scan over the Internet for companies registered in South Africa determined that. Even the address and telephone number in Johannesburg were bogus.

Someone was trying to extort her, Hauck knew. Someone familiar with her husband's dealings. Even his trustee, Lennick, whom Hauck had spoken with earlier and who appeared like a stand-up guy, agreed.

"*Incoming*, Lieutenant!"

The call rang out from the outside squad room, followed by the low, pretend *whoosh* of a mortar round exploding.

"Incoming" was how they referred to it when Hauck's ex-wife was on the line.

Hauck paused a second, phone in hand, before picking up. "Hey, Beth, how's it going?"

"I'm okay, Ty, fine. You?"

"How's Rick?"

"He's good. He just got an increase in territory. Now he's got Pennsylvania and Maryland, too." Beth's new husband was a district manager in a mortgage firm.

"That's real good. Congratulations. Jess mentioned something like that."

"It's sort of why I'm calling. We thought we'd take this long-overdue trip. You know how we've been promising Jessie we'd take her down to Orlando? The theme-park thing."

Hauck straightened. "You know I was sort of hoping she and *I* could do that together, Beth."

"Yeah, I know how you've always been saying that, Ty. But, um . . . this trip's for real."

The dig cut sharply into his ribs. But she was probably right. "So when are you planning on doing this, Beth?"

Another pause. "We were thinking about Thanksgiving, Ty."

"Thanksgiving?" This time the cut dug all the way through his intestines. "I thought we agreed Thanksgiving's mine this year, Beth. I was going to take Jess up to Boston to my sister's. To see her cousins. She hasn't been up there in a while."

"I'm sure she'd like that, Ty. But this came up. And it's Disney World."

He sniffed, annoyed. "What, does Rick have a sales conference down there then or something?"

Beth didn't answer. "It's Disney World, Ty. You can take her Christmas."

"*No.*" He tossed his pen on his desk. "I can't take her Christmas, Beth. We discussed this. We had this planned. I'm going away Christmas." He'd made these plans to go bonefishing with a group of school buddies off the Bahamas, the first time he'd been away in a long time. "We went over this, Beth."

"Oh, yeah." She sighed as if it had somehow slipped her mind. "You're right. I remember now."

"Why not ask Jess?"

"Ask Jess what, Ty?"

"Ask her where *she'd* like to go."

"I don't have to ask her, Ty. I'm her mother."

He was about to snap back, *Goddamn it, Beth, I'm her father,* but he knew where that would lead.

"We actually sort of already booked the tickets, Ty. I'm sorry. I really didn't call you to fight."

He let out a long, frustrated exhale. "You know she likes it up there, Beth. With her cousins. They're expecting us. It's good for her now—for her to see them once or twice a year."

"I know, Ty. You're right. Next time, I promise, she will." Another pause. "Listen, I'm glad you understand."

They hung up. He swiveled around in his chair, his eyes settling on the picture of Jessie and Norah he kept on the credenza. Five and three. A year before the accident. All smiles.

It was hard to remember they had once been in love.

There was a knock against Hauck's office door, startling him. *"Hey, Loo!"*

It was Steve Christofel, who handled bunko and fraud.

"What, Steve?"

The detective shrugged, apologetic, notepad in hand. "You want me to come back, boss? Maybe this isn't a good time."

"No, it's fine. Come on in." Hauck swiveled back around, mad at himself. "Sorry. You know the routine."

"Always something, right? But, hey, Lieutenant, you mind if I see that case file you always keep in here?"

"Case file?"

"You know, the one you always keep hidden on your desk over there." The detective grinned. "That old hit-and-run thing. *Raymond."*

"Oh, that." Hauck shrugged as if exposed. He

always kept it buried under a stack of open cases. Not forgotten, not for a second. Just not solved. He lifted the stack and fished out the yellow case file from the bottom. "What's going on?"

"My memory's a little fuzzy, Lieutenant, but wasn't there a name that was connected to it somewhere? Marty something?"

Hauck nodded.

The person who had called up AJ Raymond at the shop, just before he'd left to cross the street. *Something like Marty,* his boss had said. It had just never led anywhere.

"Why?"

"This wire just came in." Christofel came around and placed his notepad on Hauck's desk. "Some credit-card-fraud division has been trying to chase it down after all this time. An Amex card belonging to a Thomas *Mardy*—that's M-A-R-*D*-Y—was used to pay for a limo ride up to Greenwich. Dropped him off at the Fairfield Diner at a little before noon, Lieutenant. April ninth."

Hauck looked up, his blood starting to course.

April 9. That was the morning of the hit-and-run. *Mardy,* not Marty—*that fit!* A Thomas Mardy had been dropped off across the street from where AJ Raymond was killed.

Now every cell in Hauck's body sprang alive.

"There's just one catch, Lieutenant." The detective scratched his head. "Get this. . . . The Thomas Mardy the Amex card belonged to was actually *killed* on April ninth. In the Grand Central bombing. On the tracks . . ."

Hauck stared.

"And that was three full hours," the detective said, "before the Greenwich hit-and-run."

CHAPTER TWENTY-THREE

That night Hauck couldn't sleep. It was a little after twelve. He climbed out of bed. Letterman was on the TV, but he hadn't been watching. He went to the window and stared out at the sound. A stubborn chill knifed through the air. His mind was racing.

How?

How was it possible someone had died on the tracks and yet hours later his card had been used to pay for a ride to the Fairfield Diner? To the very spot where the Raymond kid was killed.

Someone had called him right before he left to cross the street. *Something like Marty . . .*

Mardy.

How did Charles and AJ Raymond fit together? *How?*

He was missing something.

He threw on a sweatshirt and some jeans and

slipped on some old moccasins. Outside, the air was sharp and chilly. He hopped into his Bronco. The block was dark.

He drove.

They had kept the protection on for four days now. He'd had a car in front of the house, another that followed the kids to school. Nothing had happened. Not surprising. Maybe whoever was bothering her had backed off? The temperature had already been turned up pretty high.

Hauck pulled off the highway at Exit 5. Old Greenwich. As if by some inner GPS.

He headed onto Sound Beach and into town. Main Street was totally dark and deserted. He turned right on Shore toward the water. Another right onto Sea Wall.

Hauck pulled up twenty yards down from her house. The rookie, Stasio, was on duty tonight. Hauck spotted the patrol car, lights out, parked across from the house.

He went up and rapped on the window. The young officer rolled it down, surprised. "Lieutenant."

"You look tired, Stasio. You married, son?"

"Yessir," the rookie answered. "Two years."

"Go home. Grab some sleep," Hauck said. "I'll take over here."

"You? I'm fine, Lieutenant," the kid protested.

"It's okay. Go on home." Hauck winked at him. "I appreciate your doing the job."

It took a final remonstration, but Stasio, outranked, finally gave in.

Alone, Hauck balled his fists inside his sweatshirt against the cold.

Across the street the house was completely dark, other than a dim light upstairs shining through a curtain. He looked at his watch. He had a meeting with Chief Fitzpatrick at 9:00 A.M. A replacement shift wouldn't be on until 6:00. He inhaled the crisp, damp air from off the sound.

You're crazy, Ty.

He went back to his Bronco and opened the door. As he was about to climb in, he noticed that the drapes had parted upstairs. Someone looked out. For a moment, in the darkness, their gazes met.

Hauck thought he made out the faint outline of a smile.

It's Ty, he mouthed, looking up. He had wanted to tell her that every time she called him "Lieutenant."

It's *Ty.*

And about your husband. What you're feeling, what you're going through now ... *I know.*

I damn well know.

He waved, a wink of recognition he wasn't sure she could even read. Then he pulled himself inside the Bronco, shutting the door. When he looked back up, the drapes had closed.

But that was okay.

He knew she felt safe, knowing he was there. Somehow he did, too.

He hunkered down in the seat and turned the radio on.

It's Ty. He chuckled. *That was all I wanted to say.*

CHAPTER TWENTY-FOUR

April

And then it was a year.

A year without her husband. A year spent bringing up her kids by herself. A year of sleeping in her bed alone. An anniversary Karen dreaded.

Time heals, right? That's what everyone always says. And at first, Karen wouldn't allow herself to believe it. Everything reminded her of Charlie. Everything she picked up around the house. Every time she went out with friends. TV. Songs. The pain was still too raw.

But day by day, month into month, the pain seemed to lessen each morning. You just got used to it. Almost against your will.

Life just went on.

Sam went to Acapulco with her senior class-mates and had a blast. Alex scored a game-winning goal in lacrosse, his stick raised high in the air. It was nice to see life in their faces again. Karen had to do something. She decided to get her real-estate license. She even dated, once or twice. A couple of divorced, well-heeled Greenwich financial types. Not exactly her type. One wanted to fly her to Paris for the weekend. On his jet. After meeting him the kids rolled their eyes and went "yick," too old, giving her a big thumbs-down.

It was still too soon, too creepy. It just didn't seem right.

The best news was that the whole situation with Archer gradually just died down. Maybe there was too much heat. Maybe whoever was trying to extort money from them got cold feet and gave up. Gradually things relaxed. The protection came off, their fears subsided. It was as if the whole frightening episode just went away.

Or at least that's what Karen always prayed, every night as she turned off the lights.

April 8 there was a TV documentary airing on the bombing, the night before the one-year anniversary. Shot by some camera crew that had been embedded with one of the fire teams that had responded, along with footage from hand-held cameras by people who just happened to be in Grand Central at the time, or on the street.

Even still, Karen had never watched anything about that day.

She couldn't. It wasn't an event to her—it was the day her husband was killed. And it perpetually seemed to be around: On the news. *Law & Order* episodes. Even ball games.

So they all talked it over—as a family. They made plans to be together the following night, by themselves, to recognize the real anniversary of Charlie's death. The night before was just a distraction. Sam and Alex didn't want to see it, so they hung out with friends. Paula and Rick had invited Karen out. But she said no.

She wasn't even sure why.

Maybe because she wanted to show she was strong enough. Not to have to hide. Charlie had gone through it. He'd gone through it for *real*.

So could she.

Maybe there was just the slightest urge to be part of it. She was going to have to deal with it sometime. It might as well be now.

Whatever it was, Karen made herself a salad that night. Read through a couple of magazines that had piled up, did a little work on some competitive real-estate listings on the computer. With a glass of wine. All the while it was like she had some anxious inner eye fixed to the clock.

You can do this, Karen. Not to hide.

As it approached nine, Karen switched off the computer. She flicked the TV remote to NBC.

As the program came on, Karen felt anxious. She steeled herself. *Charlie went through this,* she told herself. *So can you.*

One of the news anchors introduced it. The show began by tracing the 7:51 train to Grand Central, docudrama style, starting with its departure out of the Stamford station. People reading the papers, doing crossword puzzles, talking about the Knicks game the night before.

Karen felt her heart start to pound.

She could almost see Charlie in the lead car, immersed in the *Journal.* Then the camera switched to two Middle Eastern types with knapsacks, one stowing a suitcase on the luggage rack. Karen brought Tobey up into her arms and squeezed him close. Her stomach felt hollow. Maybe this wasn't such a good idea.

Then on the screen, the timeline suddenly read 8:41. The time of the explosion. Karen looked away. *Oh, God . . .*

A security camera on the tracks in Grand Central captured the moment. A shudder, then a flash of blinding light. The lights on the train went out. Camera phones in cars farther back recorded it. A tremor. Darkness. People screaming.

Concrete collapsing from a hundred pounds of hexagen and accelerant—the fire raging near two thousand degrees, smoke billowing into the main concourse of the station and onto the street. Aerial shots from traffic helicopters circling. The same pictures Karen saw that terrible morning, all hurtling back. Panicked people stumbling out of the station, coughing. The deadly plume of black smoke billowing into the sky.

No, this was a mistake. Karen clenched her fists and shook her head. She squeezed Tobey, tears flooding her eyes. *It's wrong.* She couldn't watch this. Her mind flashed to Charlie down there. What he must have been going through. Karen sat, frozen, thrust back to the horror of that first day. It was almost unbearable. People were dying. Her husband was down there dying. . . .

No. I'm sorry, honey, I can't do this.

She reached for the remote and went to turn it off.

That was when the footage shifted up to the street level. One of the remote entrances on Forty-eighth and Madison. Handheld cameras: people staggering onto the street, shell-shocked, gagging, blackened with char and ash, collapsing onto the pavement. Some were weeping, some just glassy-eyed, grateful to be alive.

Horrible. She couldn't watch.

She went to flick it off just as something caught her eye.

She blinked.

It was only an instant—the briefest moment flashing by. Her eyes playing tricks on her. A cruel one. *It couldn't be. . . .*

Karen hit the reverse button on the remote with her thumb, waiting a few seconds for it to rewind. Then she pressed the play arrow again, moving a little closer to the screen. The people staggering out of the station . . .

Every cell in her body froze.

Frantically, Karen rewound it again, her heart slamming to a complete stop. When she got back to the spot a third time, she took a breath and pressed pause.

Oh, my God . . .

Her eyes stretched wide, as if her lids were stapled open. A paralyzing tightness squeezed her chest. Karen stood up, her mouth like sandpaper, drawing closer to the screen. *This cannot be. . . .*

It was a face.

A face that her mind was screaming to her couldn't be real.

Outside the station. Amid the chaos. *After* the explosion. Averted from the camera.

Charlie's face.

133

Karen's stomach started to crawl up her throat.

No one might have ever noticed it, no one but her. And if she had so much as blinked, turned away for just an instant, it would have been gone.

But it was real. Captured there. No matter how much she might want to deny it!

Charlie's face.

Karen was staring at her husband.

PART TWO

CHAPTER TWENTY-FIVE

The morning was clear and bright, the suburban New Jersey road practically deserted of traffic, except for about thirty bikers cruising in unison in their colorful jerseys.

Coasting near the front of the pack, Jonathan Lauer cast a quick glance behind, searching out the bright green jersey of his friend Gary Eddings, a bond trader at Merrill. He caught a glimpse of him, boxed in. *The perfect chance!* Crouching into a tuck, Jonathan began to pump his legs and weave a path through the maze of lead riders of the peloton. When a path opened up in front of him, he broke free.

Lauer, the imaginary announcer exclaimed in his head, *a bold, confident move!*

While for the most part they were just a bunch of thirty-something dads sweating off a few carbs on a Sunday morning, privately he and Gary had this game. More than a game, a challenge. They always pushed each other to the limit. Raced each other in the final straightaway. Waited for the other to make the first move. The winner got to brag for a week and wear the pretend yellow jersey. The loser bought the beers.

Calves pistoning, leaning over the handlebar of his brand-new carbon-fiber LeMond, Jonathan built a margin of about twenty yards, then coasted freely into the curve.

The finish line, the bend after the intersection with 287, was a half mile ahead.

Looking back, Jonathan caught a glimpse of Gary trying to free himself from the pack. His blood started to pump, accelerating as the country road turned into a perfect straightaway in the last half mile. He'd moved at the right time!

Pedaling fiercely now, Jonathan's thighs were burning. He wasn't thinking about the new job he had started just a few weeks before—on the energy desk at Man Securities, one of the real biggies—a chance to earn some real numbers after the mess at Harbor.

Nor was he thinking about the deposition he had to make that week. With that auditor from the Bank of Scotland and the lawyer from Parker, Kegg forcing him to testify against his former company after taking the attractive payout deal that had been offered him when the firm shut down.

No, all that was in Jonathan's mind that morning was racing to that imaginary line ahead of his friend. Gary had maneuvered out of the pack and had made up some distance. The intersection was just a hundred yards ahead. Jonathan went at it, his quads aching and his lungs on fire. He snuck a final peek back. Gary had pulled up. Game over. The rest of the pack was barely in sight. No way he could catch him now.

Jonathan coasted underneath the 287 overpass and cruised around the bend, raising his arms with a triumphant whoop.

He'd dusted him!

A short time later, Jonathan was pedaling home through the residential streets in Upper Montclair.

The traffic was light. His mind drifted to some complex energy index play someone had described at work. He was relishing his win and how he could tell his eight-year-old son, Stevie, how his old dad had smoked everyone today.

As he neared his neighborhood, the streets turned a little winding and hilly. He coasted down the straightaway on Westerly, then turned up Mountain View, the final hill. He huffed, thinking how he'd promised he'd take Stevie to buy some soccer shoes. His house was just a quarter mile away.

That was when he spotted the car. More like a large black façade, a Navigator or an Escalade or something with a shiny chrome grille.

It was heading right for his path.

For a second, Jonathan Lauer was annoyed. *Hit the brakes, dude.* It was a residential street. There was plenty of distance between them. No one else was around. It flashed through his head that maybe he had taken the turn a little wide.

But Jonathan Lauer didn't hear the sound of brakes.

He heard something else.

Something crazy, his annoyance twisting into something else. Something horrifying, as the SUV's grille came closer and closer.

He heard acceleration.

CHAPTER TWENTY-SIX

Over the next few days, Karen must have watched that two-second clip a hundred times.

Horrified. Confused. Unable to comprehend what she was seeing.

The face of the man she had lived with for eighteen years. The man she'd mourned and missed and cried over. Whose pillow she still sometimes crept over to at night and hugged, whose name she still whispered.

It was Charlie, her husband, caught in an unexpected freeze-frame as the camera randomly swept by.

Outside Grand Central. *After* the attack.

How the hell can that be you, Charlie . . . ?

Karen didn't know what to do. Whom she could possibly tell? She went for a jog with Paula out on Tod's Point, and listened to her friend

141

going on about some dinner party she and Rick had attended, at this amazing house out on Stanwich, when all the while she just wanted to stop. Face her friend. Tell her: *I saw Charlie, Paula.*

The kids? It would shatter them to see their father there. They would die. Her folks? How could she possibly explain? Until she knew.

Saul? The person he owed everything to. No.

So she kept it to herself. She watched the captured moment, over and over, until she was driving herself crazy. Confusion hardening into anger. Anger into hurt and pain.

Why? Why, Charlie? How can that be you? How could you have done this to us, Charlie?

Karen went over what she knew. Charlie's name had been on the Mercedes dealer's transit sheet. They had found the remnants of his briefcase blown apart, the charred slip of paper from his notepad she had received. He'd called her! 8:34. It didn't make any sense to Karen.

He was there on that train!

At first she tried to convince herself that it couldn't be him. He would never, ever do this to her. Or to the kids. Not Charlie. . . . And why? *Why?* She stared at him. People look alike. Eyes, hopes—they can play crazy tricks. The picture was a little fuzzy. But every time she went back to that screen, replayed the image she had saved

142

for maybe the thousandth time—there it was. Unmistakable. The sweats coming over her. Accusation knifing up in her belly. Her legs giving out like jelly.

Why?

Days passed. She tried to pretend to be herself, but the experience made her so sick and so confused, all Karen could do was hide in her bed. She told the kids she had come down with something. The anniversary of Charlie's death. All those feelings rushing back at her. One night they even brought dinner up to her. Chicken soup they had bought at the store, a cup of green tea. Karen thanked them and looked into their bolstering eyes. "C'mon, Mom, you'll be fine." As soon as they left, she cried.

Then later, when they were asleep or at school, she'd go around the house, studying her husband's face in the photos that were everywhere. The ones that meant everything to Karen. All she had. The one of him in his beach shirt and Ray-Bans that they'd blown up for the memorial. Of him and Karen dressed in black tie at her cousin's wedding. The personal items she had never cleared off his dresser in his closet: business cards, receipts, his watches.

You couldn't do this to me, could you, Charlie? To us . . .

Not you . . .

It had to be some kind of coincidence. A freakish one. *I trust you, Charlie. . . . I trusted you in life, and I'm goddamned going to trust you now.* In a million years, he would never hurt her this way.

Karen kept coming back to the one thing she still had of him. The torn sheet from his notepad someone had found in Grand Central. *From the Desk of Charlie Friedman.*

She felt him there. Trust had to win out here. The trust of eighteen years. Whatever she saw on that screen, she knew damn well in her heart just who her husband was.

For the first time, Karen looked at the note sheet. Really looked at it. Not just as a keepsake. Megan Walsh. The random name scrawled there in Charlie's barely legible script. The scribbled phone number: 964-1650. And another number, underlined in his bold, broad strokes:

B1254.

Karen closed her eyes.

Don't even go there, she admonished herself, suspicion snaking through her. *That wasn't Charlie. It couldn't be.*

But suddenly Karen stared wide-eyed at the

scribbled numbers. The doubts kept tearing at her. Seeing his face up on that screen. It was like a piece of his past, a link to him—the only link.

Crazy as it is, you've got to go ahead and call, Karen.

If only to stop yourself from totally going insane.

CHAPTER TWENTY-SEVEN

It took everything Karen had to do it.

In a way it made her feel like she was cheating on him, on his memory. What if that wasn't even *him* up on that screen? What if she was making all this up, over someone who simply looked like him?

Her husband had been dead for over a year!

But she dialed, secretly praying inside that the number wasn't to some hotel and B1254 a room there, and this was how she would have to think of him. The weirdest doubts crossed Karen's mind.

"JP Morgan Chase. Fortieth and Third Avenue branch," a woman on the line answered.

Karen exhaled, relief mixed with a little shame. But as long as she'd gone this far, she might as well go all the way. "I'd like to speak with Megan Walsh, please."

"One moment, please."

It turned out Megan Walsh was the manager in charge of the Private Banking Department there. And after she'd explained that her husband was now deceased and that Karen was the sole beneficiary of his estate, B1254 turned out to be a safe-deposit box that had been opened at the branch a couple of years before.

In Charlie's name.

Karen drove into town the following morning. The bank was a large, high-ceilinged branch, only a few blocks from Charlie's office. Megan Walsh was an attractive woman in her thirties, with long dark hair and dressed in a tasteful suit. She took Karen back to her cubicle office along a row with the other managers.

"I remember Mr. Friedman," she told Karen, her lips pressed tightly in sympathy. "I opened the account with him myself. I'm very sorry for your loss."

"I was just piecing through some of his things," Karen said. "This wasn't even listed as part of his estate. I never even knew it existed."

The bank manager perused Karen's copy of Charlie's death certificate and the letter of execution from the estate. She asked her a couple of questions: First, the name of their dog. Karen smiled. (It turned out he had listed Sasha.) His

147

mother's maiden name. Then she took Karen back into a private room near the vault.

"The account was opened about eighteen months ago, last October." Ms. Walsh handed Karen the paperwork. The signature on the box was plainly Charlie's.

Probably just business stuff, Karen assumed. She'd see what was in there and turn whatever it was over to Saul.

Megan Walsh excused herself and returned shortly with a large metal container.

"Feel free to take as much time as you need," she explained. She placed it on the table, unlocking the clasp in Karen's presence with her own duplicate key. "If there's anything you need, or if you'd care to transfer anything into an account, I'll be happy to help you when you're done."

"Thank you." Karen nodded.

She hesitated over it for a few moments, after the door had closed and she was left alone with this piece of her husband he had never shared with her.

There was the shock of seeing his face up on that screen. Now this box that had never been mentioned as part of the estate or even come up in any of Charlie's business files. She ran her hand a little cautiously along the metal sides. *What could he be keeping from her in here?*

Karen drew open the large container from the top and peered inside.

Her eyes stretched wide.

The box was filled with neatly arranged bundles of cash. Wrapped packets of hundred-dollar bills. Bearer-bond notes bound with rubber bands with denominations scrawled on the top sheet in Charlie's handwriting: $76,000, $210,000. Karen lifted a couple of packets, catching her breath.

There's at least a couple of million dollars here.

She knew immediately this wasn't right. Where would Charlie get his hands on this kind of cash? They shared everything. Numbly, she let the packets of bundled cash drop back into the case. Why would he have kept all this from her?

Her stomach knotted. She flashed back to the two men from Archer two months before. *A considerable amount of money missing.* And the incident with Samantha in her car. *Two hundred and fifty million dollars.* This was only a fraction of that amount.

She was still gaping at the contents of the box—it started to scare her. *What the hell is going on, Charlie?*

Toward the bottom of the container, there was more. Karen dug around and came out with a manila envelope. She unfastened the clasp and slid out what was inside. She couldn't believe what she saw.

A passport.

New, unused. Karen flipped through it. It had Charlie's face inside.

Charlie's face—but with a completely different name. A fake one.

Weitzman. Alan Weitzman.

In addition, she slid out a couple of credit cards, all made out to the same false name. Karen's jaw fell slack. Her head started to ache. *What are you hiding from me, Charlie?*

Confused, Karen sank back into the chair. There had to be some reason for all this that would make sense. Maybe the face she'd seen on that screen was *not* really Charlie's.

But here it was.... Suddenly it seemed impossible to pretend anything else. She ran her eyes down the activity sheet again. The box had been opened two years before. A year before he died. Charlie's signature, plain as day. All the entries had been his. A couple shortly after the box was opened. Then once or twice a month, seemingly like clockwork, almost as if he were preparing for something. Karen skimmed to the bottom, her gaze locking on the final entry.

There was Charlie's signature. His quick, forward-leaning scrawl.

But the date . . . *April 9.* The day of the Grand Central bombing.

Her eyes fastened on the time—1:35 P.M. Karen felt the sweats come over her.

That was four and a half hours after her husband had supposedly died.

CHAPTER TWENTY-EIGHT

Karen held back the urge to retch.

She felt dizzy. Light-headed. She grabbed on to the edge of the table to steady herself, unable to free her eyes from what she saw on that sheet.

1:35 P.M.

Suddenly, there was very little that made sense to Karen in that moment. But one thing did, flashing back to his grainy image from that hand-held camera up on that screen.

Her husband was definitely alive.

Reeling, Karen ran through the contents of the safe-deposit box once again, accepting in that moment that everything she had felt and taken for granted over the past year, every shudder of grief and loss, every time she'd wondered empathetically what Charlie must have felt, every time she'd crawled over to his side of the bed at night and hugged his pillow, asking, *Why . . . why?*—it had all been nothing but a lie.

He had kept it all from her. He had planned this.

He didn't die there that day. In the blast. In the hellish flames.

He was alive.

Karen's mind shot back to that morning . . . Charlie hollering to her over the dryer, about taking in the car. In her haste, words she had barely heard.

He's alive.

Then to the shock that had gripped her at the yoga studio as, glued to the screen, panic taking over her, she slowly came to accept that he was on that train. His call—the very last sound of his voice—about bringing home dinner that night. That was 8:34 A.M. The blown-apart top piece of the briefcase with his initials on it. The sheet from his notepad that someone had sent.

It all came tumbling back—deepening with the force of a storm circling in her mind. All the pain and anguish she had felt, every tear . . .

He was there. On that train.

He just hadn't died.

At first it was like the cramp of a stomach flu forcing her insides up. She fought back the urge to gag. She should be jubilant. *He was alive!*

153

But then she just stared blankly at the cash and the fake passport. He hadn't let her know. He'd let her suffer with the thought all the past year. Her confusion turned to anger. She sat there staring at the fake passport photo. Weitzman. *Why, Charlie, why? What were you devising? How could you do something like this to me?*

To us, Charlie?

They had loved each other. They had a life together. A family. They traveled. They talked about things they were going to do once the kids were gone. They still made love. *How do you fake that? How do you possibly do this to someone you loved?*

Suddenly Karen felt jelly-legged. All that money, that passport, what did it mean? Had Charlie committed some kind of crime? The room began to close in on her.

She felt she had to get out of there. *Now.*

Karen clasped the box shut and called outside. In a moment Megan Walsh came back in.

"I'd like to just leave this here if I could for now," Karen said, brushing the perspiration off her cheeks.

"Of course," Ms. Walsh replied. "I'll just give you my card."

Karen asked her, "Did anyone else have access to this box?"

"No, just your husband." The bank official looked back quizzically. "Is everything all right?"

"Yes," Karen lied. She took her purse but before running out requested a copy of the activity sheet. "I'll be back in a few days to decide what to do."

"That's fine, Mrs. Friedman, just let me know."

Out on the street, Karen sucked a breath of cooling air into her lungs. She steadied herself against a signpost. Slowly, her equilibrium began to return.

What the hell is going on here, Charlie? She turned away from people passing by on the sidewalk, afraid they would think her a lunatic to be reeling around in such a distraught state.

Didn't I take care of you? Wasn't I good to you, baby? I loved you. I trusted you. I mourned you, Charlie. It tore me fucking apart when I thought you were dead.

How can you possibly be alive?

CHAPTER TWENTY-NINE

Saul Lennick's office was close by, on the forty-second floor of one of those tall glass office towers on Forty-seventh and Park.

Karen hurried over, without even calling, praying he was there. His secretary, Maureen, came out and immediately saw the distress and nerves all over Karen's face.

"Can I get you anything, Ms. Friedman?" she asked solicitously. "A glass of water?"

Karen shook her head.

"Please come on back. Mr. Lennick's available. He can see you now."

"Thank you." Karen exhaled with relief. *Thank God!*

Saul Lennick's office was large and important-looking, filled with a collection of African masks and Balinese burial artifacts, with a view of the Manhattan skyline and, to the north, Central Park.

He had just hung up from a call, and he stood with a look of concern as Maureen rang Karen in.

"Karen?"

"Something's going on, Saul. I don't know what it is. But Charlie's done something . . . in his business."

"What?" Lennick inquired. He came around and pulled out a chair for her in front of his large desk, then sat back down.

She was about to blurt out everything she knew and had discovered—starting with seeing Charlie's face in the documentary. And that he was alive!

But she managed to catch herself at the last second, worried that maybe Saul might think he was talking to a raving lunatic, and decided to tell him only what she'd seen today.

"I came across something, Saul. Something Charlie wrote out before he died. I don't know how to even begin to explain, but I do know it fits into all these crazy things that have been happening. Those people from Archer. Samantha. I didn't know what to do with it, Saul."

"With what?"

Agitated, Karen told him about finding the safe-deposit box. The cash and bonds. The passport. Charlie's photograph next to the fake name.

"At first I thought maybe it was another

woman, but it wasn't another woman, Saul. It's worse. Look at me, Saul, I'm a goddamn wreck." She took in a breath. "Charlie's done something. I don't know what. He was my husband, Saul. And I'm scared. I feel like those people are going to come back. People are coming after us, and now I find this box full of cash and a false ID. I'm not going to put my kids in danger, Saul. Why would Charlie be hiding this stuff from me? I know you know something. What the hell's going on here? You owe that much to me, Saul—*what?*"

Lennick rocked back in his leather chair. Behind him the vast skyline of New York spread out like a giant panoramic photo.

He exhaled.

"All right, Karen. I was hoping I'd never have to bring this up. That it had somehow all gone away."

"What, Saul? That *what* had gone away?"

He leaned forward. "Did Charles ever mention someone by the name of Coombs? Ian Coombs?"

"Coombs?" Karen shook her head. "I don't think so. I don't recall."

"What about an investment outfit called Baltic Securities? Did he ever mention them?"

"Why are you asking me all these things, Saul?

158

I didn't exactly get involved in my husband's business. You of all people know that."

"I do know that, Karen, it's just that . . ."

"It's just that *what*, Saul? Charlie's not here. All of a sudden, everybody's making these innuendos about him. *What the hell has my husband done?*"

Lennick stood up, dressed in a navy pinstripe suit with gold cuff links at his wrists. He came around the desk in front of Karen and sat back down on a corner of it. "Karen, by any chance did Charlie ever mention any other accounts he might have been managing?"

"Other accounts?"

Lennick nodded. "Completely separate from Harbor. Maybe offshore—the Bahamas or the Cayman Islands, perhaps? Things aren't governed by the SEC or the U.S. accounting laws down there." His gaze was measured, serious.

"You're scaring me a little, Saul. Charlie was a stand-up guy. He didn't keep things from anyone. Least of all you."

"I know that, Karen. And I wouldn't have brought it up. Except . . ."

She stared. "Except . . . ?"

"Except you found what you found, Karen. The cash, that passport. Which together don't look exactly stand-up to me."

Karen tensed. Her thoughts flashed to the face on that screen. Their entire lives together, they had shared pretty much everything. Stuff with the kids, their finances. When they were angry with each other. Even what was going on with the dogs. That was how they did things. It was a matter of trust. Now, in the pit of her stomach, Karen felt this doubt. Chilling her. Over Charlie. It was a feeling she'd never had before.

"Whose money are we talking about, Saul?"

He didn't answer. He simply pressed his lips together and brushed back his thinning gray hair.

"Whose money?" Karen stared at him directly.

Her husband's mentor let out a breath. His fingers drummed on the top of his walnut desk like a funeral dirge.

He shrugged. "That's the trouble, Karen. No one's exactly sure."

CHAPTER THIRTY

Karen was frantic. The next few days, she barely dragged herself out of bed, not knowing what the hell to do. Samantha was starting to act concerned. It had been almost a week since Karen hadn't been herself, since she'd seen Charlie on that screen. Her daughter's eyes reflected that they knew that something wasn't right. "What's going on, Mom?"

As much as she wanted to, how could Karen possibly tell her?

That the person she admired most in the world, who had always provided for her and kept her strong, had deceived them in this way. What had Saul said? Setting up accounts. Running money, for people she didn't know. Offshore?

What kind of people?

All that money, it terrified Karen. What was it

for? She began to think that maybe Charlie had committed some kind of crime. *Did Charlie ever mention any other accounts he might be managing?*

No, she had told him. *You know Charlie, he was an honest guy. He fretted over nickels and dimes for his clients.*

Had she been kidding herself all these years?

A few more days went by. Karen was driving herself half crazy, thinking about Charlie being out there somewhere, what all this meant. It was late one night. The kids' lights had long been turned off. Tobey was asleep on her bed. Karen went downstairs to the kitchen to make herself some tea.

Charlie's photo was on the counter. The one from the memorial: in his white polo shirt and khaki shorts, Topsiders and aviator Ray-Bans. They had always thought it was vintage Charlie, kicking back on a boat in the middle of the Caribbean—a cell phone stapled to his ear.

You knew him, Saul. . . .

Karen picked it up, for the first time restraining an urge to shatter it in anger against the wall. But then the strangest memory came to mind. From deep in the vault of their life together.

Charlie—waving.

It had been the end of a glorious week in the Caribbean, sailing. St. Bart's. Virgin Gorda. They ended up in Tortola. The kids had to be back to school the following day.

Then, strangely, Charlie announced he needed to stay on. A change of plans. Someone he had to see down there.

Out of the blue?

So he accompanied them to the local airport, the little twelve-seater shuttling them back to San Juan. It had always made Karen a bit nervous to fly those tiny planes. On takeoff and landing, she always held Charlie's hand. Everyone made a little fun of her. . . .

Why was all this coming back now?

Charlie said good-bye to them at the makeshift gate, more like a glass door leading out onto the tarmac. "You'll be fine," he told her with a hug. "I'll be back up north in two days." But buckling herself in, in the two-engine plane, Karen felt an inexplicable jolt of fear shoot through her—like she might never see him again. She had thought, *Why aren't you with me, Charlie?* a flash of being alone, reaching out for Alex's hand.

As the plane's propellers whirred, Karen's eyes went to the window, and she saw him, on the balcony of the tiny terminal, in his beach shirt and Ray-Bans, his eyes reflecting back the sun.

Waving.

Waving, with his cell phone stapled to his ear, watching the tiny plane pull away.

Offshore, Saul had said to her. *The Bahamas or the Cayman Islands.*

Now that same fear rippled through Karen, staring at his photo. That she somehow didn't really know him. Not the way it mattered. His eyes dark now, not reflecting the sun but deeper, unfamiliar—like a cave that led to many chasms. Chasms she had never explored before.

It scared her. Karen put down the photo. She was thinking, *He's out there.* Maybe thinking of her now. Maybe wondering, at this very moment, if she knew, if she suspected, felt him. It gave her the chills. *What the hell have you done, Charlie?*

She knew she couldn't keep bottling this up forever. She'd go insane. She had to know. Why he had done this. Where he was.

Karen sank down on a stool at the counter. She put her head in her hands. She'd never felt so confused or so isolated.

There was only one place she could think to go.

CHAPTER THIRTY-ONE

Hauck headed back upstairs to his office from
the holding cells down in the basement. He and
Freddy Muñoz had just taken a statement from
a scared Latino kid who was part of this group
from up in Norwalk who had been heisting
fancy cars from backcountry Greenwich homes,
a statement that could now blow the case wide
open. Joe Horner, a detective from the Norwalk
police department, was holding on the phone
for him.

As Hauck turned in from the hallway, Debbie,
his unit's secretary, flagged his attention.

"Someone's here to see you, Ty."

She was seated on the bench in the outer office,
wearing an orange turtleneck and a lightweight
beige jacket, a tote bag on the bench next to her.
Hauck made no attempt to conceal that he was
pleased to see her.

"Tell Horner I'll get back to him in a minute, Deb."

Karen stood up. She smiled, a little nervous to be here. Hauck hadn't seen her for a couple of months, since that other situation, the people harassing her, had quieted down and they'd pulled the protection. He had called once or twice to make sure everything was okay. Smiling, he went up to her. Her face was pallid and drawn.

"You said I should call." She shrugged. "If anything ever came up."

"Of course."

She looked up at him. "Something did."

"Come on in my office," he said, taking her by the arm.

Hauck called to Debbie that he'd ring the Norwalk detective back, then led Karen past the row of detectives' desks through the glass partition into his office. He pulled out a cheap metal chair at the round conference table across from his desk. "Sit down."

It was clear she was upset. "You want something? Some water? A cup of coffee?" She shook her head. Hauck pulled another chair around and sat, facing her, arms across the back. "So tell me what's going on."

Karen sucked in a breath and pressed her lips

tightly together, then reached inside her purse, the expression on her face somewhere between grateful and relieved. "Do you have a computer in here, Lieutenant?"

"Sure." Hauck nodded, wheeling around to a credenza by his desk.

She handed him a small DVR disc. "Can you put this in?"

He reached down and inserted it into the computer beneath the credenza. The disc kicked in and came to life, some kind of TV show or news report in mid-airing on the screen. A mass of people on the streets of New York. In unrest. Amateur footage, a handheld camera in the crowd. It became immediately clear he was watching the aftermath of the Grand Central bombing.

Karen asked him, "Did you happen to watch that documentary, Lieutenant? Last Wednesday night?"

He shook his head. "I was working. No."

"I did." She brought his attention back to the disc: people running out of the station onto the street. "It was very hard for me. A mistake. It was like living the whole thing all over again."

"I can understand."

Karen pointed. "Just about here I couldn't watch it anymore. I went to turn it off." She stood up and came behind his back, leaning over his shoulder, facing the screen. "It was like I was going crazy inside. Watching Charlie's death. All over."

Hauck didn't see where this was heading. She reached her hand across him for the mouse. She waited, letting the action on the screen unfold, people staggering up onto the street out of a remote entrance to the station, gagging, coughing out smoke, faces blackened. The hand-held camera jiggled.

"That's when I saw it." Karen pointed.

She positioned the mouse on the toolbar and clicked. The picture on the screen came to a stop. 9:16 A.M.

The frame captured a woman reaching out to comfort someone on the street who had collapsed. In front of her was someone else, a man, his jacket dusty, his face slightly averted from the camera, rushing by. Karen's eyes fixed on the screen, something almost steely about them, hardened, yet at the same time, Hauck couldn't help but notice, sad.

"That's my husband," she said, trying to keep her voice from cracking. She looked him in the eye. *"That's Charlie, Lieutenant."*

Hauck's pulse came to a stop. It took a second for it to fully sink in just what she meant. Her husband had died there. A year ago. He had been to her home, to the memorial. That much was clear. He turned again to the screen. The features seemed a bit familiar from the photos he'd seen at her house. He blinked back at her.

"What do you mean?"

"I don't *know* what I mean," Karen said. "He was on that train—that much I'm sure. He called me from it, just before the blast. They found pieces of his briefcase in the wreckage. . . ." She shook her head. "But somehow he didn't die."

Hauck pushed back from the desk, his eyes intent on the screen again. "A hundred people might look like that. He's covered in ash. There's no way you can be sure."

"That's what I told *myself*," she said. "At first. At least it's what I was hoping." Karen moved back to the table. "Over the past week, I must have looked at that scene a thousand times."

She reached in and drew a sheet of paper out of her bag. "Then I found something. It doesn't matter what. All that matters is that it led me to this safe-deposit box at a bank in Manhattan that I never knew my husband had."

She slid the sheet across the table to Hauck.

It was a photocopy of an account-activation form from Chase. For a safe-deposit box and, attached, what appeared to be an account history.

There was a lot of activity, going back a couple of years. All the entries bore the same signature.

Charles Friedman.

Hauck scanned down.

"Check out the last date," Karen Friedman told him. "And the time."

Hauck did, and felt a sharp pain stick him in the chest. His eyes flashed back at her, not understanding. *Can't be . . .*

"He's alive." Karen Friedman met his eyes. Her pupils glistened. "He was there, at that bank, four and a half hours *after* the bombing. Four and a half hours after I thought he was dead.

"That's Charlie." She nodded to him, glancing at the screen. *"That's my husband, Lieutenant."*

CHAPTER THIRTY-TWO

"Who have you told?"

"No one." She stared back at him. "How could I? My kids . . . after what they've been through, it would kill them, Lieutenant. How could they even begin to understand? *My friends?*" She shook her head, glassy-eyed. "What am I possibly supposed to say to them, Lieutenant? That it was all some kind of crazy mistake? 'Sorry, Charlie's not really dead. He's just been fucking deceiving me over the past year. Deceiving all of us!' At first I thought maybe you hear about people who come out of these life-altering situations, you know, *affected. . . .* " She placed her finger on the bank forms. "But then I found *these.* I thought about taking everything to Saul Lennick. Charlie was like a second son to him. But I got scared. I thought, what if he's really done something? You know, something bad. What if I was doing the wrong thing . . . ? How it would affect everybody. I got all scared. *Do you understand what I mean?*"

Hauck nodded, the stress clear in her voice.

"So I came here."

Hauck picked up the bank papers. Because he was a cop, he had learned over the years to withhold his reactions. Gather the facts, be a little circumspect, until a picture of the truth becomes clear. He looked at the bank form. *Charles Friedman was there.*

"What is it you want me to do?"

"I don't know." Karen shook her head in consternation. "I don't even know what he's done. But it's something. . . . Charlie wouldn't just do this to us. I knew him. He wasn't that kind of man, Lieutenant." She pushed a wisp of hair out of her face and wiped her eyes with the heel of her hand, tears smearing. "The truth is, I don't have any fucking idea what I want you to do."

"It's okay," he said, squeezing her arm. Hauck stared back at the screen. He ran through the usual responses. Some crazy shock reaction— amnesia—from the bombing. But the bank form dismissed that one fast. Another woman? Embezzlement? He flashed to the scene in the parking lot with Karen's daughter. *Two hundred and fifty million dollars.* Yet Saul Lennick had assured him Charles's hedge fund was perfectly intact.

"If you don't mind my asking, what did you find in there?" Hauck asked, pointing to the record for the safe-deposit box.

"Money." Karen exhaled. "Lots of money. And a passport. Charlie's picture, with a totally assumed name. A few credit cards . . ."

"He left this all behind?" A year ago. "This may have been just some kind of backup." Hauck shrugged. "I guess you understand, this wasn't unpremeditated. He was planning this."

She nodded, biting her lower lip. "I realize that."

But what Charles could never have planned, Hauck knew, was how he would execute this. Until the moment came.

His thoughts settled on another name. *Thomas Mardy.*

"Listen." Hauck swiveled to her. "I have to ask, did your husband have any history of . . . you know . . ."

"Did he *what*?" Karen stared at him. "Did he play around? I don't know. A week ago I would have said that was impossible. Now I'd be almost happy to hear that's what it was. He had that passport, those cards. . . . He was

173

planning all this. While we were sleeping in the same bed. While he was rooting for the kids at school. He somehow managed to get away from that train in the midst of the chaos and say, '*Now* it's happening. Now's the time. *Now's the time I'm going to walk out on my entire life.*'"

For a few seconds, there was only silence.

Hauck pressed his lips together and asked again, "What do you want me to do?"

"*I don't know.* Part of me wants to just put my arms around him and tell him that I'm happy he's alive. This other part . . . I opened that box and realized he's kept a whole part of his life secret from me. From the person he supposedly loved. I don't know what the hell I want to do, Lieutenant! Slap him in the face. Throw him in jail. I don't even know if he's committed a crime. Other than hurting me. But it doesn't matter. That's not why I'm here."

Hauck wheeled his chair closer. "Why are you here?"

"*Why am I here?*" Tears rushed into her eyes again. She clenched her fists and tapped them helplessly against the table. Then she looked back up at him. "Isn't it pretty obvious? *I'm here because I can't think of anywhere else to go!*"

Hauck went over to her as she just folded,

weightlessly, into his arms. She buried her head on his shoulder and dug her fists into him. He held her, feeling her trembling in his grasp, and she didn't pull away.

"He was dead! I mourned him. I missed him. I agonized on whether his last thoughts were about us. There wasn't a day when I didn't wish I just could have talked to him one last time. To tell him I hoped that he was okay. And now he's *alive. . . ."*

She sucked back a breath, wiping the tears off her dampened cheeks. "I don't want him hunted down. He did what he did, and he must have had some reason. He's not a bastard, Lieutenant— whatever you might think. I don't even want him back. It's too late now. I have no idea what I even feel. . . .

"I guess I just want to know . . . I just want to know why he did this to me, Lieutenant. I want to know what he's done. I want to see his face and have him tell me. The truth. That's all."

Hauck nodded. He squeezed her arms and let go. He kept a tissue box by his desk. He pulled a couple for her.

She sniffled back a smile. "Thanks."

"Part of the job. People always seem to be crying in here."

She laughed and dabbed her eyes and nose.

"I must be like a goddamn train wreck to you. Every time you see me . . ."

"No." He winked. "Anything but. However, you do seem to present some intriguing situations."

Karen tried to laugh again. "I don't even know what the hell I'm asking you to do."

"*I* know what you want me to do," he replied.

"I'm not sure where else to turn, Lieutenant."

"It's *Ty*."

What he said seemed to take her by surprise. For a second they just stood there, drawn to each other. She brushed a wave of auburn hair away from her still-raw eyes.

"Okay." She sucked in a breath and nodded. "*Ty* . . ."

"And the answer's yes." He sat back on the edge of his desk and nodded. "I'll help."

CHAPTER THIRTY-THREE

He'd said yes. Hauck went over the scene again.

Yes, he would help her. Yes, he knew what she needed him to do. Even though he knew in that instant it could never be accomplished with him on the job.

He took the *Merrily* out on the sound that night. He sat in the dark with the engines off, the water calm, the lights of downtown Stamford flickering on the shore.

Why? he asked himself.

Because he couldn't get the image of her out of his mind? Or the feel of her softness when she leaned into him. Her sweet scent still vibrant in his nostrils, every hair on his arm on edge, every nerve awakened from its long slumber.

Was that what it was, Ty? Is that all?

Or maybe it was the face that crept into his head as he sat with his Topsiders up on the gunnels, drinking a Harpoon Ale. A face Hauck had not brought into mind for months but that now once again came back to life for him, frighteningly real.

Abel Raymond.

The blood trickling out from under his long red hair. Hauck kneeling over him, promising he'd find out who had done this.

Charles Friedman hadn't died.

That changed everything now.

Thomas Mardy. He'd been a supervisor at a credit-checking business. He'd gotten on the 7:57 that day out of Cos Cob and had died on the tracks in Grand Central, in the blast.

Yet somehow one of his credit cards had been used for a limo ride up to Greenwich three hours later.

Now Hauck knew how.

He wondered, could the Mustang just have been a coincidence? *Charlie's Baby . . .* It had thrown him off. It would have thrown anyone off.

But now, seeing Charlie's face on the screen, he knew—more clearly than Karen Friedman could ever know—just how her husband had spent the hours between being caught by that camera coming out of that station and ending up hours later in the vault of that bank.

The son of a bitch hadn't died.

That afternoon Hauck had run Charlie's name through the NCIC system. The usual asset check—credit cards, bank accounts, even immigration. Freddy Muñoz brought it back, knocked on the door wearing a quizzical expression. "This guy's deceased, LT. On April ninth." His look sort of summed it up. "In the Grand Central bombing."

Nothing. But Hauck wasn't surprised.

Charles Friedman and AJ Raymond had been connected. And not by the copper Mustang. That much he now knew. They had lived different lives, a universe apart. Yet they had been connected.

What the hell could it be?

Hauck drained the last of his IPA. The answer wasn't here. The kid had family. Pensacola, right? His brother had come up to claim his things. His father was a harbor captain. Hauck remembered the old man's photo among AJ's things.

Yes, he would help her, he had said. Hauck pulled himself up out of the chair. He started the ignition. The *Merrily* coughed to life.

He'd help her. He only hoped she wouldn't regret whatever he found.

"Carl, I'm going to need a little time." Hauck knocked on his boss's door. "I have a bunch built up."

Carl Fitzpatrick, Greenwich's chief of police, was at his desk, preparing for an upcoming meeting. "Sure, Ty. C'mon in, sit down." He swiveled his chair around his desk and came back with a scheduling folder. "What are we talking about, a few days?"

"A couple of weeks," Hauck said, unconfiding. "Maybe more."

"Couple of weeks?" Fitzpatrick gazed at him over his reading glasses. "I can't authorize that kind of time."

Hauck shrugged. "Maybe more."

"Jesus, Ty . . ." The chief tossed his glasses on his desk, looked at him directly. "What's going on?"

"Can't say. Things are pretty clean right now. Whatever comes up, Freddy and Zaro can cover. I haven't taken more than a week in five years."

"Is everything all right, Ty? This isn't something about Jess, is it?"

"No, Carl, everything's fine." Fitzpatrick and he were friends, and he hated being vague. "It's just something that's come up I have to see through."

"Couple of weeks . . ." The chief scratched the back of his head. He pieced through the file. "Gimme a few days. I'll shuffle things around. When did you need to leave?"

"Tomorrow."

"Tomorrow." Fitzpatrick's eyes stretched wide. "Tomorrow's impossible, Ty. This is totally out of the blue."

"To you, maybe." Hauck slowly stood up. "To me it's long overdue."

CHAPTER THIRTY-FOUR

The doorbell rang. Barking, Tobey scampered to the door. Alex was at a friend's, studying for an exam. Samantha was on the phone in the family room, her legs dangling over the back of the couch, *Heroes* on the TV.

"Can you get that, Mom?"

Karen had just finished up cleaning in the kitchen. She tossed down the cloth and went to answer the door.

When she saw who it was, she lit up in surprise.

"There's a couple of things you can do for me," the lieutenant said, huddled in a beige nylon jacket against a slight rain.

"My daughter's at home," Karen said, glancing back into the family room, not wanting to involve her. She grabbed a rain jacket off the bench and threw it over her shoulders and stepped outside. "What?"

"You can look through any of your husband's personal belongings. Notes from his desk. Canceled checks, credit-card receipts. Whatever might still be around. Are you still able to access his computer?"

Karen nodded. She'd never had the urge to remove it from his study. It had never been quite the right time. "I think so."

"Good. Go through his old e-mails, any travel sites he may have visited before he left, phone records. What about his work-related things? Are they still around?"

"I have some stuff of his that was given back to me in a box downstairs. I'm not sure where his office computer ended up. What am I looking for?"

"Anything that might prove useful in determining where he might go. Even if it ends up it's not where he is now, it could at least be a starting point. Something to go on . . ."

Karen covered her head against the raindrops. "It's been over a year."

"I know it's been a year. But there are still records. Get in touch with his ex-secretary or the travel agency he used to use. Maybe they sent him brochures or made some reservations that no one would have even thought were important then. Try to think yourself, where would he go? You lived with him for eighteen years."

"You don't think I haven't already racked my brain?" The rain intensified. Karen wrapped her arms against the chill. "I'll look again."

"I'll help you arrange to get some of it done if you need," Hauck said, "when I get back."

"When you get back? Back from where?"

"Pensacola."

"*Pensacola?*" Karen squinted at him. "What's down there? Is that for me?"

"I'll let you know," Hauck said with a smile, "as soon as it's clear to me. In the meantime I want you to go through whatever you can find. Think back. There's always some clue. Something someone's left behind. I'll be in touch when I get back."

"Thank you," Karen said. She placed her hand against his slicker, rain going down her face. Her eyes suddenly full.

It had been a long time since she'd felt the presence of someone in her life, and here was this man, this man she barely knew who had come into her life in the mayhem after Charlie had died, and he'd seen her, rootless as a craft foundering in the waves of a storm. And now he was the one person she could cling to in this world, the one anchor. It was strange.

"I'm sorry I dragged you into all this, Lieutenant. I'm sure you have enough to do in your job."

"You didn't drag me into it." Hauck shook his head. "And anyway, I'm not doing this on the job."

"What do you mean?"

"You didn't want this out in the open, did you? You didn't want me to have to deal with whatever came back. I'd never be able to do that if I was there."

She looked at him, confused. "I don't understand."

"I took a few weeks," he said, rain streaming down his collar. Then he winked. "Don't worry about it. I had no idea what to do with the time anyway. But it's only me. No badge. No one else." His blue eyes glimmered in a soft smile. "I hope that's okay."

Was it okay? Karen didn't know what she was expecting when she went to him. Maybe only someone to listen to. But now her heart melted a bit at what he was willing to do.

"Why . . . ?"

He shrugged. "Everybody else—they were either really busy or just needed the paycheck."

Karen smiled, gazing back at him, a warming, grateful sensation filling up her chest. "I meant, why are you doing this, Lieutenant?"

Hauck shifted his weight from one foot to another. "I don't really know."

185

"You know." Karen looked at him. She pushed back a lock of wet hair that had fallen into her eyes. "You'll let *me* know when it's time. But thank you anyway, Lieutenant. Whatever it is."

"I thought we went through that one already," he said. "It's *Ty*."

"All right, *Ty*."

A glow of grateful warmth came into her gaze. Karen held out her hand. He took it. They stood there like that, rain pelting down on them.

"It's *Karen*." Her eyes met his. "I'm happy to meet you, Ty."

CHAPTER THIRTY-FIVE

Gregory Khodoshevsky gunned the engine on his three-wheeled, seventy-thousand-dollar T-Rex sport cycle, and the three-hundred-horsepower vehicle shot over the makeshift course he had set up on the grounds of his twenty-acre Greenwich estate.

Trailing close behind, his fourteen-year-old son, Pavel, in his own bright red T-Rex, gamely tried to keep up.

"C'mon, boy!" Khodoshevsky laughed through the helmet mike as he maneuvered around a cone, passing his son back on the other side. "You're not going to let an old *starik* like me take you, are you?"

Pavel cut the turn sharply, almost flipping his machine. Then he righted himself and sped up to almost sixty miles per hour, going airborne over a knoll.

"I'm right behind you, old man!"

They sped around the man-made pond, past the helicopter pad, then bounced back onto a long straightaway on Khodoshevsky's vast property. On the rise, his eighteen-thousand-square-foot redbrick Georgian stood like a castle with its enormous fountained courtyard and sprawling eight-car garage. Which Khodoshevsky filled with a Lamborghini Murciélago, a yellow Hummer that his wife, Ludmila, paraded around town, and a customized black Maybach Mercedes complete with bulletproof windows and a Bloomberg satellite setup. That cost him over half a million alone.

Though he was only forty-eight, the "Black Bear," as Khodoshevsky was sometimes known, was one of the most powerful people in the world, though his name would not be found on any list. In the *kleptocracy* that became the privatization spree in Russia of the 1990s, Khodoshevsky convinced a French investment bank to buy a run-down automotive-parts plant in Irkutsk, then leveraged it into a controlling seat on the board of Tazprost, Russia's largest—and ailing—automobile manufacturer, which, upon the sudden demise of two of its more uncompliant board members, dropped in Khodoshevsky's lap at the age of thirty-six. From there he obtained the rights to open Mercedes and Nissan dealerships in Estonia and Latvia, along with hundreds of Gaznost filling stations all over Russia to fill them up.

Under Yeltsin the Russian economy was carved up by a handful of eager *kapitalisti*. One big fucking candy store, Khodoshevsky always called it. In the free-for-all that became the public finance sector, he opened department stores modeled after Harrods that sold pricey Western brands. He bought liquor distributor-ships for expensive French champagnes and wines. Then banks, radio stations. Even a low-cost airline.

Today, through a holding company, Khodoshevksy was now the largest single private landlord on the Champs-Élysées!

In the course of growing his empire, he had done many questionable things. Public minis-ters on Putin's economic trade councils were on his payroll. Many of his rivals were known to have been arrested and imprisoned. More than a few had been disposed of, suffering untimely falls from their office windows or unexplained car accidents on the way home. These days Khodoshevsky generated more free cash flow than a medium-size economy. In Russia today what he could not buy, he stole.

Fortunately, his was not a conscience that kept

him troubled or awake at night. He was in touch daily through emissaries with a handful of powerful people—Europeans, Arabs, South Americans—whose capital had become so vast it basically ran the world. Wealth that had created the equivalent of a supereconomy, keeping real-estate prices booming, luxury brands flourishing, yacht makers busy, Wall Street indices high. They developed economies the way the International Monetary Fund once developed nations: buying up coal deposits in Smolensk, sugarcane fields for ethanol in Costa Rica, steel factories in Vietnam. However the coin fell, theirs always ended up on top. It was the ultimate arbitrage Khodoshevsky had crafted. The hedge fund of hedge funds! There was no way to lose.

Except maybe, as he relaxed a bit on the accelerator, today, to his son.

"C'mon, Pavel, let me see what you're made of. *Gun it now!*"

Laughing, they sped into the final straightaway, then did a lap around the massive fountain in the courtyard in front of the house. The T-Rexes' superheated engines spurted like souped-up go-carts. They bounced over the Belgian cobblestones in a father-son race to the finish.

"I've got you, Pavel!" Khodoshevsky called, pulling even.

"Believe it, old man!" His determined son gunned the engine and grinned.

In the final turn, they both went all out. Their wheels bumped together and scraped. Sparks flew, and Khodoshevsky lurched into the basin of the gigantic baroque fountain they had brought over from France. His T-Rex's fiberglass chassis caved in like crepe paper. Pavel threw up his hands in victory as he raced by. *"I win!"*

Stiffly, Khodoshevsky squeezed himself out of the mangled machine. A total loss, he noted glumly. Seventy thousand dollars down the drain.

Pavel jumped out of his and ran over. "Father, are you all right?"

"Am I all right?" He took off his helmet and patted himself around to make sure. He had a scrape on his elbow. "Nothing broken. A good pass, boy! That was fun, eh? You'll make a race driver yet. Now, help me drag this piece of junk into the garage before your mother sees what we've done." He mussed his boy's hair. "Who else has toys like this, eh?"

That was when his cell phone rang. The Russian reached in and pulled his BlackBerry out of his jeans. He recognized the number. "I'll be with you in a second." He waved to Pavel. "I'm afraid it's business, boy." He sat on the edge of the stone fountain and flipped open his phone. He ran a hand through his tousled black hair.

"Khodo here."

"I just want you to know," the caller, a private banker Khodoshevsky knew, began, "the assets we spoke of have been transferred. I'm bringing him the final shipment myself."

"That's good." Khodoshevsky snorted. "He must have pictures of you, my friend, for you to trust him after that mess he made of things last year. You just be sure you explain to him the price of doing business with us. This time you see to it he fully understands."

"You can be certain I will," the German banker said. "I'll remember to pass along your best regards."

Khodoshevsky hung up. It wouldn't be the first time, he thought, he had gotten his hands dirty. Surely not the last. The man was a good friend. Khodoshevsky had shared many meals with him, and a lot of good wine. Not that it mattered. Khodoshevsky clenched his jaw. No one loses that kind of money of theirs and doesn't feel it.

No one.

"Come, boy." He got up and went over to pat

Pavel on the back. "Help me drag this piece of shit into the garage. I have a brand-new one in there. What do you say, maybe you'd like to give your old man another turn?"

CHAPTER THIRTY-SIX

"Mr. Raymond?"

Hauck knocked at the small white, shingle-roofed home with a cheap green awning over the door in a middle-class section of Pensacola. There was a small patch of dry lawn in front, a black GMC pickup with an EVEN JESUS LOVED A GOOD BEER bumper sticker parked in the one-car garage.

The door opened, and a dark, sun-flayed man peered back. "Who're you?"

"My name's Hauck. I'm a lieutenant with the police department up in Greenwich, Connecticut. I handled your son's case."

Raymond was strongly built, of medium height, with a rough gray stubble. Hauck figured him for around sixty. His gnarled, cedar-colored skin looked more like a hide of leather and offset his clear blue eyes. He had a faded blue and red military tattoo on his thick right arm.

"Everyone knows me as Pappy," he grunted, throwing open the door. "Only people who want money call me Mr. Raymond. That's why I wasn't sure."

Hauck stepped through the screen door into a cramped, sparely furnished living room. There was a couch that looked like it had been there for forty years, a wooden table with a couple of Budweiser cans on it. The TV was on—a *CSI* rerun. There were a couple of framed pictures arranged on the wall. Kids. In baseball and football uniforms.

Hauck recognized one.

"Take yourself a seat," Pappy Raymond said. "I'd offer you something, but my wife's at her sister over in Destin, so there's nothing here but week-old casserole and warm beer. What brings you all the way down here, Lieutenant Hauck?"

"Your son."

"My son?" Raymond reached for the remote and flicked off the TV. "My son's been dead over a year now. Hit-and-run. Never solved. I understood the case was closed."

"Some information's come out," Hauck said, stepping over a pile of newspapers, "that might shed some new light on it."

"New light . . ." The old man bunched his lips together and mocked being impressed. "Just in fucking time."

195

Hauck stared at him. He pointed to the wall. "That's AJ over there, isn't it?"

"That's Abel." Raymond nodded and released a breath.

"He played defensive backfield, huh?"

Raymond took a long time before saying, "Listen, son, I know you came a long way down here and that somehow you're just trying to help my boy—" He stopped, looked at Hauck with hooded eyes. "But just why in hell are you here?"

"Charles Friedman," Hauck answered. He moved a stack of local sports pages off the chair and sat down across from Raymond. "Any chance you know that name?"

"Friedman. Nope. Never heard it before."

"You're sure?"

"Said it, didn't I? My right hand's got a bit of a tremor in it, but not my brain."

Hauck smiled. "Any chance AJ . . . *Abel* ever mentioned it?"

"Not to me. 'Course, we weren't exactly in regular conversation over the past year after he moved up north." He rubbed his face. "I don't know if you know, but I worked thirty years down at the port."

"I was told that, sir. By your other son when he came to claim AJ's things."

"Rough life." Pappy Raymond exhaled. "Just

look at me." He picked up a photo of himself at the wheel of what appeared to be like a tug and handed it to Hauck. "Still, it provided some. Abel got what I never got—meaning a little school, not that he ever had cause to do much with it. He chose to go his own way. . . . We all make our choices, don't we, Lieutenant Hauck?" He put the photo down. "Anyway, no, I don't think he ever mentioned the name Charles Friedman to me. Why?"

"He had a connection to AJ."

"That so?"

Hauck nodded. "He was a hedge-fund manager. He was thought to have been killed at the bombing at Grand Central Station in New York last April. But that wasn't the case. Afterward, I believe he found a ride up to Greenwich and contacted your son."

"Contacted Abel? Why?"

"That's why I'm here. To find out."

The father's eyes narrowed, circumspect, a look Hauck knew. He laughed. "Now, that's a pickle. One dead man going to meet another."

"AJ never mentioned being involved in anything before he was killed? Drugs, gambling— maybe even some kind of blackmail?"

Raymond brought back his legs off the table and sat up. "I know you came down here a long

197

way, Lieutenant, but I don't see how you can go implying things about my boy."

"I didn't mean to," Hauck said. "I apologize. I'm not interested in whatever he may have done, except if it sheds any light on who killed him. But what I *am* interested in is why a man who's just gone through a life-threatening situation and whose life is a world apart from your son's finds his way up to Greenwich and gets in touch with your boy directly after."

Pappy Raymond shrugged. "I'm not a cop. I expect the normal course would be to ask him."

"I wish I could," Hauck said. "But he's gone. For over a year. Disappeared."

"Then that's where I'd be putting my best efforts, son, if I were you. You're wasting your time here."

Hauck handed Pappy Raymond back the photo. Stood up.

"You think that man killed Abel?" Pappy Raymond said. "This Charles Friedman? Ran him down."

"I don't know. I think he knows what happened."

"He was a good boy." Raymond blew out air. A gleam showed in his clear blue eyes. "Headstrong. Did things his own way. Like you-know-who. I wish we'd had more time." He drew in a breath. "But I'll tell you this: That boy wouldn't have harmed the wings on a goddamn fly, Lieutenant. No reason . . ." He shook his head. "No reason he had to die like that."

"Maybe there's someone else I could ask," Hauck pressed. "Who might know. I'd like to help you."

"Help *me*?"

"Solve AJ's killing, Mr. Raymond, 'cause that's what I damn well feel it was."

The old man chuckled, a wheezy laugh escaping. "You seem like a good man, Lieutenant, and you've come a long way. What'd you say your name was?"

"Hauck."

"Hauck." Pappy Raymond flicked on the TV. "You go on back, Luh-tenant Hauck. Back to wherever you're from. *Connecticut.* 'Cause there ain't no way in hell, whatever 'new light' you may have turned up, sir, that it's ever gonna be of any help to me."

CHAPTER THIRTY-SEVEN

Pappy Raymond was holding back. Why else would he push Hauck away so completely? Hauck also knew the old guy would be a tough one to crack.

He went back to the Harbor Inn hotel overlooking Pensacola Bay, where he was staying, stopped in the gift shop to buy a T-shirt for Jess that said PENSACOLA ROCKS, then fished out a Seminole beer from the minibar and threw himself onto the bed, turning on CNN.

Something had happened. An explosion at an oil refinery in Lagos, Nigeria. Over a hundred people killed. It had spiked the price of oil all day.

He reached over and fished out the number of AJ Raymond's brother, Pete, who had come up to Greenwich after the accident to take possession of his things.

Hauck called him. Pete said he would meet him at a bar after his shift the next day.

The Bow Line was down near the port, where Pete, who had come out of the Coast Guard two years before, was a harbor pilot like his father.

"It was like something just turned off in Pop," Pete said, drawing from a bottle of Bud. "AJ was killed. No one ever called my dad a teddy bear, but one day he went to work, wanting to do everything he could about what happened. The next day it was like it was all in the past. Off-limits to even bring it up. He never shared what he was feeling."

"You think part of it's guilt?"

"Guilt?"

Hauck took a swig of beer. "I've interviewed my share of people, Pete. I think he's holding something back."

"About AJ?" Pete shrugged, pushed back his hair under a Jacksonville Jaguars cap. "Something was going on. . . . People who he talked to tell me he had this thing—this cover-up he'd stumbled into. Some ships he thought were falsifying their cargo. Like some big national-security thing. He was all worked up.

"Then the thing with AJ happened. And that was it. It was over for him." He snapped his finger. "Lights out. Whatever it was, I never heard squat about it ever again. It was as if the whole thing just got buried the next day."

"I don't mean to push it," Hauck said, tilting his beer. "All I want to do is find your brother's killer, which is precisely what I believe it was. Anyone you know who can tell me any more on this?"

Pete thought a moment. "I could give you a few names. His old pals. I'm not sure what makes you think it's all related, though."

Hauck tossed a couple of bills on the counter. "That would be a big help."

"Thirty years . . ." Pete got up and drained the last of his beer. "Pop was like a god down there in the harbor. There was nothing went on he didn't know about or hadn't done. Now look at him. He was always a hard man, but I would never call him bitter. He took it rough, what happened to my brother. Rougher than I would expect. Given that they never saw eye to eye for a goddamned second while AJ was alive."

The following day Hauck made the rounds at the docks. A couple of large freighters had come in early that morning. Huge unloading trestles and hydraulic lifts were hissing, off-loading massive containers.

He found Mack Tyler, a sunburned, broad-chested tug's mate at the pilots' station. He had just come in from a launch.

Tyler was a bit guarded at first. People protected their own down there, and here was this cop from up north asking all kinds of questions. It took a little finesse for Hauck to get him to open up.

"I remember I was out with him one day," Tyler said. He leaned against a retaining wall and lit up a cigarette. "He was about to board some oil tanker we were bringing in. Pappy was always going on about these ships he'd seen before, making false declarations. How they were riding so high in the water, no way they could possibly be full, like their papers said. I think he even snuck down into the holds of one once.

"Anyway"—Tyler blew out smoke—"this one time we had pulled up alongside and the gangway was lowered to us, and Pappy was getting ready to go aboard. And he gets this cell-phone call. Five in the fucking A.M. He takes it, and all of a sudden his legs just give out and his face gets all pale and pasty—it was like he was having some kind of heart attack. We called in another launch. I had to bring the old man in. He wouldn't take any medical attention. Just a panic attack, he claimed. Why, he wouldn't say. Panic attack, my ass."

"You remember when that was?" asked Hauck.

"Sure, I remember." The big sailor exhaled another plume of smoke. "It wasn't too long after the death of his boy up there."

Later, Hauck met with Ray Dubose, one of the other harbor pilots, at a coffee stand near the navy yard.

"It was getting crazy," said Dubose, a big man with curly gray hair, scratching the bald spot on his head. "Pappy was going around making all kinds of claims that some oil company was falsifying its cargo. About how these ships were riding so high in the water. How he'd seen them before. The same company. Same logo—some kind of a whale or shark, maybe. Can't recall."

"What happened then?"

"The harbormaster told him to back off." Dubose took a sip of coffee. "That's what happened! That this was one for customs, not us. 'We just pull 'em in, Pappy.' He'd pass it along. But Pappy, God bless, he just kept on pushing. Raised a big stink with the customs people. Tried to contact some business reporter he knew from the bar, like it was some big national-security story he was uncovering and Pappy was Bruce Willis or someone."

"Go on."

Dubose shrugged. "Everyone kept telling him just to back off, that's all. But Pappy was never one to listen. Stubborn old fool. You know the type? Came out of the womb that way. I miss the son of a bitch, though. Pretty soon after his boy died up there, he packed it in with his thirty years and called it quits. Took it hard.

"Funny thing, though . . ." Dubose crumpled his cup and tossed it into a trash bin against a wall. "After that happened, I never heard another peep out of him about those stupid tankers again."

Hauck thanked him and drove back to the hotel. For the rest of the afternoon, he sat around on the small balcony overlooking the beautiful Gulf blue of Pensacola Bay.

The old man was hiding something. Hauck felt it for sure. He'd seen that haunted face a hundred times before. *There's nothing you can do that's gonna help me now. . . .*

It might only be guilt, that he had pushed his youngest son away. And what happened afterward.

Or it could be more. That the hit-and-run up north hadn't been so accidental after all. That that was why they were unable to ever find anything resembling the SUV the witnesses had described.

Why no one else ever saw it. Maybe someone had deliberately killed Pappy Raymond's son.

And Hauck felt sure those tankers were connected.

He nursed a beer. He thought about placing a call to Karen to see what she had found.

But he kept coming back to the hardened look in the old sailor's eyes.

CHAPTER THIRTY-EIGHT

Karen went back through all of Charlie's things as Hauck had asked her. She opened the cartons she had kept piled in the basement, doing her best to avoid the attention of the kids. Heavy, boxed-up files that Heather, his secretary, had sent with a note: *You never know what's in them. Maybe something you'll want to keep.* Brochures for trips they had taken as a family. The ski house they rented one year at Whistler. Letters. A kazillion letters. A bunch of things on the Mustang, which Charlie had asked her in the will he left not to sell.

Basically, the sum of their lives together. Stuff Karen had never had the heart to go through. But nothing that helped. At some point she sat in frustration with her back against the concrete basement wall and silently swore at him. *Charlie, why the hell did you do this to us?*

Then she went through the computer that was still sitting at his desk. She turned it on for the first time since the incident. It felt weird, invasive—as if she were prying into him. His signature was everywhere. In a million years she would never have done this when he was alive. Charlie never kept a password. Karen was able to get right in. What on earth had there ever been to hide?

She scrolled through his stored Word documents. Mostly they were letters he'd written from home—to industry people, trade publications. The draft of a speech or two he'd given. She went on his AOL account. Any e-mails he might've written before he disappeared had probably long since been wiped away.

It felt futile. And dirty, going through his things. She sat there at his desk, in the messy study, much of it still just as he'd left it a year before, where he'd paid the bills and read over his trade journals and checked his positions, the desk still piled with trade sheets and prospectuses.

There was nothing. He didn't want to be found. He could be anywhere in the fucking world.

And the truth was, Karen had no idea what she was gong to do if she even found him.

She contacted Heather, who was working at a small law firm now. And Linda Edelstein, whom Karen still occasionally used as a travel agent. She asked them both to think back on whether Charlie had made any unusual purchases ("a condo somewhere, as crazy as that sounds, or a car?") or booked any travel plans in the weeks before he died. She concocted this inane story about discovering something in his office about a surprise trip he'd been planning, an anniversary thing.

How in the world could she possibly tell them what was really in her mind?

As a friend, Linda scrolled back through her travel computer. "I don't think so, Kar. I would have remembered at the time. I'm sorry, hon. There's nothing here."

This was insane. Karen sat there among her husband's things at her wits' end, growing angry, wishing she never had watched that documentary. It had changed everything. *Why would you do this to us, Charlie? What could you possibly have done?*

Tell me, Charlie!

She picked up a stack of loose papers and went to throw them against the wall. Just then her gaze fell to a memo from Harbor that was still there from a year before. Her eye ran down the office distribution list. Maybe they knew. She spotted a name there—a name that hadn't crossed her mind in months.

Along with a voice. A voice she had never responded to, but one that now suddenly echoed in her ears with the same ringing message:

I'd like to speak with you, Mrs. Friedman.... There are some things you ought to know.

CHAPTER THIRTY-NINE

The address was 3135 Mountain View Drive, a hilly residential road. In Upper Montclair, New Jersey.

Karen found Jonathan Lauer's address in one of Charlie's folders. She checked to make sure it was still valid. She didn't want to talk with him on the phone. It was a Saturday afternoon.

There are some things you ought to know. . . .

Saul had said it was just a matter of personnel issues, compensation. Karen had never heard from him again. And it wasn't that she didn't trust Saul. It was just that if they were turning over every stone, the way Ty wanted to, she thought she might as well hear it from Lauer directly. She had never called him back. It had been an awfully long time.

But suddenly Charlie's trader's cryptic words took on a more important meaning.

Karen pulled into the driveway. There was a white minivan parked in the open two-car garage. The house was a cedar and glass contemporary with a large double-story window in the front. A kid's bike lay on the front lawn. Next to a portable soccer net. Rows of pachysandra and boxwood flanked the flagstone walkway leading up to the front door.

Karen felt a little nervous and embarrassed, after so much time. She rang the bell.

"I got it, Mommy!"

A young girl in pigtails who appeared around five or six opened the door.

"Hey." Karen smiled. "Is your daddy or mommy at home?"

A woman's voice called out from inside, "Lucy, who's there?"

Kathy Lauer came to the door, holding a rolling pin. Karen had met her once or twice—first at an office gathering and, later, at Charlie's memorial. She was petite, with shoulder-length dark hair, wearing a green Nantucket sweatshirt. She stared at Karen in surprise.

"I don't know if you remember me—" Karen started in.

"Of course I remember you, Mrs. Friedman," Kathy Lauer replied, cradling her daughter's face to her thigh.

"Karen," Karen replied. "I'm sorry to bother you. I know you must be wondering what I'm doing here, out of the blue. I was just wondering if your husband might be at home."

Kathy Lauer looked at her a bit strangely. "My husband?"

There was a bit of an awkward pause.

Karen nodded. "Jon called me a couple of times, after Charlie—" She stopped herself before she said the word. "I'm a little embarrassed. I never got back to him. I was all caught up then. I know it's a while back. But he mentioned some things. . . ."

"Some things?" Kathy Lauer stared. Karen couldn't quite read her reaction, nervousness or annoyance. Kathy asked her daughter to go back into the kitchen, said she'd be along in a second to finish rolling the cookie dough with her. The little girl ran off.

"Some things about my husband's business," Karen clarified. "By any chance is he around? I know it's a little strange to be coming here now. . . ."

"Jon's dead," Kathy Lauer said. "I thought you knew."

"Dead?" Karen felt her heart come to a stop and the blood rush out of her face. She shook her head numbly. "My God, I'm so sorry. . . . No . . ."

213

"About a month ago," his wife said. "He was on his bike coming back up the road, up Mountain View. A car ran into him. Just like that. A hit-and-run. The guy who hit him never even stopped."

CHAPTER FORTY

Dock 39 was a dingy, nautical-style bar in the harbor, not far from the navy yard. A shorted-out Miller sign flickered on and off in the window, while a carving of a ship's bow hung above the entrance on the wooden façade. From the street Hauck could see a TV on inside. A basketball game. It was playoff time. A crowd of people gathered whooping around the bar.

Hauck stepped inside.

The place was dark, smoky, jammed with bodies fresh from the docks. A noisy throng at the bar was following the game. The Pistons versus the Heat. People were still in their work clothes, blowing off steam. Dock workers and seamen. No office crowd here. Ray Dubose had told Hauck that this was where he could find him.

Hauck caught the barman's eye and asked him

for a Bass ale. He spotted Pappy, huddled with a few guys drinking beer down at the end of the bar. The old man seemed disinterested in the game. He stared ahead, ignoring the sudden shouts that occasionally rang out or the jab of his neighbor's elbow when someone made a play. At some point Pappy turned around and noticed Hauck, Pappy's eyes narrowing balefully and his jaw growing tight. He picked up his beer and stood up, pushing himself away from his crew.

He came over to Hauck, pushing through the crowd. "I heard you been asking about me. I thought I told you to head back to where you came."

"I'm trying to solve a murder," Hauck told him.

"I don't need you to solve no murder. I need you to leave me alone and go back home."

"What did you stumble into?" Hauck asked. "That's why you won't talk to me, isn't it? That's why you quit your job—or were pressured to. Someone threatened you. You can't keep pretending it's going to go away. It won't go away now. Your son is dead. That's what that 'accident' up in Greenwich was about, wasn't it? Why AJ was killed."

"Get the hell away from me." Pappy Raymond

216

pushed away Hauck's arm. Hauck could see he was drunk.

"I'm trying to solve your son's murder, Mr. Raymond. And I will, whether you help me or not. Why don't you make it easy and tell me what you found?"

The more Hauck said, the more the anger seemed to build in Pappy Raymond's eyes. "You're not hearing me, are you, son?" He thrust his beer mug into Hauck's chest. "I don't want your help. I don't need it. Go on out of here. Go back home."

Hauck grabbed his arm. "I'm not your enemy, old man. But letting your son's death eat away at you by doing nothing is. Those ships were falsifying something. They were empty, right? There was some kind of fraud going on. That's why AJ was killed. It wasn't any 'accident' up there. I know it—you know it, too. And I'm not backing off. You don't tell me, someone will. I'll pitch a tent on your goddamn lawn until I know."

A roar went up from the bar. "C'mon, Pappy!" one of his buddies yelled to him. "Wade just hit a three. We're back down by six."

"This is the last time I'm telling you." Pappy glared. His gaze burned into Hauck's eyes. "Go on home."

"No." Hauck shook his head. "I'm not."

That was when the old guy raised his arm and took a swing at him. A wild one, his fist catching on the shoulder of a man nearby, but the punch of a man who was used to throwing them, and it surprised Hauck, catching him on the side of his face. The mug shot out of his hands, crashing to the floor, spilling beer.

People spun around to them. *"Whoa . . . !"*

"What is it you want from me, mister?" Pappy grabbed Hauck by the collar. He raised his fist again. "Can't you just go back to wherever the hell you're from and let what's happened here die out? You want to be a hero, solve someone else's crime. Leave my family alone."

"Why are you protecting these people? Whoever they are, they killed your son."

Pappy's face was barely an inch away from Hauck's, the smell of beer and anger all over him. He raised his fist back again.

"Why?" Hauck stared at him. *"Why . . . ?"*

"Because I have other children," Pappy said, anguish burning in his eyes. His fist hesitated. "Don't you understand? *They* have children."

Suddenly the wrath in the old man's eyes began to diminish, and what was left there, in his hot, tremoring irises, was something else. Helplessness. The desperation of someone boxed in, with nowhere to turn.

"You don't know." Pappy glared at him, lowering his fist, releasing Hauck's collar. "You just don't know. . . ."

"I do know." Hauck met the old man's eyes. "I know exactly. I lost a child, too."

Hauck pressed something into Pappy's hand as a couple of his friends finally came over and pulled him away, saying the old man had had one too many, offering to buy Hauck another beer. They dragged him back to the bar, where he sat, his face flushed with alcohol and incoherence, amid the hollering and smoke.

Dejected, Pappy opened his fist and stared. His eyes widened. Then he looked back at Hauck.

Please, his expression said, this time with desperation. *Just go away*.

CHAPTER FORTY-ONE

"Mom?"

Samantha knocked on the bedroom door.

Karen turned. "Yes, hon."

Karen was on the bed with the TV going. She didn't even know what she was watching. The whole ride back to Greenwich, it beat on her—Jonathan was dead. Struck by a car coming down from the hill while cycling back to his home. Charlie's trader had been trying to tell her something. He had a family, two young kids. And just like that boy who had Charlie's name in his pocket, who had died in Greenwich the same day Charlie disappeared—Jonathan had died the same way. A hit-and-run. If she hadn't had the thought to go and see him, she would never have known.

Samantha sat beside her. "Mom, what's going on?"

Karen turned down the volume. "What do you mean?"

"Mom, please, we're not idiots. You haven't been yourself for over a week. You don't exactly have to have a medical degree to see that you don't have the flu. Something's going on. Are you okay?"

"Of course I'm okay, honey." Karen knew that her face was saying something different. *How could she possibly tell her daughter this?*

Sam stared. "I don't believe you. Look at you. You've barely left the house in days. You haven't been working out or gone to yoga. You're pale as a ghost. You can't keep things from us. If they're important. You're not sick, are you?"

"No, baby." Karen reached for her daughter's hand. "I'm not sick. I promise."

"So what is it, then?"

What could she possibly say? That things were starting to piece together that were really scaring her? That she had seen her husband's face after he'd supposedly died? That she had come upon phony passports and money? That he may have been doing something illegal? That two people who might've shed some light on it were dead? How do you drag your children into the truth that their father had deceived them all in such a monstrous way? Karen asked herself. How do

221

you unleash that kind of hurt and pain onto someone you love so much?

"*Pregnant*, then?" Sam pressed her, with a sheepish grin.

"No, honey"—Karen smiled back—"I'm not pregnant." A tear built up in her eye.

"Are you sad about me going off to college? Because if you are, I won't go. I could go somewhere local. Stay here with you and Alex ..."

"Oh, Samantha." Karen pulled her daughter close and squeezed. "I would never, ever do that to you. I'm so proud of you, hon. How you've dealt with all this. I know how hard it's been. I'm proud of both of you. You've got lives to live. What's happened to your father can't change that."

"So what *is* it then, Mom?" Sam curled up her knee. "I saw that detective here the other night. The one from Greenwich. You guys were outside in the rain. Please, you can tell me. You always want honesty from me. Now it's your turn."

"I know," Karen said. She lifted the hair out of Sam's eyes. "I've always asked that from you, and you've given it, haven't you?"

"Pretty much." Samantha shrugged. "I've held a few things back."

"Pretty much." Karen smiled again, looking in her daughter's eyes. "That's about all I could ask for, isn't it, honey?"

Samantha smiled in return.

"I know it's my turn, Sam. But I just can't tell you, honey. Not just yet. I'm sorry. There are some things—"

"It's about Dad, isn't it? I've seen you looking through his old things."

"Sam, please, you have to trust me. I can't—"

"I know he loved you, Mom." Samantha's eyes shone brightly. "Loved all of us. I just hope that in my life I'm lucky enough to find someone who loved me the same way."

"Yes, baby." Karen held her close. Tears wound their way down her cheeks as they clung to each other there. "I know, baby, I know—"

Then in mid-sentence she stopped. Something unsettling crossed her mind.

Lauer's wife had said he was set to testify regarding Harbor the week he was killed. Saul Lennick would have known that. *Let me handle it, Karen. . . .* He had never told her anything.

All of a sudden, Karen wondered, *Did he know? Did he know Charlie was alive?*

"Yes, baby . . ." Karen kept brushing her daughter's hair. "I hope to God one day you do."

CHAPTER FORTY-TWO

Saul Lennick waited on the Charles Bridge in Prague overlooking the Vltava River.

The bridge teemed with tourists and afternoon pedestrians. Artists sat at easels capturing the view. Violinists played Dvořák and Smetana. Spring had left a festive mood in the city. He looked up at the Gothic spires of St. Vitus and Prague Castle. This was one of his favorite views.

Three men in business attire stepped onto the span from the Linhart Ulice entrance and paused underneath the east tower.

The sandy-haired one, in a topcoat and brown felt hat, wearing wire-rimmed spectacles, and with a ruddy, cheerful face, came forward holding a metal briefcase, while the others waited a few steps behind.

Lennick knew him well.

Johann-Pieter Fichte was German. He had worked in the private banking departments of Credit Suisse and the Bundesbank. Fichte possessed a doctorate in economics from the University of Basel. Now he was a private banker, catering to the highest financial circles.

He was also known to represent some of the most unsavory people in the world.

The banker was what was known in the trade as a "money trafficker." His particular skill was to be able to shift sizable assets from any part of the world in no matter what form: cash, stones, arms—even drugs on occasion—until they emerged in a completely different currency as clean and perfectly investable funds. He did this through a network of currency traders and shell corporations, a labyrinthine web of relationships that stretched from the dark corners of the underworld to boardrooms across the globe. Among Fichte's less visible clients were Iraqi clerics and Afghani warlords who had looted American reconstruction funds; a Kazakh oil minister, a cousin of the president, who had diverted a tenth of his country's reserves; Russian oligarchs, who dealt primarily in drugs and prostitution; even the Colombian drug cartels.

Fichte waved, angling through the crowd. His

two associates—bodyguards, Lennick assumed—stayed a few paces behind.

"Saul!" Fichte said, embracing Lennick with a broad smile, placing his case at Lennick's feet. "It's always a pleasure to see you, my friend. And for you to come all this way."

"The price of a service job." Lennick grinned, grasping the banker's hand.

"Yes, we are only the high-priced errand boys and accountants of the rich"—the banker shrugged—"available at their beck and call. So how is your lovely wife? And your daughter? She's still up in Boston, is she not? Lovely city."

"All fine, Johann. Thank you for asking. Shall we get on?"

"Ah, business." Fichte sighed, turning to face the river. "The American way . . . His Excellency Major General Mubuto sends you his highest regards."

"I'm honored," Lennick said, lying. "And you will return them, of course."

"Of course." The German banker amped up his smile. Then, in a soft voice, staring ahead, as if his gaze were tracking a far-off bird that had landed on the Vltava, he explained. "The funds we discussed will be in the form of four separate deliveries. The first is already on account at Zurich Bank, ready to be transferred upon your say-so to anywhere in the world. The second is currently held at the BalticBank in Estonia. It is in the form of a charitable trust designed to sponsor UN grain shipments to needy populations in East Africa."

Lennick smiled. Fichte always had a cultivated sense of irony.

"I thought you'd appreciate that. The third delivery is presently in non-cash form. Military hardware. Some of it your own, I am told. It should be leaving the country within the week. The general is quite insistent on the timing."

"Why the rush?"

"Pending the status of the Ethiopian military buildup on the Sudanese border, it's conceivable His Excellency and his family may be forced to leave the country at fairly short notice." He winked.

"I'll see to it the funds don't sit unproductive for too long," Lennick promised with a smile.

"That would be greatly appreciated." The German bowed. Then his tone turned businesslike again. "As discussed, each of the deliveries will be in the amount of two hundred and fifty million euros."

Well over a billion dollars. Even Lennick had to marvel. It crossed his mind just how many heads had had to roll and thousands of fortunes wiped out to assemble such a sum.

The banker said, "I think we've already gone over the general agreement."

"The mix of products is quite diversified and fully transparent if need be," Lennick replied. "A combination of U.S. and worldwide equities, real-estate trusts, hedge funds. Twenty percent will be retained in our private equity fund. As you know, we've been able to achieve a twenty-two and a half percent average portfolio return over the past seven years, net of any unforeseen fluctuations, of course."

"*Fluctuations . . .*" The German nodded, the warmth in his blue eyes suddenly dimmed. "I assume you're speaking of that energy hedge fund that collapsed last year. I hope it won't be necessary to revisit my clients' unhappiness over that development, will it, Saul?"

"As said"—Lennick swallowed a lump, trying to redirect the subject—"an unforeseen fluctuation, Johann. It won't happen again."

The truth was, with the amount of capital available in today's world, Lennick had learned to make money in every conceivable market environment. In times of economic strength or stagnation. Good markets or bad. Even following acts of terrorism. The panic after 9/11 would never occur again. He had billions invested on all sides of the economic ledger, impervious to the vagaries of whoever won or lost. Today geopolitical trends and shifts were merely hiccups in the global transfer of capital. Yes, there were always blips—blips like Charlie, betting on the price of oil so stubbornly and unable to cover his spots on the way down. But behind that, all one had to do was look at the vast Saudi and Kuwaiti investment funds, the world's greatest oil producers, hedging their bets by buying up all the ethanol-producing sugarcane fields in the world.

It was the greatest capital-enlarging engine in the world.

"So it doesn't bother you, my friend?" the German banker suddenly asked. "You are a Jew, yes, and yet you know that this money you take regularly finds its way into the hands of interests that are unfriendly to your own race."

"Yes, I'm a Jew." Lennick looked at him and shrugged. "But I learned a long time ago that money is neutral, Johann."

"Yes, money is neutral," Fichte agreed. "Still, my client's patience is not." His expression sharpened again. "The loss of over half a billion dollars of their funds does not sit easily with these kinds of people, Saul. They asked me to remind you—your daughter has children up in Boston, does she not?" He met Lennick's eye. "Ages two and four?"

The blood seeped from Lennick's face.

"I was asked to inquire as to their general health, Saul. I hope they're well. Just a thought, my old friend, from my own employers. Please, do not dwell. Still . . ." His smile returned with an affable tap of Lennick's arm. "A small incentive to keep those—how was it you phrased it?— *fluctuations* to a minimum, yes?"

A cold bead of sweat traveled down Lennick's back underneath his six-hundred-dollar Brioni pinstripe shirt.

"Your man lost us a considerable amount of money," Fichte said. "You shouldn't be so surprised, Saul. You know who you're playing with here. No one is above accountability, my friend—*even you.*"

Fichte put on his hat.

Lennick felt a constriction in his chest. His palms, suddenly slick with sweat, pressed deeply onto the bridge's railing. He nodded. "You spoke of four new deliveries, Johann. Two hundred and fifty million euros each. So far you've only mentioned three."

"Ah, *the fourth . . .*" The German banker

smiled and patted Lennick briskly on the back. He drew his gaze to the metal case at his feet.

"The fourth I'm giving you *today*, Herr Lennick. In bearer bonds. My men will be happy to escort you to wherever you would like it placed."

CHAPTER FORTY-THREE

By morning the welt on Hauck's face had gone down a bit. He had packed his bags, set to check out in a couple of minutes. There was no need to press the old man any longer. He had other ways to find out what he needed to know. He glanced at his watch. He had a ten o'clock plane.

When he opened the door to leave, Pappy Raymond was leaning on the outside railing.

The old man's face was haggard, eyes blood-shot and drawn. He looked like he'd spent the night curled up in some alley. Or like he'd been in a street fight with a ferret. And the ferret had won!

"How's the eye?" He looked at Hauck. Somewhere in his tone was the hint of an apology.

"Works." Hauck shrugged, rubbing the side of his face. "I was a little peeved about the beer, though."

"Yeah." Pappy smiled sheepishly. "Guess I owe you one of those." The blue in his hooded eyes shone through. "You heading home?"

"Somehow I got the sense you'd be okay with that."

"Hmphh," Pappy snorted. "How'd I ever give you that idea?"

Hauck waited. He set down his bags.

"I was a fool my whole life," Pappy said finally. He eased off the railing. "Stubborn with the best of them. Problem is, it takes getting old to find that out. Then it's too late."

From his coverall pocket, he took out the Orange Bowl ticket stub Hauck had placed in his hand the night before. He bunched up his lips. "We drove all day to see that game. Might as well have been the Super Bowl for all my son cared. It was to him. Seminoles were always his team." He scratched his head, suddenly clear-eyed. "I guess I should say thanks. I remember last night you said . . ."

"My daughter was four." Hauck gazed back at him. "She was run over by our car, in our own driveway. Five years ago. I'd been driving. I thought I'd left it in park. I was bitter, after the pain finally eased. My ex-wife still can't look me in the eyes without seeing it all over. So I know. . . . That's all I meant to say."

"Never goes away, does it?" Raymond shifted his weight on the railing.

Hauck shook his head. "Never does."

Raymond let out a breath. "I watched those goddamn tankers come in three, four times. From Venezuela, the Philippines, Trinidad. Twice I even brought 'em in myself. Even a fool could see those ships were riding way too high. Didn't have a lick of oil. Even snuck inside the holds once to see for myself." He shook his head. "Clean as a baby's ass. It's not right what they were trying to do. . . ."

Hauck asked, "You took it to your boss?"

"My boss, the harbormaster, the customs people . . . No duty on oil, so what the hell do they care? No telling who was getting paid. I kept hearing, 'You just bring 'em in and park 'em, old man. Don't stir it up.' But I kept stirring. Then I got this call."

"To push you to stop?"

Pappy nodded. "'Don't make waves, mister. You never know where they might fall.' Finally I got this visit, too."

"You remember from whom?"

"Met me outside the bar, just like you. Square jaw, dark hair, mustache. The kind of SOB who looked like he meant trouble. Mentioned my boy

234

up north. Even showed me a picture. AJ and some gal up there with a kid. I knew what he was telling me. Still I kept at it. Called up this reporter I knew. I said I'd get him proof. That's when I went aboard. A week later they sent me *this*."

Pappy dug into his trousers, the kind of navy blue work pants he'd worn on the job, and came out with his cell phone, scanning it until he found a stored call. He handed it to Hauck.

A photo. Hauck exhaled. AJ Raymond lying in the road.

Pappy pointed. "You see what they wrote to me there?"

SEEN ENOUGH NOW?

A screw of anger and understanding tightened in Hauck's chest. "Who sent this to you?"

Pappy shook his head. "Never knew."

"You take this to the police?"

Another shake of the head. "They won. No."

"I'd like to send this picture to myself, if that's okay?"

"Go ahead. I'm not standing by any longer. It's yours now."

Hauck forwarded the image to himself. Felt his phone vibrate.

"He was a good boy, my son." Pappy looked

Hauck in the eye. "He liked surfing and fishing. Cars. He'd never hurt a fly. He didn't deserve to die like that. . . ."

Hauck handed Pappy back the phone. He moved next to the old man on the railing. "These people, it was they that did this to him, not you. You were just trying to do what you thought was right."

Pappy gazed at him. "Why are you doing all this, mister? You never showed me no badge. It can't just be for AJ."

"My daughter," Hauck said, shrugging back at him, "she had red hair, too."

"So we're the same." Pappy smiled. "Sort of. I was wrong, Lieutenant, the way I treated you. I was scared for Pete and my other boy, Walker, their families. Bringing all this up again. But you get them. You get those sons of bitches who killed my boy. I don't know why they did. I don't know what they were protecting. But whatever it was, it wasn't worth this. You get them, you hear? Wherever this leads. And when you do"—he winked, a glimmer in his eye— "you don't think about throwin' 'em in no jail, you understand?"

Hauck smiled. He squeezed the man on the arm. "So what was the name?"

Pappy squinted. "The *name*?"

"Of the tanker?" Hauck asked.

"Some Greek word." Pappy sniffed. "I looked it up. Goddess of the underworld. *Persephone,* it was called."

CHAPTER FORTY-FOUR

Vito Collucci could find anything, if the matter was about money. He made his living as a forensic accountant, tracking down the buried assets of philandering husbands for vengeful ex-wives. The hidden profits of large companies trying to fend off class-action suits. Before putting out a shingle, he had been a detective on the Stamford police force for fifteen years, which was where Hauck knew him from.

Vito Collucci could spot a bad seed in a sperm bank, he liked to say.

"Vito, I need a favor," Hauck said over the phone, heading out to the airport for his flight from Pensacola.

These days Vito ran a good-size company. He was a frequent "guest expert" on MSNBC, but he had never forgotten how Hauck had thrown him cases when he first got started.

"When?" he asked. When Hauck called, Vito knew it usually involved information. Information that was hard to find.

"Today," Hauck said. "I guess, tomorrow, if you need it."

"Today's fine."

Hauck landed at two, taking his Bronco up from La Guardia. As he passed Greenwich heading to Stamford, the station a mile away, it occurred to him that he was getting deeper into something and a little further outside the law than he liked. He thought about giving Karen Friedman a call but decided to wait. There was a text message on his phone.

Usual place. From Vito. Three P.M. was fine.

The usual place was the Stamford Restaurant & Pizzeria, a no-frills cops' haunt on Main Street, past downtown, close to the Darien border.

Vito was already there, at one of the long tables covered in checkered cloths. He was short, barrel-chested, with thick wrestler's forearms and wiry graying hair. A plate of ziti with sauce was set before him, and a bowl of escarole and cannellini beans.

"I'd run up the check," he said as Hauck came in, "but you're lucky, Ellie's got me on this cholesterol thing."

"I can see." Hauck grinned and sat down. He ordered the same. "So how've you been?"

"Good," Vito said. "Busy."

"You look thinner on TV."

"And you don't seem to age," Vito said. "Except for that shiner you're carrying. You gotta realize, Ty, you can't tussle with the young dudes anymore."

"I'll keep that in mind."

Vito had a manila envelope beside him on the table. He pushed it over to Hauck. "Take a peek. I'll let you know what I found."

Hauck gazed at the contents.

"The ship was easy. I looked it up in Jane's. *Persephone,* right?" Vito stabbed at a few ziti with his fork. "ULCC-class supertanker. Built in Germany, 1978. Pretty much outdated now. What're you thinking, maybe of trading up to something a bit more seaworthy, Ty?"

"Might look good on the sound." Hauck nodded. "Be a bit of a bitch to dock, though." He scanned a photocopied page from the nautical manual that displayed an image of the ship. Sixty-two thousand tons.

"Been sold around a couple of times over the years," Vito went on. "The last time to some Greek shipping company—Argos Maritime. That mean anything to you?"

Hauck shook his head.

"Didn't think it would. So I kept at it. Pretended that I was a lawyer's assistant to the company, tracking down a claim. The past four years this scrap heap's been leased to some oil-exploration outfit I can't bring up anything on anywhere. Dolphin Oil."

Hauck scratched his head. "Who's Dolphin?"

"Fuck if I know." Vito shrugged. "Believe me, I checked. No record of them anywhere in the D&B. Then I tried a trade list of petroleum-exploration and -development companies, and it didn't show up either. If Dolphin's a player in the oil and gas business, they're keeping it pretty much on the QT."

"You think they're a real company?"

"My thoughts exactly," Vito said, pushing his plate away. "So I kept digging. I tried a directory of offshore-company listings. No record of them in Europe or Asia. I'm thinking, how does a company with no record in the industry lease a goddamn supertanker? Guess what came up? Feel free to turn the page."

Hauck did.

Vito grinned widely. "Out of Tortola—in the BVIs . . . Whaddaya know about that—*Dolphin fucking Oil!*"

"In *Tortola*?"

Vito nodded. "A lot of companies are being set up there now. It's like a mini–Cayman Islands. Avoids taxes. Keeps the funds out from under the eye of the U.S. government. As well as the SEC, if they're public. Far as I can tell, and I've only been at it a couple of hours, Dolphin's basically just a holding company. No revenues or profits of any kind. No transactions. A shell. The management seems to be just a bunch of fancy barristers down there. Check out the board—everybody's got an LLC behind his name. Far as I can tell, it basically belongs to this investment company that's situated down there as well. Falcon Partners."

"Falcon . . . never heard of it." Hauck shook his head.

"You're not supposed to have heard of it, Ty. That's why the hell it's there! It's some kind of private investment partnership. Or at least *was*. The fund was dissolved and the assets redistributed back to its limited partners earlier this year. Took me a while to figure out why. I was hoping to try to get a list of who the partners were, but it's totally private—buttoned up. Whoever they are, the money's probably long back to wherever it came from by now."

Hauck scanned over the one-page company summary of Falcon. He knew in his gut he was getting close.

242

Whoever owned Dolphin had been engaged in some kind of cover-up. They had used empty tankers but declared that they were filled with oil. Pappy had stumbled onto it, and they'd tried to shut him up, but whatever they were hiding, he wasn't the kind that shut up easily, and it had ended up costing him his son. *Seen enough now?* Dolphin led to Falcon.

Close enough, Hauck felt, the hairs raised expectantly on his arms. "How the hell do we get to Falcon, Vito?"

The detective was staring at him. "What's the point of all this, Ty?"

"The point?"

Vito shrugged. "First time since I've known you you're not up front with me. My spies tell me you're on leave from the department."

"Maybe your spies told you why."

"Something personal, is all. Some kind of case that's consuming you."

"It's called murder, Vito, no matter who I'm working for. And if this was all just so personal"—Hauck looked back at him, curling a smile—"I'd have called Match.com, not you."

Vito grinned. "Just warning an old friend to stay within the boundaries, that's all."

The private investigator took out a folded piece of paper from his jacket pocket and pushed it across the table. "Whoever Falcon is, Ty, they wanted to keep it secret. The board's pretty much the same legal functionaries as Dolphin."

Hauck scanned down the page. Nothing. Fucking close.

"One thing, though," Vito added. "I mentioned that Falcon was comprised of a bunch of limited partners who want to remain secret. But the general partner *is* listed. In the investment agreement, plain as day. It's the outfit who manages the funds."

Hauck turned the page. Staring back at him, there was a name. Vito had highlighted it in yellow.

When Hauck's gaze fell on it, his heart sank a little, as opposed to the leap he'd always imagined. He knew where this was about to lead.

Harbor Capital. The general partner.

Harbor was the firm that belonged to Karen Friedman's husband.

"That what you're looking for?" Vito asked, watching Hauck dwell on the page.

"Yeah, that's what I'm looking for, buddy." Hauck sighed.

CHAPTER FORTY-FIVE

The man broke through the surface of the glistening turquoise water in the remote Caribbean cove.

No one around. Not even a name for this place, just a speck on the map. The only sounds were the caws of a handful of frigate birds as they tumbled out of the sky into the sea searching for prey. The man looked back at the perfect half circle of white sand beach, palm trees swaying in the languid breeze on the shore.

He could be anywhere. Anywhere in the world.

Why did he choose here?

Twenty yards away, his boat bobbed on the tranquil tide. What seemed like a lifetime ago, it occurred to him, he had told his wife he could spend the rest of his life in just such a place as this. A place without markets or indices. Without cell phones or TV. A place where no one looked for you.

And where there was no one to find you.

Every day that part of his life became a more distant part of his mind. The thought had a strange appeal to him.

The rest of his life.

He raised his face into the warm rays of the sun. His hair was cut short now, shaved in a way that might make his children roll their eyes, some old guy trying to appear cool. His body was fit and trim. He no longer wore glasses. His face was covered in a stubbly growth. He had a local's tan.

And money.

Enough money to last forever. If he could manage it right. And a new name. Hanson. Steven Hanson. A name he had paid for. A name no one knew.

Not his wife, his kids.

Not those who might want to find him.

In this complicated world of computers and personal histories, he had simply gone, *poof.* Disappeared. One life ended—with remorse, regret, at the pain he knew he'd caused, the trust he'd broken. Still, he'd had to do it. It had been necessary. To save them. To save himself.

One life ended—and another sprang up.

When the moment had presented itself, he could not turn it down.

He hardly even thought of it now. The blast. One minute he had gone back from the front of the car to make a call, then flash! A black, rattling cloud with a core of orange heat. Like a furnace. The clothes burned off your back. Hurled against the wall. In a tangle of people screaming. Black smoke everywhere, the dark tide rushing over him. He was sure he was dead. He remembered thinking, through the haze, this way was best. It solved everything.

Just die.

When he came to, he looked at the ravaged train car. Every place he had been just a moment before was gone. Obliterated. The car in which he'd sat. The people around him, who were reading the paper, listening to their iPods. Gone. In a horrifying ocean of flame. He coughed up smoke. *Got to get out of here,* he thought. His brain was ringing. Numb. He staggered out, onto the platform. Horrible sights—blood everywhere, the smell of cordite and charred flesh. People moaning, calling out for help. *What could he do?* He had to get out, let Karen know he was alive.

Then it all became startlingly clear.

This was how. This was what had been presented to him.

He could die.

He stumbled over something. A body. Its face almost unrecognizable. In the chaos he knew he needed to be someone else. He felt around in the man's trousers. In the smoke-filled darkness, the whole station black. He found it. He didn't even look at the name. What did it matter? Then he began to run. His wits suddenly clearer than they'd ever been. *This was how!* Running, stumbling over the flow, not toward the entrance but to the other end of the tracks. Away from the flames. People from the rear cars were rushing there. The uptown entrances. Away from the flames. The one thing he had to do, resonating in his mind. Abel Raymond. He took a last look back at the smoldering car.

He could die.

"Mr. Hanson!" A voice suddenly brought him back, interrupting his dark memory. Leaning back in the water, Charles looked over at the boat. His Trinidadian captain was bending over the bow. "Mr. Hanson, w'ought to be pushing off about now. If we want to make it there by night."

There. Wherever it was they were heading. Another dot on the map. With a bank. A rare-stone dealer. What did it matter?

"Right, I'll be along in a moment," he called back.

Treading water, he looked at the idyllic cove one last time.

Why had he come here? The memories only hurt him. The happy voices and recollections only filled him with regret and shame. He prayed she had found a new life, someone new to love her. And Sam and Alex . . . That was the only hope open to him now. *We could spend the rest of our lives here,* he had told her once.

The rest of our lives.

Charles Friedman swam toward the anchored boat, its name painted on the stern in gold script. The only attachment he allowed himself, the only reminder.

Emberglow.

PART THREE

PART THREE

CHAPTER FORTY-SIX

Twice a week, Tuesday and Thursday, Ronald
Torbor generally took his lunch at home. Those
days Mr. Carty, the senior bank manager, covered
his desk from one to three.

As assistant manager of the First Caribbean
Bank on the isle of Nevis, Ronald lived in a
comfortable three-bedroom stone house just off
the airport road, large enough to fit his own
family—his wife, Edith, along with Alya and
Peter and Ezra, and his wife's mother, too. At
the bank, people came to him to open accounts,
apply for loans—the position came, to the view
of his fellow locals, with a certain air of import-
ance. He also took pleasure in catering to the
needs of some of the island's wealthier clientele.
Though he had grown up kicking around a
soccer ball on dirt fields, Ronald now liked golf
on the weekends over on St. Kitts. And when

the general manager, who was soon to be transferred, went back home, Ronald felt sure he had a good chance of becoming the bank's first local-born manager.

That Tuesday, Edith had prepared him his favorite—stewed chicken in a green curry sauce. It was May. Not much going on at the office. Once the tourist season died, Nevis was basically a sleepy little isle. These kinds of days, other than waving to Mr. Carty that he was back, he felt there was no urgency to hurry back to his desk.

At the table, Ronald glanced over the paper: the results from the Caribbean cricket championships being held in Jamaica. His six-year-old, Ezra, was home from school. After lunch, Edith was taking him to the doctor. The boy had what they called Asperger's syndrome, a mild form of autism. And on Nevis, despite the rush of new money and developers, the care wasn't very good.

"After work you can come watch Peter play soccer," said Edith, seated in the chair next to Ezra. The boy was playing with a toy truck, making noise.

"Yes, Edith." Ronald sighed, enjoying his peace. He focused on the box score. Matson, for Barbados, wrong-foots Anguilla for six!

"And you can bring me back some fresh-baked roti from Mrs. Williams, if you please." Her bakery was directly across from the bank, best on the island. "You know the kind I like, onion and—"

"Yes, mum," Ronald muttered again.

"And don't be 'mumming' me in front of your boy like I'm some kind of schoolmarm, Ronald."

Ronald looked up from the paper and flashed Ezra a wink.

The six-year-old started to laugh.

Outside, they heard the sound of gravel crunching, as a car drove up the road to their house.

"That is probably Mr. P.," Edith said. Paul Williams, her cousin. "I said he could come by about a loan."

"Jeez, Edith," Ronald groaned, "couldn't you have him just come by the bank?"

But it wasn't Mr. P. It was two white men, who got out of the Jeep and stepped up to the front door. One was short and stocky, with wrap-around sunglasses and a thick mustache. The other was taller, wearing a light sport jacket with a colorful beach shirt underneath with a base-ball cap.

Ronald shrugged. "Who's this?"

"I don't know." Edith opened the door.

"Afternoon, ma'am." The mustached man politely took off his hat. His eyes drifted past her. "Mind if we speak to your husband? I can see he's at home."

Ronald stood up. He'd never seen them before. "What's this about?"

"Banking business," the man said, stepping around Ronald's wife and into the house.

"Banking hours are closed—for lunch." Ronald tried not to seem unfriendly. "I'll be back down there at three."

"No." The mustached man lifted his glasses and smiled. "I'm afraid the bank is open, Mr. Torbor. *Right here.*"

The man shut the door. "Just look at these as extra hours."

A shudder of fear rippled through Ronald's body. Edith met his gaze as if to find out what was going on, then moved back around to the table, next to her son.

The mustached man nodded to Ronald. "Sit down."

Ronald did, the man flipping a chair around and pulling it up to him, smiling strangely. "We're really sorry to interrupt your lunch, Mr. Torbor. You can get back to it, though, once you tell us what we need."

"What you need . . . ?"

"That's right, Mr. Torbor." The man reached into his jacket and removed a folded sheet. "This is the number of a private account at your bank. It should be familiar. A sizable amount of money was wired into it several months back, from Tortola, the Barclays bank there."

Ronald stared at the number. His eyes grew wide. The numbers were from his bank, First Caribbean. The taller man had pulled up a chair next to Ezra, winking and making mugging faces at the boy, which made him laugh. Ronald glanced fearfully toward Edith. *What the hell are they doing here?*

"This particular account is no longer active, Mr. Torbor," the man with the mustache acknowledged. "The funds are no longer in your bank. But what we want to know, and what you're going to help us find out, Mr. Torbor, if you hope to ever get back to your lunch and this happy little life of yours, is precisely where the funds were wired— once they left here. And also under what name."

Perspiration was starting to soak through Ronald's newly pressed white shirt. "You must know I can't give out that kind of information. That's all private. Covered by banking regulations—"

"Private." The mustached man nodded, glancing toward his partner.

"Regulations." The man in the beach shirt sighed. "Always a bitch. We sort of anticipated that."

With a sudden motion, he reached over and jerked Ezra up out of his chair. Surprised, the child whimpered. The man put him on his lap. Edith tried to stop him, but he just elbowed her, knocking her to the floor.

"Ezra!" she cried out.

The small boy started crying. Ronald leaped up.

"Sit down!" The mustached man grabbed him by the arm. He also took something out of his jacket and placed it on the table. Something black and metallic. Ronald felt his heart seize as he saw what it was. "Sit down."

Frantic, Ronald lowered himself back into the chair. He looked at Edith helplessly. "Whatever you want. Please, don't hurt Ezra."

"No reason to, Mr. Torbor." The mustached man smiled. "But no point beating around the bush. What you're going to do now is call in to your office, and I want you to have your secretary or whomever the fuck you talk to down there look up that account. Make up whatever excuse or justification you need. We know you don't get those kinds of funds in your sleepy little bank very often. I want to know where it went, which country, what

bank, and under what name. Do you understand?"

Ronald sat silent.

"Your father understands what I mean,
doesn't he, boy?" He tickled Ezra's ear. "Because
if he doesn't"—his eyes now shifted darkly—"I
promise that your lives will not be happy, and
you will remember this little moment with regret
and anguish for as long as you live. I'm clear on
that, aren't I, Mr. Torbor?"

"Do it, Ronald, please, do it," Edith pleaded,
pulling herself up off the floor.

"I can't. I can't," he said, trembling. "There
are procedures for this sort of thing. Even if I
agreed, it's governed by international banking
regulations. Laws . . ."

"Back to those regulations again." The
mustached man shook his head and sighed
loudly.

The taller man holding Ezra removed something from *his* jacket pocket.

Ronald's eyes bulged wide.

It was a tin of lighter fluid.

Ronald dove out of the chair to stop him, but
the mustached man hit him on the side of the
head with the gun, sending him sprawling onto
the floor.

"Oh, Jesus Lord, no!" Edith screamed, trying

259

to wrench the man off her son. He elbowed her away.

Then, smiling, the man holding Ezra took the crying boy by the collar and began to douse him with fluid.

Ronald launched himself again, but the mustached man had cocked his gun and raised it to Ronald's forehead. "I keep remembering asking you to sit down."

Ezra was bawling now.

"Here's your cell phone, Mr. Torbor," pushing Ronald his phone from across the table. "Make the call and we just go away. Now."

"*I can't.*" Ronald held out trembling hands. "Jesus God in heaven, don't. I . . . can't."

"I know he's a bit off, Mr. Torbor." The man shook his head. "But he's just an innocent boy. Shame to hurt him in this way. For a bunch of silly regulations . . . Anyway, not a pretty thing at all for your wife to witness, is it?"

"*Ronald!*"

The man holding Ezra took out a plastic lighter. He flicked it, sparking up a steady flame. He brought it close to the child's damp shirt.

"*No!*" Edith shrieked. "Ronald, please, don't let them do this! For God's sake, do whatever the hell they're asking. *Ronald, please . . .* "

Ezra was screaming. The man holding him

drew the flame closer. The man with the mustache pushed the phone in front of Ronald and looked steadily at him.

"*Exactamente,* Mr. Torbor. Fuck the regulations. It's time to make that call."

CHAPTER FORTY-SEVEN

Karen rushed to drop Alex off at the Arch Street Teen Center that Tuesday afternoon, for a youth fund-raiser for the Kids in Crisis shelter in town.

She was excited when Hauck had called. They agreed to meet in the bar at L'Escale, overlooking Greenwich Harbor, which was virtually next door. She was eager to tell him what she'd found.

Hauck was sitting at a table near the bar and waved when she came in.

"Hi." She waved, folding her leather jacket over the back of her chair.

For a moment she moaned about how traffic was getting crazy in town this time of day. "Try to find a parking space on the avenue." She rolled her eyes in mock frustration. "You have to be a cop!"

"Seems fair to me." Hauck shrugged, suppressing a smile.

"I forgot who I was talking to!" Karen laughed. "Can't you do anything about this?"

"I'm on leave, remember? When I'm back, I promise that'll be the very first thing."

"Good!" Karen nodded brightly, as if pleased. "Don't let me down. I'm relying on you."

The waitress came over, and it took Karen about a second to order a pinot grigio. Hauck was already nursing a beer. She'd put on some makeup and a nice beige sweater over tight-fitting pants. Something made her want to look good. When her wine came, Hauck tilted his glass at her.

"We ought to think of something," she said.

"To simpler times," he proposed.

"Amen." Karen grinned. They touched glasses lightly.

It was a little awkward at first, and they just chatted. She told him about Alex's involvement on the Kids in Crisis board, which Hauck was impressed with and called "a pretty admirable thing."

Karen smiled. "Community-service requirement, Lieutenant. All the kids have to do it. It's a college application rite of spring."

She asked him where his daughter went to school and he said, "Brooklyn," the short version, leaving out Norah and Beth. "She's growing up pretty fast," he said. "Pretty soon *I'll* be doing the community-service thing."

Karen's eyes lit up. "Just wait for the SATs!"

Gradually Hauck grew relaxed, the lines between them softening just a little, suddenly feeling alive in the warm glow of her bright hazel eyes, the cluster of freckles dotting her cheeks, the trace of her accent, the fullness of her lips, the honey color of her hair. He decided to hold back what he'd learned about Dolphin and Charles's connection to it. About Thomas Mardy and how he'd been at the hit-and-run that day. Until he knew for sure. It would only hurt her more— send things down a path he would one day regret. Still, when he gazed at Karen Friedman, he was transported back to a part of his life that had not been wounded by loss. And he imagined—in the ease of her laugh, the second glass of wine, how she laughed at all the lines he had hoped she would—she was feeling the same way, too.

At a lull, Karen put down her wine. "So you said you made a little headway down there?"

He nodded. "You remember that hit-and-run that happened the day of the bombing, when I came by?"

"Of course I remember."

Hauck put down his beer. "I found out why the kid died."

Her eyes widened. *"Why?"*

He had thought carefully about this before she arrived, what he might say, and he heard himself retelling how some company was carrying on a fraud of some kind down there, a petroleum company, and how the kid's father— a harbor pilot—had stumbled right into the middle of it.

"It was a warning"—Hauck shrugged—"if you can believe it. To get him to back off."

"It was *murder*?" Karen said, a jolt of shock shooting through her.

Hauck nodded. "Yeah."

She sat back, stunned. "That's so terrible. You never thought it was an accident. My God . . ."

"And it worked."

"What do you mean?"

"The old man stopped. He buried it. It never would have come out if I didn't go down."

Karen's face turned pallid. "You said you went down there for me. How does this relate to Charles?"

How could he tell her? About Charles, Dolphin, the empty ships? Or how Charles had been in Greenwich that day? How could he hurt her more, more than she'd already been, until he knew? Knew for sure.

And being with her now, he knew why.

265

"The company," Hauck said, "the one that was doing this down there, had a connection to Harbor."

The color drained from Karen's face. "To Charlie?"

Hauck nodded. "Dolphin Petroleum. You know the name?"

She shook her head.

"It may have been part of a group of investments he owned."

Karen hesitated. "What do you mean, investments?"

"Offshore."

Karen put a hand to her mouth and looked at him. It only echoed what Saul had said. "You think Charles was involved? In this hit-and-run?"

"I don't want to get ahead of ourselves, Karen."

"Please don't protect me, Ty. You're thinking he was involved?"

"I don't know." He exhaled. He held back the fact that Charles had been up there that day. "There are still a lot more leads I have to run down."

"Leads?" Karen sat back. Her eyes had a strange, confused look to them. She pressed her palms together in front of her lips and nodded. "I found something, too, Ty."

"What?"

266

"I don't know, but it's scaring me a little—like you are now."

She described how she'd been going through some of Charles's old things, as he'd asked, his old files, had spoken to his old secretary and travel agent but been unable to find anything.

Until she came across a name.

"The guy had called me a couple of times, just after Charles died. Someone who worked for him." She described how Jonathan Lauer had tried to contact her, the cryptic messages he'd left. *Some things you ought to know . . .* "I just couldn't deal with it back then. It was too much. I mentioned them to Saul. He said it was just personnel stuff and he'd take care of it."

Hauck nodded. "Okay . . ."

"But then I thought of it in light of all that's come up, and it began to gnaw at me. So I went out to see him while you were gone. To New Jersey. To see him. I didn't know where he worked now, and all I had was this address from when he worked for Charles, with a private number. I just took a chance. His wife answered the door." Karen's eyes turned glassy. "She told me the most horrible thing."

"What?"

"He's dead. He was killed. In a cycling accident, a few months back. What made it all a

little creepy was that he'd been scheduled to give a deposition in some matter related to Harbor later in the week."

"What kind of matter?"

"I don't know. But it wasn't just that. It was the way he was killed. Coupled with the way your Raymond kid was killed, who had Charlie's name on him."

Hauck put down his glass, his antennae for these sorts of things beginning to buzz.

"A car hit him," Karen said. "Just like your guy. It was a hit-and-run."

A group of office people seated next to them suddenly grew louder. Karen leaned forward, her knees pressed together, her face a little blank.

"You did good," Hauck said, showing he was pleased. "Real good."

Some of the color returned to her cheeks.

"You hungry?" Hauck asked, taking a chance.

Karen shrugged, casting a quick glance at her watch. "Alex has a ride home with a neighbor. I guess I have a little time."

CHAPTER FORTY-EIGHT

On the way home, Hauck rang up Freddy Muñoz.

"LT!" his detective exclaimed in surprise. "Long time no hear. How's vacation?"

"I'm not on vacation, Freddy. Listen, I need a favor. I need you to get a copy of the file on an unsolved homicide in New Jersey. Upper Montclair. The victim's name is Lauer. L-A-U-E-R, like Matt. First name Jonathan. There may be a parallel investigation by the Jersey State Police."

Muñoz was writing it down. "Lauer. And what do I say is the reason we need it, LT?"

"Similar pattern to a case we've been looking at up here."

"And which case is that, Lieutenant?"

"It's an unsolved hit-and-run."

Muñoz paused. In the background there was

the sound of young kids shouting, maybe the Yankees game on TV. "Jesus, Ty, this becoming an MO with you now?"

"Have someone drop it off at my home tomorrow. If I was active, I'd do it myself. And Freddy . . ." Hauck heard the sound of Freddy's son, Will, cheering. "This stays just between us, okay?"

"Yeah, LT," the detective answered. "Sure."

New leads, Hauck was thinking.

One definitely ran through Charlie Friedman's trustee, Lennick. Karen trusted him. Almost like a member of the family. He would have known about Lauer. Did he know about Dolphin and Falcon, too?

Did Charlie ever mention he was managing any accounts offshore?

The other ran through New Jersey, this second hit-and-run. Hauck had never been one to have much faith in coincidences.

As he drove, his thoughts kept straying back to Karen. Off the top of his head, he came up with ten good, solid reasons he should stop now, before things went any further between them.

Starting with the fact that her husband was alive. And how Hauck had made a pledge to find him. And how he didn't want to cause her any more needless hurt by holding things back than she had already been through.

And how she was rich. Used to different things. Traveled in a totally different league.

Jesus, Ty, you're not exactly playing the strongest hand here.

Still, he couldn't deny that he felt something with her. The electricity when their hands brushed once or twice at dinner. The same sensation coursing through his veins right now.

He pulled his Bronco off the exit of 95 back in Stamford. It occurred to him why he couldn't tell her. Why he was holding back the whole truth. That Charles had returned to Greenwich after the bombing. That he had a hand in killing that boy. Maybe the other one, too.

Why he didn't want to bring the police into the matter. Get other people involved.

Because Hauck realized that for the last four years he'd been essentially rootless, alone. And Karen Friedman was the one thing he felt connected to right now.

CHAPTER FORTY-NINE

There was a knock on the door the following afternoon, and Hauck went over to answer.

Freddy Muñoz was there.

He handed Hauck one of those large, string-bound interoffice envelopes. "Hope I'm not bothering you. Thought I'd bring it up to you myself, Lieutenant, if that's okay?"

Hauck had just come back from a run. He was sweaty. He was in a gray Colby College T-shirt and gym shorts. He had spent most of the morning working on the computer.

"You're not bothering me."

"Place looks nice." The detective nodded approvingly. "Needs a bit of a woman's touch, don't you think? Maybe make a little sense of that kitchen over there?"

Hauck glanced at the dishes piled in the sink,

a few open containers of takeout on the counter. "Care to volunteer?"

"Can't." Muñoz snapped his fingers, feigning disappointment. "Working tonight, Lieutenant. But I thought I'd just hang around a minute while you took a look through that, if that's okay?"

Buoyed, Hauck opened the envelope's flap and slid the contents on the coffee table, while Muñoz threw himself into a cushy living-room chair.

The first thing he came upon was the incident report. The report of the accident by the lead officer on the scene. From the Essex County PD. Details on the deceased. His name, Lauer. Address: 3135 Mountain View. DOB. Description: white male, approximately thirty, wearing a yellow biking uniform, severe body trauma and bleeding. Eyewitness described a red SUV, make undetermined, speeding away. New Jersey plates, number undetermined. Time: 10:07 A.M. Date. Eyewitness report attached.

It all seemed to have a familiar feel.

Hauck glanced through the photos. Photostats of them. The victim. In his biking jersey. Hit head-on. Severe blunt trauma to the face and torso. There was a shot of the bike, which had basically been mangled. A couple of views in either direction. Up, down the hill. The vehicle was clearly heading down.

Tire marks only after the point of impact.

Just like AJ Raymond.

Next Hauck leafed through the medical examiner's report. Severe blunt-force trauma, crushed pelvis and fractured vertebrae, head trauma. Massive internal bleeding. Dead on impact, the medical examiner presumed.

Hauck paged through the detectives' case reports. They had mapped out the same course of action Hauck had up in Connecticut. Did a canvass of the area, notified the state police, checked with the body shops, tried to trace back the tread marks for a tire brand. Interviewed the victim's wife, his employer. "No motive found" to assume it might not have been an accident.

Still no suspects.

Muñoz had gotten up and gone over to a canvas Hauck was working on by the window. He lifted it off the easel. "This is pretty good, Lieutenant!"

"Thanks, Freddy."

"May get to see you at the Bruce Museum yet. And I don't mean waiting in line."

"Feel free to help yourself to any you like," Hauck muttered, flipping through the pages. "One day they'll be worth millions."

It was frustrating—just like his. The Jersey folks had never found any solid leads.

It just came down to a coincidence, a coincidence Hauck didn't believe, one that didn't lead anywhere.

"Strike you as reasonable, Freddy?" Hauck asked. "Two separate 509s? Two different states. Each with a connection to Charles Friedman."

"Keep at it, Lieutenant," Muñoz said, flopping back over the arm of the heavy chair.

All that was left was the detail of the eyewitness depositions. *Deposition.* There was only one.

As Hauck opened it up, he froze. He felt his jaw drop open, his eyeballs pulled like magnets to the name on the deposition's front page.

"See what I'm seeing?" Freddy Muñoz sat up. He swung his legs off the chair.

"Yeah." Hauck nodded and took a breath. "I sure do."

The lone eyewitness to Jonathan Lauer's murder had been a retired New Jersey policeman.

His name was Phil Dietz.

The same eyewitness as at AJ Raymond's hit-and-run.

CHAPTER FIFTY

He had slipped up. Hauck read over his testimony once, twice, then again.

He had slipped up big-time!

Immediately Hauck recalled how Pappy Raymond had described the guy who'd met him outside the bar and put the pressure on him. *Stocky, mustached.* In the same moment, it became clear to Hauck just who had taken those pictures of AJ Raymond's body in the street.

Dietz.

His heart slammed to a stop.

Hauck thought back to his own case. Dietz had described himself as being in the security business. He'd said he'd run down to the crash site after the accident. That he never got a good look at the car, a white SUV, out-of-state plates, as it sped away up the road.

Good look, my ass.

He'd been planted there.

That's why they'd never been able to locate any white SUV with Massachusetts or New Hampshire plates. That's why the New Jersey police couldn't find a similar vehicle there.

They didn't exist! It had all been set up.

It was a thousand-to-one shot anyone would have ever connected the two incidents, if Karen hadn't seen her husband's face in that documentary.

Hauck grinned. Dietz was at both sites. Two states apart, separated by over a year.

Of course, that meant Charles Friedman was connected, too.

Hauck looked back up at Muñoz, a feeling that he was finally getting somewhere buzzing in his veins. "Anyone else know about this, Freddy?"

"You said keep it between us, Lieutenant." The detective shrugged. "So that's what I did."

He looked back up at Freddy. "Let's keep it that way."

Muñoz nodded.

"I want to go over the Raymond file again. You get me a copy up here today."

"Yes, sir."

Hauck stared at the image of the gregarious, mustached face—an ex-cop—now morphed into the calculating countenance of a professional killer.

The two cases hadn't merged, they had basically crashed together. Head-on. And this time there were other people to see. His blood was racing.

You screwed up, he said to Dietz. *Big-time, you son of a bitch!*

The first thing Hauck did was forward a photo of Dietz's face to Pappy, who a day later confirmed that that had been the same man who'd been in Pensacola. That alone was probably enough to arrest Dietz right now for conspiracy to murder AJ Raymond, and maybe Jonathan Lauer, too.

But it didn't take things through to Charles Friedman.

Coincidence didn't prove anything. With a good lawyer, it could be argued that being at both crash sites was just that. He'd given his word to Karen to find out about her husband. Charles had been in Greenwich. Lauer worked for him. They both led to Dolphin. Dietz was in it, too. Hauck wasn't liking at all where this was leading. Tying Charles to Dietz would be a start. Right now he was afraid that if he blew the lid off everything, who knew where any of it would lead?

You should go back to Fitzpatrick, a voice in him

said. Swear out a warrant. Let the feds figure this out. He had taken oaths. His whole life he'd always upheld them. Karen had uncovered a conspiracy.

But something held him back.

What if Charles was innocent? What if he couldn't tie Charles and Dietz together? What if he hurt her, Karen, her whole family, after vowing to help her, trying to make *his* case, not hers? Bring him in. Put the pressure on Dietz. He would roll.

Or was it her? Was it what he felt himself falling into, these cases colliding together? Wanting to protect her just a little longer until he knew for sure. What stirred so fiercely in his blood. What he lay awake thinking of at night. Conflicted. As a cop, knowing his feelings were leading him astray.

He called her later that day, staring at Dietz's file. "I'm heading down to New Jersey for a day. We may have found something."

Karen sounded excited. "What?"

"I looked through the file on Jonathan Lauer's hit-and-run. The only eyewitness there, a man named Dietz—he was one of the two witnesses to AJ Raymond's death, too."

Karen gasped. In the following pause, Hauck knew she was putting together just what this meant.

"They were set up, Karen. This guy, Dietz, he was at both accidents. Except they weren't accidents, Karen. *They were homicides.* To cover something up. You did good. No one would ever have put any of this together if you hadn't gone to visit Lauer."

She didn't reply. There was only silence. The silence of her trying to decide what this meant. In regard to Charles. For her kids. For her.

"What the hell am I supposed to think, Ty?"

"Listen, Karen, before we jump . . ."

"Look, *I'm sorry,*" Karen said. "I'm sorry about these people. It's terrible. I know this is what you were always thinking. But *I* can't help thinking that there's something going on here, and it's starting to scare me, Ty. *What does all this mean about Charles?*"

"I don't know. That's what I'm going to find out."

"Find out how, Ty? What are you going to do?"

There was a lot he had withheld from her. That Charles had a connection to Falcon. To Pappy Raymond. That he was sure Charles was complicit in AJ Raymond's death—and maybe Jonathan Lauer's, too. But how could he tell her any of that now?

"I'm going to go down there," he said, "to Dietz's home. Tomorrow."

"You're going down there? What for?"

"See what the hell I can find. Try and figure out what our next step is."

"Our next step? You arrest him, Ty. You know he set those poor people up. He's responsible for their deaths!"

"You wanted to know how this connected to your husband, Karen! Isn't that why you came to me? You wanted to know what he's done."

"This man's a murderer, Ty. Two people are dead."

"I know that two people are dead, Karen! That's one thing you don't have to remind me of."

"What are you saying, Ty?"

The silence was frosty between them for a second. Suddenly Hauck felt sure that by admitting he was not going down to bring Dietz in he was somehow giving away everything that was in his heart: the feelings he carried for her, the braids of red hair that had pushed him here, the echo of a distant pain.

Finally Karen swallowed. "You're not telling me everything, are you, Ty? Charles is tied to this, isn't he? Deeper than you're letting on?"

"Yes."

"My husband . . ." Karen let out a dark chuckle. "He always bet against the trends. A *contrarian*, he called himself. A fancy name for someone who always thinks he's smarter than everybody else. You better be careful down there, Ty, whatever you're planning."

"I'm a cop, Karen," Hauck said. "This is what cops do."

"No, Ty, cops arrest people when they're implicated in a crime. I don't know what you're going to do down there, but what I do know is that some of it is about me. And that's scaring me, Ty. You just make sure you do the right thing, okay?"

Hauck flipped open the file and stared at Dietz's face. *"Okay."*

CHAPTER FIFTY-ONE

Something strange crept through Karen's thoughts that night. After she hung up from Ty.

About what he'd found.

It lifted her at first. The connections between the accidents. That she'd actually helped him.

Then she didn't know what she felt. An uneasiness that two people linked to her husband had been killed to cover something up—and the suspicion, a suspicion Ty wasn't clearing up for her, that Charlie was involved.

Jonathan Lauer worked for him. The fellow who was run over in Greenwich the day he disappeared had had Charlie's name in his pocket. The safe-deposit box with all that cash and the passport. The tanker that had a connection to Charlie's firm. Dolphin Oil . . .

She didn't know where any of this led.

Other than that her husband of eighteen years

had been involved in something he'd kept from her and that Ty wasn't telling her all he knew.

Along with the fact that much of the life she'd led the last eighteen years, all those little myths she'd believed in, had been a lie.

But there was something else burrowing inside her. Even more than the fear that her family was still at risk. Or sympathy for the two people who had died. Deaths, Karen was starting to believe, against her will, that were inextricably tied to Charles.

She realized she was worried for him, Hauck. What he was about to do.

It had never dawned on her before, but it did now. How she'd grown to rely on him. How she knew by the way he'd looked at her—that day at the football game, how his eyes lit up when he saw her waiting at the station, how he had taken everything on for her. That he was attracted to her.

And that in the most subtle, undetected way Karen was feeling the same way, too.

But there was more.

She felt certain he was about to do something rash, way outside the boundaries. That he might be putting himself in danger. Dietz was a killer, whatever he had done. That he was holding something back—something related to Charlie.

For her.

After he called, she stayed in the kitchen heating up a frozen French-bread pizza in the microwave for Alex, who seemed to live on those things.

When it was done, Karen called him down, and she sat with him at the counter, hearing about his day at school—how he'd gotten a B-plus on a presentation in European history that was half his final exam and how he'd been named co-chair of the teen Kids in Crisis thing. She was truly proud of that. They made a date to watch *Friday Night Lights* together in the TV room later that evening.

But when he went back upstairs, Karen stayed at the counter, her blood coursing in a disquieted state.

Strangely, inexplicably, there had grown to be something between them.

Something she couldn't deny.

So after their show was done and Alex had said good night and had gone back upstairs, Karen went into the study and picked up the phone. She felt a shifting in her stomach, school-girlish, but she didn't care. She dialed his number, her palms perspiring. He answered on the second ring.

"Lieutenant?" she said. She waited for his objection.

"Yes?" he answered. There was none.

"You just be careful," she said again.

He tried to shrug it off with some joke about having done this a million times, but Karen cut him short.

"Don't," she pleaded. "Don't. Don't make me feel this all over again. Just please be careful, Ty. That's all I'm asking. Y'hear?"

There was a silence for a second, and then he said, "Yeah, *I hear.*"

"Good," she said softly, and hung up the phone.

Karen sat there on the couch for a long time, knees tucked into her chest. She felt a foreboding worming through her—just as it had on the small plane that day as the propellers whirred in Tortola, Charlie waving from the balcony, the sun reflecting off his aviators, a sudden sensation of loss. A tremor of fear.

"Just be careful, Ty," she whispered again, to no one, and closed her eyes, afraid. *I couldn't bear to lose you, too.*

CHAPTER FIFTY-TWO

The interstate that ran barely a mile from where Hauck lived in Stamford, I-95, turned into the New Jersey Turnpike south of the George Washington Bridge.

He took it, past the swamps of the Meadowlands, past the vast electrical trellises and the warehouse parks of northern New Jersey, past Newark Airport, over two hours, to the southern part of the state, north of the Philadelphia turnoff.

He got off at Exit 5 in Burlington County, finding himself on back roads that cut through the downstate—Columbus, Mount Holly, sleepy towns connected by wide-open countryside, horse country, a universe away from the industrial congestion back up north.

Dietz had been a cop in the town of Freehold. Hauck checked before he left. He'd put in sixteen years.

Sixteen years that had been cut short by a couple of sexual-harassment complaints and two rebukes for undue force, as well as some other issue that didn't go away involving an underage witness in a methamphetamine case where Dietz had been found to apply excessive pressure for her testimony, which sounded more like statutory rape.

Hauck had missed all this. What reason had there ever been to check?

Since then Dietz was self-employed in some kind of security company, Dark Star. Hauck had looked them up. It was hard to figure out just what they did. Bodyguards. Security. Private contract work. Not exactly installing exclusive security systems, or whatever he had said he'd been doing in the area when AJ Raymond was killed.

Dietz was a bad guy.

As he drove along backcountry stretches, Hauck's mind wandered. He had been a cop for almost fifteen years. Basically, it was all he knew. He'd risen fast through the bureaucracy that was the NYPD. He'd made detective. Been assigned to special units. Now he ran his own department in Greenwich. He'd always upheld the law.

What was he going to do when he got there? He didn't even have a plan.

Outside Medford, Hauck found County Road 620.

On each side there were gently sloping fields and white fencing. There were a few signs for stables and horse farms. Merryvale Farms— home to Barrister, "World's Record, quarter mile." Near Taunton Lake, Hauck checked the GPS. Dietz's address was 733 Muncey Road. It was about three miles south of town. Middle of nowhere. Hauck found it, bordering a fenced-in field and a local firehouse. He turned down the road. His heart started to pick up.

What are you doing here, Ty?

Muncey was a rutted blacktopped road in dire need of a repaving. There were a few houses near the turnoff, small clapboard farmhouses with trucks or the occasional horse van in front and overgrown, weeded yards. Hauck found a number on a mailbox: 340. He had a ways to go.

At some point the road turned into dirt. Hauck bounced along in his Bronco. The houses grew farther apart. At a bend he came upon a cluster of RD mailboxes, 733 written on one of them. The postal service didn't even come down any farther. A tremor shot through Hauck as he knew he was near. Boundaries, he knew he'd left them behind long ago. He didn't have a warrant. He hadn't run this by the office.

Dietz was a potential co-conspirator in two homicides.

What the hell are you doing down here, Ty?

He passed a red, fifties-style ranch house: 650. A film of sweat had built up on his wrists and under his collar. He was getting close.

Now there was a huge distance between homes this far down. Maybe a quarter mile. There was no sound to be heard, other than the unsettling crunch of gravel under the Bronco's wheels.

Finally it came into view. Around a slight bend, tucked away under a nest of tall elms, the end of the road. An old white farmhouse. The picket fence in front was in need of repair. A loose gutter was hanging down. What lawn there was looked like it hadn't been mowed in months. Except for the presence of a two-seater Jeep with a plowing hitch attached in the driveway, it hardly looked as if anyone even lived here. Hauck slowed the Bronco as he drove by, trying not to attract attention. A Freehold Township Police sticker was on the back of the Jeep. A number on the column of the front porch confirmed it:

733.

Bingo.

The dilapidated two-car garage was shut.

Hauck couldn't see any lights on inside the house. Cars would be few and far between down here. He didn't want to be spotted driving by again. About fifty yards past, he noticed a turn-off, more of a horse trail than a road, barely wide enough for his car, and he took it, bouncing over the uneven terrain. Partway in, he cut a left through a field of dried hay, his path concealed by the tall, waist-high brush. A couple of hundred yards behind, Hauck had a decent view of the house.

Okay, so what happens now?

From a satchel Hauck removed a set of bin-oculars and, lowering the window, took a wide scan back at the house. No movement. A shutter hung indolently from one of the windows. No indication that anyone was there.

From the same satchel, Hauck took out his Sig automatic, safety off, checking that the sixteen nine-millimeter rounds were loaded in the clip. He hadn't drawn his gun in years. He recalled running into an alley, firing off three rounds at a suspect fleeing from a building, who had sprayed his TEC-9 at Hauck's partner in a weapons bust as he was running away. He'd hit the guy in the leg with one shot. Brought him in. Received a commendation for it. That was the only time he had ever fired his gun on the job.

Hauck rested the gun on the seat next to him. Then he opened the glove compartment and took out the small black leather folder that contained his Greenwich shield. He didn't quite know what to do with it, so he placed it in the pocket of his jacket, and took out a two-liter bottle of water and drank a long swig. His mouth was dry. He decided not to think too hard on what he was doing here. He took another sweep on the house with the binoculars.

Nothing. Not a fucking thing.

Then he did what he'd done a hundred times in various stakeouts over the years.

He uncapped a beer and watched seconds tick off the clock.

He waited.

CHAPTER FIFTY-THREE

He watched the house all night. No lights ever went on. No one ever drove up or came home.

At some point he looked up the phone number Dietz had given him along with his home address and dialed it. After four rings the answering machine came on. "You've reached Dark Star Security. . . . Please leave a message." Hauck hung up. He turned the radio to 104.3 Classic Rock and found the Who. *No one knows what it's like to be the bad man. . . .* His eyes grew heavy, and he dozed off for a while.

When he woke, it was light. Nothing had changed.

Hauck tucked the gun into his belt. Stretched on a pair of latex gloves. Then he grabbed a Maglite and his cell phone and stepped out of the Bronco. He pushed his way through the dense hayfield until he found the trail.

He decided that if Dietz was somehow there, he'd arrest him. He'd call in the Freehold police and work out the details later.

If he wasn't, he'd take a look around.

He made his way down the dirt road to the front of the dilapidated house. There was a sign on the scrabbly lawn: PRIVATE PROPERTY. BEWARE OF DOG. He climbed up the steps, his heart beginning to pound in his chest, his palms slick with perspiration. He stood to one side of the door and peeked in through a covered window. Nothing. He drew a breath and wondered if he was doing something crazy. *Here goes. . . .* He put a hand on the grip of his automatic. With the other he took his Maglite and knocked on the front door.

"Anyone home?"

Nothing.

After a few moments, he knocked again. "I'm looking for some directions. . . . Anybody home?"

Only silence came back.

The porch was a wraparound. Hauck decided to follow it around the side. On the lawn, just off the dirt driveway, he spotted a condenser box hidden in a bush and went over and lifted the metal panel. It was the main electrical feed to the house. Hauck pulled it, disabling the phone line and the alarm. Then he went back to the porch. Through the window he could see a dining room with a plain wooden table inside. Farther along he came upon the kitchen. It was old, fifties tile and linoleum, hadn't been updated in years. He tried the back door.

It was locked shut as well.

Suddenly a dog barked, the sound penetrating him. Hauck stiffened, swallowing his breath, feeling exposed. Then he realized that the bark had come from a neighboring property, a faraway woof that rifled through his bones, hundreds of yards off. Hauck looked out at the obstructed fields. His blood calmed. *Nerves . . .*

He continued around the back of the house. He passed a locked shed, a lawn mower with a protective tarp covering it, a few rusted tools scattered about. There was a step up to a cedar back porch. An old Weber grill. A bench-style outdoor table. Two French doors led to the back of the house. The curtains were drawn.

Hauck stepped carefully and paused for a moment, hidden by the curtains, in front of the door. It was locked as well. Panels of divided glass. A bolt drawn. He took his Maglite and tapped on one of the panels near the doorknob. It jiggled in its frame. Loose. He knelt down and hit the panel one more time, hard. The panel split and fell in.

Hand on his gun, he held there for a moment, waiting for any noise. Nothing. He doubted that Dietz had a security tie-in to the local police. He wouldn't want to take the chance of anybody needlessly poking around.

Hauck reached in through the open panel and wrapped his hand around the knob. He flicked the bolt back and twisted.

The door opened wide.

There was no alarm, no sound emanating. Cautiously, Hauck stepped inside.

He found himself in some kind of shabbily decorated sunroom. Faded upholstered chairs, a wooden table. A few magazines scattered on the table. *Forbes. Outdoor Life. Security Today.*

Heart pounding, Hauck took hold of his gun and went back through the kitchen, the floorboards creaking with each step. The house was dark, still. He looked into the living room and saw a fancy new Samsung flat-screen.

He was in. He just had no idea what he was searching for.

Hauck found a small room between the living room and the kitchen that was lined with bookshelves. An office. There was a small brick fireplace, a countertop desk with papers strewn about, a computer. A bunch of photos on the wall. Hauck looked. He recognized Dietz. In uniform with other policemen. In fishing clothes holding up an impressive sailfish. Another on some kind of large black-hulled sailing ship with a bare-chested, dark-haired man.

Hauck sifted through some of the papers on the desk. A few scattered bills, a couple of memos with Dark Star letterhead on them. Nothing that seemed to shed any light. The computer was on. Hauck saw an icon on the home page for Gmail, but when he clicked on it, up came a prompt asking for a password. Blocked. He took a shot and clicked the Internet icon, and the Google News homepage came on. He pointed the mouse and looked around to see what sites Dietz had previously logged on to. The last was the American Airlines site. International travel. Several seemed like standard trade sites. Farther down was something called the IAIM. He clicked—the International Association of Investment Managers.

Hauck felt his blood stir.

Harbor Capital, Charles Friedman's firm, had been queried in.

He sat in Dietz's chair and tried to follow the search. A Web file on the firm came up. A description of their business, energy-related portfolios. Assets under management, a few performance charts. A short history of the firm with a bio page of the management team. A photo of Friedman.

That wasn't all.

Falcon Partners, the investment partnership out of the BVIs, had been queried, too.

Now Hauck's blood was racing. He realized he was on the right track. The IAIM page merely provided a listing for Falcon. There was no information or records. Only a contact name and address in Tortola, which Hauck copied down. Then he swung around to the papers on Dietz's desk. Messages, correspondence, bills.

There had to be something here.

In a plastic in-box tray, he found something that sent his antennae buzzing. A photocopy of a list of names, from the National Association of Securities Dealers, of people who had received licenses to trade securities for investment purposes. The list ran on for pages, hundreds of names and securities firms, from all across the globe. Hauck scanned down—*what would Dietz be looking for?*

Then, all of a sudden, it occurred to him just what was unique about the list of licenses.

They had all been granted within the past year.

As Hauck paged through it, he saw that several names had been circled. Others were crossed out, with handwritten notes in the margins. There were hundreds. A long, painstaking search to narrow them down.

Then it hit him, like a punch in the solar plexus.

Karen Friedman wasn't the only person who thought her husband was alive!

There was a printer-copier on the credenza adjacent to the desk, and Hauck placed the security list along with Dietz's notes in it. He kept looking. Amid some scattered sheets, he found a handwritten note on Dark Star stationery.

The Barclays Bank. In Tortola.

There was a long number under it, which had to be an account number, then arrows leading to other banks—the First Caribbean Bank. Nevis. Banc Domenica. Names. Thomas Smith. Ronald Torbor. It had been underlined three times.

Who were these people? What was Dietz looking for? Hauck had always assumed that Charles and Dietz were connected. The hit-and-runs . . .

That's when it struck him. *Jesus . . .*

Dietz was searching for him, too.

Hauck picked up a scrawled sheet of paper from the tray, some kind of travel itinerary. American Airlines. Tortola. Nevis. His skin started to feel all tingly.

Dietz was ahead of him. *Did he possibly already know where Charles was?*

He placed a copy of the same sheet in the

printing bay and pressed. The machine started warming up.

Then suddenly there was a noise from outside the window. Hauck's heart slammed to a stop.

Wheels crunching over gravel, followed by the sound of a car door slamming.

Someone was home.

CHAPTER FIFTY-FOUR

Hauck's blood became ice. He went over to the window and peeked through the drawn curtains. Dietz's office faced the wrong direction; there was no way to determine who it was. He removed the Sig 9 from his belt and checked the clip. He was completely out of bounds here—no warrant, no backup.

Inside, Hauck was just praying it wasn't Dietz.

He heard a knock at the door. Someone shouting out, *"Phil?"* Then, after a short pause, something that made his pulse skyrocket. The sound of a key being inserted in the front door, the lock opening. A man's voice calling.

"Phil?"

Hauck hid behind the office door. He wrapped his fingers around the handle of the Sig and stood pressed against the door. He had no way out. Whoever it was had already come inside.

Hauck heard the sound of footsteps approaching, the creak of bending wood on the floorboards. *"Phil? You here?"*

His heart started going wild. Panicked, his mind flashed to whether or not his Bronco might have been seen. He realized that sooner or later whoever this was, if he made his way around the house, would notice the smashed rear window-pane. Would find his way back to the office. Whoever this was had access. On the other hand, Hauck was there totally unlawfully. He had no warrant. He hadn't notified the local police. He would be cited just for bringing in his gun. The footsteps came closer. He wasn't sure what to do. Only that he'd gotten himself into a sizable amount of shit, and it was getting deeper by the second. The man was walking around the house. *Should he make a run for it?*

Then something happened that sent Hauck's pulse into a frenzy.

The fucking printer began to print.

The pages Hauck had fed into the tray, they were suddenly going through. The hum of the machine was like an alarm bell.

"Phil!"

The footsteps got closer. Behind the door Hauck gripped his Sig, pressing the muzzle up against his cheek. The machine continued to print. He couldn't stop it! *Think, think, what to do?*

Hauck froze at the creak of a nearby floorboard as whoever it was came around the corner. He peeked inside the office. Hauck held, rigid as a board.

"Phil, I didn't know you were here. . . ."

The man paused, remaining in the doorway. The pages continued to feed into the machine one by one.

Hauck held his breath. *Shit* . . .

A second later the heavy office door slammed into his chest, taking him by surprise, the Sig flying out of his hand.

Hauck's eyes darted after the gun, the door barreling into him again, striking him in the side of the head, dazing him, the gun clattering across the floor.

The man crashed the door into Hauck one more time, this time following it into the room, mashing Hauck's right hand in the hinge. Hauck finally threw the brunt of his weight against it and rammed it back with all his might, sending the man reeling into the room.

The man had close-cropped hair and a large nose, his cheek bloodied from the blow. He glared at Hauck. "What the hell are you doing here? Who the fuck are you?"

Hauck stared back. He realized he had seen him before.

The second witness. The guy in a warm-up jacket at AJ Raymond's hit-and-run. A track coach or something.

Hodges.

Their eyes met in a stunned, glaring gaze.

Hodges's eyes were equally as wide. *"You!"*

Hauck's glance darted toward the gun on the floor, as Hodges took the nearest thing available, a decorative scrimshaw horn Dietz kept on a side table, and lunged in Hauck's direction, slashing the sharp point of the horn through Hauck's sweatshirt and tearing into his skin.

Hauck cried out. The horn dug through his chest, his ribs on fire.

Hodges slashed at him again, Hauck flailing desperately for the other man's arm to block the blow, pinning it back, while Hodges pushed with all his might with his other hand against Hauck's neck.

He kneed Hauck sharply in the side of his chest, his wound.

"Aaagh!"

"What are you doing here?" Hodges screamed at him again.

"I know," Hauck grunted back. "I know what's happened." Blood seeped through the ripped, damp fabric of his sweatshirt. "It's over, Hodges. I know about the hit-and-runs."

Straining, Hauck forced back his attacker's fingers, reaching for the handle of the horn. It fell, skidding away.

Hauck faced him, clutching his side. "I know they were set up. I know they were done to protect Charles Friedman and Dolphin Oil. The police are on the way." He was still dazed from the first blows, short of breath. His neck was raw and throbbing where Hodges had squeezed it. "You're done, man."

"Police . . ." Hodges echoed skeptically. "So who the fuck are you, the advance guard?"

Eyes ablaze, he darted to the fireplace and grabbed an iron poker there and swung it at Hauck as hard as he could, narrowly missing his head by inches and striking into the wall behind him, shards of dug-out plaster splintering over the floor.

Hauck dove headfirst into him, knocking Hodges back against the desk, heavy books and photos tumbling all over them, the printer crashing down from the shelf.

They rolled onto the floor, Hodges coming up on top. He was strong. Maybe a few years back Hauck could've taken him, but he was still dazed from the body blows of the door and the gash on his side. Hodges fought like he had nothing to lose. He kneed Hauck deeply in the groin, sending the air rushing out of him, and grabbed the iron poker lengthwise with both hands, pinned it across Hauck's chest like a vise, forcing it into the nook of his neck.

Hauck gagged, sucking in a desperate breath.

"You think we did it to protect him?" Hodges said, squeezing him, his face turning red. "You don't know a fucking thing." He continued to press the poker into the cavity of Hauck's neck. Hauck felt his airway closing on him, a clawing tightness taking over his lungs. Intensifying. He tried to roll his attacker off, knee him, but he was pinned and the iron rod was squeezing the life out of him. He felt the blood rush into his face, his strength waning, his lungs about to burst.

Hodges was going to kill him.

Straining, he tried with everything he had to push the poker back. His breath was desperate, his lungs clutching for blocked air. The blood was almost bursting through his head.

That's when he felt the hard mound of the gun pressing sharply into his back. Hodges had him pinned, but somehow Hauck forced a shoulder up and reached, one arm dangling back, the other vainly trying to pry Hodges's grip away from his throat. Fingers grasping, Hauck found the warm steel of the muzzle, spun it around under his body for the grip.

"*Stop*," he gasped, "lemme talk. Stop."

"*How did you get here?*" Hodges shouted at him. "How did you find out?" It was as if an iron hoe were being clawed inside Hauck's throat. Finally he managed to wrap his fingers around the Sig's handle. With the gun still underneath his body, he maneuvered it around.

"*How?*" Hodges demanded, pinning Hauck's legs with his thighs and pressing the last gulps of air out of his chest.

All Hauck could do was raise himself ever so slightly, creating the tiniest space for him to slide his gun hand around, as Hodges now saw what he was attempting. And so, exerting himself even harder, he pinned Hauck's arm back with his knee, jamming the poker tighter into his larynx.

Hauck's lungs were about to explode.

His shoulder was pressed back so tightly there was no way he could aim. He managed to wrap his finger around the trigger, but the muzzle was jammed in against his body. He had no idea where it was even pointed, only that his strength was waning, his air disappearing. . . . No more time.

He braced for the explosion in his side.

And fired—a muffled, close-in pop.

Hauck felt a jolt. The concussive shock seemed to reverberate inside both of their bodies. He tensed, expecting the rush of pain.

None came.

On top of him, Hodges grimaced. The iron rod was still pressed into Hauck's neck.

There was a sharp smell of cordite in Hauck's nostrils. Slowly, the pressure on his throat released.

Hodges's eyes went to his side. Hauck saw an enlarging flower of red oozing from under his shirt there. Hodges straightened, his hand reaching to his side, and drew it back, smeared with blood.

"Sonofafucking bitch . . ." he groaned.

Hauck pushed his legs, and, glazy-eyed, Hodges rolled off him. Heaving, Hauck gulped precious, needed air deep into his lungs. His side felt on fire. There was blood all over him—whose, he wasn't sure. Hodges crawled his way to the door.

"It's over," Hauck gasped, staring over at him, barely able to point his gun.

Clumsily, Hodges dragged himself up. A damp scarlet blotch seeped out of his shirt. He clamped it with his hand. "You don't have a fucking clue," he said, coughing back a heavy laugh.

He winced. Stood there, waiting for Hauck to pull the trigger. Exhausted, Hauck could barely raise the gun.

"You're dead! You don't know it yet, but you're dead." Hodges glared at him. "You have no idea who you're fucking with!"

Hunched over, he staggered out of the room. Hauck could do nothing to stop him. It took everything he had just to pull himself up, coughing air back into his obstructed air pipe, his clothes drenched in sweat. He lurched outside after Hodges, clutching his ribs. Everything had gone wrong. He heard the sound of Hodges's truck starting up, spotted droplets of blood leading off the porch to the driveway.

"Hodges!" Hauck came down the steps and leveled his gun at the truck. It backed out of the driveway and sped off down the road. Hauck took aim at the rear tires, his finger pulsed. "Stop!" he called after him. *Stop.* He didn't even hear his own voice.

But he just held there, watching the truck ramble down the road, his gun aimed into the retreating cloud of dust.

It took everything Hauck had to focus on a single thought.

That he was involved in something—something that had blown up in his face.

And that he was no longer representing anything. Not all the oaths, not the truth, not even Karen.

Only his own base desire to know where it led.

CHAPTER FIFTY-FIVE

His side was on fire.

His neck was swollen twice its size. He could barely swallow.

Every time he breathed, his ribs ached like he'd been through ten rounds with a heavy weight. His chest was covered with a bright red welt.

He didn't know what he had done.

He'd gone back in and grabbed the papers he'd copied out of the copier. Then he headed to his car.

As he drove back, Hauck's first thoughts centered on Jessica—how lucky he was just to be alive.

Stupid, Ty, just plain stupid. He tried to size up the situation. Everything he'd done had been outside his jurisdiction. Breaking into Dietz's house. Taking in his gun. Not informing the local authorities. And Hodges . . . he would live. But, Hauck realized, that wouldn't be the half of it. Dietz would know—and so would whoever he worked for. This thing could explode. Of course, they had no way to know he was doing this on his own. Or, the thought calmed him slightly, that Karen was in any way involved.

That was the only fucking thing about any of this that was good.

It took him over three hours to drive back home. He got back in the early afternoon. He threw himself on his couch in exhaustion and examined his side, his head rolled back, trying to make sense of what he had done. He had broken laws. A shitload of them. He had put Karen in danger. The oaths he had taken in his life, to uphold the law, to do the right thing, they were all pretty much shattered now.

Hauck peeled off his bloodstained clothes and tossed them in a ball in the pantry. Just lifting his arms made him feel incredibly sore. The gash on his side had caked with blood, the skin torn where Hodges had slashed him. Bright red welts were all over his neck and chest. He looked in the mirror and winced. He didn't know if he needed medical attention. His head was heavy. He just wanted to sleep. He felt alone. For the first time in his life, he didn't know what to do.

He eased himself back onto the couch. There was just one person he could think of to call.

"Ty . . . ?"

"Karen, listen, I need you," he huffed. "Up here." It was more of a plea than a statement. He caught his breath and sucked in air.

"Ty, are you all right?" Karen's voice was alarmed. "I was worried. I tried calling you. You didn't answer."

"Karen, something happened. . . . Just come on up. Please." In close to a daze, he told her where he lived.

"I'm on my way. You don't sound good, Ty. You're scaring me. Just tell me, is there anything you need?"

"Yeah." He exhaled, his head falling back. "Disinfectant. And a whole lot of gauze."

Hauck staggered to the door when he heard her knock. In a pair of gym shorts and a robe to conceal his wounds. He grinned, pale, his expression saying something like, *I'm really sorry for getting you into this.* Then he sort of leaned into her.

She looked at him, horrified. "What the hell's happened, Ty?"

"I found Dietz's place. I staked it out all night. I didn't think anyone was there. This morning I went in."

"He was there?"

"No." Hauck took the bag of medical supplies he'd requested out of her hands—disinfectant, tape, and gauze. He stepped back over to the couch with a bit of a limp, eased himself down. "Hodges was, though."

Her eyes screwed up. "Hodges?"

"He was the other witness at AJ Raymond's hit-and-run. I guess they were in this together. Partners."

"Together in what?"

That was when Karen's gaze focused on the welts on Hauck's neck, and she gasped. *"My God, Ty, what have you done?"* She drew back the collar of his terry robe, eyes wide, gently running her fingers across the bruised skin, inspecting the torn knuckles, aghast, carefully taking his hands in hers.

"This side's worse." Hauck shrugged, guiltily, letting his robe fall open to reveal the matted blood and tracks of torn flesh underneath his arm.

"Oh, my God!"

"It was all set up," he said, trying to explain. "Abel Raymond. Lauer. Those accidents, they were hits. Dietz and Hodges killed them both. To cover it all up."

"What!?" There was a pall of confusion on

314

Karen's face, but also something deeper—*fear*, knowing that somehow what he wasn't totally divulging related back to her. That Charlie was involved.

"What happened to Hodges?" she asked, grabbing the disinfectant and ripping open the box of gauze.

His expression was stonelike. "Hodges was shot, Karen."

"Shot?" She put the things back down, the color draining from her face. "Dead . . . ?"

"No. At least I don't think so."

He told her everything. How he had gone inside the house figuring it was safe, and how Hodges came in, surprising him, in Dietz's office. How they'd struggled, Hodges slashing him with the horn, clamping the iron poker across his neck, how Hauck thought he was dying. How he'd shot Hodges.

"Oh, my God, Ty . . ." Karen's eyes were wide and empathetic. The consternation on her face had turned to real fear. "What did the police say? It has to be self-defense, right? He was trying to kill you, Ty."

Hauck kept his gaze trained on her. "I didn't call in the police, Karen."

She blinked. *"What . . . ?"*

"I had no right to be there, Karen. The whole

315

thing was illegal from the start. I didn't have a warrant. There isn't an open case against them. I'm not even on goddamn duty, Karen."

"*Ty . . .*" Karen's hand shot to her mouth as she started to realize the situation. "You can't just pretend this didn't happen. You shot someone."

"This man tried to kill me, Karen! You want me to call the police? Don't you understand? Your husband was in bed with these people, Karen. Dietz, Hodges. When Charlie left Grand Central that morning, he made his way up to Greenwich. He stole the credit card off of someone who died on the tracks. There was a call to AJ Raymond, Karen, from the diner across the street. Charlie made that call, Karen. Your husband. Either he was directly involved in the murder of AJ Raymond or he damn well helped set it up."

"*Charlie . . . ?*" Karen shook her head. "You can't think Charlie's some kind of killer, Ty. No. *Why?*"

"To cover up what Raymond's father stumbled onto in Pensacola. That they were falsifying shipments of oil in one of the companies Charlie controlled."

Karen shook her head again defiantly.

"It's true. Have you ever heard of Dolphin Oil, Karen? Or something called Falcon Partners?"

316

"No."

"They're subsidiaries, owned by his company. Harbor. Offshore. You want me to call in the police, Karen? If I do, they're going to issue an immediate warrant for his arrest. There are ample grounds—fraud, money laundering, conspiracy to commit murder. Is that what you want me to do, Karen? To you *and* your family? Call in the police? Because that's what's going to happen."

Karen put a hand to her forehead and shook her head reflexively. "I don't know."

"Charlie was tied to them. Through the investment companies he controlled. Through Dietz. He's tied in to both murders, Karen—"

"I don't believe it! You can't expect me to believe my husband's a murderer, Ty!"

"Look!" Hauck reached over and grabbed the papers he had taken from Dietz's office and put them in front of her face. "His name is all over the place. Two people are dead, Karen. And now you have to listen to me and make a decision, because there may be more. This guy Dietz, he's looking for Charlie, too. I don't know who the hell he is or who he's working for, but he's out there, Karen, and somehow he knows Charlie's alive, just like we do, and he's searching for him, too—I found the trail! Maybe they're trying to shut him up, I don't know. But I guarantee you

if he finds him, Karen, before we do, it won't be to tearfully look him in the eyes and ask how he could've possibly done this to you."

Karen nodded haltingly, a tremor of confusion rattling her. Hauck reached over and took her hand. He wrapped his fingers around her tightened fist.

"So you tell me, Karen, is that what you really want me to do? Call in the police? Because the police *are* involved. *I'm* involved. And after today, with what's happened, I can't just reverse the clock and go back empty-handed anymore."

Her eyes were filled, tears reflecting in them. "He's the father of my kids. You don't know how many times I've wanted to kill him myself, but what you're telling me . . . a murderer? No, I won't believe it till I hear it from him."

"I'll find him for you, Karen. I promise I will. But just be sure that with what's happened now, these people know I'm onto them. We're in it now. If that's something you don't think you can face—and I'd understand it if it was—now's the time to say so."

Karen looked down. Hauck felt a finger wrap around his hand, her pinkie, cautious and tremulous. It squeezed. There was a frightened look in her eyes, but behind it something deeper, a twinkling of resolve. She looked at him and shook her head again.

"I want you to find him, Ty."

Her face dipped, ever so slightly, close to his, her hair tumbling against his cheek. Her breath was close and halting. Their knees touched. Hauck felt his blood spark alive as the side of her breast brushed his arm. Their lips could have touched right there. It would have taken only a nudge, and she would have folded into him— and a part of him wanted her to, a strong part, but another part said no. The hair on his arms tingled as he listened to her breathe.

"You knew this all along," she said to him. "About Charlie. That this led back to him. You held it back from me."

"I didn't want you to be any more hurt until I was sure."

She nodded. She locked her fingers inside his hand. "He wouldn't kill anyone, Ty. I don't care how foolish it makes me look. I know him. I lived with him for close to twenty years. He's the father of my kids. I know."

"So what do you want to do?"

Karen gently eased open Hauck's robe. He tensed. She ran her fingers along his chest. She reached for the bag of liniment she had brought. "I want to take a look at that wound."

319

"No," he said, catching her hand. "You know what I meant."

She held a moment, their hands still touching.

"I want to hear from his lips what he's done, why he walked away from us, from almost twenty years of marriage, his family. I want to find him, Ty. Find Charles. Something came up while you were down there. *I think I may know how.*"

CHAPTER FIFTY-SIX

It was the car.

She had already been through everything two times over, just as Ty had asked. Still, while he was down in Jersey, she felt she had to do something. To keep from worrying.

So Karen tore through Charlie's things all over again—the old bills, the stacks of receipts he'd left in his closet, the papers on his desk. Even the sites he'd visited on his computer before he "died."

A wild-goose chase, she told herself. Just like the one before.

Except this time some things came up. A file buried deep in his desk, hidden under a pile of legal papers. A file Karen had never noticed before. From before Charlie died. Things she didn't understand.

A small note card still in its envelope—

addressed to Charles. The kind that accompanied a gift of flowers. Karen opened it, a little hesitantly, and saw it was written in a hand she didn't recognize.

It stopped her.

Sorry about the pooch, Charles. Could the kids be next?

Sorry about the pooch. Karen saw that her hands were shaking. Whoever wrote it had to be talking about Sasha. And what did that possibly mean, that the kids could be next?

Their kids . . .

Suddenly Karen felt a tightness in her chest. *What had these people done?*

And then, in that same hidden-away file, she came across one of the holiday cards they'd sent as a family before Charlie had died. The four of them sitting on a wooden fence at a field near their ski house in Vermont. A happy time.

She opened it.

She almost threw up.

The kids' faces, Samantha and Alexander—*they had both been cut out.*

Karen covered her face with her hands and felt her cheeks flush with blood.

"What the hell is happening here, Charlie?"

She stared at the card. *What the hell were you involved in? What were you doing to us, Charlie?* All of a sudden, the incident in Samantha's car at school came hurtling back to Karen, her heart starting to race. Accusingly. She got up from the desk. She wanted to hit something. She touched her hand to her face. Looked around the room.

His room.

"Talk to me, Charlie, you bastard, talk to me!"

And then her eyes seemed to fall on it.

Amid the clutter of papers and prospectuses and sports magazines she had still never quite cleared from his office.

The stack. The neatly piled stack Charlie kept on the bookshelf. Every issue. A sure-as-hell fire hazard, Karen always called it. His little dream collection, dating back since he'd first acquired his toy, eight years earlier.

Mustang World.

She went over to it—the stack of magazines piled high. She picked up one or two, the thought now forming in her brain.

This was it! The one thing about him he could never change. No matter what name he was under. Or who he was now.

Or where.

His stupid car. *Charlie's Baby.* He read about the damn things in his spare time, checked out the prices, chatted about them online. They always joked how it was a part of him. His mistress that Karen just had to put up with. She called it Camilla, as in Camilla and Charles. Better than Camilla, Charlie always joked. "Better-looking, too."

Mustang World.

He constantly put the car up for sale, then never sold it. In the summer he drove it in rallies. Monitored the online sites. She didn't understand what these cards she'd found were about. They scared her. She didn't know for sure what he'd done.

"But that's the way," Karen said to Hauck as she went to dress his wounds now.

She reached into her bag and dropped a copy of the magazine on the table. *Mustang World.*

"That's how we find him, Ty. *Charlie's Baby.*"

CHAPTER FIFTY-SEVEN

One Police Plaza was the home of the NYPD's administrative offices in lower Manhattan, as well as of the Joint Inter-Agency Task Force that oversaw the city's security.

Hauck waited in the courtyard in front of the building, looking out over Frankfort Street, which led onto the Brooklyn Bridge. It was a warm May afternoon. Strollers and bikers were crossing the steel gray span, office workers in shirtsleeves and light dresses on their lunchtime stroll. A few years back, Hauck used to work out of this building. He hadn't been down here in years.

A slightly built, balding man in a navy police sweater waved to a coworker and came up to him, his police ID fastened to his chest.

"New York's Finest." The man winked, standing in front of Hauck. He sat down beside him and gave him a tap of the fist.

"Go, blue!" Hauck grinned back.

Lieutenant Joe Velko had been a young head of detectives in the 105th Precinct, and had gone on to receive a master's degree from NYU in computer forensics. For years he and Hauck had been teammates on the department's hockey team, Hauck a crease-clearing defenseman with gimpy knees, Joe a gritty forward who learned to use a stick on the streets of Elmhurst, Queens. Joe's wife, Marilyn, had been a secretary at Cantor Fitzgerald and had died on 9/11. Back then it was Hauck who had organized a benefit game for Joe's kids. Captain Joe Velko now ran one of the most important departments in the entire NYPD.

Watchdog was a state-of-the-art computer software program developed by the NCSA, powered by nine supercomputers at an under-ground command center across the river in Brooklyn. Basically what Watchdog did was monitor billions of bits of data over the Internet for random connections that could prove useful for security purposes. Blogs, e-mail messages, Web sites, MySpace pages—billions of bits of Internet traffic. It sought out any unusual rela-tionships between names, dates, scheduled public events, even repeated colloquial phrases, and spit them out at the command center in daily "alerts," whereupon a staff of analysts pored over them, deciding if they were important enough to act on or to pass along to other security teams. A couple of years back, a plot to bomb the Citigroup Center by an antiglobalization group was uncovered by Watchdog, simply because it connected the same seemingly innocent but repeated phrase, "renewing our driver's license," to a random date, June 24, the day of an event there highlighted by a visit from the head of the World Bank. The connection was traced to someone on the catering team, who was an accomplice on the inside.

"So what do I owe this visit to?" Velko turned to Hauck. "I know this isn't exactly your favorite place."

"I need to ask you a favor, Joe."

A seasoned cop, Velko seemed to see something in Hauck's face that made him pause.

"I'm trying to locate someone," Hauck explained. He removed a thin manila envelope from under his sport jacket. "I have no idea where he is. Or even what name he might be using. He's most likely out of the country as well." He put the envelope on Velko's lap.

"I thought you were going to give me a challenge." The security man chuckled, unfastening the clasp.

He slid out the contents: a copy of Charles Friedman's passport photo, together with some things Karen had supplied him. The phrases "1966 Emberglow Mustang. GT. Pony interior. Greenwich, Connecticut." Some place called Ragtops, in Florida, where Charles had purchased it. The Greenwich Concours Rallye, where he sometimes showcased his car. A few of what Karen remembered as Charlie's favorite car sites. And finally a few favorite expressions he might use, like, "Lights out." Or "It's a home run, baby."

"You must think just because you elbowed a few firemen out of the crease who were trying to knock the shit out of me I really owe you, huh?"

"It was more than a few, Joe." Hauck smiled.

"A '66 Mustang. Pony interior. Can't you just log on to eBay for one of these things, Ty?" Velko grinned.

"Yeah, but this is far sexier," Hauck replied. "Look, the guy may be in the Caribbean, or maybe Central America. And Joe . . . this is gonna come out in your search, so I might as well tell you up front now—the person I'm looking for is supposedly dead. In the Grand Central bombing."

"*Supposedly* dead? As opposed to really dead?"

"Don't make me go into it, partner. I'm just trying to find him for a friend."

Velko slid the paper back inside the envelope. "Three hundred billion bits of data crossing the Internet every day, the city's security squarely in our hands, and I'm looking at an Amber Alert for a dead guy's '66 Mustang."

"Thank you, guy. I appreciate whatever turns up."

"A wide goddamn hole in the Patriot Act"—Velko cleared his throat—"That's what the hell's going to turn up. We're not exactly a missing-persons search system here." He looked at Hauck, reacting to the marks on his face and neck and the stiffness in his reach.

"You still skating?"

Hauck nodded. "Local team up there. Over-forty league now. Mostly a bunch of Wall Street types and mortgage salesmen. *You?*"

"No." Velko tapped his head. "They won't let me anymore. They seem to think my brain is good for something other than getting knocked around. Too risky on the new job. Michelle is, though. You should see her. She's a goddamn little bruiser. She plays on the boys' team for her school."

"I'd like to," Hauck said with a fond smile. When Marilyn died, Michelle had been nine and

Bonnie six. Hauck had organized a benefit game for them against a team of local celebrities. Afterward Joe's family came onto the ice and received a team jersey signed by the Rangers and the Islanders.

"I know I've said this, Ty, but I always appreciated just what you did."

Hauck shot Joe a wink.

"Anyway, I better get on these, right? Top secret—specialized and classified." Joe stood up. "Is everything okay?"

Hauck nodded. His side still ached like hell. "Everything's okay."

"Whatever turns up," Joe said, "I can still find you up at your office in Greenwich?"

Hauck shook his head. "I'm taking a little time. My cell number's in the package. And Joe ... I'd appreciate it if you kept this entirely between us."

"Oh, you don't have to worry about *that*." Joe raised the envelope and rolled his eyes. "Taking a little time ..." As Velko backed away toward the police building, he cocked Ty a wary smile.

"What the hell are you getting yourself involved in, Ty?"

CHAPTER FIFTY-EIGHT

After his meeting with Velko, Hauck went to the office of Media Publishing, located on the thirtieth floor of a tall glass building at Forty-sixth Street and Third Avenue.

The publishers of *Mustang World*.

It took Hauck's flashing his badge first to the receptionist and then to a couple of junior marketing people to finally get him to the right person. He had no authority here. The last thing he wanted was to have to call in yet another old friend from the NYPD. Fortunately, the marketing guy he finally got in front of seemed eager to help and didn't ask him to come back with a warrant.

"We've got two hundred and thirty-two thousand subscribers," the manager said, as if overwhelmed. "Any chance you can narrow it down?"

"I only need a list of those who've come aboard within the past year," Hauck told him.

He gave the guy a card. The manager promised he'd get to it as soon as he could and e-mail the results to Hauck's departmental address.

On the ride back home, Hauck mapped out what he would do. Hopefully, this Mustang search would yield something. If not, he still had the leads he'd taken from Dietz's office.

The Major Deegan Expressway was slow, and Hauck caught some tie-up near Yankee Stadium.

On a hunch he fumbled in his pocket for the number of the Caribbean bank he'd found at Dietz's. On St. Kitts. As he punched in the overseas number on his cell, he wasn't sure just how smart this was. The guy could be on Dietz's payroll for all he knew. But as long as he was playing long shots . . .

After a delay a sharp ring came on. "First Caribbean," answered a woman with a heavy island accent.

"Thomas Smith?" Hauck requested.

"Please hold da line."

After a short pause, a man's voice answered, "This is Thomas Smith."

"My name is Hauck," Hauck said. "I'm a

police detective with the Greenwich police force, in Greenwich, Connecticut. In the States."

"I know Greenwich," the man responded brightly. "I went to college nearby at the University of Bridgeport. How can I help you, Detective?"

"I'm trying to find someone," Hauck explained. "He's a U.S. citizen. The only name I have for him is Charles Friedman. He may have an account on record there."

"I'm not familiar with anyone by the name of Charles Friedman having an account here," the bank manager replied.

"Look, I know this is a bit unorthodox. He's about five-ten. Brown hair. Medium stature. Wears glasses. It's possible he's transferred money into your bank from a corresponding bank in Tortola. It's possible that Friedman is not even the name he's currently using now."

"As I said, sir, there is no account holder on record here by that name. And I haven't seen anybody who might fit that description. Nevis is a small island. And you can understand why I would be reluctant to give you that information even if I did."

"I understand perfectly, Mr. Smith. But it is a police matter. If you would maybe ask around and check . . ."

"I don't need to check," the manager answered. "I have already." What he told Hauck made him flinch. "You are the second person from the States who's been looking for this man in the past week."

CHAPTER FIFTY-NINE

Michel Issa squinted through the lens over the glittering stone. It was a real beauty. A brilliant canary yellow, wonderful luminescence, easily a C rating. It had been part of a larger lot he'd bought and was the pick of the litter. Hovering over the loupe, Michel knew it would fetch a real price from the right buyer.

His specialty.

Issa's family had been in the diamond business for over fifty years, emigrating to the Caribbean from Belgium and opening the store on Mast Street, on the Dutch side of St. Maarten when Michel was young. For decades Issa et Fils had bought high-quality stones direct from Antwerp and a few "gray" markets. People came to them from around the world—and not just couples off the cruise ships looking to get engaged, though they catered to that, too, to keep up the storefront. But important people, people with things to hide. In the trade, Michel Issa was known, as his father and grandfather had been before him, as the kind of *négociant* who could keep his mouth shut, who had the discretion to handle a private transaction, no matter what its magnitude.

With the money trail between banks so transparent after 9/11, shifting assets into something tangible—and transportable—was a booming business these days. Especially if one had something to hide.

Michel put down the lens and transferred the premier stone back into the tray with the other stones. He placed them in his drawer and twisted the lock. The clock read 7:00 P.M. Time to close for the day. His wife, Marte, had an old-style Belgian meal of sausage and cabbage prepared for him. Later, on Tuesday nights, they played euchre with a couple of English friends.

Michel heard the outside door chime. He sighed. Too late. He had just sent his sales staff home. He didn't flinch. There was no crime here on the island. Not this kind of crime. Everyone knew him, and, more to the point, they were on an island, surrounded by water. There was absolutely nowhere to go. Still, he reproved himself for having to be rude. He should have locked the door.

"Monsieur Issa?"

"I'll be with you in a moment," Michel called. He glanced through the window into the show-room and saw a stocky, mustached man in sunglasses waiting by the door.

He twisted the lock of the security drawer a second time. When he went around into the shop, there were two men. The man who called out, sort of a circumspect smile in his dark features, stepped up to the counter. The other, tall in a beach shirt and a baseball cap, standing by the door.

"I'm Issa," Michel said. "What can I do for you?" He placed his left foot near the alarm behind the counter, noticing the taller man still hovering suspiciously by the door.

"I'd like you to take a look at something, Monsieur Issa," the mustached man said. He reached inside his shirt pocket.

"Stones?" Issa sighed. "This late? I was just preparing to leave. Is it possible we can reschedule for tomorrow?"

"Not stones." The mustached man shook his head. "Photographs."

Photographs. Issa squinted at him. The mustached man placed a snapshot of a man in business attire on the counter. Short, gray-flecked hair. Glasses. The photo looked like it had been cut out of some corporate brochure.

Issa put on his wire reading glasses and stared. "No."

The man leaned forward. "This was taken some time ago. He may look different today. His hair may be shorter. He may not wear glasses anymore. I have a suspicion he may have come through here at some point, seeking to make a transaction. This transaction you would remember, Monsieur Issa, I'm sure. It would have been a large sale."

Michel didn't answer right away. He was trying to gauge who his questioners were. He tried to brush it off with a modest smile.

The mustached man smiled knowingly at him. But there was something behind it that Issa didn't like.

"Police?" he questioned. He had arrangements with most of them. The local ones, even Interpol. They left him alone. But these men didn't look the type.

"No, not police." The man smiled coolly. *"Private.* A personal affair."

"I'm sorry." Michel shrugged his shoulders. "I have not seen him here."

"You're quite sure? He would have paid in

338

cash. Or perhaps with a wire transfer from the First Caribbean Bank or the MaartensBank here on the island. Say, five, six months ago. Who knows, he may even have come back."

"I'm sorry," Michel said again, the specifics starting to alarm him, "I don't recognize him. And I would if he had been here, of course. Now, if you don't mind, I have to—"

"Let me show you this one, then," the mustached man said, firmer. "Another photo. You know how these things sometimes work. It may freshen everything up again."

The man pulled a second photo out of his breast pocket and laid it on the counter next to the first.

Michel froze. His mouth went dry.

This second photo was of his own daughter.

Juliette, who lived in the States. In D.C. She had married a professor at George Washington University. They'd just had a baby, Danielle, Issa's granddaughter, his first.

The man watched Issa's composure begin to waver. He seemed to be enjoying it.

"I was wondering if that refreshed your memory." He grinned. "If you knew this man now. She's a pretty woman, your daughter. My friends tell me there's a new baby, too. This is a cause for celebration, Monsieur Issa. No reason they should ever be involved in nasty business like this, if you know what I mean."

Issa felt his stomach knot. He knew precisely what the man meant. Their eyes locked, Michel sinking back on his stool, the color gone from his face.

He nodded.

"He's American." Michel looked down, and wet his lips. "As you said, he doesn't look the same now. His hair is closely shaved to his head. You know, the way young people wear it today. He wore sunglasses, no spectacles. He came here twice—both times with local bank contacts. As you said, maybe six or seven months ago."

"And what was the nature of the business, Monsieur Issa?" the mustached man asked.

"He bought stones, high quality—both times. He seemed interested in converting cash into something more transportable. Large amounts, as you say. I don't know where he is now. Or how to reach him. He called me on his cell phone once. I didn't take an address. I think he mentioned a boat he was living on. It was just those two times." Michel looked at him. "I've never seen him again."

"*Name?*" the mustached man demanded, his dark pupils urgent and smiling at the same time.

"I don't ask for names," Michel said back.

"His name?" the man said again. This time his hand applied pressure to Michel's forearm. "He had a bank check. It had to be made to someone. You did a large transaction. You had to have a record of it."

Michel Issa shut his eyes. He didn't like doing this. It violated every rule he lived by. Fifty years. He could see who these people were and what they wanted. And he could see, by the intensity in this man's gaze, what was coming next. *What choice did he have?*

"Hanson." Issa moistened his lips again and exhaled. "Steven Hanson, something like that."

"Something like that?" The man now wrapped his stocky fingers around Issa's fist and squeezed. He was starting to hurt him. For the first time, Michel actually felt afraid.

"That's what it is." Michel looked at him. *"Hanson.* I don't know how to contact him, I swear. I think he was living off his boat. I could look up the date. There must be a record of it at the harbor."

The mustached man glanced back around to his friend. He winked, as if satisfied. "That would be good," he said.

"So that makes everything okay, yes?" Michel asked nervously. "No reason to bother us again. Or my daughter?"

341

"Why would we want to do that?" The mustached man grinned to his partner. "All we came for was a name."

Still shaking, Michel closed up his shop and left shortly after. He locked the rear entrance to the store. That's where he kept his small Renault, in a little private lot.

He opened the car door. He didn't like what he'd just done. These rules had kept his family in business for generations. He had broken them. If word got out, everything they'd worked for all these years was shot.

As he stepped into the car and was about to shut the door, Michel felt a powerful force push at him from behind. He was thrown into the passenger seat. A strong hand pressed his face sharply into the leather.

"I gave you his name," Michel whimpered, heart racing. "I told you what you wanted to know. You said you wouldn't bother me anymore."

A hard metal object pressed to the back of Issa's head. The merchant heard the double click of a gun being cocked, and in his panic, his thoughts flashed to Marte, waiting for him at dinner. He shut his eyes.

"Please, I beg you, no. . . ."

"Sorry, old man." The pop of the gun going off was muffled by the Renault's chugging engine. "Changed our minds."

CHAPTER SIXTY

The first thing that came back was the data from *Mustang World.* The list of new subscribers Hauck had asked for.

Back at home, he glanced over the long list of names. One thousand six hundred and seventy-five of them. Several pages long. It was organized by mailing zip code, starting with Alabama. Mustang enthusiasts from every part of the globe.

From the bank trail he'd found at Dietz's, it seemed a valid assumption Charles might be in the Caribbean or Central America. Karen told him they'd sailed around there. The bank manager on St. Kitts had told Hauck someone else had been looking for Charles. He'd also have to have access to these banks at some point.

But as he flipped through the long list, Hauck

realized Charles could be anywhere. If he was even in here . . .

Slowly, he started to scan through.

The next thing that he got was a call from Joe Velko.

The Joint Inter-Agency Task Force agent caught Hauck on a Saturday morning just as he had put on a batch of pancakes for Jessie, who was up with him that weekend. When she asked about the red marks on his neck and the stiffness in his gait, Hauck told her he'd slipped on the boat.

"I pulled up some hits for you on that search," Joe informed him. "Nothing great. I'll fax it out to you if you want."

Hauck went over to his desk. He sat in his shorts and T-shirt, holding a spatula as twelve pages of data came rolling in.

"Listen," Joe told him, "no promises. Generally we might get a thousand positive hits for any one that could actually lead somewhere—and *that* means merely something we can pass along to an analyst's desk. We call any correlations to key input 'alerts' and rank them by magnitude. From low to moderate to high. Most classify in the lower bracket. I've spared you most of the boilerplate and methodology. Why don't you flip over to the third page?"

Hauck picked up a pen and found the spot. There was a shadowed box with the heading "Search AF12987543. *ALERT.*"

Joe explained, "These are random hits from some online newsletter the computer picked up. From something called the Carlyle Antique Car Auction in Pennsylvania." He chuckled. "Real cloak-and-dagger stuff, Ty. You see how it says, '1966 Emberglow Mustang. Condition: Excellent. Low Mileage, 81.5. *Shines!* Frank Bottomly, Westport, Ct.'"

"I see it."

"The computer picked up the car and the connection to Connecticut. This communication took place last year—basically just someone making a random query into buying one. You can see the program assigned a rating of LOW against it. There's a bunch of other stuff like that. Idle chatter. You can go on."

Hauck flipped through the next few pages. Several e-mails. The program was monitoring private interactions. Tons of back-and-forth chatter on classic-car sites, blogs, eBay, Yahoo.com. Whatever it picked up using the reference points Hauck had provided. A few hits on the Web site of the Concours d'Elegance in Greenwich. All were assessed as LOW. There was even a rock group in Texas called Ember Glow that opened for the singer Kinky Friedman. The priority against that hit was labeled "ZERO."

There were twelve whole pages of this. One e-mail was literally a guy talking about a girl named Amber, with the comment, "She glows like an angel."

No Charles Friedman. Nothing from the Caribbean.

Hauck felt frustrated. Nothing to add to the list from *Mustang World.*

"Dad?" An acrid smell penetrated Hauck's nostrils. Jessie was standing by the stove in the open kitchen, her pancakes going up in smoke.

"Oh shit! Joe, hold on."

Hauck ran back into the open kitchen and flipped the black pancakes off the skillet and onto a plate. His daughter's nose turned up in disappointment. "Thanks."

"I'll make more."

"Emergency?" Joe inquired on the line.

"Yeah, an eleven-year-old emergency. Dad screwed up breakfast."

"That takes precedence. Look, go through it.

It's only a first pass. I just wanted you to know I was on it. I'll call if anything else comes in."

"Appreciate it, Joe."

CHAPTER SIXTY-ONE

Karen pulled her Lexus into the driveway. She stopped at the mailbox and rolled down her window to pick up the mail. Samantha was home. Her Acura MPV was parked in front of the garage.

Sam was in the last days of school, graduating in a week. Then she and Alex were heading to Africa on safari with Karen's folks. Karen would have loved to be going along as well, but when the plans were made, months earlier, she had just started at the real-estate agency, and now, with all that was happening, how could she just walk away and abandon Ty? Anyhow, she rationalized, what was better than the kids going on that kind of adventure with their grandparents?

As the commercials said, *Priceless!*

Karen reached through the car window and

pulled out the mail. The usual deadweight of publications and bills, credit-card solicitations. A couple of charity mailings. An invitation from the Bruce Museum was one of them. It had a fabulous collection of American and European paintings and was right in Greenwich. The year before, Charlie had been appointed to the board.

Staring at the envelope, Karen drifted back to an event there last year. She realized it was just two months before Charlie disappeared. It was black-tie, a carnival theme, and Charlie had gotten a table. They had invited Rick and Paula. Charlie's mother, up from Pennsylvania. Saul and Mimi Lennick. (Charlie had harangued Saul into a considerable pledge.) Karen remembered he'd had to get up in his tux and make a speech that night. She'd been so very proud of him.

Someone else invaded her thoughts from that night, too. Some Russian guy from town, whom she'd never met before, but Charlie seemed to know well. Charles had gotten him to donate fifty thousand dollars.

A real charmer, Karen recalled, swarthy and bull-like with thick, dark hair. He patted Charlie on the face as if they were old friends, though Karen had never even heard his name. The man had remarked that if he'd known that Charles had such an attractive wife, he would have been happy to donate more. On the dance floor, Charlie mentioned that the guy owned the largest private sailboat in the world. A financial guy, of course, he said—a biggie—friend of Saul's. The man's wife had on a diamond the size of Karen's watch. He had invited them all out to his house—in the backcountry. More of a palace, Charlie said, which struck Karen as strange. "You've been there?" she asked. "Just what I've heard." He shrugged and kept dancing. Karen remembered thinking she didn't even know where in the world he had known the guy from.

Afterward, at home, they took a walk down to the beach at around midnight, still in their tuxedo and gown. They brought along a half-filled bottle of champagne they'd taken from the table. Trading swigs like a couple of teenagers, they took off their shoes and Charles rolled up his pant legs, and they sat on the rocks, peering out at the faraway lights of Long Island, across the sound.

"Honey, I'm so proud of you," Karen had said, a little tipsy from all the champagne and wine, but clearheaded on this. She placed her arm around his neck and gave him a deep, loving kiss, their bare feet touching in the sand.

"Another year or two, I can get out of this,"

he replied, his tie hanging open. "We can go somewhere."

"I'll believe that when it happens," Karen said laughingly. "C'mon, Charlie, you love this shit. Besides . . ."

"No, I mean it," he said. When he turned, his face was suddenly drawn and haggard. A submission in his eyes Karen had never seen before. "You don't understand. . . ."

She moved close to him and brushed his hair off his forehead. "Understand *what*, Charlie?" She kissed him again.

A couple of months later he was gone in the blast.

Karen put the car into park and sat there in front of her house, suddenly trying to hold back an inexplicable rush of tears.

Understand what, Charlie?

That you withheld things from me all our lives, who you really were? That while you went in to the office every day, drove to Costco with me on weekends, rooted for Alex and Sam at their games, you were always planning a way to leave? That you may have even had a hand in killing innocent people? *For what, Charlie?* When did it start? When did the person I devoted myself to, slept next to all those years, made love with, loved with all my heart—when did I have

352

to become afraid of you, Charlie? When did it change?

Understand what?

Wiping her eyes with the heels of her hands, Karen gathered the stack of letters and magazines on her lap. She put the car back into gear and coasted down to the garage. It was then that she noticed something standing out in the pile— a large gray envelope addressed to her. She stopped in front of the garage and slit it open before she climbed out.

It was from Tufts, Samantha's college, where she was headed in August. No identifying logo on the envelope, just a brochure, the kind they had received early in the application process, introducing them to the school.

A couple of words had been written on the front. In pen.

As she read them, Karen's heart crashed to a stop.

CHAPTER SIXTY-TWO

A day later Hauck and Karen arranged to meet.
They decided on the Arcadia Coffee House on
a side street in town, not far away. Hauck was
already at one of the tables when she arrived.
Karen waved, then went to the counter and
ordered herself a latte. She joined him by the
window in the back.

"How's the side?"

He lifted his arm. "No harm, no foul. You did
a good job."

She smiled at the compliment, but at the same
time looked at him reprovingly. "You still should
let someone take a look at it, Ty."

"I got a few things back," he said, changing
the subject. He pushed across a copy of the list
of *Mustang World* subscribers. Karen turned
through a couple of pages and blew out her
cheeks, daunted at the size.

"I was able to narrow it down. I think it's a good bet to assume that Charles is out of the country. If he has funds kept in the Caribbean, at some point he'd have to access those banks. There's sixty-five new names in Florida alone, another sixty-eight international. Thirty of them are in Canada, four in Europe, two in Asia, four in South America, so let's forget them. Twenty-eight of them were in Mexico, the Caribbean, or Central America."

Hauck had highlighted them with a yellow marker.

Karen cupped her hands around her coffee. "Okay."

"I have a friend who's a private investigator. I went to him for the information I showed you on Charles's offshore company in Tortola. We eliminated four of the names right away. Spanish. Six others were commercial—auto dealerships, parts suppliers. I had him do a quick financial search on the rest."

"So what did you find?"

"We scratched off six more because of issues like length of stay at their residence and stuff we could glean from credit cards. Five others listed themselves as married, so unless Charles has been really very busy in the past year, I think we're safe to can them, too."

Karen nodded and smiled.

"That leaves eleven." He had highlighted them page by page. Robert Hopewell, who lived on Shady Lane, in the Bahamas. An F. March—in Costa Rica. Karen paused over him. She and Charles and Paula and Rick had once been there. A Dennis Camp, who lived in Caracas, Venezuela. A Steven Hanson, who was listed at a post-office box in St. Kitts. Alan O'Shea, from Honduras.

Five more.

"Any of these names seem familiar to you?" Hauck asked.

Karen went through the entire list and shook her head. "No."

"A few have phone numbers listed as well. I can't imagine that anyone trying to be invisible would do that. Most are just post-office boxes."

"Assuming he's even here?"

"Assuming he's here." Hauck nodded with a sigh. "The one advantage we have is that he doesn't know there's any reason for anyone to assume he's alive." He looked at her. "But I have a couple more irons in the fire, before you even think of having to make that call."

"It's not that." Karen nodded, fretful, massaging her brow.

"What's wrong?"

"There's something I have to show you, Ty."

She reached inside her bag. "I found a couple of things last week, buried in Charlie's desk drawer, when you asked me to go through stuff. I should have showed them to you then, but they were old and they scared me. I wasn't sure what to do. They're from before the bombing."

"Let me see."

Karen took them out of her purse. One was a small note card still in its tiny envelope, addressed to Charles. Hauck flipped it open. It was one of those cards that would accompany a floral delivery.

Sorry about the pooch, Charles. Could your kids be next?

He looked back up at Karen. "I'm not sure I understand."

"Before he died"—Karen wet her lips—"*left* . . . we had another Westie. Sasha. She was run over by a car, right on our street. Right in front of our house. It was horrible. Charlie was the one who found her. A couple of weeks before the bombing . . ."

Hauck looked back at the note. *They were threatening him.*

"And *this* . . ." Karen pushed forward the other item. She rubbed her forehead, her eyes strained.

It was a holiday card. A picture of the family on it. A happier time. *From the Friedmans.* Charlie, in a blue fleece vest and knit shirt, his arm around Karen, in a windbreaker and jeans, sitting on a stockade fence in the country somewhere. She looked bright-eyed and proud. Pretty. *Wishing you the season's best for the coming year . . .*

Hauck winced, as if a blunt force had punched him in the belly.

Samantha's and Alex's faces—they had both been cut out.

He looked up at her.

"Someone was threatening Charles, Ty. A year ago. Before he left. Charlie kept these things hidden away. I don't know what he did, but I know it has to do with the people at Archer and all this money offshore."

Someone *was* threatening him, Hauck thought, placing the cards on top of each other and handing them back to Karen.

"Then yesterday I got this."

Karen reached into her bag and came out with something else, this time a large gray envelope. "In the mail."

Her eyes were worried. Hauck thumbed the top open, slid out what was inside. It was a brochure. Tufts. Where Sam was heading in the fall, he remembered.

There was some writing on the front. The same forward-leaning script as on the floral note.

You still owe us some answers, Karen. No one's gone away. We're still here.

"They're threatening my children, Ty. I can't let that happen."

He placed his palm over her hand. "No. We won't."

CHAPTER SIXTY-THREE

The cell call came in just as Hauck was getting ready to go in to visit Chief Fitzpatrick, to request that a patrol car be assigned to watch Karen's house again.

"*Joe?*"

"Listen," the JIATF man said, "I have something important here. I'm faxing it out to you now."

The pages started to flow before Hauck even arrived back at his desk. "What I'm sending you is a transcript of a series of online conversations taken off a car-enthusiast site," Velko explained. "The first exchange took place in February." Three months earlier. Joe sounded excited. "I think we got something here."

Hauck started to read the transcript as fast as he could tear the pages from the machine. The first page was headed ALERT. In the shadow box, there was a transcript number and a date, February 24. There was also a listing of the key "trigger phrases" Hauck had given Joe: "1966 Ford Mustang. Emberglow. Greenwich, Ct. Concours d' Élégance. *Charlie's Baby*." A few of his favorite phrases.

The alert box was marked "HIGH."

Hauck sat down at his desk and read, his blood pulsing expectantly.

KlassicKarMania.com:

Mal784: Hey, trading a 66 Ember Glow 'Stang in for a 69 Merc 230 Cabriolet. Any1 interested?

DragsterB: Saw one of those in a movie out last year. Sandra Bullock. Looked fine.

Xpgma: The car or the girl?

DragsterB: Real funny, dude.

Mal784: Lake House. Yeah, except mine's a ragtop, GT. 62,000 miles. 280hp. Near mint. Any1 interested? Take $38.5.

DragsterB: I know someone who might be.

SunDog: Where is it?

Mal784: Florida. Boynton Beach. Rarely sees the light of day.

SunDog: Maybe. Had one once myself. Up north. What's the VIN code? C or K?

Mal784: K. High performance. All the way.

SunDog: How's the inside?

Mal784: Orig Pony leather. Orig radio. Not a scratch. Little bastards have a way of getting under your skin, right?

SunDog: Had to sell. Moved. Used to show it around.

Mal784: Where?

DragsterB: This a private conversation? Anyone out there got a line on a set of Crager 16" rims????

SunDog: A few places. Stockbridge, Mass. The Concours in Greenwich. Once down your way, in Palm Beach.

Mal784: Hey, you used to be on here a while back? Different name, though. CharlieBoy or something, wasn't it?

SunDog: Change of life, man. Lemme see the car. Post a picture.

Mal784: Gimme your address.

SunDog: Put it on this site, Mal. I'll look.

That was all. Hauck read through the exchange again. Every instinct told him he was onto something. He flipped the page over. There was another exchange. This one was two weeks later, March 10.

Mal784: You don't know your Mustangs for

shit, bro. Check out the VIN#. K's are higher horsepowers. Command higher price. Yours is a J. 27–28K tops.

Opie$: Okay, I'll check.

Mal784: You'll learn something. Some people don't know what they have.

SunDog: So, Mal, you still got that Ember Glow????

Mal784: Hey!!! Look what the tide dragged in. What happened to you, guy? I posted a shot, like you said. Never heard back.

SunDog: Saw it. Lights-out machine, no doubt. No luck, huh? Anyway, not for my life now.

Mal784: I can deal. My middle name.

SunDog: Not that. I'm more on water than dry land now. Then I got to find a way to get it through customs down here.

Mal784: Donde?

SunDog: Caribbean. No matter. Would only rot in the sun down here. But I may come back to you. Thx.

Mal784: You late, you wait, man. Putting it up through the auctions now.

SunDog: Best of luck. From an ol' short seller, another time. I'll keep checking.

Opie$: Hey, I just looked. What about VINS beginning with N?

"Ty, you read them yet?" Joe Velko asked.

Hauck shuffled the pages. "Yeah. I think we hit the jackpot here. So how do we trace this dude, SunDog?"

"I already put out an IP user trace through the Web site's server, Ty. You understand, I wouldn't be doing this if it wasn't for you?"

"I know that, Joe."

"So I went to the blog site. They didn't put up a lot of resistance. It's amazing what a government agency can do, post-9/11, even without a subpoena. Got a pen?"

Hauck scrambled around the desk. "I'm feeling safer already, Joe. Shoot."

"SunDog is just a user name. We traced it back to a Web address, which they supplied us. Oilman0716@hotmail.com."

CHAPTER SIXTY-FOUR

Hauck fixed on the name. *Oilman*. He knew without needing anything else that they had found him. Everything inside him told him this was Charles.

"Is this traceable, Joe?"

"Yes . . . and no. As you know, Hotmail is a free Internet site. Therefore you don't need anything but a given name to register, and it doesn't even have to be a real one to get that done. Or even a real address. But we can go back to them and trace what was on the application. And there's a communication history we can go back on. What I *can't* do, however, is narrow that down to a specific place."

Hauck's blood surged with optimism. "Okay . . ."

"The activity seems to be coming from the

365

Caribbean region. Not to a specific location though, but on a wireless LAN. There's been activity picked up around St. Maarten, the BVIs. Even as far away as Panama."

"The guy's been traveling?"

"Maybe, or on a boat."

A boat. That made sense to Hauck. "Can we narrow *that* down?"

"With time," the JIATF man explained. "We can set up a surveillance and monitor future activity and triangulate a point of origin. But that takes manpower. And paperwork. And other countries involved. You understand what I mean. And I gather that's something you're not eager to deal with, are you, Ty?"

"No," he admitted. "Not if I can help it, Joe."

"That's what I thought. So this is the next-best step. We traced the application information through the Hotmail people. That much I can do, but after that you're on your own."

"That's great!"

"The address on the account is to a post-office box at the central post office on the island of St. Maarten in the Caribbean. I went as far as I could without getting anyone else involved and checked down there. It's registered to a Steven Hanson, Ty. That ring a bell?"

"Hanson?" At first it was a blank, but then

something went off inside him. "Hold on a second, Joe. . . ."

He swiveled around the desk, rifling through a stack of papers. Until he found it.

The list of new subscribers from *Mustang World.*

He had narrowed it down to just a handful of names. From all over the region: Panama. Honduras. The Bahamas. The BVIs. . . . It took a few seconds, scanning the list. Hopewell, March, Camp, O'Shea.

But there it was!

S. Hanson. Date of subscription: 1/17. *This year!* The only address given was a post-office box on St. Kitts.

Steven Hanson.

A surge of validation ran through Hauck's veins.

Steven Hanson was Oilman0716. And Oilman0716 had to be Charles. Too much fit.

The car. The Concours. The little phrases. Karen had been right. This was the part of him that could not change. *His baby.*

They had found him!

CHAPTER SIXTY-FIVE

The doorbell rang, and when Karen went to answer it, she stood fixed in surprise. "Ty . . ."

Samantha was in the kitchen, polishing off a yogurt, watching the tube. Alex had his feet slung over the couch in the family room, alternately groaning and exulting loudly, engrossed in the latest Wii video game.

Hauck's face was lit up with anticipation. "There's something I have to show you, Karen."

"Come on in."

Karen had tried to shield the kids from all that was going on—her shifting moods, the worry that seemed permanently etched in her face right now. Her frustrated, late-night rummaging through Charles's old things.

But it was a losing fight. They weren't exactly stupid. They saw the unfamiliar circumspection, the tenseness, her temper a little quicker than it had ever been before. Ty's showing up un-announced would only arouse their suspicions even more.

"C'mon in here," Karen said, taking him into the kitchen. "Sam, you remember Detective Hauck?"

Her daughter looked up, her knees curled on the stool, dressed in sweatpants and a Greenwich Huskies T-shirt, her expression somewhere between confused and surprised. "Hi."

"Good to see you again," Hauck said. "Hear you're gearing up for graduation?"

"Yeah. Next week." She nodded. She shot a glance toward Karen.

"Tufts, right?"

"Yeah," she said again. "Can't wait. What's going on?"

"I need to speak with Detective Hauck a second, hon. Maybe we'll just go . . ."

"It's okay." She got down from the stool. "I'm leaving." She tossed her yogurt container into the trash and tossed the spoon into the sink. "Good to see you again," she said to Hauck, tilting her head and screwing her eyes toward Karen, like, *What's going on?*

Hauck waved. "You, too."

Karen flicked off the kitchen TV and led him toward the sunroom. "C'mon, we'll go in here."

She sat down on the corner of the floral couch. Ty took a seat in the upholstered chair next to her. She had her hair up in a ponytail and was wearing a vintage heather gray Texas Longhorns T-shirt. No makeup. She knew she looked a mess. Still, she knew he wouldn't show up like this, at night, unless it was about something important.

He asked her, "Do they know?"

"About what I found in the mail?" Karen shook her head. "No. I don't want to worry them. I've got my folks coming up next week for the graduation. Charlie's mom, coming in from PA. They're going to Africa on safari with my folks a few days later. Sam's graduation present. I'll feel a whole lot better the minute I get them on that plane."

Ty nodded. "I'm sure. Listen. . . ." He pulled some papers out of his jacket. "I'm sorry to bother you here like this." He dropped them on the table in front of her. "You might as well read it yourself."

Warily, Karen picked them up. "What is it?"

"It's a transcript. Of two Internet conversations. From one of your husband's car sites. They took place back in February and March. One of the outfits I gave the information you found managed to pick them up."

The tiny hairs on Karen's arms stood on end.

She read through the transcripts. *Emberglow. Concours. Greenwich.* Her heart picked up a beat each time she encountered a familiar phrase. Suddenly it dawned on Karen just what this was. *SunDog.* The mention of a change of life, in the Caribbean. A reference to Charlie's old screen name, *CharlieBoy.*

An invisible hand seemed to clutch her heart in its icy fist and not let go. She focused on the name for a long time. Then she looked up. "You think this is Charlie, don't you?"

"What I think is that there's an awful lot that sounds pretty familiar," he replied.

Karen stood up, a jolt of nerves winding through her. Until now it had been safe to feel that it was all some abstract puzzle. Seeing his face on the screen; finding the safe-deposit box in New York. Even the horrible death of that person on his staff, Jonathan . . . It all just led somewhere nebulous, somewhere she never thought she'd actually have to confront.

But now . . . Her heart raced. SunDog. Karen could actually see him coming up with something like that. Now there was the possibility that everything that had happened was real. Now she could read words and phrases he might have said and almost hear his voice—familiar, alive. Out there—doing the same things, having the same conversations he'd once had with her.

A pressure throbbed in Karen's forehead. "I don't know what to do with this, Ty."

"I had my contacts trace the name," he said. "It's a free Internet site, Karen. Hotmail. There's no name registered against it, just a post-office box out of St. Maarten. In the Caribbean."

Karen held her breath and nodded.

"The P.O. box was registered under the name of Steven Hanson."

"Hanson?" Karen looked anxious.

"Does it mean anything to you?"

"No."

Hauck shrugged. "No reason it should. But it did strike something in me. I checked it back against the list we got from *Mustang World*." He handed her another sheet. "Look, there's an S. Hanson right here. No address, but a P.O. box. This one's in St. Kitts."

"That doesn't prove it's him," Karen said. "Only someone who's interested in the same kind of cars—from down there. Lots of people might be."

"Who's keeping an awfully low profile, Karen. Post-office boxes, assumed names. I did a credit check on the name down there, and you know what came back? *Nothing.*"

"That still doesn't mean it's Charles!" Her voice carried an edge of desperation in it. *"Why?* Why are you doing this, Ty? Why did you quit your job?" She came back to the couch and sat down on the arm, staring at him. "What's in it for you? *Why the hell are you making me face this?"*

"Karen . . ." He put his hand on her knee and gently squeezed.

"No!" She pulled away.

His deep-set eyes were unwavering, and for a second she thought she might just start to cry. She wanted him to hold her.

"You said there was an e-mail address?"

"Yeah. There is." He reached over and handed her a slip of paper. Karen took it, her fingers shaking.

Oilman0716@hotmail.com.

She read it over a couple of times, the truth slowly sinking in. Then she looked up at him with a half smile, as if stung, wounded.

"Oilman . . ." She sniffled, feeling lifted for a second, and at the same time let down.

A moist film burned in her eye.

"It's him." She nodded. "That's Charlie."

"You're sure?"

"Yeah, I'm sure." She exhaled, as if fortifying herself against the dam burst of tears about to come down. "That number, 0716—we always used it for our passwords. That's our anniversary—July sixteenth. . . . The date we were married. In 1989. *That's Charlie, Ty*."

CHAPTER SIXTY-SIX

The house was dark. Karen sat in Charlie's office. The kids had long since closed their doors and gone to sleep.

Karen stared over and over at the e-mail address. Oilman0716.

Waves of anger and uncertainty coursed through her veins. Anger mixed with accusation, uncertainty at what she should do. She wasn't sure if she even knew what she was feeling inside, but the more she stared at the familiar number, the more all doubt was gone. She knew it had to be Charlie.

And that took something out of her. The last ember of faith she still had in him. In the life they'd led. Her last hope.

You bastard, Charlie . . .

Contact him? She didn't know what she could possibly even say to him.

How could you, Charlie? How could you have left us like that? We were a team. We were soul mates, right? Didn't we always say how we completed each other? How could you have done these horrible things?

Karen's head felt like it weighed a thousand pounds. She thought of AJ Raymond and Jonathan Lauer. Deaths her husband was tied to. It repulsed her, sickened her.

Is it all true?

Over the past year, she had learned to make her peace with the fact that her husband had died. She'd done whatever it had taken. And now he was back. *Alive*—just as she was alive.

She could confront him.

Oilman0716.

What could she possibly say?

Are you alive, Charlie? Are you reading this? Do you know how I feel? How we would all feel if the children even knew? How badly you've hurt me? How you cheapened all those years we spent together. Charlie, how . . . ?

She logged on to her own AOL account. KFried111. Twice she even summoned the courage to go as far as type in his address. *Oilman.*

Then stopped herself.

What was there to be gained from opening

376

this all up? To have him say he was sorry. To have him admit to her that he was someone other than the person she knew. That he had done these things—while living with her, sleeping with her. Planned his way out. To hear the pretense that he had once loved her, loved them . . .

Why? What was to be gained? To drag her family through it all over again. This time it would be much worse.

A tear burned down Karen's cheek. A tear filled with doubt and accusation. She stared at the address on the screen and started to cry.

"Mom?"

Karen looked up. Samantha was in the doorway, in her oversize Michigan T-shirt and panties. "Mom, what's going on? What are you doing here sitting in the dark?"

Karen brushed away the tear. "I don't know, baby."

"Mom, what's happening?" Sam came over to the desk and knelt next to her. "What are you doing at Dad's desk? You can't tell me it's nothing—something's been bothering you for over two weeks." She put her hand on Karen's shoulder. "It's about Dad, isn't it? I know it. That detective was here again. Now there's a car outside down the street. *What the hell's going on,*

Mom? Look at you—you're in here crying. Those people are bothering us again, aren't they, Mom?"

Karen nodded, drawing in a breath. "They sent another note," she said, wiping the wetness out of her eyes. "I just want you to have a day to yourself we'll all be proud of, honey. You deserve that. And then go on that trip."

"And then what happens, Mom? What the hell has Dad done? You can tell me, Mom. I'm not six."

How? How could she tell her? Tell her all? It would be like stealing her daughter's innocence in a way, the warm memory she carried of her father. They had mourned him, laid him to rest. Learned to live without him. *Damn you, Charlie,* Karen seethed. *Why are you making me do this now?*

She cuddled Sam by the waist and took a breath. "Daddy may have done some things, Sam. He may have run some people's money. Bad people, honey. Offshore. *Illegally*. I don't know who they were. All I know is now they want it."

"Want *what*, Mom?"

"Money that's unaccounted for, honey. That Daddy may have lost. That's the message they wanted you to pass along to me."

378

"What do you mean, they want it, Mom? *He's dead.*"

Karen brought her daughter to her lap and squeezed her, the way she did when she was little, even drawing in a breath of Sam's familiar fresh-scrubbed scent. She shuddered against what she was about to say.

"Yes, honey, he's dead." Karen nodded against her.

"There's stuff you're not telling me, isn't there? I know, Mom. Lately you're always down there rifling through his old things. Now you're here, in the middle of the night, in his office, in front of his computer. Daddy wouldn't do something wrong. He was a good man. I saw the way he worked. I saw the way the two of you were with each other. He's not here to defend himself, so it's up to us. He would never have done anything that would cause us harm. He may have been your husband, Mom, but he was our dad. I knew him, too."

"Yes, baby, you're right." Karen hugged her. "It is up to us." She stroked Sam's hair as her daughter folded into her.

It's up to us that this has to end. Whatever it was these people wanted from her. Sam had a life to live. They all did. What was this nightmare going to do—follow them *forever*?

379

Would you really want to know, baby, if I told you? What he'd done. Would you really want your memories and love destroyed? *Like mine.* Wouldn't it just be better, simply to love him, to remember him as you do? Taking you to skating practice, helping you with your math. Being there in your heart, as he was now?

"This is scaring me a little, Mom," Sam said, pulling close.

"Don't let it, honey." Karen kissed her hair. But inside, she said to herself, *It scares me, too.*

Damn you, Charlie. Why did I ever have to see your face on that screen?

Look at what you've done.

CHAPTER SIXTY-SEVEN

The day finally came for the kids to leave. Karen helped pack up their bags and drove them to JFK, where they connected with her folks, who had come up the day before, at the British Air terminal.

She parked the car and went inside with them to check in, where she met up with Sid and Joan. Everyone was excited. Karen hugged Sam with everything she had and told her to take care of her brother. "I don't want him to be listening to his iPod and get carried off by a pack of lions."

"It's a portable DVR, Mom. And in his case more likely a pack of baboons."

"Funny." Alex scrunched his face, elbowing her. He'd always had to be dragged a little to go on this trip, always moping about large bugs and contracting malaria.

"C'mon, guys . . ." Karen gave them both a

381

big hug. "I love you both. You know that. You have a blast. And be in touch."

"We can't be in touch, Mom," Alex reminded her. "We're in the bush. We're on safari."

"Well, pictures then," she said. "I expect lots and lots of pictures. Y'hear?"

"Yeah, we hear." Alex smiled sheepishly.

The kids both put their arms around her and gave her a real hug. Karen couldn't help it—tears welled in her eyes.

Alex snorted. "Here goes Mom."

Karen wiped them away. "Cut it out."

She hugged her parents, too, and then she watched them go off, waving as they headed to security—Alex in a Syracuse baseball cap with his backpack containing his car magazines, Sam in a pair of sweatpants with her iPod, waving a last time. Karen barely held it together.

She thought of the warning she had just received and of Charles's e-mail. And how she wanted her kids to be safe—so what was she doing, sending them to Africa? Back in her car, she sat for a moment in the garage before turning on the ignition. She pressed her face against the steering wheel and cried, happy that her kids were gone but at the same time feeling very alone, knowing that the time had finally come.

The time to face him.
It's up to us, right?

That night Karen sat over Charles's computer.

There was no more fear, no more question of what she had to do. Only the resolve that she now felt to face it.

The thought occurred that she should call Ty. In the past weeks, she had grown close to him, feelings stirring in her, feelings mixed in with the confusion over what was happening with Charles, that seemed better to deny. And she'd never given Ty an answer about what she was prepared to do with what he'd found.

She logged on to her e-mail account.

KFried111. A name Charlie would recognize in an instant.

She was giving him her answer.

It's just the two of us now, Charlie. And the truth.

What could she possibly say? Every time she thought about it, everything came back. The anguish of losing him. The shock of seeing him again on the screen. Finding the passport, the money. The realization that he wasn't dead but had abandoned her. Her daughter's fear after she'd been accosted in her car.

Everything came back, but Ty was right. It wasn't going to go away.

People had died.

Hesitantly, she typed in the address. Oilman0716. Karen had done it several times before, but this time there was no turning back. She wondered, with a faint smile, what he would think, how his world would change, what door she was opening, a door maybe better off shut.

Not any longer, Charlie.

Karen typed out two words. She read them over and swallowed. Two words that would change her life a second time, reopen wounds that had barely healed.

She clicked send.

Hello, Charlie.

CHAPTER SIXTY-EIGHT

In a spot called Little Water Cay, near the islands of Turks and Caicos, Charles Friedman flicked on his laptop. The satellite broadband beamed in.

An unsettling dread deepened in him.

First it had been a week ago on Domenica. A teller he sometimes flirted with there mentioned how someone had been into the bank the week before, a short, mustached man, inquiring of one of the managers about an American who had wired in funds. Describing a person similar to him. The man had even showed a photo around.

Then there was the article that he now unfolded in his lap.

From the *Caribbean Times*. Regional News section. About a murder on the island of St. Maarten. An old-line diamond merchant had been shot in his car. Nothing had been broken into or stolen. The man's name was Issa. He had been on the island for fifty years.

His diamond merchant. *His* contact. In the past year, he had made two transactions with Issa. Charles's eyes drilled in on the headline. A crime of that nature hadn't happened there in ten years.

Somehow they knew. It was getting too close. He'd have to change venues. They must have followed him through his network of banks, discovered that his fee account from Falcon had been drawn down. Now the death of this diamond merchant. It saddened Charles that he might be responsible for the old man's fate. He had liked Issa. Soon Charles would need funds. But it was getting too dangerous to show his face right now. Even here.

He always knew that it was likely one day they would latch onto the trail of the money.

It had rained heavily during the night. A few puffy clouds still loitered in the crisp blue sky. He sat on the deck of his boat with a mug of coffee and fired up his Bloomberg account, his early-morning ritual. Checked his overnight positions, just as he'd been doing for twenty years, though now he traded only for himself. Soon he'd have to stop that as well. Maybe they could trace his activity—his investment signature was on every trade. Still, it was all he could do to keep sane. Now he would lose that, too.

His laptop came to life. His server announced that he had four new messages.

He didn't receive many e-mails under his new account. Mostly just spam that managed to reach him—mortgage solicitations and Viagra ads. An occasional electronic trading update. He didn't dare draw attention to his new identity. That's the way it had to be.

And that's what he was thinking, spam, as, sipping his coffee, he scanned the list of messages.

Until his eyes stopped.

Not stopped—*crashed* was more like it, his stomach seizing, into the address of the sender of the third one down.

KFried111.

Charles's feet fell off the gunwales. His spine arched, as if a jolt of high voltage had been shot through it. He focused on the name again, blinking, as if his eyes were somehow playing tricks on him.

Karen.

Heart pounding, he double-checked, just to make sure he hadn't managed to log on to his old e-mail address, which he knew was impossible. But what else could it be?

No, it was all correct. *Oilman.*

His throat went dry. Worse, then came the bowel-tightening realization that in a flash everything had just caught up with him. His past. His deceptions. What he had done. *How was this possible? How could she have found his name? His address?* No, he realized those weren't even the right questions.

How was it possible she even knew he was alive?

A year had passed. He had covered his tracks perfectly. He had no connection to his old life. He had never once run into anyone they knew—always his greatest fear. Charles's fingers were shaking. *KFried111.* Karen. *How would she have been able to track him there?*

A mix of emotions swept over him: panic, fear, longing. Memory. Seeing all their faces, missing them in this moment as much as he had missed them all so terribly those first months.

Finally Charles summoned the nerve. He clicked on the name. All that was there were two sparse words. He read them, the color draining from his face, his eyes welling up, stinging with guilt and shame.

Hello, Charlie.

CHAPTER SIXTY-NINE

When the call found him, Saul Lennick had just climbed into bed in his silk Sulka pajamas. He was glancing over a financial prospectus for a meeting he had in the morning, his attention diverted by the late TV news.

Mimi, who was in the midst of an Alan Furst novel next to him, sighed crossly, glancing at the cell phone. "Saul, it's after eleven."

Lennick fumbled for his phone on the night table. He didn't recognize the number, but it was from out of the country. *Barbados*. His heart picked up. "Sorry, dear."

He removed his reading glasses and flipped it open. "Can't this wait until the morning?"

"If it could, I would've," the caller, Dietz, replied. "Relax, I'm on a phone card. It can't be traced."

Lennick sat up and put on his slippers. He

uttered a guilty sigh to his wife, pretending that it was business. He took the phone into the bathroom and shut the door. "All right, go ahead."

"We've got problems," Dietz announced. "There's a homicide detective in Greenwich who handled that thing we did up there. The one who interrogated me. I may have mentioned him before."

"So . . . ?"

"He knows."

"He knows *what*?" Lennick stood in front of the mirror, picking at a pore on the side of his face.

"He knows about the accident. He also knows about that other thing in New Jersey. He somehow broke into my house. He's linked me with one of the other witnesses. You beginning to get an idea what I'm talking about now?"

Under his breath Lennick gasped, "Jesus Christ!" He was no longer staring at the pore but at his face, which had turned white.

"Sit down. It gets worse."

"How the hell can it get worse, Dietz?"

"You remember Hodges? One of my men."

"Go on."

"He's been shot."

Lennick's chest began to feel like he was having a heart attack. Dietz told him how

390

Hodges had gone to Dietz's house and found the cop. *Inside.* How the two of them had tussled.

"Now, listen, before you bust an artery, Saul, there's some good news."

"What can be good about this?" Lennick sat down.

"He has no grounds. The Greenwich detective. Whatever he's doing, he's doing it alone. It's not part of any official investigation. He broke into my house. He brought a gun in there and used it. He didn't make a move to arrest Hodges. You see what this means?"

"No," Lennick said, panicked, "I don't see what this means."

"It means he's completely out of his jurisdiction, Saul. He was simply sneaking around. Before I called you, I called up his station up in Greenwich. *The guy's on fucking leave!* He's freelancing, Saul. He's not even on active duty. If it came out what he did, they'd take his badge. They'd arrest *him*, not me."

A dull pain flared up in Lennick's chest. He ran a hand through his white hair, sweat building up underneath his pajama top. He immediately retraced the steps of what anyone could have known that could have led back to him.

He exhaled. It was all Dietz.

"Here's the kicker," Dietz went on. "I had

391

someone I know up there keep an eye on him. At night he's been watching over a house in Greenwich in his own car."

"Whose?"

"A woman. Someone you know well, Saul."

Lennick blanched. "Karen?"

He tried to piece it together. *Did Karen somehow know?* Even if she had found out about the incident with Lauer, how would she possibly have connected it with the other? A year ago. She had found the safe-deposit box, the passport, the cash.

Did Karen somehow know that Charles was alive?

Lennick moistened his lips. They had to speed this up. He pressed Dietz. "How are things going down there?"

"We're making progress. I've had to do some 'off-road' stuff, if you know what I mean. But that never seemed to bother you before. I think he's on a boat somewhere. But somewhere close. I've traced him through three of his banks. He'll need money. I'll have him soon. I'm closing in.

"But, listen," Dietz said, "regarding the detective, he may have found certain things in my office . . . related to what I'm doing here. Maybe even about you. I can't be sure."

A police detective? Things were growing deeper than Lennick was comfortable with. That was surely crossing the line. Still, what choice did he have?

"You know how to handle these things, Phil. I've got to go."

"One more thing," Dietz said. "If the detective knows, there's always the chance that she knows, too. I realize you're friendly. That you have something to do with her kids."

"Yes," Lennick muttered blankly. He was fond of Karen. And, having been like an uncle to them since they were small, in charge of their family trusts, you could say he did have something to do with the kids.

But it was business. Lauer had been business, the Raymond kid had been business, too. The furrows on his face were carved deep and hard. They made him seem older—older than he'd felt in years.

"Just do whatever it is you have to do."

Lennick clicked off. He splashed some water on his face, smoothed back his hair. Shuffling in his slippers, he trudged back to bed.

The evening news had finished. Mimi had turned off the light. David Letterman was on. Lennick turned to her to see if she was asleep. "Shall we catch the monologue, dear?"

CHAPTER SEVENTY

Karen waited two days. Charles didn't reply.

She wasn't sure he ever would.

She knew Charles. She tried to imagine the shock and dismay that her e-mail must have caused.

The same shock he had caused when she saw his face up on that screen.

Karen checked her e-mails several times a day. She knew what must be going through him now. Sitting in some remote part of the globe, the careful construct of his new life suddenly crumbling. It must be killing him—retracing every step, running through a thousand possibilities.

How could she possibly know?

How many times, Karen imagined, he would have read over those two words. Replaying everything in his mind, racking his brain, all the preparations he had made. His bowels acting up. Not sleeping. Things always affected Charles that way. *You owe me*, she said to him silently, relishing this image of him, panicked, rocked. *You owe me for the hurt you put me through. The lies . . .*

Still, she couldn't forgive him. Not for what he'd done to her—to the kids. She no longer knew if there was love between them. If there was anything still between them, other than the memory of a life spent together. Still, it didn't matter. She just wanted to hear from him. She wanted to see him—face-to-face.

Answer me, Charlie . . .

Finally, after three days, Karen typed out another message. She closed her eyes and begged him.

Please, Charlie, please. . . . I know it's you. I know you're out there. Answer me, Charlie. You can't hide any longer. I know what you've done.

CHAPTER SEVENTY-ONE

I know what you've done!

Charles sat in the corner of a quiet Internet café in the harbor on Mustique, where he had put in, staring in horror at Karen's latest message.

A collection of dreadlocked locals drinking Jamaican beer and a party of itinerant German surfers in tattoos and bandannas. He had a pressing fear, even here, that everything was closing in on him.

I know what you've done!

What? What do you know I've done, Karen? And how? Hidden behind his shades, he took a sip of a Caribe and read the message over for the tenth time. He knew she would keep at it. He knew her. This was no longer something he could just ignore.

396

And how in hell did you find me?

What do you want me to say to you, Karen? That I'm a bastard? That I betrayed you? Charles could sense the anger resonating in her words. And he didn't blame her. He deserved whatever she felt. To have left them as he did. To have put them through that anguish. The loss of a husband, a father. Then, after it all finally subsided, to suddenly find out he was alive!

Answer me, Charlie.

What do you know, Karen?
If you knew, truly knew, you would understand. At least a little. That it was never to hurt you. That would have been the last thing in my heart.

But to protect you, Karen. To keep you safe. To keep Sam and Alex safe as well. You would know why I *had* to stay away. Why, when the door opened and the path presented itself, I had to "die."

Please, Charlie, please. . . . Answer me, Charlie.

The surfers were cackling loudly in German at something they had found on YouTube. A heavyset island woman in a colorful shift sat down across from him, towing a young daughter sipping on a Fanta. Charles realized he had spent so much of the past year hiding, in shadows, turning away from who he was. From everything he once loved.

But all of a sudden it was like he felt alive again. For the first time in a year! It was clear to him, you could never fully kill it. What was inside you. Who you are.

And now Charles realized that if he only touched this key, a flick of his hand, sent this message back, answered her, it reopened everything. The whole world changed again.

I know what you've done.

He took a swig of beer. Maybe it was time to move on again. To Vanuatu in the Indian Ocean. Or back to Panama. No one would find him. He had money there.

He lifted his shades. He looked closely at the words he had written. Pandora's box was about to open again. For her and for him. And this time there would be no closing it. No sudden bomb blast interfering—nowhere to hide.

The hell with it, he said. He finished the last of his beer. She had found him. *The iron fist in the velvet glove . . .* he recalled fondly.

She would never let up.

Yes, I'm here. Yes, it's me, he said. With one last reflection, he pushed the send key, sending his world spinning again.

Hello, baby. . . .

CHAPTER SEVENTY-TWO

Hauck had gone out for an evening run around the cove. He'd sat at home for a couple of days, and still he hadn't heard from Karen. The night was hot, sticky. The cicadas were buzzing. Finally he just had to calm the frustration that was bursting in his chest.

He knew it wasn't right to push. He knew how hard this had to be for her, to face her husband. It would be like a part of Norah suddenly brought up for him again. Ripping open wounds that hadn't healed. He wasn't sure whether to wait and see if she still wanted to find Charles. Or now that she knew the truth—at least parts of it—to simply pack it in. Bring what they'd found into Fitzpatrick.

He'd have to reopen the case. AJ Raymond's hit-and-run.

That's what had started him on it in the first place, right?

To his surprise, as he headed back down Euclid toward his house, he spotted the familiar Lexus parked on the street. Karen sitting on his front stairs. When he came to a stop, she stood up.

A slightly awkward smile. "Hey . . ."

She was dressed in a fitted black shirt worn out over nice jeans, her caramel hair a little messy, a chunky, quartzlike bracelet dangling loosely from her wrist. It was a warm summer night. She looked great to him.

"I'm sorry to barge in," she said, a look that was almost forlorn, little-girl-ish, coming through on her face. "I just needed to talk to someone. I took a chance."

Hauck shook his head. "You're not barging in."

He walked her up the steps and unlocked the door. He grabbed a towel off the kitchen counter and wiped down his face. He asked if she wanted a beer from the fridge.

"No. Thanks."

Karen was like a bundle of nerves, and she walked around like she was holding something deep inside. She went up to the easel by the window. He followed her over, taking a seat on the stool.

"I didn't know you paint."

Hauck shrugged. "You better look at it closely before you use that word."

She stepped up to the easel. So close that Hauck could smell her scent—sweet, blossomy—his pulse climbing. He held back the urge to touch her.

"It's nice," she said. "You're always full of surprises, aren't you, Lieutenant?"

"That's about the nicest thing anyone's ever said about it." He smiled.

"You probably cook, too. I bet you—"

"Karen . . ." He had never seen her so wound up. He swiveled around and went to grab her arm.

She pulled away.

"*It was him,*" she said. Her eyes were liquid, angry, almost glaring at him. "He answered me. It took three days. I had to write him twice." She put a hand to the back of her neck. "I didn't know what to say to him, Ty. What the hell *could* I say? 'I know it's you, Charles. Please answer me'? Finally he did."

"What did he say?"

"What did he say?" She sniffed, blew out a derisive blast of air. "He said '*Hello, baby.*'"

"That's all?"

"Yeah." She smiled, hurt. "That was all." She took a few steps around, as if she were holding back some torrent, checking out the view of the cove off the deck. She went over to a console against the wall. He kept a couple of pictures on it. She picked them up, one by one. A shot of the two girls when they were babies. He saw her staring at it. Another of Hauck's boat, the *Merrily*.

"Yours?"

"Mine." Hauck nodded. He stood up. "Not exactly like the sultan of Brunei's, but Jessie likes it. In the summer we go up to Newington or out to Shelter Island. Fish. When the weather's nice, I've been known to—"

"You do it all, don't you, Ty?" Her eyes were ablaze, flashing at him. "You're what they call a good man."

Hauck wasn't sure if that was a compliment. Karen compressed her lips tightly, ran a hand through her tousled hair. It was like she was ready to explode.

He stepped forward. "Karen . . ."

"'Hello, baby,'" she said again, her voice cracking. "That's all he fucking said to me, Ty. Like, *'What have you been up to, hon? Anything new with the kids?'* It was Charles! The man I buried. The man I slept next to for eighteen years! *'Hello, baby.'* What the hell do I say to him now, Ty? What the hell happens now?"

Hauck went to her and took her in his arms. This time as he had always dreamed of holding her tightly, pressing her close to his chest, hard. His blood almost burst out of his veins.

At first she tried to pull away, anger coursing. Then she let him, tears smearing on his shirt, her hair honey-scented and disarrayed, her breasts full against his chest.

He kissed her. Karen didn't resist. Instead she parted her lips in response, her tongue seeming just as eager to seek out his, something beyond their control taking hold of them, her scent deep in his nostrils—an intoxication, something sweet, jasmine—driving him wild.

His hand traveled down the curve of her back, his fingers crawling underneath the belt on her jeans. Arousing him. He drew it back, her blouse loose, finding the warmth of the exposed flesh of her belly, drew it past the breathless sigh of her breasts, and cupped her face in his hands.

"You don't have to do anything," he said.

"*I can't.*" Karen looked at him, tears glistening off her cheeks. "I can't be there alone."

He kissed her again. This time their tongues lingered in a sweet, slow dance. "*I just can't. . . .*"

Hauck wiped the tears off her face. "You don't have to," he said. "You don't have to do anything."

Then he picked her up in his arms.

* * *

They made love in the bedroom.

Slowly, he unbuttoned her shirt, ran his hands over the black lace of her bra, tenderly down to her groin, as she drew back, a little afraid, parts of her that hadn't been touched in a year.

Her breathing heavy, Karen tilted her head against his bare chest. "Ty, I haven't done this in a long time."

"I know," he said, gently pulling her arms through her sleeves, running his hand along her thigh, underneath her jeans.

She tensed with anticipation.

"I mean with someone else," she said. "I've been with Charles for twenty years."

"That's okay," he said. "I know."

He laid her back on the bed, drew her jeans out from under her firm thighs a leg at a time, slipped his hand underneath her panties, felt the tremor of anticipation there. The throbbing in her womb was driving Karen wild. She looked up at him. He had been there for her, steadied her, when everything else was just insanity. He had been the one thing in which she could believe. She reached up and gently touched his side, the marks healing, and kissed them, his perspiration sweet. Hauck, tensing, unbuckled his shorts. He was the one thing that held her together. Without him she didn't know what she would have done.

She put her face close to him. *"Ty . . ."*

He moved his body firmly over hers, his buttocks tight, arms strong, athletic. Their bodies came together like a warm wave, electricity shooting down Karen's spine. She arched her back. Her breasts, his chest came together, a hundred degrees.

Suddenly there was nothing holding them back. She felt this yearning rising up from her center. Karen let her head fall back, fall from side to side as he entered her, a tremor shooting through her from the tips of her fingers to her toes, like a current, a long-awaited prize. She cupped his rear and drew him into her deeply. A wildness taking over. Gasping, their bodies became a tangle of pelvises and thighs. She clung to him. This man had risked everything for her. She didn't want to hold anything back. They rocked. She wanted to give him everything. A part of her she had never given to anyone. Even Charles. A part of her she had always held back.

Everything.

CHAPTER SEVENTY-THREE

Afterward they lay on the bed, spent, Karen's body slick with lovely sweat, still radiating fire. Hauck cooled her, blowing on her chest, her neck. Her hair was a tangled mess.

"Must be your lucky day," she mused, with an ironic roll of her eyes. "Normally I never give out until at least the third date. It's a hard-and-fast rule at Match.com."

Hauck laughed, lifting a leg up on his other knee. "Listen, if it means anything, I promise I'll still come through with a couple of meals."

"*Whew!*" Karen blew out a breath. "That's a load off my mind."

She glanced around the cramped bedroom, looking for things about him she didn't know. A simple wooden bed frame, a night table with a couple of books stacked—a biography of Einstein, a novel by Dennis Lehane—a pair of jeans tossed over a chair in the corner. A small TV.

"What the hell is *that*?" Karen said, pointing to something against the wall.

"Hockey stick," Hauck said, falling back.

Karen propped up on her elbow. "Tell me I didn't just sleep with a man who keeps a hockey stick in his bedroom."

Hauck shrugged. "Winter league. Guess I never moved it."

"Ty, *it's fucking June.*"

He nodded, like a little boy discovered with a stash of cookies under his bed. "You're lucky you weren't here last week. My skates were in here, too."

Karen brushed her hand against his cheek. "It's good to see you laugh, Lieutenant."

"I guess we could say we're both a bit overdue."

For a while they lay like two starfish on the large bed, barely covered, just the tips of their fingers touching, still finding each other.

"Ty . . ." Karen raised herself up. "There's something I need to ask you about. I saw something when I came to your office that day. You had a picture on the credenza. *Two* young girls. When I saw you at the game that day, I met your daughter and you told me she was your only

408

one. Then tonight I saw another of her, outside."
She leaned close to him. "I don't mean to open
something up—"

"No." He shook his head. "You're not opening
anything up."

Facing the ceiling, he told her. About Norah.
At last. "She'd be nine now."

Karen felt a stab of sadness rush over her.

He told her how they'd just come back from
the store and forgotten something and had been
in such a rush to get back there. There was his
shift, he was running late. Beth was mad at him.
They were living out in Queens then. He had
bought the wrong dessert. "Pudding Snacks . . ."

How he had somehow left the car in a rush,
his shift in half an hour, rushing back in to grab
the receipt.

"Pudding Snacks," Hauck said again, shrugging at Karen, an empty smile.

"They'd been playing on the curb. Tugboat
Annie, Jessie told us later. You know the song—
'Merrily, merrily, merrily . . .'" He inhaled a
breath. "The car backed out. I hadn't put it in
park. All we ever heard was Jessie. And Beth. I
remember the look she gave me. 'Oh, Ty, oh, my
God!' It all happened so suddenly." He looked
up at her and wet his lips. "She was four."

Karen sat up, and brushed her hand across

his slick face. "You're still carrying it, aren't you? I can see it in your eyes. I saw it there the first time we met."

"You were the one who was forced to deal with something then."

"Yes, but I still saw it. I think that's why I thanked you. For what you said. You made me feel like you understood. I don't think you ever let it go."

"How *do* you let that go, Karen?"

"I know." Karen nodded. "I know. . . . What about your wife? Beth, right?"

Hauck leaned up on his side, hunched his shoulders sort of helplessly. "I don't think she's ever forgiven me. The irony was, she was the reason I was running back to the store." He turned and faced her. "You know how you always asked me why I'm doing this, Karen?"

She nodded again. "Yeah."

"And one reason is that I think I was drawn to you from the first time we met. I couldn't get you out of my mind."

Karen took his hand.

"But the other," he said, and shook his head, "that Raymond kid, lying there on the asphalt. I knew there was something about it from the get-go. Something about him just brought me back, to Norah. I couldn't put it away . . . his image. I still can't."

"Their *hair*," Karen said, cupping Hauck's curled hand close to her breast. "They both had the same red hair. You've been trying to make up for that accident all this time. By solving this hit-and-run. By playing the hero for me."

"No, that part was just my plan to get in your pants," he teased, deadpan.

"Ty." She looked into his sorrowful eyes. "You are a good man. That part I could see the first time we met. Anyone who knows you can see that. We all do things every day—walk off the curb into traffic, drive when we've had a bit too much to drink, forget to blow out a candle when we go to sleep. And things just go on, like they always do. Until one time they don't. You can't keep judging yourself. This happened a long time ago. It was an accident. You loved your daughter. You still do. You don't have to make up for anything anymore."

Hauck smiled. He pressed his hand to her cheek and stroked Karen's face. "This from a woman who walked in here tonight having found out that her once-deceased husband was her new AOL pen pal."

"Tonight, yes." Karen laughed. "Tomorrow . . . who the hell knows?"

She dropped back onto the bed. Suddenly she remembered why she had come. The frustration

411

that bristled in her blood. *Hello, baby . . .* It all overwhelmed her a little. She grasped his hand.

"So what the hell are we gonna do now, Ty?"

"We're gonna let it drop," he said, running his finger along the slope of her back and letting it linger on her buttock. "Anyway, it's not exactly conducive, Karen."

"Conducive? Conducive to *what*?" she asked, aware of the renewed stirring in her belly.

He turned toward her and shrugged. "To doing it again."

"*Doing it again*?" He pulled Karen on top of him, their bodies springing alive. She brushed her nose against his, her hair cascading all over his face like a waterfall, and then she laughed. "You know how long it's been since I've heard those words?"

CHAPTER SEVENTY-FOUR

In the morning Hauck put on coffee. He was out on the deck when Karen stepped outside after nine, wearing an oversize Fairfield University T-shirt she'd grabbed from the drawer, wiping sleep from her eyes.

"Morning." He looked up, his hand brushing against her thigh.

She leaned against him and rested her head on his shoulder. "Hi."

It was a bright, warm, early-summer morning. Karen looked across the row of modest homes to the sound. Boaters were readying their craft in the marina. An early launch to Cove Island was going out. A few gray gulls flapped in the sky.

She went over to the railing. "It's nice out here." She nodded toward the painting, still on its easel. "Feel like I've seen this before."

Hauck pointed to a stack of canvases against the wall. "All the same view."

Karen raised her face to the sun and ran a hand through her tangled hair against the breeze. Then she sat down next to him, cupping her hands around the mug.

He said, "Listen, about last night . . ."

She put out her hand and stopped him. "Me first. I didn't mean to throw myself at you. I just couldn't face being alone. I—"

"I was about to say last night was a dream," he said, winking into her sleepy eyes.

"I was about to say something like that, too." Karen smiled back sheepishly. "I hadn't been with anyone else in almost twenty years."

"It was crazy. All that pent-up energy . . ."

"Yeah, *right*." She rolled her eyes.

He shifted himself around to her. "You know that yoga move, where you arch your spine back like that and—"

Karen slapped at his wrist, rebuking. "Oh, you're a stitch!"

Ty caught her hand. He looked at her, directly now. "I meant it, Karen. What I told you about why I started in on this. Because of you. But you knew that. I've never been much of a poker player."

Karen leaned her head on his shoulder again.

"Ty, listen, I don't know if this is such a smart idea for us right now."

"That's a risk I'll have to take."

"There's just too much going on that I have to sort out. What we do about Charlie, my kids? My goddamn husband's out there, Ty!"

"Have you made up your mind?"

"About what? Help me out. It's like a fucking Costco of things to choose from."

"About Charles," Hauck said. "About what you want me to do."

Karen drew in a breath. There was something firm in her gaze, replacing the coiled anxiety of last night. She nodded. "I've made up my mind. He owes me answers, Ty, and I want them. *When* he first started lying to me. When whatever it was he was chasing became more important to him than me or the kids. And I'm not gonna turn the page on almost half my life without hearing them. From him. By letting him off the hook. I want to find the man, Ty."

After she got home and took a shower and brushed out her hair, Karen sat back down at the computer. All the anxiety she'd been feeling last night had hardened into a new resolve.

She clicked on to AOL and found Charlie's reply to her. She read it over one more time.

415

Hello, baby. . . .

She started to type.

I'm not your "baby," Charles. Not anymore. I'm someone you've terribly hurt—beyond what you could ever imagine. Someone very confused. But you already know that, Charles, don't you?

You knew that when you wrote me back. You must've known that since the day you left. So here's the deal—I want to see you, Charles. I want to hear why you did this. Why you used us, Charlie, the people you supposedly loved. Not over the Internet. Not like this. I want to hear it directly from you. Face-to-face. Who you really are, Charlie.

She had to hold herself back.

So you tell me—how. You tell me where I can meet you, Charlie. You make it happen, so I can go forward in my life—if that's something you at all might still care about. Don't even think about saying no. Don't even think about hiding, Charlie. Tell me how.
Karen.

CHAPTER SEVENTY-FIVE

Charles was inside the South Island Bank on St. Lucia when Karen's message came in over his BlackBerry.

Her words stopped him like a shot of epinephrine into his heart.

No. He couldn't do this. He couldn't see her. This wasn't going to work. He had opened the door, but that had been a moment of weakness and stupidity. Now he had to slam it shut.

He had made out an account-transfer form. Filled in the routing numbers and the new accounts. He was cleaning house here, transferring the funds he kept to the Banco Nacional de Panama in Panama City and the Seitzenbank in Luxembourg, and from there on to safer ground.

It was time to be leaving.

Charles waited for a brightly clad local woman to finish, then sat down at the manager's desk.

The manager was an amiable islander he had worked with before, who seemed pleased to see Charles again, as he did every few months.

And he was disappointed to see him closing out his accounts.

"Mr. Hanson," the manager said, dutifully fulfilling his request, "so it seems we will not be seeing you here anymore?"

"Maybe not for a while," Charles said, standing up. "Thanks." The two shook hands.

As he left, his mind weighing Karen's urgent message—resolving to tell her no, not to contact him anymore—Charles never noticed the manager reaching for a slip of paper he kept hidden in his desk. Or picking up the phone before Charles had even stepped out the door.

Karen was still at the computer when Charles's reply came in.

No, Karen. It's way too dangerous. I can't let that happen. The things I did that you may think you know about . . . you simply don't. Just accept that. I know how you must feel, but please, I beg you, just go on with your life. Don't tell anyone you found me. No one, Karen! I loved you. I never meant to hurt you. But now it's too late. I accept that. But please, please, whatever you may feel, don't write me anymore.

Anger bristled through Karen's blood. She wrote back:

Yes, Charlie, I'm afraid you ARE going to let that happen! When I say I know about what you've done, I don't just mean that you're alive. I know. . . . I know about Falcon and all the money you were managing offshore, Charlie. That you kept from me all those years. And Dolphin. Those empty tankers, Charlie. That person in Pensacola who uncovered your fraud. What the hell did you try to do to him, Charlie?

This time his reply came back in seconds—a tone of panic:

Just who have you been talking to, Karen?

What does it matter who I've been talking to, Charlie?

Now they were going back and forth, real time. Karen and the man she had thought was a ghost.

419

You're not seeing it. All that matters is, I know. I know about that boy who was killed in Greenwich. The day you disappeared. The day we were up here bleeding for you, Charlie. And I know you were there. Is that enough yet? I know you came up here after the bombing. The bombing when you were supposed to have been killed, Charlie. I know you called him under an assumed name.

How, Karen, how?

And I know who he was, Charlie. I know he was that man from Pensacola's son. What your own trader, Jonathan Lauer, probably found out himself and was trying to tell me. Is that enough yet, Charlie? Fraud. Murder. Covering it all up.

Seconds later Charlie wrote back:

Karen, please . . .

She wiped her eyes.

I haven't told any of this to the kids. If I did, it would surely kill them, Charlie. Like it's been fucking killing me. They're away now. On safari with my folks. Sam's graduation present. But people have been threatening us, Charlie. Threatening THEM! Is that what you wanted, Charlie? Is that what you wanted to leave behind?

She drew in a breath and went on typing.

I know there are risks. But we're going to take those risks. Otherwise, I'm going to pass all this on to the police. You'll be charged, Charlie. We're talking murder. They'll find you. If I could, believe me, so can they. And that's what your kids will think of you, Charlie. That you were a murderer. Not the person they admire now.

Karen was about to push send, but then she hesitated.

So that's the price, Charles, for my silence. To keep all this quiet. You always loved a fair exchange. I don't want you back. I don't love you anymore. I don't know if I have any feelings for you. But I am going to see you, Charlie. I am going to hear why you did this to us, from your lips, face-to-face. So you just tell me how it's going to get done. Nothing else. No apologies. No sorrow. Then you can feel free to disappear for the rest of your miserable life.

She pressed send. And waited. For several minutes. There was no reply. Karen began to grow worried. What if she had divulged too much? What if she had scared him away? For good. Now that she'd finally found him.

She waited for what seemed forever. Staring at the blank screen. *Don't do this to me again, Charles. Not now. C'mon, Charlie, pretend that you once loved me. Don't put me through this again.*

She shut her eyes. Maybe she even dozed off for a while, totally enervated, spent.

She heard a sound. When Karen opened her eyes, she saw that an e-mail had come in. She clicked on it.

Alone. That's the only way it happens.

Karen stared at it. A tiny smile of satisfaction inched onto her lips.

All right, Charles. Alone.

CHAPTER SEVENTY-SIX

Another day passed while Karen waited for Charles's instructions. This time she wasn't nervous or afraid. Or surprised when she finally received them.

Just resolved.

Come down to the St. James's Club on St. Hubert's in the BVIs.

Karen knew the place. They had sailed around there a couple of times. It was a beautiful spot on a horseshoe cove, a cluster of thatched bungalows nestled right on the beach. Completely remote.

Charles added:

Soon. Days, not weeks, Karen. I'll contact you there.

There were many things Karen thought to say to him. But all she wrote back was:

I'll be there.

Ronald Torbor wrestled with what to do. That very morning he had looked up and seen Steven Hanson, the American, standing in front of his desk.

Come to close out his accounts.

The bank manager tried to camouflage his surprise. Since the two Americans had been to his house, he had prayed he would never see this man again. But here he was. All the while they talked and conducted business, Ronald's heart was hammering out of his chest. As soon as the man left, Ronald rushed into the office bathroom. He splashed cold water all over his burning face.

What should he do?

He knew it was wrong—what those awful men had asked him to do. He knew it violated every fiduciary oath. That he would be fired if anyone found out. Lose everything he had worked for all these years.

And Ronald liked him. Mr. Steven Hanson. He was always cheerful and polite. He always had a good word to say about Ezra, whose picture was on Ronald's desk and whom Hanson had seen once before when Ezra and Edith had been visiting in the bank.

But what choice did he have?

It was for his son that he was doing this.

The mustached man had promised—if he ever found out that Ronald had screwed him, they would be back. And if they had traced Hanson this far, they could trace him further. And if they found out his accounts had been transferred out, it would be worse for them. Edith and Ezra.

Far, far worse.

Ronald realized there was a lot more at stake than just his job. There was his family. They had threatened to kill him. Ezra. Ronald had vowed he could not see that look of fear in his wife's eyes again.

Mr. Hanson, please understand. What choice do I have?

There was a pay telephone on the far end of the square outside the bank. Next to a bench, with an election poster on it, a picture of Nevis's corrupt incumbent minister over the slogan TIME COME FOR DEM TO GO.

He put a pay card in the slot and punched in the international number he'd been given. *Make sure I hear from you, Ronald*, the mustached man had said as he left, patting Ezra's head. "Nice boy." He winked. "I'm sure he'll have quite a future in life."

The call connected. Ronald swallowed back his fear.

"*Hello*," a voice answered. Ronald recognized its tone. Just hearing it again sent a shiver of shame and revulsion down his spine.

"It's Ronald Torbor. From Nevis. You said to call."

"Ronald. Good to hear from you," the mustached man replied. "How's Ezra? Getting along?"

"I've seen him," Ronald said without responding. "The man you're looking for. He was here today."

CHAPTER SEVENTY-SEVEN

"I'm going alone," Karen explained to Hauck.

They met for coffee again at Arcadia in town. Karen told him how Charlie had contacted her at last, and about his instructions. "He said just me. That was the deal I made. I've got to do it, Ty."

"No. You're not." He put down his coffee and shook his head. "That doesn't fly, Karen. You don't have any idea who else he may be involved with. There's no way I'm going to let you put yourself at risk."

"That's the deal, Ty. I agreed."

"*Karen.*" Hauck leaned in close, lowering his voice so people at the nearby tables wouldn't hear. "This man walked away from you and your family. You know precisely what he's done. You also know what he has to protect. This is dangerous, Karen. This isn't some high-school stunt. You told Charlie exactly what you'd uncovered about him. People have died. No way in hell would I let you go down there alone."

"You don't have to remind me what the stakes are, Ty." Karen's voice was strained, and growing louder. She looked at him pleadingly. "When I came to you, I trusted you. I told you things I could never tell anyone else."

"I think I've earned that trust, Karen."

"Yes." Karen nodded. "I know you have. But now you have to trust *me* just a little, too. *I'm going*," she said, her eyes lucid, unwavering. "This is my husband, Ty. I know him, whatever it may seem. And I know he would never harm me. I told him yes, Ty. I'm not going to lose this chance."

Hauck exhaled a deep breath, his stern gaze reflecting his resistance. He could stop her, he knew. He could blow the whole thing wide open today. Take the heat he had brought upon himself. But this was what he'd always promised her. From the beginning. To find Charles. And as he ran through his remaining options, he realized that in many ways he was already in too deep.

"It has to be somewhere very public," he said

finally. "I have to be able to watch out for you. That's the only way."

She widened her eyes. "Ty . . ."

"That's not negotiable, Karen. If the situation seems safe once we know all the details, you can go see him. Alone. I give you my word. But I'm going to be around. That's the deal."

Karen's face carried an admonition. "You can't use me to get to him, Ty. You have to promise."

"You think I'm going down there to arrest him, Karen? What do you think, I'm going to call in Interpol and set up a sting like on *Miami Vice*?" He fixed on her. "The reason I'm going there is that I'm probably in love with you, Karen—don't you understand that?—or something pretty damn close. I'm going there because there's no way in hell I'm going to let you get in over your head and get yourself killed."

The look in his eyes was determined and unbending. The shining blue in them had hardened into more of an intractable gray resolve. For a while the two of them just sat there, Hauck bristling.

Then slowly Karen smiled. "You said 'probably.'"

"Yeah, probably." Hauck nodded. "And while I'm at it, probably a little jealous, too."

"Of Charles?"

"Of eighteen years, Karen. This is the person you built your life with, whatever the hell he's done."

"That part is over, Ty."

"I don't know what's over." He looked away for a second, then sucked in a frustrated breath. "Anyway, I said it, stupid as it sounded, what the hell."

Karen reached over to his hand. She pressed his palm inside both of hers, massaging the soft cushions. Eventually he met her eyes.

"You know, I probably love you, too." She shrugged. "Or something close."

"I'm overwhelmed."

"But if we do this, Ty, we can't do it like that. *Please*. This is the most important thing for me now. That's why I'm going down there. Afterward . . ." Karen pressed her thumb into his palm. "Afterward we'll see. Is that a deal?"

He wrapped his pinkie around hers and granted his reluctant agreement. "Do you know this place?"

"The St. James Club? We were there once. We pulled in at the dock for lunch." She saw his concern. "It's like in *Condé Nast Traveler*, Ty. It's not exactly the setting for an ambush."

"So when do you go?"

"*We* go, Ty. *We*. Tomorrow," Karen said. "I already booked the tickets."

"Tickets?"

"Yeah, Ty, *tickets*." Karen grinned. "You honestly think I thought you'd ever let me go down there on my own?"

CHAPTER SEVENTY-EIGHT

Rick and Paula were away. As were Karen's kids. She e-mailed the lodge where Sam and Alex were staying and told them she would also be away for a few days. The dog would be left with the neighbors. She realized she should let someone know where she was going. She dialed a number and a familiar voice picked up, at home.

"Saul?"

"*Karen?*" Lennick sounded surprised but pleased. "How are you? How's that gang of yours?"

"We're all good, Saul. It's why I'm calling. I'm heading out of town for a few days. The kids are off in Africa, if you can believe it. On safari. Sam's graduation present. With my folks."

"Yes, I remember you talking about that," he said blithely. "It certainly pays to be young now, doesn't it?"

"Yes, Saul," Karen said, "I guess it does. Listen, they're a little hard to reach there, so I left your office number at their next lodge. You know, just in case anything comes up. I wasn't sure who else to call."

"Of course. I'm delighted, Karen. You know I'll do what I can do. So where are you heading? Just in case I need to reach you," he explained.

"Down to the Caribbean. The British Virgin Isles. . . ."

"Excellent. The islands are nice this time of year. Any specific place?"

"I'll leave my cell number with you, Saul." She decided to hold the rest back. "If you need me, you can reach me there."

Saul was Charlie's mentor. He had overseen the shutdown of Charlie's firm. He had learned things about him. Archer. The offshore accounts. He'd never said anything about it to her. With a chill, Karen suddenly wondered, *Does he know it all?*

"I know that Charlie was up to some things, Saul."

He paused. "Just what do you mean, Karen?"

"I know he was handling a lot of money. Those accounts we spoke of, offshore. That's what those passports and the money were about, weren't they? You never got back to me, but I know you know that, Saul. You knew him better than I did. And you'd protect him, Saul, wouldn't you, if something came out? Even now?"

"I never wanted to worry you, Karen. That's part of my job. And I'd protect you, too."

"Would you, Saul?" Suddenly Karen felt she understood something. "Even if it threatened you?"

"Threatened me? How could it possibly threaten me, Karen? What do you mean?"

She was about to press him—ask him if he knew. Did he know that her husband was alive? Was Saul part of it? Part of why Charlie was hiding or, as a foreboding thought flashed through her, even the person he was running from? Was he a part of what came between them? *Saul?* He would have known about Jonathan Lauer. He never told her about that. Karen felt a nervousness snake through her, as if she had crept into a forbidden space, a closed vault, chilly and tightly sealed.

Saul cleared his throat. "Of course I would, Karen."

"Of course you would *what*, Saul?"

"Protect you, Karen. And the kids. Isn't that what you asked?"

Suddenly Karen felt sure. He did know. Much, much more than he was telling her. She could feel it in the quiver of his voice. Saul was Charlie's mentor.

He knew. He had to know.

And now Saul knew that she knew, too.

"You never told me." Karen wet her lips. "You knew that Jonathan Lauer had died. You knew he'd tried to contact me. You knew that Charlie was handling this money. Charlie's dead, right, Saul? He's dead—and you're still protecting him."

There was a pause.

"Of course he's dead, Karen. Charlie loved you. That's all you should be thinking about now. I think it's best to keep it like that."

"What did my husband do, Saul? What is it with you people? Why are you holding things back from me?"

"You enjoy yourself down there, Karen. Wherever you're heading. You know I'll take care of whatever needs to be done up here. You know that, don't you, dear?"

"Yes," Karen said. Her mouth was dry. A chill of uncertainty passed through her, a window left open to a world she once trusted.

"I know that, Saul."

PART FOUR

CHAPTER SEVENTY-NINE

The twelve-seater Island Air Cessna touched down on the remote island strip, its wheels barely finding the slip of land in the green-blue Caribbean Sea. The small plane coasted to a stop at the terminal, basically a Quonset hut with a tower and a wind indicator.

Hauck winked to Karen across the aisle from him. "Ready?" Two baggage handlers in T-shirts and shorts ran out as soon as the propellers stopped.

The young pilot in wraparound sunglasses helped passengers out onto the tarmac at the bottom of the landing steps.

"Nice flight," Hauck said.

"Welcome to paradise." He grinned back.

They had taken the morning flight down to San Juan from JFK, caught the American Eagle connection to Tortola, and now the cramped puddle jumper over the glasslike sea to St. Hubert. Karen had been quiet for much of the trip. She slept, fidgeted through a paperback she'd brought along. Anxious. To Hauck she could not have looked prettier in a tight-fitting brown tank and white capris, an onyx pendant around her neck, and tortoiseshell sunglasses perched on her head.

Hauck helped her off the steps and flipped down his own shades. Whyever they had come here, it was beautiful. The sun was dazzling. A cool trade wind off the sea caressed them.

"Friedman? Hauck?"

A local representative from the resort, dressed in an epauletted white shirt and holding a clipboard, called out to them.

Hauck waved him over.

"Welcome to St. Hubert." The young black man grinned amiably. "I'll be taking you to the resort."

They loaded their bags into a hotel Land Cruiser. The island seemed barely more than a large ribbon of sand and vegetation in the middle of the sea. Only a few miles from end to end. There was a small mountain splitting the island, some makeshift food stands, locals selling fruit and homemade rum, a few goats. A couple of colorful billboards for a local rent-a-car service and Caribe beer.

The trip to the hotel took a little more than fifteen minutes of bouncing over the uneven road. Soon they were pulling into the St. James's resort.

The setting was beautiful, lush with vegetation and tall palm trees. It took about two seconds to establish that this wasn't the type of place Hauck could afford on his own. A week here probably cost more than a month's pay. At the open-air front desk under a thatched roof, Karen asked for the two adjoining rooms she'd reserved in the hotel part of the resort. They had discussed it. That was okay with Hauck. This wasn't a holiday. It was important to remember just why they were here.

"Any messages?" Karen inquired as they checked in.

The pretty island desk clerk behind the counter scanned the computer. "I'm sorry, Ms. Friedman, none."

A bellman took them out to their rooms, each tastefully decorated with a large canopied bed and expensive rattan furniture. A large marble bathroom with a big tub. Outside, palm trees swayed right up to the terrace, which looked over the perfect white-sand beach.

They met on their adjoining decks, gazing out at the sea. There were a few tented cabanas dotting the beach. And a gorgeous white thirty-foot yacht moored at the pier.

"It's beautiful," Hauck said, looking around.

"Yeah," Karen agreed, inhaling the ocean breeze, "it is."

"No point in just sitting around until you hear from him." Hauck shrugged. "Want to meet for a swim?"

"What the hell?" Karen smiled. "Sure."

A short while later, Karen came down in a stylish bronze one-piece and a tie-dyed sarong, her hair pinned above her head. Hauck had on a pair of "designer" Colby College shorts.

The water was warm and foamy. Tiny white waves lapped at their feet. The beach was pretty much deserted. It was June and the resort didn't seem exactly filled. There was a small reef a couple of hundred yards out, a handful of sunbathers camped out on it. A young couple was playing paddleball. The sea was almost as calm as glass.

"God, it's gorgeous." Karen sighed, as if in heaven, wading in.

"Man," Hauck agreed, diving into the surf. When he came up, he pointed. "Want to swim out to that reef?"

"Swim? How about I race you?" Karen grinned.

"Race me? You know who you're talking to,

lady?" Hauck laughed. "I'm still the third-leading all-time rushing leader for Greenwich High."

"Oh, I'm quaking." Karen rolled her eyes, unimpressed. "Watch out for sharks."

She dove in gracefully ahead of him. Hauck let her get a couple of strokes' head start, then went in after. He pulled hard, a few small waves breaking against him. Karen cut through the surf in an effortless crawl. He wasn't gaining. No matter how he pushed he couldn't seem to make up ground. Once or twice he tried to lunge and grab her legs. It took about three minutes. Karen beat him to the reef by a mile. She was already waiting as he climbed out, sucking air.

"I've been had."

She winked. "Atlanta AAU twelve-and-under freestyle champion." She shook the water out of her hair. "What the hell took you so long?"

"Ran into a shark," he snorted, grinning coyly at her.

Karen lay back on the fine sand. Hauck sat with his arms wrapped around his knees, looking back at the thatched roofs and swaying palms on the beautiful tropical isle.

"So what else do you do well?" he asked, feigning dejection. "Just so I know."

"Chili. Tennis. Large donors." She grinned.

"I've been known to successfully raise a few bucks in my time. You?"

"Clear out a hockey crease. Get cats out of trees. Munch on doughnuts," he replied. "Catch the occasional blue."

"You paint," Karen said encouragingly.

"You saw it."

"That's true." She poked at him playfully with her toe. "You could call it that!"

Hauck watched the beads of water drying on her wet skin.

"So what happens?" Karen asked, her tone suggesting that the subject had changed. "After?"

"After?"

"After I see Charles. Then what happens to him, Ty? All those things he's done . . ."

"I don't know." Hauck exhaled. He shielded his eyes from the sun. "Maybe you can convince him to turn himself in. We found him—someone else could also. He can't run forever."

"You mean go to jail, right?"

Hauck shrugged.

"I don't think that would happen. I don't see that, Ty."

He tossed a pebble into the water. "First let's see what he has to say."

She nodded. They looked at each other a few

seconds, neither of them wanting to put into words their fears for a future they didn't know. Then Karen prodded him again with her toe, smiled. "So . . . uh, double or nothing on the way back?"

"Not a chance. You should know, I don't take defeat very well."

"Your loss!" Karen chimed in with a conspiratorial grin, looking back at him as she pushed herself up and into the waves.

He jumped in after her. "On the other hand, I don't take being shown up particularly well either!"

Later they met for dinner. The dining terrace overlooking the cove was barely half filled. A few honeymoon couples and a couple of European families.

Hauck ordered a local spicy fish dish; Karen had lobster. Hauck insisted he pay, and ordered a fancy bottle of Meursault. Karen, already slightly tanned, was dressed in a black lace dress. Hauck knew the ground rules, but he could hardly keep his eyes off her.

Afterward they walked back along the pathway to the front desk. She checked her BlackBerry, disappointed. Then she asked at the desk for her messages.

Nothing there either.

"This was a nice day," he said.

Karen smiled sweetly. "Yeah."

Upstairs, he walked her to her door. There was an awkward moment until Karen leaned close and gave him a soft kiss on the cheek.

She smiled at him again, with a grateful twinkle and a wave of a finger, as she closed the door. But Hauck could see the worry in her eyes.

Still no word from Charles.

CHAPTER EIGHTY

There was nothing the next day either. Karen grew increasingly tense.

Hauck felt it, too. In the morning he went for a run outside the grounds, then came back and lifted some weights. Later he tried to distract himself with some departmental reviews he'd taken with him before he left.

In her room Karen checked her BlackBerry for messages a hundred times.

What if she had scared him off? she wondered. What if Charles had gone back into hiding? He could be a million miles away.

He would let her know, she told herself. He wouldn't torture her again.

In the afternoon Hauck swam out to the reef again, floated on his back for what seemed an hour. He thought about what Karen had said, what he would do regarding Charles—*after*. Back at home.

He knew he had to lay it all out. Dietz. Hodges. The money offshore. The empty tankers. Pappy Raymond. The hit-and-runs.

Everything.

Even if she begged him not to. There'd be an investigation. Into Hauck's behavior. He'd be suspended for sure. He might even lose his job.

He put it off and went back up to the room and lay down on the bed. His insides felt as if a jagged wire had been dragged through them. Charles's silence was killing both of them. And the thought of "what after." All of a sudden, the future, and everything it held, didn't seem so far off.

He tossed the stack of work papers onto the bed, slid open the sliding door, and stepped out onto the balcony.

He spotted Karen across from him on her terrace. She was facing the ocean, doing yoga, in tight leggings and a short cotton tank.

He watched.

She was graceful, moving from one pose to another as in a dance. The curve of her finely cut arms, her fingers reaching toward the sky. The steady rhythm of her breaths, her chest expanding and contracting, the delicate deep arch of her spine following the movement of her arms.

His blood stirred.

He knew he was in love with her. Not probably as he had kidded—but completely. He knew she had awakened him from a deep slumber, the sweet lure of something that had been dead inside him for a long time.

It was bursting through him now.

She didn't notice him at first, so intent was she in the precision of her movements. The arc of her leg, the lift of her pelvis, stretching. Her hair tumbling forward in its ponytail. The glimpse of her exposed midriff.

Goddamn it, Ty. . . .

She brought her arms back in a wide semi-circle and seemed to open her eyes. Their gazes met.

At first Karen just smiled, as if she'd been exposed in some private ritual, like taking a bath.

Hauck saw the blotch of sweat on her top, the shoulder strap off her shoulder, the wisp of honey-colored hair that had fallen across her eyes.

He couldn't stand it anymore. It was like a fire blazing through him. Through the urgency of his nod. They didn't say a thing, but something wordless and breathless was communicated between them.

"Karen . . ."

He was at her door the very second that it opened, pushing it wide, taking her and forcing her back inside the room and up against the wall before she whispered, "What the hell do you want from me, Ty?"

He pressed his mouth on hers, stifling any objection, tasting the sweetness of her breath. Karen pulled his shirt out in the same necessity, tugging at his shorts. He cupped his rough palm to the curve of skin underneath her leggings, heat radiating out of every pore, unable to stop himself.

Her chest heaved. *"Jesus, Ty . . ."*

He yanked down her leggings. Her skin was slick and sweaty from outside. He lifted her there, setting her straight against the weight of the high-backed rattan chair, hearing her murmur, her arms around his neck, lifting, until he was inside her, like two starved people ravaging for food, her legs straddling his thighs.

This time there was no softness, no tenderness. Only a yearning that rose up from deep within their core. She buried her face in his chest and rocked in his arms. He clung to her as tightly as he had ever held anything in his life. And when it was over, with a last, unembarrassed gasp, he continued to hold her, pressing her shape against his, and letting her drop easily into the big chair, Hauck leaning up against the wall, sliding to the floor, spent.

"So much for the conditions." Karen groaned, brushing her damp hair out of her face.

"Didn't work too well. . . ." Hauck exhaled, raising a knee up off the floor.

"We could just leave," he said to her. "We don't have to wait around for him, Karen. I know there are things you want to hear from him, but the hell with it—all it's going to do is hurt you, Karen, whichever way it falls. We could just leave. Let Charles go back to wherever the hell he wants to."

Karen nodded. She forced a smile. "That doesn't exactly sound very policelike, coming from you, Ty."

"Maybe because I don't feel very policelike. Maybe because for the first time in five years I feel whole. I've spent my entire goddamn life trying to do the right thing, and I'm scared—for once I'm scared—of what seeing him will do. What we're doing here, Karen, this may be the biggest lie in the world. But whatever it is, it's a lie I don't want to end."

"I don't want to end it either, Ty."

A sharp ringing cut her off. It came from the table where Karen's bag was. Both sets of eyes flashed to it. She pulled her top over herself and ran and rummaged for her BlackBerry.

451

It was vibrating.

She looked up, anxious. "It's him."

Karen opened the message. "'A boat will be at the St. James dock at eight A.M.,'" it read. "'The captain's name is Neville. He'll take you to me. You alone, Karen. That's the only way. No one else. Charles.'"

She came over and passed the phone to Hauck. He read it for himself. Inside, he felt everything slipping away.

"He's my husband," Karen said. She slid down next to him. "I'm sorry, Ty, I have to go."

CHAPTER EIGHTY-ONE

Forty miles away Phil Dietz sipped a black cactus margarita in the Black Hat Bar in Tortola. There was a band playing Jimmy Buffett and Wyclef Jean, a throng of young people dancing, spilling beers, their carefree brains buzzing with rum. Dietz noticed a pretty gal in a low-cut halter sitting at the other end of the bar and thought, what the hell, he might just make a move as the evening developed, even if, by the looks, he had to pay. He'd earned it. He'd charge it off on Lennick's account, he decided. Sort of a celebration, because tomorrow the fun was over. It was going to get native again.

He'd found his man.

It had been a breeze to track the itinerary of Karen Friedman. Lennick had alerted him. He knew that the fish had caught the line. If she was heading to the BVIs, it was likely she'd pass through San Juan, so he called with a question about the reservation. Airlines still gave out shit like that. Made his job easy. So he had Lenz, who had driven the hit car in Greenwich, but whose face was unknown to them, watching out for her in Tortola. He tracked the Island Air single-engine to St. Hubert's. There was only one place they could go there.

What he hadn't planned on was the cop. Dietz knew this wasn't exactly a lovers' getaway. Charles wouldn't be far behind.

He had led them there.

Whatever would happen next, that part was right up Dietz's alley. Charles would show himself soon. He had Lenz installed at the club, keeping a watchful eye on them. Dietz had a small plane rented. The rest was routine. What they paid him for. The kinds of skills he'd honed his whole life.

Dietz took another sip of his drink. The girl with the boobs in the halter smiled his way. He grew aroused.

He knew he wasn't exactly handsome. He was short and stocky and had military tattoos up and down his thick arms. But women always managed to notice him, and they were drawn to him in a hard-edged way.

He thought of the cop. He complicated things.

If they knew about Dolphin, they might have found the old geezer in Pensacola. And if they had, coupled with Lauer, maybe it wasn't as much of a fishing expedition down at his house as he'd thought.

Charles knew things. More than they could let him divulge. He had been sloppy, but the sloppiness was going to have to end.

Dietz scratched his mustache and pushed out his cigar. *Time to pay up, Charles.*

But in the meantime he had this little diversion. He took another look at the girl and finished off his drink. He flipped open his cell phone. One last call.

He dialed the number that was in his memory. A gravelly, accented voice picked up. *Always play both ends against the middle*, Dietz thought. He'd been told to give a progress report, stay in touch.

"Good news," Dietz said, keeping an eye on the girl. "I think we've found him."

"Excellent," the voice replied. "Was it through the accounts?" The banks, the electronic transfers. The diamond merchant they had painstakingly tracked.

"No need," Dietz said. "Ultimately, I found another way. His wife led us right to him."

Dietz stood up and tossed a twenty on the bar. Tomorrow . . . tomorrow it was back to business.

He'd take care of Hodges, too. But tonight . . .
The girl was talking to a tall, blond surfer dude.
He passed by a group of bone fishermen, bragging about their catch. When he got in front of
her, she looked up.

"Where are you?" Dietz asked into the phone.

"Don't you worry," the brusque voice replied.
"I'm around."

CHAPTER EIGHTY-TWO

The morning broke hazy and warm.

Karen woke early and ate a light breakfast in her room. She sat out on the balcony and sipped her coffee, watching the sun rise over the calm sea. Trying to settle her nerves. A flock of birds circled out by the reef, honking and diving for an early meal.

Around seven-thirty she saw a white launch pull up at the St. James's dock. A captain jumped off. She stood and tried to relax her restless stomach. *Here goes. . . .*

She put on a print sundress and a pair of espadrilles. She clipped her hair up off her neck and applied a touch of blush to her cheeks and gloss to her lips, just to make herself look pretty. Then she packed her bag, sun cream, lip balm, a couple of bottles of water. She took along some pictures of the kids she'd brought with her.

Downstairs, Ty was waiting on the walkway to the beach. He gave her a supportive wink. What else was there really to say?

"I have something for you," he said, taking her under the loggia to a private spot where he sat her down in a wooden beach chair. He pressed a small disk into her palm. "It's a high-powered GPS receiver. Hide it in your purse. That way I can find you. I want you to call me on the hour. *Every hour.* Just so I know you're safe. You promise you'll do that for me, Karen?"

"Ty, I'll be fine. It's Charles."

"I want you to promise," he said, not a question this time, more of a command.

"Okay." She relented and smiled at him. "I promise."

From his pocket Hauck took out something else—a dark, metal object, small enough to fit into the palm of his hand—that made her shudder. "I want you to take this along, too, Karen."

"No."

"I mean it, Karen." He pressed it into her hand. "Just in case something happens. It's a Beretta .22. The safety's off. It may be nothing. But you don't know what you're walking into. You said it yourself—people have died. So take it. *Please.* Just in case."

458

Karen gazed at the gun, her heart quickening. She tried to push it back. "Ty, please, it's Charles . . ."

"It's Charles," he said, "and you have no idea what else you're walking into. Take it, Karen. It's not a request, it's an order. You can give it back to me this afternoon."

She stared at the gun, and it reminded her that no matter how she tried to play this, he was right—she was a little scared.

"I'm reluctant to bring it, 'cause I just might use it on him," she chortled. But she tucked it into her bag.

"Karen, listen." Ty lifted his shades. "I do love you. I think I have from that first day I came to your house. You know that. I don't know what happens after this, between you and me. We'll work that out. But now it's my turn, and I want you to hear me clearly. You be careful, Karen. I want you to stay as public as you can. You don't go anywhere with him—*after*. You don't take any risks, you understand?"

"Yessir." Karen nodded, a small smile creeping through the nerves.

"What the hell would you want me to say, Karen? I'm a cop."

The captain of the boat, a black man of about thirty in surf shorts and a baseball cap, jumped off the launch. It was called the *Sea Angel*. He seemed to be checking his watch.

Karen said, "I think I have to go."

She leaned close to him, and he hugged her. She gave him a kiss on his cheek and squeezed him tightly. "Don't worry about me, Ty." She stood up and did her best to smile. "It's Charlie. We'll probably be drinking a beer in some café by ten."

She hurried toward the dock, turning once and waving, her heart pounding all the same. Ty came out and followed her a few steps over the sand, a wave back. Then she ran up the dock to the *Sea Angel*'s captain, an affable-looking man. "You're Neville?"

"Yes, ma'am," he said. He took her bag from her. "We should be heading out." He noticed Ty, taking a step or two toward them. "He said just *you*, ma'am. Just you or we don't go."

Karen took his hand and jumped aboard. "It *is* just me. Go *where*?"

Neville stepped aboard, tossing the bowline back onto the dock. "He said you would know."

CHAPTER EIGHTY-THREE

She did know. Somewhere deep in her heart. It came to her on the water, the islands growing familiar. With a rising anticipation in her blood.

They headed west. As they cleared the reef, the twin-engine launch picked up speed. Karen went to the back of the boat. She waved at Hauck, who had come out onto the pier. A minute later the boat skidded around a bend, and he disappeared.

She was in Charlie's hands now.

It was a beautiful ride. Lots of white-beached islands, small, uninhabited slivers of sand and palms. The water was a soft green-blue, dotted with whitecaps. The sun beat down on them, clear and warm. The craft kicked speedily over the waves, leaving a wide wake, the captain clearly at home in the local waters. Karen's hair whipped in the salty breeze.

"Do you know Charles?" she shouted to Neville over the loud engines.

"You mean Mr. Hanson?" he said. "Yes. I man his boat."

"This one?"

"No, ma'am." Neville grinned broadly, as if amused. "Not at all."

The boat passed inhabited beaches. A few towns tucked into coves. Places they had been to. All of a sudden, she knew why Charles had asked her to come here. Once in a while, they shot past a beautiful yacht in the open sea. Or little fishing skiffs, manned by shirtless fishermen. Once Neville grinned and pointed out toward the horizon. "Sailfish."

Whatever agitation Karen felt, it began to ease.

The ride took fifty minutes. The launch started to come closer to tiny, uninhabited islands.

Suddenly she realized that Neville had been right. A bizarre familiarity began to overtake her. Karen recognized a beach restaurant they had once pulled into—no more than a large thatched hut with an open-kettle grill, where they had had lobsters and chicken. A few small boats moored there. Farther along, a lighthouse she remembered, striped blue and white. The name came back to Karen.

Bertram's Cay.

Now she knew where he was taking her. A last gulf of open blue sea and she saw it.

Her heart expanded.

The isolated cove where they'd once sailed, where the two of them had anchored. She thought of Charlie and his floppy hair and Ray-Bans at the helm. They had to swim into the beach, brought a basket of food and some beer, lay around like beachcombers on the fine white sand, protected by wavy palms.

Their own personal cove. What had they called it? The Never Mind Lagoon.

Where the hell did Charlie and Karen go? everyone would ask.

Karen went up to the bow as the boat slowed, and she shielded her eyes. Pulse quickening, she scanned the small horseshoe beach. Neville guided the launch, which must have drawn around three feet, to within a few yards of the beach.

It looked the same. Just as when they'd discovered it eight years earlier. There was a yellow inflatable raft drawn up on the sand. Karen's heart beat faster. She looked around. She didn't see anybody. Just heard a caw—a few gulls and pelicans hovering above the trees.

Charlie . . .

She didn't know what she was feeling. She

didn't know what her reaction might be. Karen took off her sandals, crept up on the bow, steadying herself on the railing. She glanced back at Neville, and he gave her a cautioning hand to wait as he coasted in a little closer and came around sideways. Then he nodded for her to go. *Now* . . .

Karen jumped off, her bag strapped around her shoulder. The water was warm and foamy, coming halfway up her thighs, soaking the bottom of her dress. She waded in to the beach. She didn't see anybody there. She turned around to look as Neville started to back the *Sea Angel* away from the shore. He waved to her. Karen spun around again and for the first time actually began to feel afraid.

She was alone. On this totally deserted strip. Hardly even on a map.

What if he never even came for her?

She realized she had not called Ty. *Stay in a public place,* he had insisted. Public? This was the most deserted spot in the whole fucking world.

Karen stepped tentatively up the low dune. The morning sun had baked the sand, and it felt warm and fine underneath her bare feet. There was no sound, only some chirping from the trees and the soft lapping of the tide.

She went to grab her phone from her bag as

a tiny tingling of fear rippled on the surface of her skin.

She heard the brush move and then his voice before she saw his shape.

Soft, eerily familiar. It sliced through her.

"Karen."

She felt her chest tighten, and she turned.

CHAPTER EIGHTY-FOUR

Like a ghost, Charles stepped out of the thick, close brush.

Karen's heart came to a stop.

There was a strange tentative smile on his lips. He looked at her and took off his sunglasses. "Hello, baby."

A knifepoint of shock stabbed through her. "Charles . . . ?"

Staring back at her, he nodded.

Karen's hand shot to her mouth. She didn't know what to do at first. Her breath was stolen away. She just stared. He looked different. Completely changed. She might not have recognized him if she'd passed him on the street. He had on a khaki baseball cap, but underneath Karen could see that his hair was virtually shaved. He had a stubbly growth over his cheeks, his eyes hidden. His body looked leaner, more built. And tanned. He wore pink and green floral beach trunks, water sandals, and a white tee. She couldn't tell if he looked older or younger. Just different.

"Charles?"

He stepped toward her. "Hello, Karen."

She stepped back. She didn't know quite what to feel. She was a jumble of confused emotions, suddenly seeing the man with whom she had shared every joy and important moment in her adult life, whom she had mourned as dead, and feeling the disgust that now burned in her for the stranger who had abandoned her and their children. She felt herself rear back. Just hearing his voice. The voice of someone she had buried. Her husband.

Then he stopped. Reflexively, she took a couple of awkward steps to narrow the distance. His gaze was tentative, uneasy. She stared through him like an X-ray. "You look so different, Charles."

"Comes with the territory," he shrugged, a thin, wiry smile.

"I bet it does. Nice touch, Charles, this spot." Continuing to walk toward him, absorbing the sight of him, like sharp, uncomfortable light slowly settling into shade.

He winked. "I thought you'd like that."

"Yeah." Karen stepped closer. "You always had a good antenna for irony, didn't you, Charles? You sure outdid yourself here."

"Karen"—his complexion changed—"I am so sorry. . . ."

"Don't!" She shook her head. "Don't you say that, Charles." Her blood was hot now, the shock over. The truth came back to her, why she was here. "Don't you tell me you're sorry, Charles. You don't understand where sorry even begins." A powerful current of anger and disbelief roared through her. She felt her fists close. Charles nodded, accepting the blow, removing his sunglasses. Karen stared, teeth clenched, narrowing her gaze into his familiar gray eyes.

She slapped him. Hard, across the face. He flinched, taking a step backward, but didn't cover up.

Karen hit him again—harder, confusion boiling over into unleashed rage. "How could you? *Goddamn you, Charles!* How can you be standing here in front of me?" She raised her hand and struck him again. This time in the chest, with her fist, sending him reeling back. "Goddamn you to hell, Charles! How could you do this to me? *To us?* To Alex and Sam, Charles, your family. It killed us. You took a part of us with you, Charles. We can never get that back. But *you*, you're here. . . . You'll never know. We mourned you, Charles, as deep as if it were a part of ourselves that had died." She pounded his chest again, tears of anger glistening in her eyes, Charles now deflecting the blows, which continued to rain on him, but not moving away. "We cried for you every day for a goddamn year. We lit candles in your memory. *How can you be standing here, Charles?*"

"I know, Karen," he said, bowing his head. "I know."

"No, you don't know, Charles." She glared. "You have no fucking idea what it is you've stolen from us. From Sam and Alex, Charles. And for what? But *I* know. I know exactly what you've done. I know what a lie you've lived. I know what you've kept from me. Dolphin. Falcon. Those tankers, Charles. That old guy in Pensacola . . ."

His eyes fixed on her. "Who have you been talking to, Karen?"

She hit him again. "Go to hell, Charles. Is that what you want from me here? You want me to tell you what I know?"

Finally he caught her arm, his fingers wrapping around her wrist.

"You say you know! You don't, Karen. You've

got to listen to me and hear me out. I never meant to hurt you like this. God knows, in a million years, I never meant for you to find out. Whatever I did, I did it to save you, Karen. All of you. I know how you must hate me. I know what it must feel like for you to see me here. But you have to do one thing for me, Karen. Please, just hear me out. Because whatever I did, and why I'm standing here *now,* taking my life in my hands, I did for you."

"For me?"

"Yes, for you, Karen. And the kids."

"All right, Charles." Karen sniffed back tears. They moved out of the sun, near the brush. They sat down in the sand, cooler there. "You've always been able to charm me, haven't you, Charlie? Let me hear your best shot at the truth."

He swallowed. "You say you know what I've done. The offshore trading, Falcon, Dolphin Oil . . . It's all true. I'm guilty of all of it. I ran money for years I never told you about, Karen. I ran into some problems. Liquidity problems. Big ones, Karen. I had to cover myself. I panicked. I concocted this elaborate fraud."

"Those empty tankers . . . You were falsifying oil."

Charles nodded and sucked in a breath.

"I needed to. My reserves were so low, if the banks found out, they would call in my loan agreements. I was leveraged up eight to one, Karen. I had to create collateral. Yes."

"Why, Charlie, why? Why did you have to do these things? Didn't I love you enough, Charlie? Wasn't I there for you? Didn't we have a good enough life together? The kids . . ."

"It was never that, Karen. It had nothing to do with you." He shook his head. "You remember years ago when I got overleveraged and Harbor was about to go under?"

Karen nodded.

"We would have been totally underwater. I would have had *nothing*, Karen. I would have ended up on some trading desk again, with my tail between my legs, trying to work myself back. I would've spent years paying off that debt. But it all came at a price, Karen."

"A price?"

"Yeah." He told her about the funds he'd been overseeing. "Not the birdshit little accounts I had at Harbor." The private partnerships. Falcon. Managed offshore. "Billions, Karen."

"But it was dirty money, Charles. You're a money launderer. Why don't you call it what it is? Who did this to you, Charles?"

"I'm *not* a money launderer, Karen. You

don't understand—you don't judge these kinds of funds. You run them. You manage the money. That's what I do, Karen. It was our way out. And I took it, Karen, for the past ten goddamn years. I didn't know where the hell it all came from or who they fucking robbed or stole it from. Just that it was there. And you know what? I didn't care. They were accounts to me. I invested for them. It was the same, the same as the Levinsons and the Coumiers and Smith fucking Barney. I've never even met these people, Karen. Saul found it all for me. And what do you think, there aren't others? There aren't people doing this every day, respected people who come home every night and toss the ball with the kids, and watch *ER*, and take their wives to the Met. People like me! It's out there, Karen. Drug financiers, mobsters, people siphoning off their country's oil pipelines. So I grabbed it. Like anyone else would have. It was our way out. I've never laundered a penny, Karen. I just managed their accounts."

Karen looked at him—like a laser, looked through him. The truth, like some haze in the sky, melting away. "You didn't just manage their accounts, Charlie. That sounds so good, doesn't it? But you're wrong. *I know.* . . . This is what

Jonathan Lauer wanted me to know, Charlie. After you so conveniently 'died.' But now *he's* dead, Charlie. For real. He's not coming back on some island. Like you . . . He was set to testify at some hearing a few weeks back, but he was killed, run over, just like that innocent boy in Greenwich, Charlie."

Charles averted his face.

"The one you went to see, Charlie, after Grand Central, when you stole that person's identity. The kid you helped kill, Charlie. Or *did* kill for all I know. I have no fucking idea.

"What was he going to do, Charlie, turn you in? Blow your little scam out of the water? You're not some money launderer—you're a whole lot worse, Charlie. These people, they're not coming back. Not to mention how many thousands were ruined or murdered in the name of all this money you so sacredly invested. Oh, Charlie . . . *what the hell did you do?* How did you lose your way? This was your big way out, right, baby . . . ? Well, look at you! Look at what the hell it's done."

Charles stared at her, eyes pleading. He shook his head and moistened his dry lips. "I didn't do that, Karen. What you think. I swear. You can hate me if you want, just hate me for the things I've done." He took off his cap and ran his hand

473

over his shaved scalp. "I didn't kill that boy, Karen. No matter what you think. I went up there to try to save him."

CHAPTER EIGHTY-FIVE

"Save him?" A surge of anger flared up in Karen. "Like you were going to save *me*, Charlie?"

"I went there to stop him, Karen! I knew what they were threatening to do."

"*Who*, Charles?" Karen shook her head in frustration. "Tell me who?"

"I can't spell it out for you, Karen. I don't even want you to goddamn know." Charles's face dimmed, and he drew in a harried breath and puffed his cheeks, slowly exhaling. "I had met with him once before. Near his shop. I tried to persuade him to convince his bullheaded father to simply let things go. If it got out, what we were doing with the tankers, it could unravel everything. You don't have a fucking clue where it would go. So I went there. Back to Greenwich. After the bombing. I was totally rattled. Part of me saw this as a chance to simply disappear.

I should've died there anyway. These people had threatened me, Karen. You have no idea. Another part of me just wanted to make this whole thing go away.

"So I called him. Raymond. To come and meet me. I rang him from across the street, using the dead guy's name. And I sat there, in that goddamn booth, not knowing what I was going to do or what I was going to say. Just thinking, this whole thing has to end. *Now*. These people are bad. I can't have this poor kid's blood on my hands.

"And then I saw it." Charles looked through her, staring blankly. "I saw that kid through the goddamn window, coming toward me, crossing the street, flipping open his phone. . . . I saw the car, a black SUV, coming down the Post Road parallel to him, picking up speed.

"The vehicle veered around the corner. The kid, these locks of red hair in a ponytail, real-izing what was about to happen. That moment I knew that the door had closed for me, Karen. I had lost all that money. Falsified my reserves. These bastards wanted blood. And now I had this kid's blood on my hands." He looked at her. "You have to see it, Karen, I was at risk. *You* were at risk, the kids. . . . There was no turning things back for me. I wasn't going to spend ten years in jail. I might as well have perished in that train. So I did."

"For what, Charles? To protect those monsters?"

"You don't understand." He shook his head at her. "I lost over half a billion dollars, Karen! Every day I watched, having to cover my long contracts, the spread between my position growing larger. Our life sliding away. I crashed through my reserves. I could no longer cover my loans. They were going to kill me, Karen. I needed to hold them off. So I started to fake things. I had these goddamn tankers criss-crossing the fucking globe—Indonesia, Jamaica, Pensacola. . . . All empty! And this goddamn bullheaded fool in Pensacola who wouldn't go away . . ."

Karen touched his arm. He flinched slightly. "You could have told me, Charles. I was your wife. We were a family. You could have shared this with me."

"How could I *share* it with you, Karen? They sent me Christmas cards with the kids' faces cut out. Would you have liked me to share that? They killed Sasha. They sent me this note saying the kids were next. *How about that, Karen?* These kinds of people, you don't just send them out a report promising you're going to make it up next quarter. Our home, that fancy life of ours—it all came at a price, Karen. Should I have *shared* that? Who I was? What I did? These people are killers, Karen. That's the deal I made."

"The deal you made? Goddamn it, Charlie, look at it now. Look at us. Are you happy with it?"

Charles drew in a deep, painful breath. "You know, I thought about leaving a hundred times. Taking us all. I even went as far as to get us passports. Fake ones. You remember, when I had us all take pictures? I said they were for visas to Europe, a trip we never took?"

Karen blinked, biting back tears. "Oh, Charlie . . ."

"So tell me," Charlie went on, "should I have come to you, Karen? Is that the life you would have wanted? If I told you what I was and what we had to do, uprooting the kids, you, in days. Taking them out of school in the dark, away from everything they knew. Put all of you at risk. Made you all a part of this, too. What would you have said to me, Karen? Tell me, honey, would you have gone along?"

Charles looked at her, his gaze reflecting a shattered ray of understanding, answering the question for her. "These people have the means to track anyone, Karen. You would always have been at risk, the children. . . . When the bombing occurred, it was almost like a gift. The answer suddenly seemed so clear. I know you can't see it like that. I know you think there were ways I could have dealt with this, and maybe there were. But not one that was safer, Karen. Not for you."

"But it hasn't been safe for us, Charlie." Harried, she told him about the visit of the people from Archer that first scared her, then the man who accosted Sam in her car. And recently how she'd been sent that brochure from Tufts, where Sam was going to go, with the words *We're still here.* "They keep demanding all that money."

"Just who have you been talking to, Karen?"

"No one, Charlie. This detective who's been helping me. Saul. That's all."

Charlie's jaw went tight. He took her hand. "How did you find out about me here? How did you first know I was alive?"

"I saw your face, Charlie!" Karen's eyes shone moist and wide, and she looked at him, fighting back a rush of tears.

"My face . . . ?"

"Yes." She told him about the documentary. How for a year she'd grieved for him, kept the parts of his life intact that she couldn't put away, tried to heal the hole in her heart. "You don't

479

know what it was like, Charlie." And then the documentary, on the anniversary. How she forced herself to watch but it was too much, and she went to shut it off.

And then the instantaneous flash of him. On the street. After the explosion. Looking away from the camera. "I saw you. Rushing by, in the crowd. I must have watched it a thousand times. But it was you. Impossible as it was for me to believe. I knew you were alive."

Charles leaned back, his palms outstretched behind him. He chuckled, almost amusedly at first, in disbelief. Their lives, separated by death, crossing in a captured moment, despite a thousand precautions. "You saw me."

"I didn't know what to do. I was going crazy, Charlie. I didn't tell the kids. How could I, Charles? They love you. They would die."

Moistening his lips, he nodded.

"Then I found your safe-deposit box."

His eyes grew wide.

"The one with your other passport, Charlie. In a different name. And all that money."

"You found it how?"

Karen told him about the framed note sheet she'd received. From after the blast. Someone had found it at Grand Central. With all that scribbling on it. "Part of it was the information on the box. I had nothing else to go on, Charlie."

Charles looked back at her. His face in shock. Almost ashen. A note pad. That had led her to him. Something that hadn't been destroyed in the blast. Then he stiffened. His eyes grew hooded and dark. He squeezed her hand, but this time there was a coldness there, the pressure firmer than just support.

"Who else knows about this, Karen?"

CHAPTER EIGHTY-SIX

Anxious, Hauck decided to take a run, leaving the hotel's grounds and heading up along the coast road in a steady jog. He had to do something. Sitting around watching the GPS, letting his mind wander to inescapable conclusions, he was going insane.

The GPS had stopped a while back. Fixed. 18.50° N, 68.53° W. Some tiny sand reef in the middle of the Caribbean. Twenty miles away. About the least public place she could be. He had told her to call him and let him know she was going in.

That had been two hours ago.

In his job Hauck had been partnered on dozens of stakeouts and surveillances. Waited anxiously in cars while partners put themselves on the line. It was always better to be the one to go in himself. Still, he had never felt so helpless or responsible as he did now. He ran up the long, unevenly paved road that traveled the circumference of the tiny island. He had to do something.

Move.

His strong thighs picked up the pace. There was a large rise that loomed in front of him, green with vegetation and sharply ascending, jutting out of the sea. Hauck headed up the hill toward it, his heart rate rising, a sheen of sweat matting the back of his T-shirt, building up on his skin. The sun baked down on him. Whatever breeze there was remained on the beach.

Every once in a while, he stopped and checked the screen of the GPS, which he had strapped to his waist. Still 18.50 and 68.53 degrees. Still at the same spot. Still no word. It was going on two hours now. He had tried to call. Just her recording. Maybe there was no signal where she was. What could he do, set out in a boat after her? He had given her his word.

So he ran. The seascapes were beautiful, vistas of wide-open stretches of green-blue water, a few verdant knolls rising precipitously from the beaches, an occasional white boat dotting the sea, the hazy outline of a distant island on the horizon.

But Hauck wasn't absorbing all that. He was

angry at himself for letting her go. For succumbing. The muscles in his thighs burned as the topography rose. He took off his shirt and wrapped it around his waist as sweat coated his skin. *C'mon, Karen, call. . . . Call!* His lungs grew tight.

Another hundred yards . . .

Finally he reached the top of the rise. Hauck pulled to a stop, doubled over, feeling angry, helpless, responsible.

He shouted out to no one, "Goddamn it!"

He doused himself with water. He seemed to be at the highest point. He looked back in the direction he had come from and saw the resort, tiny, far off, seemingly miles away.

Something caught his attention out on the sea.

Off the opposite side of the island. Hauck put his hand over his eyes to shield them from the sun.

It was a huge black ship. A sailing vessel. Like something he'd never seen before. Vast—it must have been as long as a football field, ultramodern, with three gleaming, metallic masts reflecting the sun. He was mesmerized.

He reached into his pouch and took out the binoculars he'd brought along. He looked out at the water and zeroed in.

Spectacular. Sleek and sparkling black. The name was on the stern. He focused.

The Black Bear.

The boat filled Hauck with awe, but also with a sense of unrest. From the edges of his memory, he knew he had seen it somewhere before.

He took out his cell phone and snapped a picture.

He *had* seen it—he tried to recall.

He just couldn't place where.

CHAPTER EIGHTY-SEVEN

"Listen, Charles, this is important." Karen reached out and touched his arm. "We're not the only people who know you're alive."

He ruffled his brow. "'We'?"

She nodded. "Yes, 'we.'" Karen told him about Hauck. "He's a detective. From Greenwich. He was trying to solve the Raymond hit-and-run that happened the same day. The boy had your name and number in his pocket. He looked after me a bit in the days when we weren't sure if you had died. Then all these crazy things began to happen."

"What kinds of crazy things?"

"People were suddenly trying to find you, Charles. Or at least all that money. I told you, they were talking about millions. They were coming to the house. Then they threatened Samantha. At school. I didn't know who else to turn to, Charles."

He looked concerned. "People as in *who*, Karen?"

"I don't know. We didn't find out. The police, or Saul. But that doesn't really matter now. What does matter is, this detective, Hauck, *he* found out. Listen, Charles, they seem to be looking for you, too. Not just for the money. *You!* They're tracing you through these bank accounts down here. This person, his name is Dietz. . . . Do you know him?"

"*Dietz?*" Charles shook his head.

"He was a part of the Raymond hit-and-run. He was a witness, in Greenwich. But the thing is, he was also there at Jonathan Lauer's, too! They were both arranged hits, Charles. Not accidents. But you know that, don't you? You know what they were trying to protect. And now I think they're down here, Charles, trying to find you. They somehow know, Charles. You're in danger."

Charles pushed up his cap and massaged his brow, as though running back in his mind through a series of events, and the conclusion he seemed to come to alarmed him. "They know about the fees," he said, looking at her glumly.

"What fees, Charles?"

"A lot of money, Karen. Money I *earned*," he said, "I didn't steal. One and a quarter percent,

487

on a couple of billion dollars. Accumulating over the past eight years. I always kept it offshore. It was for our island," he said. "Remember? *We're talking over sixty million dollars, Karen.*"

Karen's eyes grew wide.

"I never cared about the money, Charlie. I never cared about your stupid island. That was never going to happen. That was just our stupid dream." She looked at him. "What I cared about was *you*, Charlie. I cared about us, our family. These people are onto you. They can trace you, as I did. What are you going to do, Charlie, run from them the rest of your life?"

He hung his head, ran a troubled hand across his scalp. A wistful smile appeared in his gray eyes. "You know I came back once, Karen. Sam's graduation. I looked up the date on the school's Web site."

"You were there?"

He nodded fondly. "In a way. I took a car up and watched you come out after the ceremony from across the street. You had on a short yellow dress. Sam had a flower in her ear. I saw my folks there. Alex . . . He's gotten so tall. . . ."

"You were there!" Karen felt a pang grab at her heart. "Oh, Charlie, how long can you let this mess keep going on?"

"I don't know. I don't know," he said. Then,

"Tell me"—his eyes brightening—"how's his lacrosse?"

"His lacrosse?" Tears of confusion formed in her eyes. "I don't know, Charlie, he's second string, attack. He's on the bench mostly. Sam had a good year, though. She scored the winning goal against Greenwich Academy. She—" Then she caught herself. "Oh, Charlie, why are we doing this? You want to know how it was? It was hard, Charlie. It was fucking hard. Do you know how they would feel if they could see you here now? It would kill them, Charlie. Sam, Alex—they would die."

"Karen . . ."

Some strange force impelled her, and she leaned toward him, Charlie scared and confused, and they both took the other into their arms. It felt so strange, to have his arms wrapped around her. So familiar, yet so awkward. Like a ghost. "It's been hell, Charlie. First with you gone, then . . . You hurt me so." She pulled away, something between pain and accusation flashing in her eyes. "I can't forgive you, Charlie. I'm not sure I ever will. *We had a fucking life, Charles!*"

"I know it's been hard, Karen." He nodded, swallowing. "I know what I've done."

Karen sniffled back some tears and wiped her eyes with the heel of her hands. "No," she said, "no, you don't know. You don't even have a clue what you've done."

He looked at her. For the first time, he seemed to look her *over*. Her face. Her figure. How she looked in her dress. A faint smile came to his eyes. "You still look good, Karen."

"Yeah, and you don't wear glasses anymore?"

"Lasik." He shrugged. "Occupational necessity."

She smiled. "Finally drummed up the nerve, huh?"

"You got me."

Karen's smile broadened, a ray of sun reflecting brightly off her freckles.

"I want you to be happy, Karen. I want you to move on. Learn to love somebody. You ought to have happiness in your life."

"Yeah, well, you picked a wonderful time to suddenly have all this concern for me, Charlie."

He smiled ruefully.

"Listen, Charlie, it doesn't have to be like this. You can turn yourself in. This detective, Hauck, he's here with me now, Charlie."

Charles looked concerned.

"You can trust him, Charlie. I promise. He's my friend. He's not here to bring you in. You can explain what you did. You didn't kill anyone. You falsified collateral, Charlie. You lied. You can give back the money. Pay a fine. Even if you have to spend time in jail, you can get back your life. The kids, they deserve their father, Charlie. Even if we can't go back the same, they'll forgive you. They will. You can do this, Charlie."

"No." He shook his head weakly. "I can't."

"Yes you can. I know you, Charlie."

"I can't do it, Karen. I'll be in jail for twenty years. *I can't*. Besides, I'd never be safe. Nor would you. This is better, whatever it seems." He looked at her and smiled. "And just to be honest, Karen, neither of us would want to explain this to the kids."

"They would want their father, Charlie." She drew in a breath. "What are you going to do, run for the rest of your life?"

"No." He shook his head. Then a light of understanding seemed to go on in his eyes. "Listen, there are some things, Karen. You say these people are looking for me. If anything happens to me, I have these safe-deposit boxes, in different places around. St. Kitts. Panama. Tortola . . ."

"I don't want your money, Charles. What I want is for you to—"

"Ssshh . . ." He took her hand and stopped her. Squeezed. "You still have the Mustang, don't you?"

"Of course I have it, Charlie. That's what you said. In your will."

"Good. There are things you'll want to know. Important things, Karen. If anything should happen to me. The truth. The truth has always been right inside my heart. You understand that, Karen. Promise me you'll look. It'll explain a lot of things."

"What the hell are you talking about, Charlie? You have to come in with me. You can testify against these people. You can go into custody if you have to. But they're going to find you, Charlie. You just can't keep running."

"I'm not going to keep running, Karen."

"What do you mean?"

He glanced at his watch. "It's time to be getting back. I'll think about what you said. No promises." He got up, looked out at the water, and waved. On the *Sea Angel*, Neville signaled back. Karen heard the engine start. Farther out, a larger craft had come into view from around the bend. "That one's mine," Charlie pointed. "Pretty much my home for the past year. Check it out on the way back. You might get a kick out of the name."

Karen's heart kicked up, worried, as she watched her launch putter in. She was positive there was something she had failed to say.

"Promise me about the car."

"Promise you *what*, Charlie?"

"You'll need to get in." He took her by the shoulders and put a hand softly to her cheek. "I always thought you were beautiful, Karen. The most beautiful thing in the world. Except for maybe the color of my baby's eyes."

"Charlie, I can't just leave you here."

He took a glance up at the sky. "You have to leave me, Karen."

Neville coasted the *Sea Angel* back in near the shore. Charles took Karen by the arm, led her into the warm cove water. She went ahead, wading into the lapping surf, reaching for the bow. Grinning, Neville pulled her up onboard. She turned back to Charlie. The small boat began to move away. She looked at him standing on the shore. A wave of sadness swept over her. She felt she was leaving something there, a part of herself. He looked so lonely. She was sure she was seeing him for the last time.

"*Charlie!*" she called out over the engine.

"I'll think it over." He waved. "I promise. If I change my mind, I'll send Neville back for you tomorrow." He took a step into the shallow water and waved again. "The Mustang, Karen . . ."

Then he flipped his dark Ray-Bans down over his eyes.

Karen held on to the railing as the *Sea Angel*'s twin engines kicked up, creating a wake. Neville backed the craft around, and Karen ran to the stern as the boat picked up speed, the sight of Charlie on the beach growing smaller. He waved to her one last time. Karen finally gave herself over to the urge to cry. "I did miss you," she said softly. "I did miss you so much, Charlie."

As the *Sea Angel* sped away from the cove, it passed within close distance of Charlie's boat—larger, the kind he'd always dreamed of, heading in. As they drew near, Karen was able to make out the name, written in an ornate gold script on the wooden hull.

Emberglow.

It almost made her laugh, as warm, fond tears welled in her eyes. She took out her cell phone and framed a shot to remember, not knowing what she would do with it, or who she would ever show it to.

Karen never noticed the small plane circling high in the sky above her.

494

CHAPTER EIGHTY-EIGHT

Karen didn't arrive back at the hotel until well into the afternoon. Hauck was in his room by then, seated in a cane chair, his feet propped on the bed, going over some work to distract himself. His worst fears had faded. Karen had called in as soon as she hit open water to let him know she was all right. She sounded vague, even a bit distant emotionally, but she told him she would say more about it when she got to the hotel.

There was a knock on his door.

"It's open," he said.

Karen stepped into the room. She looked a little weary and conflicted. Her hair was tousled, out of place. She dropped the bag she was carrying onto the table by the door.

He asked, "So how did it go?"

She tried to smile. "How did it go?" She could

read it—anyone could read it, what he was really asking. *Had anything changed?*

"Here," she said, placing the gun he'd given her on the table by the bed. "He didn't kill those people, Ty. He committed fraud with those tankers to cover up his losses, and he admitted he went up to Greenwich after the bombing like you said—with that man's ID. To *meet* with Raymond, Ty, not to kill him. To try to get him once and for all to convince his father to stop."

Hauck nodded.

She sat down across from him on the edge of the bed. "I believe him, Ty. He said he saw the whole thing happen and that he realized there was no turning back. These people had threatened him. I showed you that Christmas card. The note about what they did to our dog. He thought he was saving us, Ty, however it sounds. But everything he said—it fits."

"What fits is that he's up to his ankles in a shitload of trouble, Karen."

"He knows that, too. I tried to get him to come in. I even told him about you. I told him he hadn't killed anyone, that all he'd done was commit fraud, that he could give back the money, pay a fine, do some time, whatever anyone would want. Testify."

"And . . . ?"

"And he said he'd think about it. But I'm not sure. He's scared. Scared to face what he's done. To face our family. I think it's just easier to run. When the boat pulled away, he waved. I have the feeling that was his answer. I don't think I'll see him anymore."

Hauck drew his legs back, tossed his papers on the table. "Do you want him to come back, Karen?"

"*Do I want him back*?" She looked at him and shook her head, eyes glazing. "Not the way you're thinking, Ty. It's over between us like that. I could never go back. Nor could he. But I realized something there. Seeing him, hearing him . . ."

"What's that?"

"My children. They deserve the truth. They deserve their father, whatever he's done, as long as he's alive."

Hauck nodded. He understood that. He had Jessie. Whatever he'd done. He drew a breath.

Karen looked at him, aching. "You know how hard it was for me to do that, Ty?"

Something held him back. "Yeah, I know."

"To see him." Her eyes filled up. "To see my husband, in front of me again. To hear him out. After what he's done . . ."

"I know how it was, Karen."

"*How*? How was it, Ty?"

497

"What is it you want me to do, Karen?"

"I want you to hold me, goddamn it! I want you to tell me I did the right thing. Don't you see that?" She let her hand fall to his leg. "Anyway, I realized something else out there as well."

"What was that?"

She got up and sat down on his lap. "I realized I do love you, Ty. Not something close." She smiled, sniffing back a tear. "The whole shebang."

"Shebang?"

"Yeah." Karen nodded and drew herself close across his chest. "Shebang."

He wrapped his arms around her, squeezing her face against his shoulder. He realized she was crying. She couldn't help herself. He held her, feeling her warm body and the lift in his own heart as hers beat steadily against him. The dampness of a few warm tears pressed against his neck.

"I do," she whispered, cuddling against him. "Impossible as that may seem."

He shrugged, bringing her face gently against his chest. "Not so impossible."

"Yes it is. Totally frigging impossible. You don't think I can read you, mister? Like an open book." Then she pulled away. "But I can't let him simply disappear again. I want to bring him home to the kids. Whatever he's done. Their father's alive."

Hauck wiped a bead of moisture from her freckled cheek with his thumb. "We'll find a way," he said. "We will."

She kissed him lightly on the lips, rested her forehead against his. "Thank you, Ty."

"Not so impossible to me," he said again. "Of course, for the kids maybe . . ."

"Oh, man!" Karen shook her head, brushing a wave of hair out of her face. "Am I gonna have a bunch to explain when they get back or what?"

That night they stayed together in his room. They didn't make love. They just lay there, his arm around her waist, her body tucked closely to him, the shadow of her husband hovering ominously, like a front coming in across the sea, over their calm.

Around one, Hauck got up. Karen lay curled on the bed, sleeping heavily. He drew the covers off and pulled on his shorts and stepped over to the window, looking out at the moonlit sea. Something gnawed at him.

The Black Bear.

The boat he'd seen. It was in his sleep. His dreams. A dark presence. And it had come to him in his dream, where he had seen it before.

Dietz's office. A photo pinned there.

Dietz's arms wrapped around the shoulders of a couple of cronies, a sailfish dangling between them.

Dietz had been on it.

CHAPTER EIGHTY-NINE

Charles Friedman sat alone on the *Emberglow*, which was now moored offshore near Gavin's Cay. The night was quiet. His legs rested up on the gunnels, and he was halfway through a bottle of Pyrat xo Reserve rum that was trying to help him make up his mind.

He should just take off. Tonight. What Karen had told him, about people on his tail, worried him. He had a house he'd bought, on Bocas del Toro, up in Panama. No one knew about that. No one would trace him there. Then from there maybe on to the Pacific if he had to . . .

The way she had looked at him. *What are you going to do, Charles, run the rest of your life. . . .*

He shouldn't involve them now.

Yet a new stirring rose up in him. The stirring of who he was, who he'd been. Seeing Karen had awakened it. Not for her—that part was over. He'd never again regain her trust. And didn't deserve it. That, he knew.

But for the children. Alex and Sam.

Her words echoed: *They'll forgive you, Charles . . .*

Would they?

He thought back to the sight of them leaving the graduation. How hard it was just to look, aching, and then drive on. How deeply the sight of them burned in his memory, and the longing in his blood. It would be nice to reclaim his life. Was that a fantasy? Was it just a drunken hope? To seize it back, no matter what the cost. Who he was. From these people.

Why do they get to win?

What had he done? He hadn't killed anyone. He could explain. Serve time. Pay back his debt. Steal back his life.

Seeing what he'd lost made Charles realize just how sorry he was to have let it go.

Neville was on shore. At a sailors' party. In the morning they were supposed to head to Barbados. There he would leave the boat, fly to Panama.

Seeing her had suddenly made things hard.

A year ago he'd had a similar choice to make. He had watched the boy get killed. Run over in front of his eyes. Watched in horror as the black

SUV drove away. Something inside told him there that he could never turn back. That that world was closed to him. The grave already dug. *So why not use it?* For a moment he'd given some thought to calling a car. Directing the driver to head up the Post Road. To his town—Old Greenwich. Then down Soundview onto Shore—in the direction of the water. *Home . . .* Karen would be there. She'd be worried, panicked, hearing word of the bombing. After he hadn't called. He would say he'd been confused. Confess everything to her. Dolphin. Falcon. No one would have to know where he'd been. That was where he belonged.

Instead he had run.

The question continued to stab at him. *Why do they get to win?*

The image of Sam and Alex shone in Charles's mind with the answer: *They don't.* He thought of the joy he'd felt with Karen, just hearing her speak the sound of his own name.

They don't. Charles put down the rum. The answer suddenly clear in his head.

He ran below. He found his cell phone in his cabin and left a detailed message for Neville, telling him just what he needed him to do. The words kept ringing: *They don't.* He went to the small pull-out counter he used as a desk,

503

switched on his laptop. He scrolled to Karen's e-mail address and typed out the quick, heartfelt words.

He read it over. Yes. He felt lifted. He felt alive in his own body again for the first time in a year. *They don't.* He thought of seeing her again. Holding his kids again. He could reclaim his life.

He pressed send.

A noise came to him from up on deck, like a boat tying up. Neville, back from his reveling. Charles called out the captain's name. Excited, he headed up to the deck. His heart was racing. He ran out from under the bridge. "Change of plans—"

Instead he stood facing two men. One was tall, lanky, in a beach shirt and shorts, holding a gun. The other was shorter, barrel-chested, with a small mustache.

Both were looking very satisfied, as if a long search had ended and they were staring at a prize they'd waited to see for a long time. The man with the mustache wore a grin.

"Hello, Charles."

CHAPTER NINETY

"Ty, wake up! Look!" Karen stood at the side of the bed, shaking him.

Hauck sat up. He'd been unable to get back to sleep for much of the night, troubled by his realization about the boat.

"There's a message from Charlie," Karen said excitedly. "He wants us to come."

Hauck glanced at the clock. He saw it was going on eight. He never slept this late. "Come where?"

Karen, in a hotel robe, just out of the shower, shoved her BlackBerry in front of him as he tried to shake the sleep out of his eyes.

Karen. I've been going over what you said. I didn't tell you all I knew. Neville will be at the dock at ten and will bring you to me. You can bring who you like. Maybe it's time. Ch.

She latched onto Hauck's hand and clasped it victoriously. "He's gonna come in with us, Ty."

They dressed quickly and met in the breakfast room downstairs. That was where Hauck informed Karen, afraid of undercutting her excitement, that Charles would have to be arrested. Shaving, he had determined that the only way to make this work was to have Charles come back to the States with them of his own accord. Hauck could take him into custody there. Here, Charles would have to remain in a jail awaiting extradition. They'd have to produce a warrant, which meant going through everything with the people back home, including, in no small way, Hauck's own part and what he'd done. That could take days, weeks. The extradition could be challenged. Charles might get cold feet. And Dietz and his people were already circling nearby.

Shortly before ten he and Karen made their way to the dock. Neville, at the helm of the white-hulled *Sea Angel*, was just cruising in.

Karen waved to him from the pier.

"Hello, ma'am." The captain waved back as the boat pulled close. A dockhand from the hotel grabbed the line. He helped Karen climb aboard, Hauck following on his own.

"You're taking us to Mr. Friedman?"

"To Mistuh Hon-son, ma'am. That's what he ask me," Neville replied dutifully.

"Are we going back to the same place?"

"No, ma'am. Not this time. The boat is at sea. It's not far."

Hauck took a seat in the rear, and Karen sat across from him as the dockhand threw Neville the line. Hauck felt in his pocket for the Beretta he'd brought along. Anything could happen out here.

They headed west, never more than a quarter mile out at sea, hugging the coastlines of tiny, speckled islands. The sky was blue but breezy, and the boat bounced, the twin engines kicking up a heavy wake.

Neither of them said much on the journey out. A new uneasiness had settled over them. Charles could give Hauck the line onto AJ Raymond's killer, why he had started out in this from the beginning. Karen was quiet, too, maybe dealing with how she was going to explain all this to her kids.

About four islands east from St. Hubert, Neville brought the engines to a crawl. Hauck checked the map. It was a strip of land called Gavin's Cay. There was a town on the north side of the island, Amysville. They were on a barely inhabited part, on the south. They came around a bend.

507

Neville pointed. "There he is!"

A large white boat sat at anchor in an isolated cove.

Hauck steadied himself on the railing and headed up to the bow. Karen followed. The boat was maybe sixty feet. Probably slept eight, Hauck figured. A Panamanian flag flew from the stern.

Neville slowed the engines to under ten knots. He traversed around a reef expertly, obviously knowing the way. Then he picked up a walkie-talkie receiver at the controls. "*Sea Angel* comin' in, Mistuh Hon-son."

No reply.

Charlie's boat was about a quarter mile away. At anchor. Hauck couldn't make out anyone on deck. Neville picked up the walkie-talkie again. The tone was scratchy.

"What's going on?" Hauck called back to him.

The Trinidadian captain glanced at his watch and shrugged. "No one there."

"What's wrong, Ty?" Karen asked, suddenly worried.

He shook his head. "I don't know."

At a slow speed, they crept up on the bobbing craft from the port side. An anchor cable stretched underwater from the bow. No sign of life on deck. Nothing.

"When is the last time you spoke with him?" Hauck called to Neville.

"Didn't." The captain shrugged. "He left me a message on my cell phone last night. Said to pick you up at ten and bring you here." He brought the *Sea Angel* around to within about fifty feet.

Still nobody visible.

Hauck climbed as high as he could on the railing and peered over.

Neville coasted the *Sea Angel* closer in. He called out, "Mistuh Hon-son?"

Only silence. Worrisome silence.

Karen placed her hand on Hauck's shoulder. "I don't like this, Ty."

"Neither do I." Hauck took the Beretta from his pocket. He grasped for the railing of the larger boat as the *Sea Angel* came abreast. He said to Karen, "Just stay where you are."

He jumped on board.

"*Hello?*" The main deck of Charlie's boat was completely empty. But in troubling disarray. The seat cushions were upended. Compartment drawers were open. Hauck noticed an empty bottle of rum on the deck. He bent down and picked his finger at a small stain he noticed on one of the displaced cushions, and didn't like what he saw.

509

Traces of blood.

He turned to Karen, who was still on the *Sea Angel* with a worried look on her face. "Stay on board."

Shifting the gun off safety, Hauck climbed down to the cabin below. The first thing he encountered was a large galley. *Someone* had been here. The sink was filled with mugs and pots. Cabinets were open, pawed through, condiments strewn all over the floor. Farther along, toward the stern, Hauck ran into three staterooms. In the first two, the beds had been tossed, drawers open, empty. The larger one looked like the Perfect Storm had hit it. The mattress was askew, sheets ripped all about, drawers rifled through, clothes thrown everywhere.

Hauck knelt. His eye was caught by the same traces of red on the floor.

He went back up on deck. "It's clear," he called to Karen. Neville ran a line and helped her climb aboard. "No one's here."

"What do you mean, no one's here? Where the hell is Charles, Ty?" said Karen, agitated now.

"Zodiac's still here," Neville said, pointing to the yellow inflatable raft, the one Karen had seen the day before, meaning that Charlie had not taken it ashore.

"Who knew he was here?" Hauck asked Neville.

"No one. Mr. Hanson kept to himself. We just moved our location yesterday afternoon."

Karen's face grew tense. "I don't like this, Ty. He wanted us to come to him."

Hauck gazed across the bay, toward the island, maybe about two or three hundred yards away. Charles could be anywhere. Dead. Taken. On another boat. He didn't want to tell Karen about the blood, which complicated things.

"Where's the nearest police station?" he asked Neville.

"Amysville," the captain replied. "Six miles or so. Around north."

Hauck nodded soberly. "Radio them in."

"Oh, Charlie . . ." Karen shook her head, exhaling a troubled breath.

Hauck went up to the bow and examined the overturned forward seat cushions, looking at the drops of blood. They seemed to lead right to the edge. He leaned over the side. The anchor line went under the surface from there. Hauck ran his hand along the cable. "Neville, hang on!"

The captain turned back from the bridge, the radio in his hand.

Hauck asked, "Do you know where the anchor switch is?"

511

"Of course."

"Raise it up for me."

Karen inhaled nervously. "What?"

Neville stared quizzically himself, then flicked a switch at the helm. Instantly, the anchor cable began to slowly wind back up. Hauck leaned over as far as he could, holding on by the railing.

"Stay back," he said to Karen.

"Ty, what do you think is going on?" she asked, a rising anxiousness in her tone.

"Just stay back!" The anchor motor whirred. The tightly threaded cable rewound. Finally something broke the surface. Like a kind of line. Fishing wire. Seaweed wrapped around it.

"Ty . . . ?"

A grave dread ran through Hauck as he looked it over.

The wire was wound around a hand.

"Neville, *stop!*" he called, throwing up his own hand. Hauck turned back to Karen. The solemn feel in his gaze communicated everything.

"Oh, Jesus, Ty, *no* . . ."

She ran to the side to look, panicked. Hauck came back over and caught her, tucking her face firmly into his chest, hiding her from the ugly sight.

"No . . ."

He held on to her as she flinched, trying to

break away from him. He motioned to Neville for him to raise the line a little higher.

The cable wound a few more turns. The hand that came out of the water locked tightly around the cable. Slowly, the rest of the body began to emerge.

Hauck's heart sank.

He had never seen Charles except in Karen's photos. What he was staring at now was a swollen, ghostly version of him. He hid Karen's face away and held her firmly to his chest.

"Is it him?" she asked, eyes averted, unable to look.

Charles's bloated white face rose above the surface—staring widely.

Hauck raised his hand and signaled for Neville to stop.

"Is it him, Ty?" Karen asked again, fighting back tears.

"Yeah, it's him." He nodded. He pressed her face close to his chest and held her as she shook. *"It's him."*

CHAPTER NINETY-ONE

A launch of white-uniformed officers from the town of Amysville arrived an hour later with a local detective on board.

Together, they raised him.

Karen and Hauck stood by, watching Charles's body pulled up on deck, stripped of the oily seaweed and debris that had clung to him and the wires that had bound him to the anchor line.

Hauck identified himself as a police detective from the States and spoke with the local official, who was named Wilson, while Karen stood by, holding her face in her hands. Hauck identified her as Hanson's ex-wife and said they had gotten back in touch after a year and had come to visit. They both said they had no idea who would want to do such a horrible thing. Robbers, maybe. Look at the boat. That seemed easiest, without opening everything up. Whatever happened next, Hauck determined it was important that he control the investigation from the States, and if they came entirely clean with the local authorities, that wouldn't happen. They gave their names and their addresses back in the States. A brief statement. They told the detective what line of work Hanson had been in—investments. Hauck knew, once they checked, that Charles's new name wouldn't yield much.

The detective thanked them cordially but seemed to regard their stories with a skeptical eye.

Two of his men lifted Charles over to a yellow body bag. Karen asked if she could have a moment. They agreed.

She knelt down next to him. She felt she had already said her good-byes to him so many times before, shed her tears. But now, as she looked into the strange calm of his face, the puffy, bluish skin, recalling both the anguish and the resigned smile he had displayed on the beach the day before, the tears began to flow, all over again. Unjudging this time. Hot streaming rivers down her cheeks.

Oh, Charlie . . . Karen picked a piece of debris out of his hair.

So many things hurtled back to her. The night they first met—at the arts benefit—Charlie all decked out in his tux, with a bright red tie. The horn-rim frames he always wore. What had he said that charmed her? "What did you do to deserve to sit with this boring crowd?" Their wedding at the Pierre. The day he opened Harbor, that first trade—Halliburton, she recalled—everything so full of hope and promise. How he would run along the sidelines at Alex's lacrosse games, living and dying with each goal, shouting out his name—"Go, Alex, go!" clapping exuberantly.

The morning he'd called to her up in the bathroom and said he had to take the train into the city.

Karen brushed her fingers along his face. "How did you let this happen, Charlie? What do I tell the kids? Who's gonna mourn you now, Charlie? What the hell do I do with you?"

As much as she tried, she could not forgive him. But he was still the man with whom she'd shared her life for almost twenty years. Who'd been a part of every important moment in her life. Still the father of her kids.

And she had seen, in the repentance of his eyes yesterday, a picture of what he so desperately missed.

Sam. Alex. *Her.*

What the hell am I gonna do with you, Charlie?

"Karen . . ." Hauck came up behind her and placed his hands softly on her shoulders. "It's time to let them do their job."

She nodded. She put her fingers on Charlie's eyelids and closed them for the last time. That was better. That was the face she wanted to carry with her. She lifted herself up and leaned ever so slightly against Hauck.

One of the officers stepped over to Charles and zipped up the protective bag.

And that was all. He was gone.

"They're going to let us go," Hauck said in her ear. "I gave them my contact info. If stuff comes out, and it's likely it will, they'll want to talk with us again."

Karen nodded. "He came back to the States, you know." She looked at him. "For Samantha's graduation. He sat there in a car across the street and watched. I want him home, Ty. I want him back with us. I want the kids to know what happened. He was their dad."

"We can request that the body be sent back once the medical examiner has gone over it."

Karen sniffed. "Okay."

They climbed back onto the *Sea Angel* and watched Charles being lifted into the police launch.

"Those people found him, Ty. . . ." Karen

fought back a rising anger in her blood. "He would've come back with us. I know it. That's why he called."

"They didn't find him, Karen." The troubling image of the large black schooner he'd seen grew vivid in his mind. "*We* did. We led them directly to him." He looked over Charles's ransacked boat. "And the real question is, what the hell would they be looking for?"

CHAPTER NINETY-TWO

Maybe they had been, Karen finally admitted as she went over and over the horrible image of Charles the next few days.

Maybe they had been set up. Maybe they did lead them directly to him.

Who?

Hauck told her about the black sailing ship he'd seen the day before. That he'd also seen on Dietz's wall. Karen even remembered a plane circling high above the island as she and Charles said good-bye, though it hadn't registered at the time.

Still, none of that mattered to her now.

Seeing Charlie—his poor, bloated body, whatever he'd done, whatever pain he'd caused, that's what haunted her. They'd spent half their lives together. They had shared just about every joyful moment in each other's life. As Karen reflected, it was hard to even separate her life from his, they were so intertwined. The tears returned, and they came back with mixed, hard-to-understand emotions. He had died all over again for her. She could not have imagined, having lost him a year ago, then having held in such pent-up anger toward him, that it could be so cruel. The who or the why—that was for Ty to solve.

They flew home the following day. Hauck wanted to get back into the country, before the investigation there rooted out that Steven Hanson had no past. Before they would have to explain things in full.

And Karen . . . she wanted to get out of that nightmare world as quickly as possible. When they got home, Hauck left her with her friend Paula. No way she could be alone. She had to finally open up to someone.

"I don't even know how to begin," Karen said. Paula took her hand. "You just have to swear, Paula, this is something between *us*. Us alone. You can't tell anyone. Not even Rick."

"Of course I won't, Karen," Paula vowed.

Karen swallowed. She shook her head and let out a breath that felt like it had been kept inside her for weeks. And it had. She looked at her friend with a flustered smile. "You remember that documentary, Paula?"

That same afternoon Hauck went into Greenwich. To the station. He bypassed saying hello to his unit and went straight to Chief Fitzpatrick's office on the fourth floor.

"Ty!" Fitzpatrick stood up, as if elated. "Everyone's been wondering when we'd see you again. We got a few doozies waiting for you if you're ready to come back. Where you been?"

"Sit down, Carl."

The chief slowly retook his seat. "Not sure I like the sound of that, guy."

"You won't." Before he started in, Hauck looked his boss firmly in the eye. "You remember that hit-and-run I was handling?"

Fitzpatrick inhaled. "Yeah, I remember."

"Well, I have a little more information I can add."

Hauck took him through everything. From the top.

Karen. Charles's number in the victim's pocket. His trip down south to Pensacola. Finding the offshore accounts, how they all tied back to Charles. Soberly, he took Fitzpatrick through his escapade down at Dietz's house. The

521

chief's eyes grew wide. Then his scuffle with Hodges . . .

"You must be fucking shitting me, Lieutenant." The chief pushed back from his desk. "What sort of evidence did you have? What went on down there—not to mention not reporting back immediately that you fucking *shot* someone—was totally illegal."

"I don't need a handbook refresher, Carl."

"I don't know, Ty." The chief stared. "Maybe you do!"

"Well, before that, there's more."

Hauck went on and told him about the second hit-and-run in New Jersey. How Dietz had been a witness at that one, too.

"They were hits, Carl. To keep people silent. To cover up their investment losses. I know that what I did was wrong. I know I may have to be cited. But the accidents were set up. *Murders,* Carl."

The chief put his fingers over his face and pressed the skin around his eyes. "The good news is, you may have found enough to reopen the case. The bad news is—it may be part of the case against *you*. You know better, Ty. Why the hell didn't you stop right there?"

"I'm not quite done, Carl."

Fitzpatrick blinked. "Oh, Jesus, Mary . . ."

Hauck took him through the last part. His trip to St. Hubert. With Karen. How they'd located Charles.

"*How?*"

"Doesn't matter." Hauck shrugged. "We just did." He told his boss about finding Charles's body on the boat. Then how he'd slightly misled the investigators there.

"Jesus, Ty, were you *trying* to break every fucking rule in the book?"

"No." Hauck smiled and shook his head, finally done. "Just seemed to happen naturally, Carl."

"I think I'm gonna need your badge and gun, Ty."

Before he left, Hauck went over to a computer on the second floor. Members of his squad came up to him excitedly. "We got you back now, LT?"

"Not quite," he said with an air of resignation, "not just yet."

He did a Google search—something that had been bugging him for days.

The Black Bear.

The search yielded several responses. About a dozen wildlife sites. An inn in Vermont.

It took to the third page until Hauck finally found the first real hit.

From the Web site of Perini Navi, an Italian boatbuilder.

The Black Bear. Luxury sailing yacht. The 88-meter clipper (290 ft.) is the largest privately owned sailing yacht in the world, using the state of the art DynaRig propulsion concept. 2 Duetz 1800 HP engines. Max Speed 19.5 knots. Sleek black ultramodern design with three 58-meter carbon fiber masts, total area under sail 25,791 sq. ft. The boat has six luxury staterooms, complete with full satellite, Bloomberg, communications, oversize plasma TVs, full gym, 50" plasma in main salon, B/O sound system. A 32" twin-engine Pascoe tender. Sleeps 12 with a crew of 16.

Impressive, Hauck thought, scrolling on. A page later, in an online boat-enthusiast magazine, he found what he was looking for.

Hauck pushed back from the computer. He paused a long time on the name. It hit home. Once he'd even been out to the house. *Some house.*

The Black Bear was owned by Russian financier Gregory Khodoshevsky.

CHAPTER NINETY-THREE

We led them to him, Karen.

The whole first day back, after telling Paula and swearing her to secrecy, Karen racked her brain for how that might be.

Led whom?

She hadn't told anyone where they were going. She'd made the reservations herself. Sitting around trying to divert her thoughts from Charles, she backed through everything from the beginning.

The documentary. The horror of seeing his face on TV. Then the note sheet from his desk she'd been sent—with no return address. Which led to the passport and the money.

Then the men from Archer, the creep who terrified Sam in her car. The horrible things Karen had found in Charles's desk—the Christmas card and the note about Sasha. Her mind kept unavoidably flicking back to him. On the beach. Then the boat.

What was anyone trying to find there, Charles?

"Who? Charlie, *who*? Tell me?" Who were you running from? Why would they want to keep after you now? She knew that Ty had gone into the office, come clean. They'd have to reopen the hit-and-runs. They'd be able to find out now who his investors were.

Tell me, Charlie. How did they know you were alive? They must have seen the fee account drawn down, he had said. Followed the bank trail. A year later, what did they need from him? What did they think he had? All that money?

Karen let her mind run as she gazed out the office window. She'd been answering a couple of e-mails she'd received from the kids. Which excited her, made things feel normal. They were having a fabulous time.

The garage doors were open. She noticed Charlie's Mustang, parked in the far bay.

Suddenly it came back to her. Just what Charlie had said: *The truth, it's always been right inside my heart, Karen.*

Something did *happen to you, Charlie.*

Why weren't you able to tell me? Why did you have to hide it, Charlie, like everything else? What did he say when she pressed him? *Don't you understand, I don't want you to know, Karen.*

Don't want me to know what, Charles?

She was about to sign off on her message to the kids when her mind wandered back once again.

This time her whole body seemed to rattle.

The truth . . . it's always been right inside my heart.

Karen stood up. A sweat came over her. She looked out the window.

At Charlie's car.

You still have the Mustang, don't you, Karen?

She thought he was just babbling!

Oh, my God!

Karen ran out of the office, Tobey trailing after her, and out the front door to the open garage.

There it was. On the rear fender of the Mustang. Where it had always been. The bumper sticker. She had seen it, passed it by—every day for a year. The words written on it: LOVE OF MY LIFE.

Written on a bright red heart!

Karen's whole body seemed to convulse. "Oh, Charlie," she moaned out loud. "If you somehow didn't mean it like this, please don't think I'm the biggest fucking idiot in the world."

Karen knelt beside the rear bumper. Curious,

Tobey nuzzled up. Karen pushed him away. "Gimme a second, baby, please." She crouched down, her back to the ground, reached up underneath the chrome bumper, and felt around.

Nothing. What did she expect? Just a bunch of dust and grime, her hand showing black streaks all over it. She pretended she wasn't feeling like a total fool.

It'll explain a lot of things, Karen.

Karen reached up again. This time farther. "I'm trying, Charlie," she said. *"I'm trying."*

She groped blindly just behind the "inside" of the heart.

Her fingers wrapped around something. Something small. Fastened to the inside of the fender.

Karen's heart started to race. She pushed herself farther underneath and stripped the object away from the edges of the chrome.

Whatever it was peeled off.

It was a small bundle, tightly bound in bubble wrap.

Karen stared incredulously at Tobey. *"Oh, my God."*

CHAPTER NINETY-FOUR

Karen brought it into the kitchen. She went through the pantry drawer and took out a package blade and cut at the tape, carefully unfolding the protective wrapping. She held it in her hand.

It was a cell phone.

Not any phone she'd ever seen before. Thinking back, she remembered that Charlie used a BlackBerry. It had never been found. Karen stared at it—almost afraid to keep it in her hands. "What are you trying to tell me, Charles?"

Finally she pressed the power button. Amazingly, after all this time, the LCD screen sprang to life.

HANDSET LOCKED.

Damn. Disappointed, Karen placed it down on the counter.

She ran through a mental file of what Charlie's

password might be. Several possibilities, starting with the obvious. She punched in their anniversary, 0716. The day Harbor opened. His e-mail name. She pressed enter.

Nothing. HANDSET LOCKED.

Shit. Next she punched in 0123, his birthday. Nothing, again. Then 0821. Hers. Wrong—a third time. So Karen tried both of the kids' birthdays: 0330. Then 1112. No luck. It began to exasperate her. Even if her thinking was right, there could still be a hundred variations. A three-digit number—eliminate the zero for the month. Or a five-digit number—include the year.

Shit.

Karen sat down. She took a notepad from the counter. It had to be one of them. She prepared to go through them all.

Then it hit her. What else did Charlie say that day? Something about "You're still beautiful, Karen."

Something about "the color of my baby's eyes."

Charlie's Baby.

On a whim Karen punched in the word—the color of his "baby." *Emberglow.*

To her shock, the LOCKED icon on the readout disappeared.

CHAPTER NINETY-FIVE

Saul Lennick sat in the library of his home on Deerfield Road, on the grounds of the Greenwich Country Club.

He had Puccini's *Turandot* on the sound system. The opera put him in the right mood, as he was going over the minutes of the most recent board meeting of the Met that he'd attended. From his leather chair, Lennick looked out at the expansive garden in back, tall trees, a pergola leading to a beautiful gazebo by the pond, all lit up like a colorful stage set.

His cell phone trilled.

Lennick flipped open the phone. He'd been awaiting the call.

"I'm back," Dietz said. "You can rest a little now. It's done."

Lennick closed his eyes and nodded. "How?"

"Don't worry your buns off how. It seems that

your old friend Charlie had a penchant for the late-night swim."

The news left Lennick relieved. All at once the weight he'd been carrying seemed to rise from his tired shoulders. This hadn't been easy. Charles had been his friend. Saul had known him twenty years. They'd shared many highs and lows together. He'd felt sadness when he first heard the news after the bombing. Now he just felt nothing. Charles had long ago grown into a liability that had to be written off.

Lennick felt *nothing*—other than a frightening new sense of what he was capable of.

"Were you able to find anything?"

"Nada. The poor bastard took it to the grave, whatever he had. And you know that I can be highly persuasive. We searched his boat from top to bottom. Ripped out the fucking engine block. Nothing."

"That's okay." Lennick sighed. "Maybe there never was anything. Anyway, it was due." Perhaps it was just a fear. *Survival*, Lennick reflected. It's truly astounding what one can do when it becomes threatened.

"There may still be a problem, though," Dietz said, breaking into his thoughts.

"What?" The detective, Lennick recalled. Now that he was back.

"Charles met with his wife. Before we were able to get to him. She and the cop, they found him."

"No," Lennick agreed sadly, "that's not good."

"They talked for a couple of hours on this island. I would've tried to do something down there, but the local cops were all over. He knows about both accidents. And Hodges. And who can guess what your boy Charles may have said to her?"

"No, we can't let that linger," Lennick concluded. This was something he had let fester far too long. "Where are they now?"

Dietz said, "Back here."

"Hmmph . . ." Lennick had gone to Yale. In his day he'd been one of the youngest partners ever at Goldman Sachs. Now he knew the most powerful people in the world. He could call anybody, and they would take it. He had the fucking secretary of the treasury on his speed dial. He had four loving grandkids. . . .

Still, when it came to business, you couldn't be too careful or too smart.

"Let's do what we have to do," Lennick said.

CHAPTER NINETY-SIX

"I was placed on disciplinary leave," Hauck said at Arcadia, warming his fingers around his coffee cup.

Karen had called him an hour earlier. She'd told him she had something important to show him. He met her in town.

"What about your job?" she asked.

"I'm not sure." Hauck let out a breath of resignation. "I'm not exactly up for Officer of the Year. I told them everything," he said, then smiled. "The whole shebang. There'll be a review. The problem is, I didn't help my case with what I let go on down in New Jersey. Still, we have the hit-and-runs. . . . I'm pretty sure Pappy Raymond will testify it was Dietz who forced him to back off the tankers. That'll have to do—until something else plays out."

"I'm sorry," Karen said. She placed a hand

on his. Her eyes were sparkling, round. And they came with a smile. "But I think I may be able to help you, Lieutenant."

"What do you mean?" His heartbeat picked up, looking at her.

She grinned. "Something else played out."

Karen reached inside her bag. "A present. From Charlie. He left it for me to find. He mentioned something about it when he was walking me back to the boat on the island, about things I would want to know if anything happened to him. About the truth being somewhere inside his heart. I thought he was just babbling. I never even gave it a second thought until I saw it."

"Saw what?"

"The heart." Karen beamed triumphantly. "Charlie's Mustang, Ty. His *baby.*"

She held out the phone. He looked at her a bit uncomprehendingly.

"It was taped inside the rear bumper of his car. That's why he didn't want me to get rid of it. He had it hidden there all along. It's what he wanted me to find."

"What, Karen?"

She shrugged. "I wasn't sure either. So I checked through the entire contact log. It didn't tell me much. Maybe you'll find a number or two you could trace. Then I thought, a cell phone—*pictures.* Maybe he had some photos in there, you know, implicating someone. There had to be some reason for him to have hidden it there. So I went into Media . . . into Camera." Karen flipped open the phone. "But there wasn't anything there either."

Hauck took it. "I can have someone go through it at the lab."

"Don't have to, Lieutenant—I found it! It was a voice recording. I never even knew these things did that, but it was there, next to Camera. So I clicked." Karen took back the phone and scrolled into Voice Recording. "*Here.* Here's your some-thing else, Ty. A present from Charlie. Straight from the grave."

Hauck looked at her. "You don't seem very pleased about it, Karen."

"Just listen." She pressed the prompt.

A tinny voice came on. "*You think I like having to be here.*"

Hauck looked at Karen and Karen said, "That's Charles."

"*You think I like the predicament that I'm in. But I'm in it. And I can't let it go on.*"

"*No,*" a second voice replied. This one Hauck was sure he'd heard somewhere before. "*We're in it together, Charles.*"

Karen looked at him, the shock evaporated, replaced by a glint of vindication. "That's Saul Lennick."

Hauck blinked.

The recording continued. *"That's the whole problem, Charles. You think you're the only one whose life you're going to drag down because of your own bungling. I'm in this straight as you. You knew the stakes here. You knew who these people are. You want to play at the big table, Charles, you've got to put up the chips."*

"I got a holiday card back, Saul. Where the hell else could it have come from? For God's sake, my kids' faces were cut out."

"And I have grandchildren, Charles. You think you're the only one whose neck is on the line?" A pause. *"I told you what to do. I told you how to handle this. I told you you had to shut up that redneck fuck down there. Now what?"*

"It's too late," Charles replied with a sigh. *"The bank, they already suspect—"*

"I can handle the bank, Charles! But you . . . you have to clean up your own mess. If not, I assure you there are other ways, Charles."

"What other ways?"

"He's got a boy, I'm told, who lives up here."

Pause.

"It's called leverage, Charles. A concept you seemed to grasp quite clearly when it came to taking us down the well."

"He's just an old geezer, Saul."

"He's going to the press, Charles. You want them sticking their noses into some national-security story and finding out what they will? I'll make sure the old man doesn't talk. I've got guys who specialize in this kind of thing. You clean up your balance sheet, Charles. We've got a month. A month, Charles, no more fuckups. You understand what I'm saying, Charles? You're not the only one with his head in the noose here."

A hushed reply. "I get it, Saul."

Hauck stared at Karen.

"It was Saul," she said, tears fighting their way into her eyes. "Dietz, Hodges—they work for him."

He covered her hand. "I'm sorry, Karen."

A sadness darkened Karen's face. "Charlie loved him, Ty. Saul was there at every turn in our lives. Like an older brother to him." She clenched her teeth. "He fucking spoke at Charlie's memorial. And he could do this to him. . . . It was Saul, Ty. Jesus Christ, I even went to him when the Archer people came. When Sam got accosted. It makes me sick."

Hauck squeezed.

"I went to him, Ty—before we left. I didn't tell him exactly where I was going, but maybe he could have put it together." Her face was ashen. "Maybe we were followed, I don't know."

"You didn't do anything wrong, Karen."

"You're the one who said we led them to him." She lifted the phone. "This is what they were looking for when they trashed the boat. Charles could have told him he had evidence. Before the bombing. Insurance. Then somehow they found out he was alive."

She let out a breath, one filled with a feeling of betrayal and anger. "So what are we going to do?"

"You're going to go home," Hauck said. He looked at her firmly. "I want you to go and pack some clothes and wait for me to come over. If these people followed us to Charles, they must also know that you met with him there."

"Okay. What about you?"

He reached for the cell phone. "I'm going home to make a copy of this, just in case. Then I'm going to call Fitzpatrick. I'll have a warrant for them by tomorrow. Before this goes one step further."

"They killed Charles," Karen said, her fists

curling slightly. She handed the phone over. "Make it worth something, Ty. Charlie wanted me to have this. Don't let them win."

"I promise, they won't."

CHAPTER NINETY-SEVEN

Karen drove home.

Her fingers trembled on the wheel. Her stomach had never felt quite so hollow or so uncertain. Was she in danger now?

How could Saul have done this to her? To Charles?

Someone she'd trusted like family over the past ten years. Someone she'd run to for support herself. It almost made her retch. He had lied to her. He had used her to get to Charlie, just as he'd used her husband. And Karen knew she had brought it on herself. She suddenly felt complicit in everything that had happened.

Even in Charlie's death.

Her mind flashed to Saul, standing up at the memorial, speaking so lovingly about Charles. How it must have amused him, Karen seethed, for fate to have intervened so beautifully. To get such a potential liability out of the way.

And all the while Charlie was alive.

Did Charlie know? Did he ever realize who it was who was after him? He thought it was his investors, in retribution. *These are bad people, Karen.* . . . But Dietz and Hodges, they worked for Saul. All along it was just his frightened longtime partner. Trying to protect his own cowardly ass.

Oh, Charlie, you always did get it wrong, didn't you?

She turned onto Shore, heading toward the water. She thought of going straight to Paula's but then remembered what Ty had told her. She turned onto Sea Wall. No sign of anybody. She pulled the Lexus into the driveway of her house.

The house lights were off.

Karen hurried in through the entrance off the garage and flicked on a light as soon as she got into the kitchen.

Immediately something didn't feel right.

"Tobey!" she called. She straightened the mail she'd left on the kitchen island. A few bills and catalogs. It always felt a little different with Alex and Sam out of the house. Since Charlie was gone. Coming back to a darkened house.

She called again, *"Tobey? Hey, guy?"* He was usually scratching at the door.

No answer.

Karen removed a bottle of water from the fridge and went into the house with the mail.

Suddenly she heard the dog—but somewhere distant, yelping.

The office, upstairs? Karen stopped, thought back. Hadn't she left him in the kitchen when she went out?

She headed through the house, following the sound of the dog. She flicked on a light near the front door.

An icy jolt traveled up her spine.

Saul Lennick sat facing her in a living-room chair, legs crossed.

"Hello, Karen."

CHAPTER NINETY-EIGHT

Her heart crawled up her throat. She looked back, frozen, the mail falling to the floor.

"What the hell are you doing here, Saul?"

"Come over here and sit down." He motioned, patting the cushions of the couch next to him.

"What are you doing here?" Karen asked again, a tremor of fear tingling across her skin.

Something in her shouted that she should immediately run. She was near the door. *Get out of here, Karen. Now.* Holding her breath, her gaze darted toward the front door.

"Sit down, Karen," Lennick said again. "Don't even think of leaving. I'm afraid that's not in the cards."

A figure stepped out of the shadows from down the hallway to her office, where Tobey was loudly barking.

Karen froze. "What do you want, Saul?"

"We have a few things to go over, you and I, don't we, dear?"

"I don't know what you're talking about, Saul."

"Let's not pretend, shall we? We both know you saw Charles. And now we both know he's dead. Finally dead, Karen. C'mon. . . ." He patted the couch as if he was coaxing over a niece or nephew. "Sit across from me, dear."

"Don't call me 'dear,' Saul." Karen glared at him. "I know what you've done."

"What I've done?" Lennick's fingers locked together. The avuncular warmth in his eyes dimmed. "What I'm asking you isn't a request, Karen." The man down the corridor moved toward her. He was tall, wearing a beach shirt, his hair gathered up in back in one of those short ponytails. Somehow she thought she'd seen him before.

"I said come here."

Her heart starting to pound, Karen moved toward him slowly. Her mind flashed to Ty. How could she get word to him? What were they going to do with her? She lowered herself onto the couch where Lennick had indicated.

He smiled. "I want you to try to conceptualize, Karen, just what the figure 'a billion' really means. If it were time, a million seconds would be about eleven and a half days. *A billion,* Karen—that's over *thirty-one years*! A trillion—" Lennick's eyes lit up. "Well, that's hard to even contemplate—thirty-one *thousand* years."

Karen looked at him nervously. "Why are you telling me this, Saul?"

"*Why?* Do you have any idea just how much money is on deposit offshore in banks on Grand Cayman and in the British Virgin Islands, Karen? It's about 1.6 trillion dollars. Hard to imagine just what that is—more than a third of all the cash deposits in the United States. It's almost as much as the GNP of Britain or France, Karen. The 'turquoise economy,' as it's referred to. So tell me, Karen, a sum so vast, so consequential, how can it be wrong?"

"What is it you're trying to justify to me, Saul?"

"*Justify.*" He was wearing a brown cashmere V-neck sweater, a white dress shirt underneath. He leaned forward, elbows resting on his knees. "I don't have to justify anything to you, Karen. Or to Charles. I have ten Charleses. Each with sums under investment just as large. Do you have any idea who we represent? You could Google them, Karen, if you wished, and find some of the most prominent and influential people in the world. Names you would know. Important families, Karen, tycoons, *others . . .*"

"*Criminals*, Saul!"

"Criminals?" He laughed. "We don't launder money, Karen. We invest it. When it comes to us, whether from the sale of an Old Master painting or from a trust in Liechtenstein, it's just plain old cash, Karen. As green as yours or mine. You don't judge cash, Karen. Even Charlie would have told you that. You multiply it. You invest it."

"You had Charles killed, Saul! He loved you!"

Saul smiled, as if amused. "Charlie *needed* me, Karen. Just as, for the purpose of what he did, I needed him."

"You're a snake, Saul!" Tears trembled in Karen's eyes. "How is it I could be hearing you like this? How could I have gotten it so wrong?"

"What do you want me to admit, Karen? That I've done things? I've had to, Karen. So did Charles. You think he was such a saint? He defrauded banks. He falsified his accounts—"

"You had that boy killed, Saul, in Greenwich."

"*I* had him killed? *I* kept fucking around with those tankers?" Lennick's face grew taut. "*He lost over a billion dollars of their fucking money, Karen!* He was playing a shell game with his own bank loans. Loans I set up. *I* killed him? What choice did we have, Karen? What do you think these people do? Pat you on the back? Tell you, 'Jolly good run of it, we'll do better next time'? We're all at risk here, Karen. Anyone who plays this game. Not just Charles."

Karen glared at him. "So who was *Archer*, Saul? Who was that man in the back of Samantha's car? Did they come from you? You bastard, you used me. You used my children, Saul. You used Sam. To get to my husband, your friend. *To kill him, Saul.*"

He nodded, a bit guiltily, but his eyes were cold and dull. "Yes, I used you, Karen. Once we discovered that Charles was somehow alive. Once we realized that all the fees that had remained in his accounts offshore after he supposedly died had been withdrawn. Who else could it have been? Then I found that note sheet on his desk with the numbers of that safe-deposit box. I had to find out what was in them, Karen. We weren't getting anywhere tracing the accounts. So we tried to frighten you a bit, that's all. Put you in play, in the hope, slim as it was, that Charles might contact you. There was no other choice, Karen. You can't blame me for that."

"You preyed on me?" Karen gasped, her eyes

wide. *Why, Saul, why?* "You were like a brother to him. You got up and eulogized him at his memorial—"

"He lost over a billion dollars of their money, Karen!"

"No." She gazed at him, this man who had always seemed so important, so wielding of control. And in a strange way, she suddenly felt she was stronger than him, no matter who was standing behind her. No matter what he might do. "It was never, ever about the money, was it, Saul?"

His face softened. He didn't even try to hide it. "No."

"It wasn't all that missing money you were looking for, why your people trashed his boat." Karen smiled. "Did you find it, Saul?"

"We found whatever we needed, Karen."

"No." Karen shook her head, emboldened. "I think not. He beat you, Saul. You may not realize it, but he did. You had that young boy killed. To protect your own interests. To keep silent what his father had managed to find out. Because you were behind it all, weren't you, Saul? The big, important man pulling all the strings. But then when you realized that Charlie's accounts had been drawn down, you suddenly understood he was alive. That he was out there, right,

Saul? Your friend. Your partner. Who knew the truth about you, right?"

Karen chuckled. "You're pathetic, Saul. You didn't kill him for money. That might even give you some dignity. You had him killed out of cowardice, Saul—fear. Because he had the goods on you and you couldn't trust him. Because one day he might testify. And it was like a ticking bomb. You would never know when. One day, when he simply got tired of running . . . What do they call that, Saul, in business circles? A deferred liability?"

"*A billion dollars, Karen!* I gave him every chance. I put my life on the line for him—*my own grandkids' lives!* No*—*I couldn't have that hanging over me, Karen. I could no longer trust him. Not after what he'd done. One day, when he got tired, tired of running, he could just come in, make a deal." Saul's gray eyebrows narrowed. "You get used to it, Karen. Influence, power. I'm truly sorry if when you look at me, you don't like what you see."

"*What I see*?" She stared at him, eyes glistening with angry tears. "What I see isn't someone powerful, Saul. I see someone old—and scared. And pathetic. But guess what? *He won.* Charles won, Saul. You knew he had something on you. That's why you're here now, isn't it? To find out just what I know. Well, here it is, Saul, you fucking, cowardly bastard: He made a tape. Of your voice, Saul. Your clear, conspiring voice going over what you were getting ready to do to that boy. How'd you say it? With your people, who take care of these things? And right now—and I hope you find the same amusement I do in this, Saul—that tape is in the hands of the police, and they're swearing out a warrant against you. So whatever you and your lackeys had in mind to do to me, there's no point anymore. Even you can see that, Saul, not that that would cause you to lose even an hour of sleep. It's too late. *They know.* They know it's you, Saul. They already do."

Karen stared with a fierceness burning in her eyes. And for a second, Saul looked a little weak, unsure of what to do now, the arrogance melting. She waited for the composure to crack on Lennick's face.

It didn't.

Instead he shrugged and his lips curled into a smile. "You don't mean that detective friend of yours, Karen. Hauck?"

Karen's glare remained on him, but in her stomach a worm of fear began to squirm through.

"Because if that's what you had in mind, I'm

afraid he's already been taken care of, Karen. Good cop, though—dogged. Seems to genuinely care about you, too." Saul stood up, glanced at his watch, and sighed.

"Unfortunately, I don't think he's even alive now, as we speak."

CHAPTER NINETY-NINE

Hauck headed home from the coffeehouse in Old Greenwich, about five minutes up the Post Road. He planned to copy the recording onto a tape, then take it over to Carl Fitzpatrick, who lived close by in Riverside, that very night. Karen had found exactly what he needed—evidence that was untainted. Fitzpatrick would have to open everything back up now.

In Stamford he veered off the Post Road onto Elm, soaring. He crossed back under the highway and the Metro-North tracks to Cove, toward the water, Euclid, where he lived. There were lights on across the street from his house, at Robert and Jacqueline's, the furniture restorers. It looked like they were having a party. Hauck made a left into the one-car driveway in front of his house.

He opened his glove compartment, pulled out

the Beretta he had given Karen, and shoved it into his jacket. He slammed the Bronco's door shut and bounded up the stairs, stopping to pick up the mail.

Taking out his keys, he couldn't help but smile as his thoughts flashed to Karen. What Charles had told her before he died, how she'd put it all together and found the phone. Wouldn't make a half-bad cop—he laughed—if the real-estate thing didn't work out. In fact . . .

A man stepped out of the darkness, pointing something at his chest.

Before he fired, Hauck stared back at him, recognizing him in an instant, and in that same instant, his thoughts flashing to Karen, he realized he'd made a terrible mistake.

The first shot took him down, a searing, burning pain lancing through his lower abdomen as he twisted away. He reached futilely into his pocket for the Beretta as he started to fall.

The second struck him in the thigh as he toppled backward, tumbling helplessly down the stairs.

He never heard a sound.

Frantic, Hauck grasped out for the banister and, missing it, rolled all the way to the bottom of the stairs. He came to rest in a sitting position in the vestibule, a dull obfuscation clouding his head. One image pushed its way through, accompanied by a paralyzing sense of dread.

Karen.

His assailant stepped toward him down the stairs.

Hauck tried to lift himself up, but everything was rubbery. He turned over to face Richard and Jacqueline's and blinked at the glaring lights. He knew something bad was about to happen. He tried to call out. Loudly. He opened his mouth, but only a coppery taste slid over his tongue. He tried to think, but his brain was just jumbled. A blank.

So this is how it is. . . .

An image of his daughter came into his mind, not Norah but Jessie, which seemed strange to him. He realized he hadn't called her since he'd been back. For a second he thought that she was supposed to come up or something this weekend, wasn't she?

He heard footsteps coming down the stairs.

He put his hand inside his jacket pocket. Instinctively, he fumbled for something there. Charlie's phone—he couldn't let him take that! Or was it the Beretta? His brain was numb.

Breathing heavily, he looked across the street again to Richard and Jacqueline's.

The footsteps stopped. Glassily, Hauck looked up. A man stood over him.

"Hey, asshole, remember me?"

Hodges.

"Yeah . . ." Hauck nodded. "I remember you."

The man knelt over him. "You look a poor sight, Lieutenant. All busted up."

Hauck felt in his jacket and wrapped his fingers around the metal object there.

"You know what I've been carrying around the past two weeks?" Hodges said. He placed two fingers in front of Hauck's face. Hazily, Hauck made out the dark, flattened shape he was holding there. A bullet. Hodges pried open Hauck's mouth, pushed in the barrel of his gun, all metallic and warm, smelling of cordite, clicked the hammer.

"Been meaning to give this back to you."

Hauck looked into his laughing eyes. "Keep it."

He squeezed on the trigger in his pocket. A sharp pop rang out, followed by a burning smell. The bullet struck Hodges under the chin, the smile still stapled to his face. His head snapped back, blood exploding out of his mouth. His body jerked off of Hauck, as if yanked. His eyes rolled back.

Hauck pulled his legs from under the dead man's. Hodges's gun had fallen onto his chest.

He just wanted to sit there a while. Pain lanced through his entire body. But that wasn't it. That wasn't what was worrying him.

Dread that fought its way through the pain.

Karen.

Using all his strength, Hauck pushed his way up to his feet. A slick coating of blood came off on his palm from his side.

He took Hodges's gun and staggered over to the Bronco. He opened the door and reached for the radio. He patched into the Greenwich station. The duty officer answered, but Hauck didn't recognize the voice.

"This is Lieutenant Hauck," he said. He bit back against the pain. "There's been a shooting at my house, 713 Euclid Avenue in Stamford. I need a local team dispatched there."

A pause. "Jesus, Lieutenant Hauck . . . ?"

"Who am I speaking to?" Hauck asked, wincing. He twisted the key in the ignition, closed the door, and backed out of the driveway, crashing into a car parked on the street, and drove.

"This is Sergeant Dicenzio, Lieutenant."

"Sergeant, listen, you heard what I just said— but first, this is important, I need a couple of teams, whoever's closest out there, sent immediately to 73 Surfside Road in Old Greenwich.

I want the house secured and controlled. You understand, Sergeant? I want the woman who lives there, Karen Friedman, accounted for. Possibly dangerous situation. *Do you read me, Sergeant Dicenzio?*"

"I read you loud and clear, Lieutenant."

"I'm on my way there now."

CHAPTER ONE HUNDRED

A blade of fear knifed through Karen as the blood drained from her face. Disbelieving, she just shook her head. "No, that's a bluff, Saul." *Ty couldn't be dead.* He'd just left her. He was headed to the station. He was going to come back and pick her up.

"I'm afraid so, Karen. We had an old friend of his awaiting his arrival at home. He might even have been carrying something of interest to us on his person. Am I right, dear?"

"No!" She stood up. Her blood stiffened in denial and rage. *"No!"* She went to lunge at Lennick, but the ponytailed man who had crept up behind grabbed her by the arms and held her back.

She tried to wrench them away. *"Go to fucking hell, Saul!"*

"Maybe later." He shrugged. "But in the mean-time, Karen, I'm afraid it's simply back to my house for a late dinner. And you . . ." He smoothed out the wrinkles from his sweater and straightened his collar. He had a look on his face that was almost sad. "You know I don't take any pleasure in doing this, Karen. I've always been fond of you. But you must realize there's just no way we can afford to let you go."

At that moment the French doors to the back-yard opened and another man stepped in—shorter, dark-haired, with a graying mustache.

Karen knew him instantly from the descriptions. *Dietz.*

"All clear," he said. Karen noticed that his shoes were caked with dirt and sand.

Lennick nodded. "Good."

Fear swelled up in Karen. "What are you going to do with me, Saul?"

"A little late-night swim, maybe. Overcome with grief and dismay at finding your husband alive—then dead again. It's a lot for anybody, Karen."

Karen shook her head. "It's not gonna hold up, Saul. Hauck's already been to his boss. He told him everything. About the hit-and-runs, Dietz, and Hodges. They're gonna know who did this. They're gonna come after you, Saul."

"After *me*?" Lennick headed toward the door as Karen struggled against the man who pinned her arms. "Don't worry your little head about it, dear. Our friend Hodges is going to have a rather difficult go of it tonight himself. And Mr. Dietz here"—Lennick nodded conspiratorially—"well, I might as well let him explain his situation to you himself."

She pulled against her assailant's grip, tears of hate burning in her eyes. "How did you ever become such a reptile, Saul? How can you ever look at my children again after this?"

"Sam and Alex." He brushed his thin hair back. "Oh, rest assured they'll be very well taken care of, Karen. Those kids will have a lot of money coming to them. Your late husband was a very wealthy man. *Didn't you know?*"

"*Rot in hell, Saul!* You bastard!" Karen twisted around as he closed the front door.

He left. Karen started to sob. Hauck. Charles. Never seeing Sam and Alex again. The idea of Saul "grieving" over her. The anger burning inside her that her kids would never know. She thought of Ty, and a sharp sadness came over her. *She* had gotten him into this. She thought of his own daughter, who would never know.

Then she turned to Dietz, petrified. Hot tears and mucus were running down her face.

"You don't have to do this," she begged.

"Oh, don't get yourself into such a state," the

man with the mustache sneered. "They say it's like falling asleep. Just give yourself over to it. It's sort of like sex, right? Do you want it rough? Or do you want it easy?" He chuckled to his partner. "We're not exactly savages here, are we, Cates?"

"Savages? No," the man holding her said. He kneed her in the back of the legs, and Karen cried out, her weight crumbling. "C'mon. . . ."

Dietz picked up a roll of packing tape that was sitting on the table. He tore a piece off and placed it firmly over Karen's mouth. It cut off her breath. Then he ripped a longer strip and wrapped it tightly around her wrists. "C'mon, doll. . . ." He took her by the arms. "Shame about your boyfriend, though. I mean, after busting into my house like that—I'd have liked to have done that one *myself*."

They dragged her through the open French doors out onto the patio in back. Karen could hear Tobey barking wildly from where he was locked up, fighting them, forced into the dark against her will, his helpless yelps filled her not only with worry but with a rising sadness, too.

Why the hell do they get to win?

They pulled her off the deck into the back-yard. There was a path behind her property through a wooden gate that led to the town road

562

to Teddy's Beach, restricted to local residents, just a block away.

Teddy's Beach. Suddenly a new fear swept through Karen's body. That beach was tiny and deserted. It had a protective rock-wall jetty, and other than a few teenagers who might've gone down there at night to make a bonfire or smoke some pot, Karen realized that it would be totally deserted. And blocked from the other homes.

That's what Dietz had meant when he'd said "All clear."

Goddamn it, no. She kicked Dietz in the shins with the point of her shoe, and he spun, angry, and smacked her in the face with the back of his rough hand. Blood spurted out Karen's nose. She choked on it.

Dietz glared at her. *"I said behave!"*

He hoisted her over his shoulder like a sack of flour and ripped off her shoes. He thrust the barrel of a gun up into her nose. "Listen, bitch, I told you what the choice was. You want it easy—or rough? You can fucking decide. Me, I can do it either way. My advice is to lie back and enjoy the ride. It's gonna be over before you even know it. Trust me, you got a much better ticket than your boyfriend."

He carried her through the tightly wooded path, thorns and brambles scratching her legs.

Her only hope was that someone would see them. She screamed and fought against the tape, but she could barely make a sound. *Please, let someone be down here,* she begged, *please. . . .*

But what would that even get her? Probably only a bullet in the head.

They came out of the woods onto the end of the town road. Totally dark and deserted. No one. The salty breeze crept into her nostrils. A few lights shone from houses in the distance, across the cove.

Dietz dropped her and pulled her by the arms. "Let's go."

No . . . Karen was crying. Fiercely, she wrenched her bound wrists away from him, but there was nothing she could do. Tears rolled down her cheeks. She thought of Ty, and the tears grew heavier and uncontrollable, choking her, making her unable to breathe. *Oh, baby, you can't be dead. Please, Ty, please, hear me. . . .* Her heart almost split in two at the thought that she had caused him harm.

They dragged her down through the sand, and she shook her head back and forth, screaming inside, *No!*

Cates, the ponytailed bastard, yanked her into the water.

Karen kneed him in the groin. He howled

and then spun in rage. "Goddamn it!" and kicked her in the stomach. He dropped her at last, face-first, in the shallow water. Exhausted, out of resistance. Forcing Karen's face under the warm foam.

"Heard the jet stream's nice this time of year." Cates chuckled. "Shouldn't be too bad."

CHAPTER ONE HUNDRED ONE

It took just minutes, Hauck's Bronco speeding down Route 1 with its top hat flashing, for him to pull outside the house on Sea Wall.

Two local blue-and-whites had already beaten him there.

Hauck noticed Karen's white Lexus parked in front of the garage. He grabbed his gun and slid out of the Bronco, favoring his right leg. Two uniformed cops, each carrying lit Maglites, were exiting the front door. He recognized one from the station, Torres. Hauck went up to them, clutching his side.

"Anyone inside?"

Torres shrugged. "There was a dog locked in one of the rooms, Lieutenant. Other than that, negative."

That didn't wash. Karen's car was here. If they had come after him, it seemed inevitable that they had come after her. "What about Mrs. Friedman? Did you check upstairs?"

"All over the house, Lieutenant. O'Hearn and Pallacio are still in there." The officer's eyes fell to Hauck's side. "Jesus, sir . . ."

Hauck headed past him into the open house, the patrolman left staring at the trail of blood.

He called out, "*Karen?*" No reply. Hauck's heart started to beat wildly. He heard barking. Officer Pallacio came down the stairs, with his gun drawn.

"Fucking dog." He shook his head. "Shot by me like a Formula One." He looked surprised to see Hauck. "Lieutenant!"

"Is anybody here?" Hauck demanded.

"No one, sir. Just Rin Tin Tin out there." He pointed out back.

"Did you check the basement?"

The cop nodded. "All over, sir."

Shit. Karen's car was here. Maybe she had gone to her friend's. . . . He racked his brain. What was her name? *Paula.* Hauck's gaze fixed on a roll of packing tape on a chair. A pile of mail and magazines were scattered about the floor. The French doors leading to the patio were ajar—Tobey barking like crazy out there.

He didn't like what he was feeling at all.

He went through the doors and looked out

567

at the yard. The night was bright, clear. He smelled the nearby sound. The dog was on the deck, barking nonstop. Clearly upset.

"Where the hell is she, Tobey?" Hauck sucked in a breath. Every time he did, it killed him.

Limping, he made his way into the backyard. There was a small pool out there, a couple of chaises. Every instinct in his body told him Karen was in danger. She had talked with Charles. She knew. He should never have let her come back here without him. *Why would it make sense to silence only him?*

Farther along, his eyes were drawn to something lying in the grass.

Shoes. *Karen's*. The ones she'd been wearing earlier tonight. A pattering of nerves drummed up in him. The beating in his heart intensified.

"Karen?" he called.

Why would they be out here?

He looked further. There was some gardening equipment on the ground, a plastic watering jug. Near the end of the yard, he came upon a wooden gate—unlatched. It opened to a narrow wooded path. He went through it. Hauck suddenly realized what it was.

It led around to the end of the town road off Surfside.

To Teddy's Beach.

He heard a voice from behind him. "Lieutenant, you need any help out there?"

Clutching his gun, forcing the pain out of his mind, Hauck stepped along the path. He pushed a few branches out of his way. After thirty or forty yards, weaving behind other houses on Sea Wall, he saw the opening to the town road.

He cupped his hands over his mouth. "*Karen!*"

No reply.

Something on the ground caught Hauck's eye. He knelt, almost buckling from the surge of pain shooting through his thigh.

A sliver of fabric. Orange.

His heart stopped still. Karen had been wearing an orange top.

A tremor of dread rose up in him. He looked out toward the beach. *Oh, Jesus.* He did his best to run.

CHAPTER ONE HUNDRED TWO

Her face was pressed under the surface, breath tightening in her lungs, flailing at him with her arms, Cates's strong hands pinning the back of her head.

Karen had fought him with everything she had. Clawing, trying to bite his arm, gasping to suck a gulp of precious air into her lungs. Once she even pulled him over on top of her, amusing Dietz, getting Cates all soaked, and he drew his fist to her face in a menacing rage. "Jesus, Cates, what a fucking woman!" she heard Dietz cackle.

Karen spit water out of her mouth and tried to scream. He dunked her under again.

Now it was ending. Cates had finally ripped off the tape from her mouth, and she was taking in water, gasping for breath with every last ounce of strength, coughing, but he cupped his hand over her mouth and forced her back down before she could scream.

And who would hear anyway? Who would hear in time? Her thoughts flashed to Ty. *Oh, please . . . please . . .* Now water was pouring in. She twisted away from his grasp a last time, gagging. This was it. She could no longer fight it. In desperation, Karen reached back, vainly trying to claw at the bastard's leg.

She heard him shout, "How's the temperature, bitch?"

A desperate will fought the urge to simply open her mouth, just surrender. Give herself over to the dark tide. She thought of Sam and Alex.

No, Karen, no . . .

Don't think of them. Please . . . That would mean this is it. *Don't give in.*

Then the denial inside her slowly relaxing, her mind wandering amid her last futile throes to an image that even in her greatest fear surprised her: an island, palms bending in the breeze, someone on the white sand, in a baseball cap, stepping toward her.

Waving.

Karen stepped toward him. *Oh, God . . .*

Just as the hand that pinned her under the dark water suddenly seemed to release.

* * *

Hauck staggered up out of the grasses over the dune, his leg exploding in agony.

From thirty yards away, he spotted the man kneeling above her in the water, pressing her face down. Someone else—Dietz, he was certain—standing a few yards back on the beach, seemingly amused by things.

"Karen!"

He stepped forward, steadying his gun with two hands in a shooter's position, just as the man kneeling over Karen looked up.

The first shot hit him in the shoulder, jerking him backward in surprise. The second and the third thudded solidly into his print beach shirt, spewing red. The man toppled into the water and didn't move.

Karen rolled over and put a hand up in the soft tide.

"Karen!"

Hauck took a step toward her and at the same time spun on Dietz, who was scrambling along the sand, drawing his weapon. The bright moon had illuminated the first guy on the water, but it was dark. Dietz was like a shadow on the move. Hauck squeezed off a shot. It missed him. The next struck him in the knee as he tried to make a run toward the jetty. He pulled up, hobbling like a colt that had broken its leg.

Hauck ran, labored, toward Karen.

Slowly, she rolled over in the shallow surf, gagging, coughing up water. She pushed herself up on her elbows and knees. In horror, she stared at Cates's wide-eyed shape—next to her, faceup in the water, and backed away as if it were something vile. She turned to Hauck, tears and disbelief in her wet eyes.

But Dietz had moved into position behind her, placing her directly in Hauck's line of sight. He had his gun aimed at Hauck, momentarily shielded behind Karen.

"Let her go," Hauck said. He kept stepping forward. "Let her go, Dietz. There's no way out." He steadied his gun at Dietz's chest. "You might imagine just how much I'd relish doing this."

"You better be good." Dietz chuckled. "You miss, Lieutenant, the next one goes in her."

"I am good." Hauck nodded.

Hauck took a step toward him. More of a stagger in the sand. It was then he realized that his knees were growing weak and that his strength was waning. He had lost a lot of blood.

"No reason to die here, Dietz," he said. "We all know it was Lennick who was behind the hits. You've got someone to roll on, Dietz. Why die for him? You can cut a deal."

"*Why . . . ?*" Dietz circled behind Karen,

573

keeping her in his line of sight. He shrugged. "Guess it's just my nature, Lieutenant."

Using her as a screen, he fired.

A bright streak whizzed just over Hauck's shoulder, the heat burning him. His wounded leg buckled as he staggered back. He winced, his arm lowering, exposed.

Seeing an advantage, Dietz stepped forward ready to fire again.

"No . . . !" Karen screamed, lunging out of the water to stop him. "No!"

Dietz shifted his gun to her.

Hauck hollered, *"Dietz!"*

He fired. The round caught Dietz squarely in the forehead. The killer's arm jerked as his own gun went off in the air. He fell back onto the sand, inert, landing like a snow angel, arms and legs spread wide. A trickle of blood oozed from the dime-size hole in his forehead into the lapping surf.

Karen turned, her face wet, glistening. For a moment Hauck just stood there, breathing heavily, two hands wrapped around the gun.

"You didn't leave," she said, shaking her head.

"Never," he said, with a labored smile. Then he dropped to his knees.

"Ty!"

Karen pushed herself up and ran over to him.

Dark blood leaked from his side into his hand. Shouts emanated from behind them, flashlights raking over the beach.

Exhausted, Karen hugged him, wrapping her arms around him, a sob of laughter and relief snaking through her tears of fear and exhaustion. She started to cry.

"It's over, Ty, it's over," she said, wiping the blood off his face, tears flooding her eyes.

"No," he said, "it's not over." He collapsed into her, sucking back his pain against her shoulder. "There's one last stop."

CHAPTER ONE HUNDRED THREE

The call came in just as Saul Lennick settled down for a late meal in his kitchen at his house on Deerfield Road.

Ida, the housekeeper, had heated up a pain du champignon meat loaf before she left. Lennick poured himself a glass of day-old Conseillante. Mimi was on the phone upstairs, going over donors for this season's Red Cross Ball.

He caught his face in the reflection from the window that overlooked Mimi's gardens. It had been close. A few days later, he didn't know what might have happened. But he had tidied it all up. Things had worked out pretty well.

Charles was dead, and with him the fear that anything might fall on Lennick. The heavy losses and the violations of the loans, those would be pinned on Charles. The poor fool had simply fled in fear. The cop was dead. Hodges, another loose end, would be dealt with the same way that very night. The old geezer in Pensacola, what did it matter what he went on about now? Dietz and Cates, as soon as he got the call, they would be rich men and out of the country. Out of anyone's sight.

Yes, Lennick had done things he never thought himself capable of. Things his grandchildren would never know. That was what his career was all about. There were always trade-offs, losses. Sometimes you just had to do things to preserve your capital, right? It had come close to all tumbling down. But now he was safe, his reputation unimpeachable, his network intact. In the morning there was money to be made. That was how you did it—you simply turned the page.

You forgot your losses of the day before.

At the sound of the phone, Lennick flipped it open, the caller ID both lifting him and making him sad at the same time. He washed down a bite of food with a sip of claret.

"Is it done?"

The voice on the other end made his heart stop.

Not just stop—*shatter*. Lennick's eyes bulged at the sight of the flashing lights outside.

"Yes, Saul, it's done," Karen said, calling from Dietz's phone. "Now it's completely done."

Three Greenwich blue-and-white police cars were pulled up in the courtyard of Lennick's stately Normandy that bordered the wooded expanse of the Greenwich Country Club.

Karen leaned against one, wrapped in a blanket, her clothes still wet. With a surge of satisfaction running through her, she handed Dietz's phone back to Hauck. "Thank you, Ty."

Carl Fitzpatrick himself had gone inside—as Hauck was under the care of a med tech—and the chief and two uniformed patrolmen pulled Lennick out of the house, his wrists bound in cuffs.

The banker's wife, dressed in just a night robe, ran out after him, frantic. "Why are they doing this, Saul? What's going on? What are they talking about—*murder?*"

"Call Tom!" Lennick shouted back over his shoulder as they led him onto the brick circle to one of the waiting cars. His eyes met Hauck's and cast him a contemptuous glare. "I'll be home tomorrow," he reassured his wife, almost mockingly.

His gaze fell upon Karen. She shivered despite the blanket but didn't break her gaze.

Her eyes contained the hint of a wordless, satisfied smile.

As if she were saying, *He won, Saul.* With a nod. *He won.*

They pushed Lennick into one of the cars. Karen came over to Hauck. Exhausted, she rested her head against his weakened arm.

It's over.

The sound came from behind them. Only a sharp ping of splintering glass.

It took a moment to figure it out. By that time Hauck was screaming that someone was shooting and had pressed his body over Karen's on the driveway, shielding her.

"Ty, what's going on?"

Everyone hit the pavement or ducked protectively behind vehicles. Police guns came out, radios crackled. People were yelling, *"Everyone get down! Get down!"*

It all stopped as quickly as it began.

The shot had come from up in the trees. From the grounds of the club. No car starting. No footsteps.

Guns trained, the officers looked for a shooter in the darkness.

Shouts rang out. *"Is anyone hurt?"*

No one answered.

Freddy Muñoz got up and got on the radio

to order the area closed off, but there were a dozen ways to get out from back there. Onto Hill. Deerfield. North Street.

Anywhere.

Hauck pulled himself up off Karen. His eye was drawn to the waiting police car. His stomach fell. "Oh, Jesus, God . . ."

There was a spiderweb of fractured glass in the rear passenger window. A tiny hole in the center.

Saul Lennick was slumped against it, as if napping.

There was a widening dark spot on the side of his head. His white hair was turning red.

CHAPTER ONE HUNDRED FOUR

Illegal search. Breaking and entering. Unauthorized use of official firearms. Failing to report a felony act.

These were just some of the offenses Hauck knew he might be facing from his bed in Greenwich Hospital. Not to mention misleading a murder investigation in the BVIs, but at least, for the moment, that was out of the jurisdiction here.

Still, as he lay attached to a network of catheters and monitors, recuperating from surgeries on his abdomen and leg, it occurred to him that a continuing career in law enforcement was pretty much of a morphine drip right now.

That next morning Carl Fitzpatrick came to visit. He brought an arrangement of daffodils with him and placed it on the sill next to the flowers sent by the local policemen's union, shrugging at Hauck a bit foolishly, as if to say, *The wife made me do it, Ty.*

Hauck nodded and said, straightfaced, "I'm actually a bit more partial to purples and reds, Carl."

"Next time, then." Fitzpatrick grinned, sitting down.

He inquired about Hauck's injuries. The bullet to his side had had the good fortune of missing anything vital. That would heal. The leg, however—Hauck's right hip, actually—with all the running and limping around as he went after Dietz and Lennick, was basically shot.

"The doctor says those end-to-end rushes on the rink are pretty much a thing of the past now." Hauck smiled.

His boss nodded like that was too bad. "Well, you weren't exactly Bobby Orr." Then after a pause, Fitzpatrick shifted forward. "You know, I'd like to be able to say, 'Good work, Ty.' I mean, that was one sweet mother of a bust." He shook his head soberly. "Why couldn't you have just brought it in to me, Ty? We could have done it by the book."

Hauck shifted. "Guess I just got carried away."

"Yeah." The chief grinned, as if appreciating

the joke. "That's what you could call it, getting carried away." Fitzpatrick stood up. "I gotta go."

Hauck reached over to him. "So be honest with me, Carl, what are the chances I'll be back on the job?"

"Honest?"

"Yeah." Hauck sighed. "Honest."

The chief blew a long blast of air. "I don't know. . . ." he swallowed. "There'll definitely have to be a review. People are going to look to me for some kind of suspension."

Hauck sucked in a breath. "I understand."

Fitzpatrick shrugged. "I don't know, Ty, whaddaya think? Maybe a week?" He curled a bright smile. "That was one fucking kick-ass of a bust, Lieutenant. I can't exactly stand behind the way you went about it. But it was sweet. Sweet enough that I want you back. So rest up. Take care of yourself. Ty, I probably shouldn't be saying this, but you should be proud."

"Thank you, Carl."

Fitzpatrick gave Hauck a tug on the forearm and headed to the door.

"Hey, Carl . . ."

The chief turned at the door. "Yeah?"

"If I *had* done it by the book . . . If I had come to you and said I wanted to reopen the Raymond hit-and-run. Before I had something. Tell me straight, would you have agreed?"

"*Agreed?*" The chief squinted in thought. "To open it back up? On *what*, Lieutenant?" He laughed as he went out the door. "No effing way."

Hauck napped a little. He felt restored. Around lunchtime there was a knock at the door. Jessie came in.

With Beth.

"*Hey, honey. . . .*" Hauck grinned widely. When he tried to open his arms, he winced.

"Oh, Daddy . . ." With tears of worry, Jessie ran over and put her face against his chest. "Daddy, are you going to be all right?"

"I'm okay, hon. I promise. I'm going to be okay. Strong as ever."

She nodded, and Hauck pressed her against him. He looked over at Beth.

She curled her short brown hair behind her ear and leaned against the door. Smiled. He was sure she was about to tell him, something like, *Nice job, Lieutenant*, or, *You sure outdid yourself this time, Ty.*

But she didn't.

Instead she came over and stood by the bed. Her eyes were liquid and deep, and it took her a while to say anything at all, and when she did, it was with a tight smile and a fond squeeze of his hand.

"All right," she said, "you can *have* Thanksgiving, Ty."

He looked at her and smiled.

And for the first time in years, he felt he saw something there. In her moist eyes. Something he'd been waiting for for a long time. Something that had been lost and had eluded him for many years and now, with their daughter's wet cheeks pressed into him, had been found.

Forgiveness.

He winked at her and held Jessie close. "That's good to hear, Beth."

That night Hauck was a little groggy from all the medications. He had the Yankees game on but couldn't follow. There was a soft knock at the door.

Karen stepped in.

She was dressed in her gray Texas Longhorns T-shirt, a jean jacket thrown around her shoulders. Her hair was pinned up. Hauck noticed a cut on the side of her lip where Dietz had slapped her. She carried a single rose in a small vase and came over and placed it next to his bed.

"My heart." She pointed to it.

He smiled.

"You look pretty," he told her.

"Yeah, right. I look like a bus just ran over me."

"No. Everything looks pretty. The morphine's kicking in."

Karen smiled. "I was here last night when you were in surgery. The doctors talked to me. You're Mr. Lucky, Ty. How's the leg?"

"It was never exactly what you'd call limber. Now it's just completely shot." He chuckled. "The whole—"

"Don't say it." Karen stopped him. "Please."

Hauck nodded. After a pause he shrugged. "So what the hell is a shebang anyway?"

Karen's eyes glistened. "I don't know." She squeezed his hand with both of hers and stared deeply into his hooded eyes. "Thank you, Ty. I owe you so much. I owe you everything. I wish I knew what the hell to say."

"Don't . . ."

Karen pressed his fingers in her palms and shook her head. "I just don't know if I can pick up the same way."

He nodded.

"Charlie's dead," she said. "That's gonna take some time now. And the kids . . . they're coming back." She looked at him. Amid all these tubes,

586

the monitor screens beeping. Her eyes flooded over.

"I understand."

She placed her head down on his chest. Felt his breathing.

"On the other hand"—she sniffed back a few tears—"I guess we could give it a try."

Hauck laughed. More like winced, pain rising up in his belly.

"Yeah." He held her. He stroked her hair. The fleshy round of her cheek. He felt her stop shaking. He felt himself start to feel at ease, too.

"We could try."

CHAPTER ONE HUNDRED FIVE

Two weeks later

Hauck drove his Bronco up to the large stone gate.

He lowered his window and leaned out to press an intercom button. A voice responded. "Yes?"

"Lieutenant Hauck," Hauck said into the speaker.

"Drive up to the house," the voice replied. The gates slowly opened. "Mr. Khodoshevsky is expecting you."

Hauck made his way up the long paved drive. Even applying the slightest pressure on the gas, his right leg still ached. He had begun some therapy, but there were weeks ahead of him. The doctors told him he might never again walk without the trace of a limp.

The property was massive. He drove past a

huge pond. There was a fenced-in field—for horses, maybe. At the top he drove up to an enormous redbrick Georgian with a magnificent courtyard in front, an ornately crafted fountain in the center, with water spilling out of sculptured figures into a marble pool.

Billionaires ruining things for millionaires, Hauck recalled. Even by Greenwich standards, he'd never seen anything quite like this.

He stepped out of the car. Grabbed his cane. It helped. He climbed up the steps to the impressive front doors.

He rang the bell. Loud choral peals. That didn't surprise him. A young woman answered. Attractive. Eastern European. Maybe an au pair.

"Mr. Khodoshevsky asked me to bring you to the den," she said with a smile. "This way."

A young boy, maybe five or six, raced past him riding some kind of motorized toy car. "Beep, beep!"

The au pair yelled out, "Michael, no!" Then she smiled apologetically. "Sorry."

"I'm a cop." Hauck winked. "Tell him to try and keep it under forty in here."

He was led through a series of palatial rooms to a family room at the side of the house, featuring a curved wall of windows overlooking the property. There was a large leather couch, a recognizable contemporary painting over it that Hauck took to be immensely valuable, though he wasn't exactly sure about the guy's use of blue. A huge media console was stacked against a wall, a stereo that went on forever. The requisite sixty-inch flat-screen.

There was an old-time western movie on.

"Lieutenant."

Hauck spotted a set of legs reclining on an ottoman. Then a large, bushy-haired body rose out of a chair, wearing baggy shorts and an oversize yellow T-shirt that read MONEY IS THE BEST REVENGE.

"I'm Gregory Khodoshevsky." The man extended a hand. He had a powerful shake. "Please, sit down."

Hauck eased against a chair, taking his weight off. He leaned on his cane. "Thanks."

"I see you're not well?"

"Just a little procedure," Hauck lied. "Bum hip."

The Russian nodded. "I've had my knee worked on several times. Skiing." He grinned. "I've learned—man is not meant to ski through trees." He reached for the clicker and turned down the volume. "You like westerns, Lieutenant?"

"Sure. Everyone does."

"Me, too. This is my favorite: *The Good, the Bad and the Ugly*. Never quite sure exactly who I identify with, though. My wife, of course, insists it's the ugly."

Hauck grinned. "If I remember, that was one of the film's themes. They all had their motives."

"Yes." The Russian smiled. "I think you're right—they all had motives. So what do I owe this visit to, Lieutenant Hauck?"

"I was working a case. A name came up that I hoped might mean something to you. Charles Friedman."

"Charles Friedman?" The Russian shrugged. "I'm sorry, no, Lieutenant. Should it?"

The guy was good, Hauck thought. A natural. Hauck looked back at him closely. "I was hoping so."

"Although, now that you mention it"— Khodoshevsky brightened—"I do remember someone named Friedman. He ran some benefit in town I went to a year or two ago. The Bruce Museum, I think. I made a donation. I remember now, he had an attractive wife. Maybe his name was Charles, if it's the one. So what did he do?"

"He's dead," Hauck said. "He had a connection to a case I was looking into, a hit-and-run."

"A hit-and-run." Khodoshevsky grimaced. "Too bad. The traffic up here is unbearable,

Lieutenant. I'm sure you know that. Sometimes I'm afraid to cross the street myself in town."

"Especially when someone doesn't want you to succeed," Hauck said, staring into the Russian's steely eyes.

"Yes. I imagine that's true. Is there some reason you connected this man to me?"

"Yes." Hauck nodded. "Saul Lennick."

"Lennick!" The Russian drew in a breath. "Now, Lennick I did know. Terrible. That such a thing could happen. Right in the man's own home. Right here in town. A challenge, I'm sure, for you, Lieutenant."

"Mr. Friedman was killed himself a couple of weeks back. In the British Virgin Isles . . . Turns out he and Mr. Lennick were financial partners."

Khodoshevsky's eyes widened, as if in surprise. *"Partners?* Crazy what's going on around here. But I'm afraid I never saw the man again. Sorry that you had to come all the way out here to find that out. I wish I could have been more help."

Hauck reached for his cane. "Not a total loss. I don't often get to see a house like this."

"I'd be happy to show you around."

Hauck pushed himself up and winced. "Another time."

"I wish you good luck with your leg. And

finding who was responsible for such a terrible thing."

"Thanks." Hauck took a step toward the door. "You know, before I go, there's something I might show you. Just in case it jogs something. I was down in the Caribbean myself a week ago." Hauck took out his cell phone. "I noticed something interesting—in the water. Off this island. I actually grabbed a snapshot of it. Funny, only a couple of miles from where Charles Friedman ended up killed."

He handed the cell phone to Khodoshevsky, who stared curiously at the image on the screen. The one Hauck had taken on his run.

Khodoshevsky's schooner. *The Black Bear.*

"Humph." The Russian shook his head, meeting Hauck's gaze. "Funny how lives seem to intersect, isn't it, Lieutenant?"

"No more," Hauck said, looking at him.

"Yes, you're right." He handed back the phone. "No more."

"I'll find my way out," Hauck said, placing his phone back in his pocket. "Just one last piece of advice, Mr. Khodoshevsky, if you don't mind. You seem to be partial to westerns, so I think you'll understand."

"And what is that?" The Russian looked at him innocently.

Hauck shrugged. "You know the expression 'Get out of Dodge'?"

"I think I've heard it. The sheriff always says it to the bad guys. But of course they never do."

"No, they never do." Hauck took a step toward the door. "That's what makes westerns. But just this once, you know, they should, Mr. Khodoshevsky." Hauck looked at him closely. "*You* should. If you know what I mean."

"I think I understand." The Russian smiled.

"Oh, and by the way"—Hauck turned, tilting his cane at the door—"that's one hell of a sweet boat, Mr. Khodoshevsky—if you know what I mean!"

EPILOGUE

"Flesh becomes dust and ash. Our ashes return to the soil. Where, in the cycle set before us by the Almighty, life springs up again."

It was a warm summer day, the sky a perfect blue. Karen looked down at Charlie's casket in the open grave. She had brought him back home, as she promised she would. He deserved that. A tear burned in the corner of her eye.

He deserved that and more.

Karen held tightly onto the hands of Samantha and Alex. This was so hard for them, harder than for anyone. They didn't understand. How he could have kept such secrets from them? How he could just walk away, whatever he'd done? Whoever he was?

"We were a family," Samantha said to Karen, confusion, even a measure of accusation, in her trembling voice.

"Yes, we were a family," Karen said.

She had come to forgive him. She had even come to love him again—in a way.

We were a family. Maybe one day they would love him again, too.

The rabbi said his final prayers. Karen's grip tightened on their hands. Her life came back to her. The day they met. How they fell in love. How one day she had said to herself he was the one.

Charlie, the captain—at the helm of the boat sailing in the Caribbean. Waving to her from their private cove at the end.

Her blood coursed with the warming current of eighteen years.

"Now it is our custom to pay our last respects to the dead by throwing a handful of dirt, reminding us that all life is transitory and humble before God."

Her father came up. He took the shovel from the rabbi and tossed a small patch over the casket. Her mom, too. Then Charlie's mother Margery, his brother steadying her arm. Then Rick and Paula.

Then Samantha, who did it in a quick, wounded manner, turning away, She handed the shovel to Alex, who stood over the grave for a long time, finally facing Karen and shaking his young head. "I can't, Mom. . . . *No.*"

"Honey." Karen squeezed him tighter. "Yes you can." Who could blame him? "It's your father, baby, whatever he's done."

Finally he picked up the shovel and tossed in the dirt, sniffling back tears.

Then it was Karen's turn. She picked up the shovelful of soil. She had already said her good-byes to him. What more was there to say?

I did love you, Charlie. And I know you loved me, too.

She tossed it in.

So it was over. Their life together. *I just buried my husband today*, Karen said to herself. Finally. Irrevocably. She had earned the right to say that.

Everyone came up and gave her a hug, and the three of them waited a moment while the rest started to go down the hill. Karen looped her hand through Alex's arm. She wrapped her other around Samantha's shoulder, bringing her close. "One day you'll forgive him. I know it's hard. He came back, Sam. He stood outside on the street and watched us at your graduation. You'll forgive him. That's what life is all about."

As they headed back down the hill, she saw him under a leafy elm, standing off to the side. He was wearing a navy sport jacket and looked nice. Still with his cane.

Their gazes met.

Karen's eyes filled with a warm feeling she hadn't felt in many years.

"C'mon," she told the kids, "there's someone I want you to meet."

As they approached him, Alex glanced at her, confused. "We already know Lieutenant Hauck, Mom."

"I know you do, hon," Karen said. She lifted her sunglasses and smiled at him. "I want you to meet him again. His name is Ty."

ACKNOWLEDGMENTS

Each book is a mirror reflecting the outside world, and I'd like to say thanks to the following, all of whom have brought the outside world to life for me far more vividly through the creation of *The Dark Tide:*

Mark Schwarzman, Roy and Robin Grossman, and Gregory Kopchinsky, for their help on hedge funds and the movement of money across continents—all aboveboard, naturally.

Kirk Dauksavage, Rick McNees, and Pete Carroll of Riverglass, designers of an advanced security software far more sophisticated than that portrayed herein, for their help with information about ways the Internet is mined for national security. As one character says, "I feel safer for it."

Vito Collucci Jr., an ex–Stamford, Connecticut, police detective turned cable news consultant, and an author in his own right, for his help on police and investigative matters.

Liz and Fred Scoponich, for who you are and for the assists on classic Mustangs, too.

Simon Lipskar of Writers House for his support, and my team at William Morrow: Lisa Gallagher, Lynn Grady, Debbie Stier, Pam Jaffee, Michael Barrs, Gabe Robinson, and, mostly, David Highfill, who throws me just enough praise to make me believe I know what I'm doing now and then, and enough direction to steer clear of my worst traits. And also Amanda Ridout and Julia Wisdom over at HarperCollins in London.

Maureen Sugden, once again, for her diligence and steadfastness in waging the good fight against italics.

To my wife, Lynn, with me every step of the way, and who always lifts me up to do my best.

But mostly to Kristen, Matt, and Nick, whom I am more proud of now, for who they've become as adults in the world, than all the dance recitals, college acceptances, and squash matches of their youth. Your reflection is on every page.

Lose yourself
in a good book with Galaxy

Curled up on the sofa,
Sunday morning in pyjamas,
just before bed,
in the bath or
on the way to work?

Wherever, whenever,
you can escape
with a good book!

So go on...
indulge yourself with
a good read and the
smooth taste of
Galaxy chocolate

The Blue Zone

Andrew Gross

They were the perfect family. And he was the perfect family man. One day changed it all.

Arrested for racketeering, Ben Raab must take his family into America's Witness Protection Programme. Only his eldest daughter, Kate, chooses to stay on the outside.

But the Programme's perfect success rate is about to come to a shocking end. A case agent is tortured to death and Ben vanishes. The one person who might be able to find him is Kate.

Pursued by killers, forced to question everything she knows about her life so far, Kate is plunged into a terrifying existence for which nothing has prepared her.

Most people would call it certain death.

The FBI calls it the Blue Zone.

"A tense and chilling thriller with a whole lot of heart"
JAMES PATTERSON

"Real fear, real thrills, real suspense...real good"
LEE CHILD

ISBN 978-0-00-724251-1

Coming soon from
HarperCollins

The new
Ty Hauck thriller

THE FINAL ANGEL